Sundown Safari

Emmett Doyle departed Ireland on an agricultural adventure to a far off land within the continent of Africa. Perhaps he was a tad naïve in his expectancy but the family motto of "Try anything once: try hard at everything" kept his thoughts focused on a life in the wild. A life coloured with equatorial warmth and beauty, which would broaden his mind and lead him to adventures exotic and carefree.

Little did he know that the country he had chosen was about to erupt into a land of terrorism and evil, instead of happily farming his acres of wheatland he would be gobbled up in an ongoing war, the likes of which he had only read about and would not have wished on his worst enemy.

However, there were times of passion, sex and lust, and even love, interwoven into a web of uncertainty. This African enclave boiled over with volatile corruption and terrorism providing the main ingredients of a recipe from Hell.

Emmett was a survivor, a lover and a fighter.

Sundown Safari, set in the mid sixties, is a magnificent story of passion, intrigue, ambition and revenge – Henry Grattan-Bellew at his compelling, provocative best.

i

Henry Grattan-Bellew, originally from Mount Bellew, East Galway and now living between Counties Wexford and Dublin, was educated in Ireland and England.

Having the wanderlust from an early age he took off for Africa in 1952 with the offer of a farm management job in the White Highlands of Kenya and immediately fell in love with that continent. An affair that has lasted over fifty years.

Agriculture, journalism and publishing blended with radio and television presentation helped to fill a highly eventful and varied life under breathtaking African skies.

He was Founder Editor of *Nedbank Sportsman* in South Africa and followed this popular monthly with *Horse and Hound, SA*, a complete monthly journal of everything equestrian, canine and social.

His first book was *Sustagen Supersport*, a pictorial essay of sports played and enjoyed in Africa. His most recent book was *A Pinch of Saltee* (2003 best seller) a true story encompassing the refurbishment and restocking of their family island off Kilmore Quay, County Wexford.

Henry Grattan-Bellew

with best wishes

SUNDOWN SAFARI

NELSON

Sundown Safari

ISBN 1-900913-12-7

A CIP catalogue for this book is available
from the British Library

First published in 2005 by
Justin Nelson Productions.
www.justin.nelson1 @ntlworld.ie

Acknowledgements

I owe a debt of gratitude to those who were so generous with their time and expertise:

Shirley, who cajoled me into finishing each chapter and then put them to bed inside her world of technological jargon of computerised discs, et al. A world I am much too frightened to enter!

Shelia, Emjie, Eileen, Nancy, Jean and Sean – all "idiolects" in their respective worlds who gave their invaluable inputs.

My many friends remaining in those African countries, Kenya, Zimbabwe and South Africa – in which I spent such memorable times.

And lastly, to Ukenza – my total figment of imagination which managed to magically reappear in nightly excursions to the writing desk.

I somehow wish it all did exist.

The Author

This is for Mbudzi,
a real lady of Africa

Prologue

Emmett Doyle never realised how lucky he had been. Escaping a web of intrigue by a needle's eye he had saved his Irish pelt from the century's worst kind of torture - the peeling off of his sun hardened skin whilst still alive. This ritual would have been ogled by the hierarchy of *Makinto* (they who fear nothing), Africa's most foul and bestial of secret societies.

Rural Ireland in the mid sixties showed a propensity for emigration and young Doyle followed the tide.

But then Emmett Doyle was no ordinary being. Luck had played an immense part in the time he had spent away from Ballyvaughan, in the west of Ireland. Now he was back into watching hookers of another species plying their age old trade on less troubled waters. He also had a story to tell.

1

"Where the hell is Ukenza?"

Someone was driving with purpose. Perhaps, with a mission in mind? Clouds of sandy amber dust spiralled in the vehicle's wake as it approached at great speed, only slowing down at the farm compound's entrance. These dust clouds enveloped the vehicle for a few brief moments.

Emmett Doyle, sitting on his veranda, after breaking for lunch, watched this approach with interest. The dusty blue Peugeot Estate halted at his garden gate. Emmett rose from his chair, stretched his now well bronzed arms above his head, stepped off the raised veranda and walked nonchalantly towards the driver who was only a few yards away from him.

She was vibrant, about five feet and a few inches, with jet black hair and an ample athletic figure. Bright red lipstick glistened on a well-formed smile. Her eyes sparkled. They were a deep purple. Her movement was definite in a sultry snakelike way.

Shirra Thomson was the first lady to call on Emmett since his recent luncheon and plant party. He remembered her well for she talked about tennis and the amateur dramatic society whenever she cornered him. Her theatrical use of words and body language seemed so out of place on these vast wheatland plains.

"I'm only here to make you say yes to being my partner in the mixed doubles at the club championships. They start in two weeks time. Please say yes darling," as she drew his face to hers and kissed voluptuously full lips to lips. She wasn't afraid of who was watching.

"My goodness," was all Emmett could reply as he caught his breath "what a lovely offer. Come on in and let's discuss it."

She continued in a breathless rush

"I've just been to the Club and put my name down for all three – that is singles, doubles and mixed. I told the silly old secretary that I would contact him about you. You will say yes darling, please?" and she plonked herself down on his settee. "I'd love a G & T and ice if you've got it, darling."

"Certainly, yes." Christopher, hovering in the background, had almost read her mind as he entered with water, ice, lemon and limes.

"God it's dusty on that road. Can I freshen up darling – I'll smell better then?"

"Of course, go ahead – you know the way don't you – here, first on the right," as he showed her down the passage.

"You're the perfect halfway house you know from town to us, out in the bush. You'll be seeing lots of me on my travels. I promise."

After a few minutes Shirra called to him from the bathroom, "any chance of another towel, Emmett darling?"

"No problem, I'll get you one. Just a mo."

He tapped on the half open door.

"Come on in there's no worry on my side darling," came a muffled reply. She was bent over the hand basin with her face in water, she was bare from the waste upwards, her full breasts hanging beside the edge of the basin.

As she straightened she turned to face Emmett signalling him to wrap the towel around her wet head. She hadn't washed her hair but a lot of it was dripping wet.

With her own towel she gently tapped her face and upper body obviously protective of the peaches and cream texture of her slightly off white skin. Perhaps well-worn ivory would be a more correct description Emmett felt as he self-consciously ogled the vision .

She wore no shoes and was tiny beside him. Her body was suddenly in front of and below as she sidled close into him.

Her freshened face peered up into his eyes. For a moment his hands stopped drying her hair, his face lowered onto her pleading lips. He held her head tightly to him. Their lips parted, tongues entwining as she began to murmur sweet mating noises. Her towel fell to the floor as hands grasped his firm buttocks.

He could feel his starved Irish pillar telescoping into a colossus. Their mouths welded, her hands leapt from buttocks to his fly, top button of his shorts already deftly opened, she struck for gold. With his jewels encased in gentle hands she dropped to the floor and took him into a devouring mouth with slightly sharp teeth grazing the tender throbbing almost virginal skin of his manhood.

Emmett moaned a mighty moan. Dogs rushed into the bathroom inquisitive as to these previously unheard noises. They smelt the two bodies but realised nothing was amiss and departed to lie, on guard, in the passage. He couldn't believe this was happening – her method was new to him – but God was it good! He never wished it to stop. His desires reached a seemingly unending series of climaxes. His need had been even greater than he first realised.

"God, you're enormous darling Irishman and such strength too. Please save this for me alone. I'll keep you supplied."

She rose from her knees drawing his head down to her and kissed him once again. This time he tasted a slight salinity in her all devouring mouth.

2

It was Emmett's turn now as he cupped her breasts and buried them both with kisses and sucks that made her moan and embrace him vicelike. His tool rose again becoming cushioned in her ample cleavage as he arched above her in adulation of such an erotic experience.

She showered kisses and little bites on his still rampant organ. She gently lead it to the basin and washed it down in soothing warm water. She towelled it softly, drew up his pants from around his ankles and cosseted it back into its special cubby hole.

From a few of his expatriate friends he had been forewarned that "are you married or do you live in Kenya" was a phrase he would have to contend with. Round one was a welcoming success and this was only Ukenza!

Emmett called for tea as he returned to normality with dogs craving his attention.

Shirra had a certain radiance as she settled into the settee and finished her long awaited G & T in double quick time.

"Don't get all dreamy eyed over this darling Emmett. I adore sex – have to have it and as often as possible. We can be an item but only an orgasmic one. I really am happily married and adore my two children – I would never leave Buster. So if you can stomach that, then we can look forward to many, many connubial episodes. You needed that, I could feel it right through your taut body – a lovely one my darling."

"I'm just dumbfounded, elated, satisfied and expectant of our next meeting. I'll take it as you dish it out. No strings."

"Good my darling. We'll play magical tennis together. Just wait and see. I have a flat I can use in Urukan so we're set up for the tournament."

In came Christopher with a tray of tea and sponge cake. He placed it on the table between them.

"I have such a thirst after that sort of exercise – wonder if it will affect you in that way. Pour a gallon of sweet tea please darling," gushed a dreamy eyed conqueror.

Emmett found he too had a massive thirst. They sat in silence devouring cups and cups of this welcome brew. Up she jumped after about fifteen minutes, and with feline ease mouthed in hushed tones:

"Must be on my way. You will play with me won't you? I'll contact the secretary tomorrow to confirm. Loved every moment. See you soon darling Irishman."

She hooted madly for her driver who had accompanied her. He came running from the labour lines. They departed in a cloud of dust.

"Wow," thought Emmett. He had certainly worked hard since he had arrived in Africa. Now it seemed he could play hard for the foreseeable future.

That night he knew exactly what it was like 'to be fucked'. What an experience. He really felt he was still quite naïve in the realms of passion. Perhaps Shirra was the catalyst for the future. He slept a satiated sleep that night.

As Emmett sat on his veranda next morning savouring yet another mug of tea his thoughts returned to Ireland and how he had fortuitously fashioned his passage to Ratilli, his home on the Punjabi Plains. He rummaged through his memories of yesterday. Those electrifying moments of pent up passion. If this was a sample of what Africa had to offer then let the full menu be served. His appetite was ready for it.

Over breakfast his mind turned to the other four of the Irish quintet and wondered whether their experiences in any way matched his?

School and university days weld friendships that span lifetimes. Or so it transpired for the "fractious five" who had met one July evening in an upstairs room of Larry Murphy's on Baggot Street, Dublin.

Drawn together by the foresight of five Irish families, their respective sons met in preparatory school at seven years of age, moved on to three different public schools, meeting up again during holidays. Two universities in Ireland and one in the United Kingdom still did not fragment the link of youthful exuberance. They each completed satisfactory degrees and then one night, at a black tie affair during August Show week, in Dublin, decided to test and taste the diaspora. They each had been on a year's sabbatical, had sewn some oats and were ready for anything.

They decided that Ireland in the sixties was too parochial, too drab and too lacking in "je ne sais quoi" – get up and go. It was a depressing time. This group decided to break out.

An upstairs room in the inn was hired. Privacy was essential. Behind closed doors an extraordinary plan was conceived.

Justin Matthews was now a doctor as were both his parents and one sister. They practised in Ireland and had never been further than Paris. He would change that style.

An architectural future coloured the canvases of Bob "Napper" McGahan's childhood. His graphic designs set teachers and tutors imaginations a whiz with delight. His mother dabbled in church fete art shows. His father was an accountant.

Isaac "Spike" Vard was an actor. His performances in school productions were legend. He was so 'camp' and played it to the full. RADA had moulded this youthful zest into an Olivier look-a-like.

Whenever a bird, mouse, dog or cat was hurt at school or its surrounds Al (Aloysius Loyola) Collins would be called to administer TLC. His future had to be

4

veterinary, wild life, ecology or the like. He studied and degreed in the former.

Emmett Doyle was rural. His physique showed the influence of Albert Finney's performance as Tom Jones in the movie of the same name. At university, reading agriculture, he grew his pony tail. It became his trademark. His family were landowners in the west of Ireland and his father had a passion for the sea. Their Galway hooker An Grainne was moored in the scenic harbour at Ballyvaughan, Co. Clare. Young Emmett had spent many hours plying the waters of Galway Bay to the Aran Isles.

That night in Larry Murphy's they decided to leave Ireland and explore the world. They drew lots for countries and vowed to set up shop wherever their allotted ticket took them.

Two pewter beer mugs contained their destiny. They, respectively, held the names of continents and their own. It was decided that alphabetically spelt names would govern the order of the draw. Slithers of paper were written up, folded and placed in the mugs.

Collins dipped first. He drew Vard who then picked Europe. Doyle was next. He brought out Collins who got South America. Matthews picked McGahan who went ecstatic when drawing Asia. Matthews was next out of the mug and he got Australia. Doyle was last to be drawn and he won Africa.

It was agreed that a three month period should be allowed to make arrangements for departure to their respective destinations. A final meeting was arranged and each set off to make contacts, peruse the appointments pages or however they wished to set up their segment of the venture.

Emmett was an avid reader of the National Geographic Magazine and loved the worlds of nature reserves and wild game that inhabited them in far off mystical lands. Now he was en route to one of these, darkest Africa.

Having picked Africa it was now up to him to find a job in any of its colourful countries. His rural background and BSc (Ag degree) coupled with his love of the outdoors and zest for living shouldn't make the search too difficult, he mused.

Calling a couple of fellow Galwegians and he invited them to lunch at the Great Southern, to pick their brains.

Whilst awaiting their arrival Emmett chanced on an English Sunday Times lying on the coffee table in the reception. Its appointments section was vast as he slowly paged through it. Under Foreign his eye was attracted by an advertisement in the bottom right hand corner.

Farm Manager/Partner required. Large wheat acreage Ukenza.

Contact London Tel......

First thoughts were "where the hell is Ukenza? Have heard its name but haven't the foggiest idea its situation." He must have said this out loud as a number of other guests looked up in surprise and fixed him with a variety of quizzical stares. He had a loud voice.

His two friends, James a vet and Simon a farmer, probably wouldn't be able to find Africa on the world map at first glance he ventured? They were both totally blank about Ukenza. Both thought the idea outrageous but Emmett felt they secretly envied his courage. Not many in rural Ireland had the getup and go attitude he had. They wouldn't easily change their cultural inheritance.

"And sure there won't be any pubs there I bet" offered Simon as a definite negative. Both were slightly red of hair and prone to freckles so too much sun wouldn't be appreciated, thought Emmett.

They were close childhood mates and wished him "all the very best, be careful of catching you know what out there and don't return with a black woman. Sure there'd be hell to pay in the village" and a wink, wink, nudge, nudge sort of attitude prevailed during the bar lunch and over a couple of pints.

"We'll keep your corner seat warm for you – never fear. Good luck and God bless". They each hugged him with true friendship expressed in the warmth and strength of their clasp as they departed across Eyre Square.

"Mind they don't string you up by your pony tail!!" was their farewell afterthought.

Later that day Emmett thought of the banter in Mullins' pub that night. Simon's sister owned their local watering hole where the two lads would meet up at 10.00 pm for their nightly pints. The entire parish would know of Emmett's journey to the dark continent by morning.

An interview in London took place the next week, followed closely by an acceptance phone call. Emmett had landed the job. His ticket to Nairobi would arrive in approximately one month's time. That should give him enough space to settle affairs at home and to extricate as much information as was possible on Ukenza and its inhabitants.

Emmett phoned the other four and explained his good fortune. Justin had also got himself organised in a hospital in Perth, Western Australia. It was therefore decided to meet up ahead of the original date to hear of all their plans and bid everyone farewell.

Dublin's Trinity College library provided a cornucopia of delights and not so delectable facts about Ukenza.

A landlocked haven – some described it – governed by a megalomaniac president, corrupt, full of poverty and with only agriculture as its main income. A total population of 12,000,000 with 100,000 Asians and 15,000 Europeans. All imports had to come via Mombasa and travel through Kenya and Uganda before reaching their border. Asians controlled transportation. There was no railway. The nearest railhead was Kampala, 600 miles away.

Tea, coffee, cotton and wheat were the main export crops.

Seven ethnic tribes made up the population. The President was from one of the minor tribes. He therefore had much opposition.

According to many political analysts he had been shrewd enough, however, to juggle the best brains from all nationalities and tribes so maintaining a power base that could eradicate any upstart opposition.

Ukenza had broken away from its mother colony in the forties and had, by and large, progressed favourably along the Independence route 'till present day. Its majority was Catholic and missions (probably Irish Emmett thought) therefore played a strong part in its education module.

Entry visas were not easy to come by but those in the know made applications look simple. Obviously Emmett's employers fitted into that bracket. They leased many thousands of acres in the bread basket region of Koram which was 200 miles from the capital city, Kenzi, and 80 miles from the provincial capital Urukan, the home of the Bhogal family, the Asian conglomerate now about to employ one slightly flamboyant but perhaps naïve Irishman.

Emmett had been interviewed by the head of the family and one of his sons, a London lawyer. They seemed nice enough in the two hours Emmett spent with them. Polite, to the point and impressive in their financial holdings. He held out for more than their initial offer. In fact, his demands for house, car, medical insurance and general expenses got cold looks from the both of them. Great poker faces as Emmett silently summed them up.

All his questioning of ex-pats he had managed to meet in the intervening weeks had prepared him well. This would be his first real job, in a foreign land and under a very different culture. He had to be prepared. So ask for the moon and the stars might get thrown in. Perhaps the luck of the Irish might well play a part?

When Amrik Bhogal phoned to confirm Emmett's appointment the only point he needed to clarify was the car. It wouldn't be a sedan. It would be a Landrover as they held the franchise for them. Emmett was chuffed as he immediately saw himself as a colonial God with dogs and servants crammed into the vehicle as he drove around the territory. He had seen and read about his dream occupation – an East African game ranger. Perhaps this first step in Africa was Emmett's route to paradise?

Saying farewell to friends and family proved a nightmare as each wanted to outdo the other with a party. Emmett met people he hadn't seen for decades – some he knew, for sure, others he could not recall but who recounted instances in his youth too gall making for repetition.

On departing for Africa he stood 5ft. 10ins tall and weighed 11 stone. He had maintained this weight right through public school and university.

"An athlete through and through," one of his lecturers had described him. With sparkling sapphire eyes, a mop of light brown hair drawn into a ponytail, his cherub-face looks attracted the female sex like male eyes to a page three babe! This inevitably provided grounds for untold jealousy. His naivety, however, usually got him out of serious trouble. Laughing it off combined with total innocence allowed him to conquer another day. His 'Mam' worried about him moving off into the great wide and perhaps Wild World, especially in darkest Africa

Finally all relatives were seen to, and a farewell booze up at Larry Murphy's with the other four intrepids saw him on his way to London for a week's jollity prior to departure.

One of his school chums was now in practice in Harley Street and he invited Emmett to stay with him. Hugh was also Irish but had chosen the London road to medical fame. And he was doing mighty well for himself too – in so few years.

Hugh's parents had spent many years in West Africa. They were both doctors in Sierre Leone and over a couple of gargantuan dinner parties managed to direct him towards kitting out his new wardrobe and instructing him just where to go in London to purchase the necessary tropical gear.

Escorted by Hugh's sensual sister, Siobhann, who was between husbands at that juncture, Emmett put together khaki bush jackets, shorts and desert boots. Lots of colourful cravats augmented a range of short sleeved shirts from Carnaby Street.

A party at the Taj Mahal on Frith Street was Hugh's idea of seasoning Emmett into oriental Indian cuisine. Getting into conversation with the Indian Maitre'd, Emmett offered a snippet of information on his impending trip to Ukenza. A smile as long as the pool in front of the real Taj Mahal in India lit up his olive black deep set eyes and spread all over his circular countenance.

"I gotting uncle in Ukenza, in Kenz. He will help you making it in far off land. I give you his name address and numbers. He very important person I'm told." No one at the table could believe Emmett's luck. Any contact surely is better than none they concluded?

The conversation rocked from whether he might be Indian Mafia, a cobbler or a chef to the more mundane of civil servant or bus driver? Emmett promised to report back to them.

As the party collected their coats Emmett was handed an envelope with a name and address. Inside the Maitre had written a hurried note to his uncle. He then wished Emmett "safe journey and may Allah guide you". He was thoroughly chuffed about this extraordinary coincidence.

The meal was superb. He felt he could get a real taste for oriental food. On leaving, Emmett palmed a further fiver of his own into the Maitre's hand.

"See you on my return. And thanks."

Flying East African Airways to Nairobi, Emmett overnighted in the Norfolk Hotel. Next morning he flew Inter-Air to Ukenza. This was in a tiny plane of sixteen passengers. It didn't seem to fly too high as it was quite easy to follow different terrain, spotting rivers, lakes and the odd salt pan. Very few roads could be seen and then nothing but cloud.

Emmett's seating companion, a turbaned Asian with a smattering of English, did manage to explain they were climbing over the mountain range that ran down the middle of the country. We would be landing very shortly. Emmett must have slept as two hours had flown quite miraculously by.

Kenzi Airport was tiny – rather like Baldonnel back home. Two or three gasoline trucks were parked close to the main buildings which looked like the Nissen huts he had seen in films from the war years.

Luckily it wasn't raining as there was a hundred yard hike from plane to buildings. Emmett lugged his overweight cabin baggage and was sweating by the time he reached the door which opened into a scant hall with a long wooden counter running the length of one side. Behind it were a dozen men in drab pale green bush shirts each looking less efficient than his neighbour.

A rather swankish turbaned Indian walked forward and enquired "Emmett Doyle I am thinking?"

"Yes indeed."

"Welcome to our beautiful country. Don't bother about customs, etc. It's all sorted."

"How nice and friendly," Emmett replied looking sheepishly at the other fifteen passengers who had formed a queue.

"Your luggage won't take long and our transport is waiting outside."

It all seemed so grand to Emmett who had only experienced the drudgery of going places in the UK and on the continent on the cheap. No VIP treatment had he ever enjoyed before this trip. Long may it last.

The Ambassador was the one decent hotel in the city he was informed by Arjan who had met him. He would be their guest for four days whilst he got the feel of things in their offices.

The hotel was a poor three-star establishment with creaking doors, occasional water, cardboard towels and rock hard pillows Ancient fans noisily circled overhead like jaded daddy longlegs attempting touch down. Extremely black staff slippered around the polished cement floors in flowing off white kanzus gathered at the waist by wide red belts which complimented the red fez each wore

9

on his head. They appeared meek but did smile when approached. All had a smattering of English. Emmett reckoned that the aroma which 'hung' all about the place was from the contents of the large tins of Cobra polish that stood silently in room corners.

The bar had a Wild West theme which Emmett thought quite bizarre. Saloon swing doors at either end of a rectangular room hosted a semi-circle of a bar counter with a mirrored background. Murals of Custer, Cochise, Earp were all there amongst dead and dying American Red Indians and blue coated cavalry.

Who on earth would know about that period of American history and would appreciate it over a beer or more in a tiny African country – in the back of beyond – mused Emmett over his first cold Tusker lager? Obviously the owner loved western movies – as did Emmett.

He was happy to just sit there and relax. Looking and listening, and getting a feel of the language he assuredly would have to master before too long, made it all so harmonious. Outside it was hot. Something else Emmett would have to cope with.

Virtually everything in the way of luxury goods had to be imported and he noticed that the beer was from East African breweries, Kampala. It was an excellent light lager which he had sampled in Nairobi and was the tipple of the majority. It was served cold from fridges beneath the counter. East Africa also produced an excellent range of spirits – Vodka, Gin and Brandy – so there would be no shortage on the liquor front.

Bhogals' offices, garages and workshops were a little out of town, very efficiently run and tastefully decorated. Not only were they Rover agents but also handled MAN trucks, Peugeot, and Toyota. It was an enormous operation.

Without prying too much it was easily seen that government was their number one client with heavy transport hauliers as close runners up. Various sons and nephews ran the business under the disciplined eye of Jaswant – head of the house and Chairman of the empire.

Emmett had enough time in Nairobi to walk the main streets and gauge the shopping sense so he could now compare the two. Kenzi was very low market in comparison. This, of course, was his initial impression. He had yet to discover the delicacies, if such were to be found.

Emmett had negotiated a three year contract with the option, from both sides, of renewal of a further three years. They had initially said it should be only a two year duration but he pointed out that any changes in the farm setup would most probably only bear fruit in the third season and thereafter.

He had agreed to a share of the crops annual profit, as his partnership deal, on top of all the other expat benefits that befitted a posting such as this in the back of beyond. In fact he went quite overboard on his beliefs, prowess and essentialities. What the hell, he argued – if he didn't land this one there would be plenty of others. Such was the optimism and enthusiasm of this almost arrogant Irishman.

"Try anything once and try hard at everything," was Emmett's motto.

He kept quiet during the hours spent at head office wanting to absorb all information possible whilst summing up the personnel he would be working with and reporting back to. His landrover was being prepared – a long wheel base model, green in colour, with a half open back-end for transporting items of varying height, length and weight. Emmett was simply dying to drive it and set sail for his new life.

2

Christopher, Zungus and Hindis

The farm was named Ratilli – an ethnic word meaning weighbridge. One of Bhogals' nephews from Kampala had originally opened up the land ten years previously and had given it the name. Emmett thought it had a good ring to it and was pleased it wasn't some obscure unpronounceable name. Ratilli ran easily off his tongue.

It was a three hour drive from Kenzi to the farm and one had to pass through the provincial capital Urukan to reach it. Bhogal had a large setup there too as it was the centre of the agricultural heartland and their original starting off place. The elders of the family still resided there.

Evidently most of the large farms were owned or leased by ex Brits, Portuguese, French, Belgium or South Africans. Emmett was told by Jaswant that the President didn't mind what nationality farmed the land as long as they were profitable and it all went toward the Forex (foreign exchange) account. He was a very forward thinking President but ruthless in many respects when things didn't run his way. No one was spared his wrath.

Emmett was warned to toe the line and not be above the law. The country's jail's were not pretty places. He was already earning sideways glances with his unusual hair style. But what the hell he thought, I am me. Let them get used to it! He wondered what hair styles lay under these Indian's dark turbans?

On the drive to Urukan he was accompanied by two of Bhogals' drivers who were returning to their homes on leave. Natives of the country are known as Kenzies but they can be divided into seven different tribes, each with their own ethnic name. These two were mines of information and Emmett felt he had learnt more about the country in one and a half hours than he had from the office staff in three days. Both were of the Tukulu tribe and spoke passable English. Tuks, as Emmett was told the tribe was referred to, were the most populous, best educated and held many of the top jobs. But the President was from a minor tribe and promoted his brothers and sisters over the rest. This was a major bone of contention he was informed.

They knew most of the staff on Ratilli and informed him that his mechanics, drivers and bookkeeper were all Tuks. He was very lucky in this, they told him.

The set up in Urukan was similar to Kenzi but smaller. All Emmett had to do there was pick up some spares for his workshop, purchase his household needs and set sail for his 'new home on the range'. His companion this time was Gilbert, the farm's secretary/bookkeeper with the month's wages onboard for the staff. Distributing this would be Emmett's first major job the following morning. This had been well planned, he thought, as it would give him an eye to eye with his entire workforce.

An hour out of Urukan they turned off the wide tarmacadam road onto an even wider sand surface.

"This is murram," said Gilbert "and it gets graded quite regularly, usually before the rains. You must beware of pot holes and on some corners the corrugations are very bad. Hard on the steering."

Emmett thanked him profusely and slowed his pace appreciably. Glints of sun on glass with clouds of dust billowing behind, signalled an oncoming vehicle. When the first one got quite close Gilbert put the palm of his hand on the windscreen in front of him until the vehicle had passed.

"Why that?" Emmett questioned.

"To stop stones from cracking the glass, fendi."

"Thanks for the tip, Gilbert, I'll have to remember that."

Emmett had heard the word, fendi, being used in Bhogals' office but hadn't asked about it. Now he realised it meant friend or master in which ever context used. He felt he was that step closer to his new life – new world – a new African person. Wait 'till the lads back home hear about this!

Only one small town, Koram, was sighted on the way. This was a main street lined on either side with African and Indian dukas (small shops). Along the pavements in front of these were men and women at sewing machines, cobblers tools, ironmongery, basket weaving and other crafts. One section was devoted to carpentry with all sizes and shapes of chairs, tables and stools on display. Many were painted in the gaudiest of colours.

Tall lean men dressed in reddish blankets, each carrying a stick, stood in groups surveying the dusty passers by. These were of the Kipsis tribe and were stockmen he was told. They had herds of Zebu cattle, coupled with black-headed Persian sheep and goat flocks. Once again it was Gilbert supplying all the information which Emmett desperately tried to store away in a jumbled brain full of new characters and designs. The Kipsis were distant relatives of the Maasai of Kenya Colony.

There were little or no trees or shrubs in the plateau they now travelled along and all land seemed to be devoid of grass.

"You are now in breadbasket of Ukenza" announced Gilbert as Emmett looked out on miles and miles of emptiness. A landscape devoid of anything. One of the ex pats Emmett had befriended explained this very phenomenon he remembered.

"It's known as M.M.B.A. – miles and miles of bloody Africa!"

Occasionally as they approached a dried up river bed and descended onto a narrow, one vehicle only, concrete path, would one notice African thorn trees and scrubland along the river banks.

"These must be dangerous in the rainy season," Emmett remarked.

"Oh yes, fendi. You can be halted for hours on either side waiting for swollen rivers to go down. A great worry if you are in a hurry."

After a further thirty minutes Gilbert pointed out the northern boundary of the farm. There was a barbed wire fence running off into the distance – one of the few such fences Emmett had noticed in the past hour of driving. On leaving Urukan's suburbs he had seen many herds of dairy cattle on intensive cultivated lands. Lots of red roofed bungalows surrounded by tall Australian blue gums (Eucalyptus trees) acted as wind brakes. These were mainly European owned farms and provided milk and vegetables for the town. After them was a native reserve where labour for the town lived and farmed. Then came the wheat lands and they evidently stretched for nearly one hundred miles.

Emmett couldn't have been more pleased when on the horizon he noticed a tall narrow building. He was about to ask when Gilbert beat him to it.

"That's the Ratilli. We are almost home, fendi. Please stop at it as I have some papers for Japhet who runs the weighbridge."

Emmett jumped out to stretch his legs and take a good look at this top heavy corrugated iron monstrosity, which wasn't in action but a group of people stood and sat around on the ground nearby. He was introduced to Japhet who showed him inside his office and explained the mechanism of the weighbridge. Gilbert told him that Japhet was on the farm's payroll and was one of his responsibilities.

All hauliers transporting wheat from the area had to weigh in empty, have it recorded, hand written in a book, and then weigh out with the load on their return trip to the grain silos in Koram and Urukan. Each farmer would thereby have a record of his crop prior to checking in for payment at the silo. This supposedly stopped any fiddling along the way. The Bhogals had built the weighbridge and charged a fee for its use.

The farm's entrance was an ornate wrought iron gateway next to the Ratilli and Emmett could see his farmhouse, adjacent buildings and labour lines down a straight avenue, devoid of trees, about a mile away.

He drove slowly savouring the moment, and approaching the compound a pack of dogs of all sizes and colour raced towards the vehicle and followed it to the front gate of the house.

A very tall thin African, shiny clean in starched khaki bush shirt and long trousers greeted them.

"Welcome fendi to your new home. I am Christopher your major domo."

Everything looked drab, even the little garden gate hung at a limp angle. The garden was under grown with weeds battling for existence in their own tiny sun drenched desert.

From the outside the house seemed spacious. It was a timber clapboard construction with a corrugated iron roof, which needed a coat of paint. It was a bungalow.

Emmett's heart sank a bit as he followed Christopher up onto the veranda. Fly screened double doors lead into a sparsely fitted sitting room. There was lots of light from two large windows. The floor was polished cement, green in colour, fading in places.

Christopher lead on down a corridor to a corner bedroom with two windows. The furniture was basic wooden – wardrobe, dressing table, double bed, foam mattress and two bedside tables. None of the light fittings had shades.

Emmett's two cases were plonked on the floor as he set out to explore the rest of the dwelling. There were two other bedrooms with single beds and wardrobes, a toilet, shower room and a wash hand basin on the wall in the passage.

The kitchen was tiny with an ancient wood stove in one corner and a small two-ring gas unit on a work table, with cylinder below. Some cupboards with drawers filled the other wall.

Next to the kitchen was an old fashioned pantry, rather like Emmett's mother had at home. Well shelved, it housed a fly screened open cupboard. There was a small window, fly screened again, which allowed for a through draft. It was cool in there.

This then was Emmett's little home and he would just have to make do with what was offered. Not, however, at all like Ballyvaughan? Every wall was painted a faded yellow.

It was mid afternoon and tea was on the brew. Emmett had pointed out to Christopher the boxes of food stuffs, so he was busy putting the various commodities away in the kitchen.

In four days he had become used to long life milk in his tea, coffee and breakfast cereal. It certainly was an acquired taste and one that needed gentling into. He saw no grass in the area so obviously there was no chance of fresh milk in this barren land.

The house was well dusted and almost clinically clean. After unpacking and arranging his gear he took a stroll out and around the farm compound. It was rectangular in design with the house holding pride of place on one of the short sides. Next to it, on its left, was the office where Gilbert and an assistant were already at work.

Running down the long side adjacent to the office were the mechanical workshops and machinery sheds. At the far end, and opposite his house and office, ran the staff labour lines (living quarters).

Grain stores made up the other long side. At a guess and having strode around, down and along the area, Emmett figured it was a hundred and fifty by seventy-five yards of a rectangle.

The workshops and grain sheds had concrete floors. A yellowy clay made up the remainder of the area. There was no wind so no dust flew. It must be hell, however, in a storm and in the rainy seasons.

Christopher produced a venison casserole for supper that night which went down well with a few glasses of Bordeaux red, which Emmett had bought in Kenzi and was highly recommended by the bottle store. They imported it from the Congo, their westerly neighbour across Lake Nduga.

Things were extraordinarily quiet save for the odd dog fight and accompanying yelps from the labour lines. Sitting out on the veranda prior to his first meal watching the African sunset, straight in front, illustrated to Emmett the compass points of the rectangle. He realised his bedroom was therefore facing east and would be blessed with the rising sun.

Emmett slept soundly that first night in his new home. He was at peace with the world.

A loud clanging noise woke him with a start. His travelling clock showed 6.00am. He waited a further fifteen minutes before venturing to draw the curtains.

There was a pale blueish grey tinge to the texture of the morning. Birds were chirping. Some sounded like house sparrows, others like starlings. Definitely songs attuned to his ear.

After shaving and dressing in shorts, shirt and desert boots, Emmett noticed his first African sunrise on the farm. It reminded him of the Country Style butter advertisement he used to see in the cinemas back home. A big round yellow ball fashioned into a smiling face rising gracefully from its slumbers, its heat exuding from three hundred and sixty degree rays onto an earth craving its first warm kiss of the day. It only took ten minutes or so to appear completely in the round, thence to continue its twelve hour journey before bowing down to sleep once again – its batteries being recharged in the still of the night – on the other side of the world.

Emmett craved his early morning 'cuppa' so this was a routine he had to get established before anything else. An old blackened kettle half full of water was on the side of the stove whose embers were still 'in' as his mother used to say about their old Aga. A couple of rakes with the poker, two small logs to add to the kindling and the kettle was whistling away in no time. The water smelt smoky which gave the tea leaves an extra special flavour. It reminded him of harvesting time in County Clare when the ladies would light a fire at the side of the field and distribute scalding hot sweet tea with ham and cheese sandwiches to the workers. Nice thoughts for his first morning at work.

Christopher arrived just before 7.00am and gave him the outline of the farm's routine.

That clanging noise was to awaken everyone and at 7.00am it would be sounded again. This summoned the staff to their respective jobs.

The compound was like an ant's nest, people tooing and frowing, chattering as they went. Tractors started up, generators, compressors sprung into life. Welding rods spewed sparks. Dogs barked.

All eyes followed Emmett as first he called on Gilbert and his assistant, Eddison. Wages would be paid at 2.00pm he was informed. It would be a short working day allowing the staff to be transported by farm lorry to Koram for shopping and imbibing after they were paid.

Eddison was given the task of escorting him into all the different sectors. He introduced only the senior personnel which in itself was quite sufficient for him to comprehend. He felt he had all the time in the world ahead to get to know the entire complement anyway.

After an hour of investigating the workings of the farm compound he returned to breakfast. Christopher enquired whether he wished his main meal in the middle of the day or in the evening?

Emmett pondered this, over his fourth cup of tea, and decided on having it in the middle of the day. He felt he might well be too exhausted at days end to enjoy heavy food.

Christopher questioned him on his likes and dislikes, explaining the problems of always having enough of everything in the store room.

There was a daily bus running to Urukan and by bribing the driver one could get goods collected there. It, however, didn't always work out the way it was meant to as the bus regularly broke down or crashed. Sometimes it was ambushed with all goods taken by the attackers!

The farm was 12,000 acres in extent. Absolutely enormous in Irish terms but by no means one of the larger spreads out here. Emmett asked Gilbert for a guide. He wished to drive around whatever roads or tracks were laid out in this flat uninteresting land. It was late September, the end of the winter, and not a semblance of greenery was evident anywhere. The harvest had been taken off to the silos and work was almost at a standstill.

This was the time of year when farm labour went home for a month's holiday to their families. It was, however, a time of repair and maintenance of plant, machinery and boundaries on the farm.

Fencing gangs took off in the morning and only returned at 4.00pm in the afternoon. The farm was ring fenced with thirteen strand barbed wire reaching up to seven feet high. This was evidently to try and restrain the movement of wild animals – game, in African terms. Lots of different species of antelope roamed these lands coming in from the foothills of the Mandara mountains which ran spine-like down the centre of the country. These reached heights of 10,000 ft. and Emmett learnt that there was wonderful trout fishing up in their higher reaches.

Tea and coffee estates took up a major portion of their fertile lower ridges. These two products, together with wheat, were the country's main exports. Cotton was a minor crop but also a very important one. The government, therefore, looked after the producers of these commodities.

Jaswant had explained, in great detail, how well they, the farmers, were protected and this must in turn, be respected at all times.

He got the impression that everything, everyone, every move, every strategy was under constant scrutiny. These snippets of information went straight to number one – the President, Victor Ubugu.

Emmett was therefore being given due warning to cooperate and produce a maximum crop. He wondered who was the government informer on Ratilli and how would he get to know him without the other realising. It would be an interesting game. He wished he had taken more interest in the chess club at school and university!

Right next to the compound and running for a thousand yards east to west was a runway (landing strip) with a raggedy torn orange windsock. Nobody, strangely, had mentioned this. The soil was parched with, in places, large cracks crisscrossing areas of hundreds of acres and more.

Certain areas were undulating and gave Emmett the chance of viewing parts of the farm from an elevated position.

A few dry riverbeds crossed the farm. Along their banks grew thorn trees (Acacias) and bushes but they petered out some fifty yards from the sandy beds. Guinea fowl and lizards, apart from a few hornbills, were the only things moving.

The short rains should arrive within a month he was told and a certain amount of green growth would then blossom forth. It was a barren world for these few months – something one just had to endure. A parched dry sandy smell tested his nostrils as his vehicle turned latent areas of soil into billowing dustclouds.

Emmett covered two of the four sections of the farm that morning and would study the map up on one of the walls in the office that afternoon. There probably wouldn't be much difference in the remainder but he felt he must get to know every corner of the ring fenced boundary line. Another day would see to that he estimated.

By 1.30pm that afternoon a queue was forming outside the office when he joined Gilbert for the distribution of wages.

There would only be a staff of approximately thirty-five as most of the casual labour had departed for their homelands on leave. Drivers, mechanics, maintenance staff and fencing teams together with farm security personnel made up this total.

In theory the short rains should arrive next month, October, enough to germinate all weeds and various grasses, then a month later the tractors would start ploughing the lands. Harrowing and preparing the seed beds for planting would be in January and early February.

Jaswant had been adamant in telling Emmett that the entire crop had to be planted within one month from starting day to finishing hour and all must be completed by March 17th – give or take a day or two.

The 'long' rains hopefully should then arrive, germinate the crop which would have four to four and a half months to grow to maturity. Harvesting usually commenced mid August, which was mid winter in this part of Africa.

That was the timetable Emmett had been given but obviously local knowledge and the 'feel' of the weather around those commencement times would determine the actual dates.

He noted that the majority of drivers and mechanics were indeed Tuks like Gilbert. Fencing staff and maintenance gangs were equally divided between the Mandi and Wasti tribes.

There was so much to discover in this climatically strange land which seemed serene on the outside but full of intrigue within. Emmett resolved to keep a chameleonic view of the situation. Although never a Boy Scout he felt that Baden Powell's motto 'be prepared' should be heeded at all times. He was a lone white man amongst a throng of natives miles from anywhere. In Emmett's naivety he hadn't factored the loneliness and isolation from other Europeans into his initial equation.

This was summarily interrupted three days later when he noticed a dust storm speeding down the avenue. He kept his eyes on the vehicle which slowed appreciably on entering the compound. It was a Landrover driven by a European.

"Ye Gods and little fishes – manna from heaven," thought Emmett as he was approached by a very bouncy man in raggedy old shorts, shirt and boots with socks just above his ankles. A well-tanned farmer no doubt, a local perhaps?

"Hi, I'm your neighbour. Ian Poultney is my name and welcome."

Emmett introduced himself and lead him over to the house.

"What do you think of the place, eh? A bit rundown but all Asian farms are like this – unless they have a Zungu – a European manager on them. The Hindi take no pride in the place – just want to drain it of all its crops and put little back in return."

Ian had a strange accent which Emmett couldn't place – very clipped and flat in places.

"Coffee or tea or beer?"

"Oh coffee – kawa as we call it here will be fine."

"I'm from Ireland and it is certainly very different from back home. It's good of you to drop in."

"Oh you'll see plenty more of us once you've settled in. We are a tight community of eleven European farms and there are another five Zungu managers in the district. You make six."

Ian was obviously keen on explaining just about everything so Emmett sat back whilst Christopher made a pot of kawa and opened a packet of biscuits. They sat on the veranda.

"Our place is across the road from the Ratilli – that's it over there," pointing to a rising piece of land all along the other side of the road.

"Do you see that kopi – knoll - over there to the left, well that's one boundary and the next farm to us is owned by my brother-in-law. And his neighbour, further on down to the south, is Todd Beaton. Are you a pilot by any chance?"

"No, I'm afraid not. Why?"

"Well my brother-in-law Howard Wood, he is a superb pilot and he's now teaching me. It's almost essential to have a plane out here. Most of the farmers fly Cessna's, a few have Pipers. Your fellow, Bhogal, he flies in with his Cessna and after planting he imports a couple of Ethiopian pilots to crop spray for him and others in the district, on contract. They live here for three months – suppose he hasn't told you about that though – he's a very slimy operator, our Jaswant. You'll find out soon enough. Anyway thanks for kawa and my main reason for dropping in was to invite you to supper tomorrow night. Jan, that's my wife, will ask Howard and Rachel to come over too."

After a second cup with plenty of friendly banter thrown in they walked back to his landrover and it was then that Emmett noticed all the extra halogen lights he had arranged on a bar above the cab.

"Why those?" Emmett asked pointing to them.

"Oh, they're for night shooting and patrolling the farm after dark. Okay? 7.30 tomorrow night. Cheerio." They bade each other au revoir 'till tomorrow evening. He left, once outside the compound gate, in a cloud of dust.

As Emmett returned to his veranda he started remembering the few snide comments that Ian had made about Asians in general and Jaswant in particular.

20

Perhaps he had got into something way over his head? His arrival and first few days in Kenzi had all been very hospitable. The majority of those he had met showed friendliness toward him. Perhaps it was just a facade and the crunch would come later?

"Oh stop worrying," he said to himself as he busied with redesigning the garden – or more correctly, the area, now a mini desert, that was supposed to be a garden.

If he was going to reside here for three years or more he would darn well live in maximum comfort within the circumstances prevailing.

Christopher was a great help fetching a ball of twine and various implements as well as some small stakes.

The little wooden gate needed fixing. Obviously a hinge had broken. How about an archway over it he mused to himself? He could then have climbing roses. And the arch could be made in the workshop. A good idea. Now the path up to the veranda – it was fifteen strides – should be paved or cemented. That would save dust and mud from being dragged into the house.

Either side of the path should have a flower bed. So after measuring and staking all this out Emmett asked Christopher where was the nearest tap – in fact where did water come from?

"Nearest tap is outside back door, fendi. Water, she come from borehole over behind workshop. Diesel engine pumps it. Maju is in charge. Very good person. He will help with garden."

Emmett was beginning to realise that all he had to do was the brainwork and design. The manual side would be taken care of. A lot easier than back home.

On his next trip to Urukan he would get seeds and fertiliser and if a nursery could be located collect some shrubs and creepers.

Christopher obviously wanted to be the gardener, in other words he wished to rule over everything in and around Emmett. House and garden would be his domain.

"It no trouble and I enjoy it fendi."

Emmett quizzed him on how and where did the hot water come from? He couldn't work this out at all.

"Follow me fendi. I show you." They went to the back of the house and situated halfway between kitchen and shower room was a contraption the likes of which Emmett had never envisaged. Two small walls of brick, both about two feet high, supported a forty-four gallon oil drum. Beneath the drum was a wood fire. Into the drum and out of it ran a series of pipes. Obviously, when he looked closely at it, Emmett could see how cold water was fed in, and hot water piped out to the various outlets in the house. One very tall pipe, like a periscope, jerked and spewed boiling water all around from a height of approximately ten feet. That would be the safety vent. Absolutely ingenious he thought. So simple and yet completely practicable and efficient. The barrel itself was caked in three inches of cement and mud combined.

"This one has worked for last six years. No troubles fendi."

"As long as the fire is kept in," replied Emmett in jest.

"That's my job fendi. No trouble."

"Thanks Christopher – now I've learnt something new today."

With that he returned inside, found the brand new diary that he had bought in Nairobi and set about updating his first days in Africa. He was determined to maintain a daily record of his African adventure. Also it would be an excellent method of self-discipline – having to actually remember to write for twenty to thirty minutes a day.

He informed Christopher that he wouldn't need any meal the following evening as he was going over to Ian's for supper.

"That's a very good man fendi. He is best farmer in district. Also his madam has cow for milk. Very nice place."

Emmett felt that was probably high praise from Christopher and he was really looking forward to meeting his neighbours. He could learn a lot from them.

Ian's wife Jan was a tall slim redhead with wavy hair touching her shoulders. She was dressed in a silk lime green blouse over pencil slim well tailored tan slacks. She moved like a gazelle and flowed over the ground so gracefully that Emmett felt he watched in awe, mouth open, gob smacked.

He hadn't been in the company of any smartly manicured ladies for quite sometime and Jan had quite taken his breath away.

Ian was still showering as he was late coming in, she explained. Cold beer was immediately offered by an elegantly attired servant as Jan relocated her half full glass of white wine, and sat in one of the abundantly cushioned armchairs. She pointed to another next to her and invited Emmett to sit and relax.

"We hope you will feel at home with us. Must be quite lonely down there with no one to talk to. Cheers," and she raised her glass.

After five minutes of 'tittle-tattle' a very fresh Ian arrived with a beer and immediately offered Emmett another drink. Slightly hot and recently cooked cashew nuts were passed around. This was a 'first' for Emmett and one he immediately took to.

Their sitting room was sunken, two steps down from the entrance hall. A large stone fireplace with a tiered stone seat either side of the hearth was the dominant factor in the room. Various fine pieces of furniture, corner cabinets, large wooden legged coffee table with glass inlay, offered a spectacular selection of bird books, Homes and Gardens and motor journals. Pictures, in silver frames, of children on horseback, rally cars, Ian and Jan and most probably their parents in separate poses adorned a long Sheraton-like sideboard.

Bright lights swept across the room as a vehicle pulled up in their curved driveway. A couple of moments later a tall blond women, elegantly dressed in a flowing garment to her ankles entered in front of a lean dark haired gentleman.

"Meet Rachel and Howard," said a retreating Ian. He was obviously off to get their drinks.

Kisses on right and left cheeks were exchanged and then they all fell back into their seats. Emmett thought it was sensible to get his background history across first as he would have the rest of the evening to hear about theirs and their respective farms. He would have lots of questions to be answered.

After about forty-five minutes their servant appeared announcing the meal was 'tari' – ready. They had a round dining table and Emmett was placed between the two ladies. Farm topics took up the first two courses as Ian had just received delivery of his new Fordson tractor with a new Australian air seeder. These were evidently the biggest models yet produced and Ian expected to be able to plant two hundred and fifty acres and more per day with them. He evidently had his tractors working eighteen hours a day in the busy season.

"You'll have to change Bhogals' ideas. Otherwise you'll never get good yields," addressing Emmett with a mile wide smile.

"Why is that?"

"Well, that farm has been disced instead of tyne ploughed for the past ten seasons and becomes a ruddy dust bowl when the winds blow. You probably have no top soil left. But he won't listen to any of us and we are only trying to help the idiot."

"What seems the problem in the main?" Emmett enquired.

"Firstly he's as mean as a church mouse, and secondly he's a Hindi and they don't like being told what to do by us Zungus. Why he's got you now is hard to fathom out? We've been pondering this conundrum since we learnt on the grapevine that a Zungu was to be installed."

"But we'll assist you in everyway," prompted Howard "and you will need all the help and luck possible as quite seriously you have a mountain to climb, especially if you want to see a good bonus cheque after harvest."

Rachel then brought some lightness to the conversation by asking Emmett "Have you heard what that side of the road is known as?"

"No, not a whisper."

"Well, its known as the Punjabi Plains as most of the farms over there are leased by Hindi. There are a few rich Africans and the President's son Jonathan has a big acreage quite near us."

"How many Zungus farmers are there up here then?" asked Emmett.

"Oh I think it was eleven on the last count, wasn't it Ian?" enquired Howard.

"Yes, something like that," he answered "and we'll give you a list and map of the district to make it easier for you."

"Have you told Emmett about the clubs?" enquired Jan.

"No not yet. All in good time. How often do you think you'll need to go to Urukan in a month?" looking at Emmett.

"Hadn't really thought about it in truth but I suppose once a month for a weekend or something like that."

"Well that's when you'll use the club to stay and participate in sports and social life. It is predominantly Zungu and is very adequate. Great fun in fact, not so ladies?"

"At times, yes darling" replied Jan "but not when you get so pissed you can't remember anything."

"Anyhow that's a delight for you for the future, Emmett" said Howard rising from his armchair and following with "time to go Pix, I have an early flight to Kenzi at first light."

They all rose and thanked Jan and Ian for a fun evening. Rachel invited Emmett over anytime and they all wished him luck.

Following Emmett to his vehicle Ian said he would pop down in a day or two and would be happy to give his advice on the farm.

It had been a wonderful evening for Emmett. He now didn't feel so very far away from the outside world and although they were a good fifteen years his senior, age didn't seem to matter out here.

Jan arrived down before lunch the very next day with a load of homemade goodies – marmalade, cheese, rusks, milk and thick cream.

"I forgot to mention these last night. I can keep you supplied with them virtually all year around."

Emmett couldn't believe his eyes as they were laid out on the dining table. Christopher was ecstatic and spoke to Jan in bounteous tones.

"How about some fresh cold lime juice, Christopher's special," Emmett offered.

"That would be lovely. I won't stay long as 'the master' must have his meal at one o'clock – Ian is rigid in his timing. The entire farm is programmed on time. He's right too as hours can slip away when least needed."

Jan spoke to Christopher in some strange dialect while they sat on the veranda.

"I have been asking him about the layout in the garden and was it your idea?"

"Yes, I adore colour and want to fill the area with flowers and shrubs."

"No problem at all. I'll arrange a plant party for you and get all our friends to chip in with bits and pieces from their gardens. You mustn't buy a thing. Just tell me when you have the beds and borders sorted out – all you have to do is provide a salad lunch and some drink. It'll be a great way to meet everyone too and now is the right time – not a busy period. Okay, that's fixed then."

She rose to leave and Christopher brought out her basket which had been taken inside. Looking at it Jan said "you must get a few of these in Koram – they're cheap and will last a lifetime. They are called kikoos" and she spelt out the word.

"Many thanks for last night and again for all these goodies. Will you keep an account for me and I'll pay weekly or whatever you wish?"

"Don't worry – Christopher knows the score. Bye for now."

Jan drove a Subaru estate and had two small African children with her. They scuttled to the car from beside the office when they saw her coming.

Things personal and pleasurable were certainly looking up. Emmett felt almost at peace with himself for the decision he had taken. He wondered how the other four were progressing? He decided to communicate by post after three months. Things would be sorting themselves out by then. He was eminently satisfied with his beginning.

3

"Rule with an Iron Fist"

𝒪𝑡 was mid afternoon Sunday when Ian arrived. He carried an ancient leather briefcase which looked totally incongruous with his regular attire of shorts, shirt and ragged old oil-stained dust hat. More like 'the man from the Pru' safari style!

"I hope this is a good time for you as I have come armed with all the info we can think of?"

"Certainly is" Emmett responded as they met by the garden gate.

"Jan's told me about the plant and shrub party. A great idea. Whenever you're ready she'll organise it – brilliant organiser is my wife. She keeps the farm accounts for me on top of everything else. Anyways, lets get down to brass tacks," as he opened the case and took out a file of papers.

This time of the day is pure magic as the heat has abated but the sun is still warm enough to sit out. About an hour later Emmett offered a cold beer which Ian gasped for jokingly.

"Thought you'd never ask!"

They had gone through all the names of the farmers, on both sides of the road, and on a hastily sketched map visualised their whereabouts. Ian explained the working of the club system throughout the country and how he and Howard would propose him for membership. Once a member of one club you had reciprocity with the others in Ukenza and with one in London, Nairobi and Kampala. Then they got onto the farm.

"First thing you must do is put in contours. Its divided into sections isn't it?"

"Yes, there are four."

"It's plain madness not having them as the rains take away all your top soil every season. Now, you have a grader I know so half the problem is solved. Ever used a theodolite?"

"No siree. What in God's name is that?"

"Well I'll lend you mine and instruct you in its use. I'll also lend you a good worker who knows about measuring and staking out the contours. You can pay him a bonus when you've finished with him."

"Gosh, that's smashing," replied Emmett not really able to realise his good fortune. Christopher had certainly been correct in his assessment of Ian all right.

"I suggest you concentrate on the two nearest sections this season and then next year tackle the remainder. That will keep you occupied, up until planting, on that one job."

He produced some more beer and brought with him a note pad this time. He mustn't miss any of this free wisdom being dispensed.

"Your staff, in the main, are fairly good. We all have a few bad buggers and each farm pretty well knows these fellows who tend to drift from farm to farm season after season."

Emmett was all ears and was sure his eyes were wider now than at any time in his life. It was all going to be a thrilling experience – no matter what. He was determined to make it work.

"Anyone tell you about the guy who was here before you?"

"No, it was never mentioned."

"Well he was an Israeli pilot cum farmer. He was here for three years and unfortunately killed himself in a flying crash whilst crop spraying on this farm. Funny Boghal .never told you about him? Nice chap really but he neglected the farm management in preference to flying."

"When was this tragedy?"

"Two seasons ago. So nothing has been done properly ever since. We all think the farm is a tax dodge for Bhogal who is stinking rich. This has only been a plaything and a means of keeping in with the President and being politically correct in essence."

"Oh my God what have I let myself in for?"

"Not to worry Emmett. Keep your head down and get on with life. We still have an extremely high standard of living – we are really lucky when you read about other independent African countries. Peace has reigned for the past decade but we do hear rumblings in the bush. Not everything is rosy in the house of Victor Ubugu."

"The Tukulu are not happy with the distribution of important positions. They are the biggest tribe in a country ruled by the leader of a minority tribe. Not an easy balancing act."

"Are there unions or radical factions in the country?" enquired Emmett.

"No unions but yes to your second part. And they need heeding. There is a ground swell of bad feeling creeping in. It's all since the last election two years ago. Lots of vote rigging and corruption."

"Where have I not heard of that in the third world? Do you know Ian that Ireland is the most generous country to the underdeveloped. We give thousands and yet haven't sorted out our own poverty back home. I suppose our missions

27

have been out in Africa decades and the Church back home still pulls the strings. They determine where the budget is spent – not necessarily for the benefit of the most needy."

"Oh ya, missions have been top dogs out here since even before the turn of the century. A majority of school leavers have good English. Perhaps they should have stuck to education and hospital care and let each person designate their own beliefs and follow them. Don't get me wrong now, I'm not anti missions or religion but no one wants things – dogmas I think you call them – rammed down one's throat."

"I was brought up in Rhodesia in the Catholic faith and respected it then as I do today. But my belief is that everyone must have the right to follow their own beliefs. We are all Christians after all – aren't we?"

"You are probably right and I certainly haven't had enough worldly experience to offer comment. I too am R.C. educated but luckily didn't have it pushed down my throat so I've that to be thankful for." They paused a while and savoured their beers.

"Wow, we've covered some ground young Emmett in the past few hours. It's been great talking with you. I know we will have wonderful times together my friend and as the Afrikaners say "Tot siens – goodbye and good luck."

As they walked to his vehicle he sounded adamant in his request "don't hesitate to pop over at any time. I'd love to show you my new toys. All the best, hey!"

What a fund of knowledge Emmett thought about his new found friend. It would be interesting to see how Jaswant took to Ian's ideas but as sure as wheat is corn "I'm going to follow his plans" Emmett thought to himself.

He had established with Jaswant that he had the complete run of the place and only when large expenditure was mooted would he have to discuss it with the boss.

Getting the grader going and restructuring the farm was run of the mill work so he would get started on that the coming week.

His garden was the other priority.

Emmett decided to check out the complete inventory of the farm. He didn't think any one knew just exactly what was in stock – and he might find some hidden treasures?

Gilbert and Eddison, with various stock books in hand, accompanied him from shed to shed.

He saw tractors, the size of which would find it difficult to travel along Irish roads, others were more recognisable in size and form. A lot were Steyr – an Austrian make which Bhogal had the agency for. Most of the machinery looked old and forlorn – unkempt would be the word. This all needed seeing to – put the rubbish on a scrap heap and strip them for spares, he thought.

He thought it was time the farm made a new start. The head mechanic, Gideon, discussed each and every item in great detail. He had been on the farm for ten years having started as a grease boy, and agreed that it needed updating and especially the seeders. These were old style drills like those used at home in Ireland, on small acreages, and were now totally inadequate and uneconomical.

Only one Kvernland mouldboard plough was found amongst a dozen disc harrows. These were evidently ruination for the ground as both Ian and Howard had warned him. Some were enormous in size – at least twenty foot in width – and could obviously cover a big acreage per hour. But at what cost Emmett wondered – especially after hearing what Ian and Howard had to say?

The combine harvesters – seven in number – looked antique but they had just completed the latest harvest so looks perhaps didn't matter. He would hear about it all from the locals no doubt.

The farm lorry, a five ton MAN, was in good order. It was the main contact with Urukan and Kenzi. The monthly transportation of staff to Koram was another of its services.

There was also a very aged red jeep – American World War ll type – which the mechanics used to travel the farm tending repairs in the field.

Out behind the southern wing of the compound was the wrecked remnants of the crop spraying plane that had ended the pilot's life. It was a tiny yellow wasp-like thing, the likes of which Emmett had not seen before. The wreck was a grim reminder of the dangers of that arm of agriculture - not one that Emmett wished to participate in. Flying yes – for pleasure – and that might well be an idea for the future he thought.

The compound had three generators and a 2000 gallon diesel storage tank. Only the office staff could issue fuel to respective drivers who signed for their off take. Here was an obvious scam area which would have to be monitored regularly by Emmett, he felt.

Ian had said something the other evening that struck home "rule with an iron fist, they respect discipline. Praise when the job is well done. You'll get their trust and loyalty then."

A number of ex-pats had told Emmett that the African, when in power, treated his own really badly and totally lost their trust. This was evidently beginning to happen in Ukenza. It would be intriguing to live through the further evolution of the State. Emmett thought that in some ways he was blessed with the chance to experience the coming passage of time, and all because of an advertisement in the Sunday Times!

Gideon reported, a couple of days later, that the giant yellow CAT grader had been serviced and it was ready for use. Emmett decided to give the runway a 'smooth-over' and tidy up the runoffs on each side in anticipation of the coming rains.

The driver certainly knew his stuff and made an excellent job of both areas. This prompted Emmett to drive over to Ian and tackle him about the Theodolite and some contour staff.

He found him in his workshop tinkering with an engine that had gone on the blink. Ian had a short strong body with colossal arms. Emmett felt he could lift a full bag of grain off the floor and over his head. He exuded strength from every pore, and certainly didn't mind getting himself covered in oil or dirt of any kind. Ian definitively lead from the front showing his staff how the job should be done. This was partly why he was such a successful farmer. Emmett took note.

"I'll be finished with this in ten minutes or so, take a look around in the meantime."

Close to his workshop Emmett found some Jersey cows and calves in well constructed but simple paddocks. They were friendly and came over to him probably hoping for a titbit.

Two bay ponies and one grey horse were in a paddock next to the cattle. All animals were in the rudest of health. A large stack of hay stood between both paddocks.

Emmett only saw one large disc harrow amongst the range of implements but there were plenty of tynes. He was fascinated by the yellow octopus styled machines that were lined up behind one another in a large three-sided shed. These had to be pneumatic seeders or planters, he surmised. He would enquire once Ian had completed his work.

Another massive open shed housed four Claas combines – each one was twice the size of anyone at Ratilli.

So this was what it took to be a successful wheat farmer? Would Jaswant ever agree an update to this level of machinery? More and more questions whizzed around Emmett's already befuddled head.

"I'm all yours now Emmett so where do we start?"

"Firstly, please explain what these yellow jobs over there are, will you?"

"Oh they are Australian air operated seeders – Murdox, the only way to guarantee a good crop. Impressive aren't they but wait 'till you see my new one – it's even bigger!"

They then passed a shuttered shed which Ian opened by pushing a switch which electrically operated a folding door which itself slid up and into the roof.

"Those are my latest toys," pointing to a range of spanking newly painted implements. "Impressive, eh? The Ford is the only one in the country and the seeder is just an upgraded model of the best in their range. They'll make planting a lot easier and more efficient and that's after all, what farming is all about. Lets go to the office."

They walked back through his sheds to a low building not far from the dwelling. One room housed the office, with next to it a store room.

From a cupboard Ian produced the theodolite and tripod. Emmett had seen them being used on the realignment of roads back home. Now he would learn a new trade.

Ian introduced Emmett to Wilson who had entered the office.

"He is my right hand here like your chap Gilbert, isn't it? They all know each other – there's a sort of bush network that goes on among farms up here. If someone needs something urgently they borrow it and return the favour another time."

"That sounds mighty sensible. I'm all for compatibility – count us in."

"Great. Oh Wilson, please see if Induna is around and ask him to come here. Thanks. Lets go and have tea while we wait."

Emmett hadn't noticed the dogs that first evening but now he counted two Rothweilers, an Alsatian and a couple of Jack Russells. Perhaps they had been locked away? The latter stayed close to Jan in the house whilst the three big ones patrolled the outside.

This was something he had to organise in quick time. He missed his family's pets terribly but hadn't dared mention the idea so soon in his residency here. Now that he had friends close at hand he was feeling more confident in himself. Jan, he was sure, would point him in the right direction and perhaps there was a SPCA or some sort of similar organisation in the country? He would be happy to 'home' a few lost souls.

Induna arrived down from Ian two days later. Emmett picked two flagmen from his labour force and the four of them started to work the grader on Section 3 which was on the north side of the compound taking in the landing strip.

The group worked for the next month and became adept at measuring out the contours which ran approximately 60 yards apart. Tuli, the grader driver, took to the task without a worry and despite lots of backchat from the other drivers one could see he was proud of his work and was enjoying each day as it came. Emmett established a routine which worked out really well for the team. If he was satisfied with progress in the first few hours of the day he gauged the amount he wished completed whether by 3pm or 5pm. This 'setting a target' tickled the team and they finished early on the majority of occasions.

This attitude permeated through the work force and a genuine team spirit seemed to be establishing itself.

Within that same month he graded a soccer pitch close to their living quarters, bought a couple of balls, had timber goal posts erected and lime dust spread as outlines for the pitch. Each evening the staff enjoyed an hour and more at play – all trying to be another Pele!

Christopher kept telling Emmett that the staff were 'so happy' having a Zungu as their master. He wished for the farm to be a success and that everyone could be recognised for their work "like what happens on the other Zungu farms."

He talked to Christopher each evening, explaining his plans, routines and goals. The farm must become profitable. When it did then everyone, including himself, would get good bonuses. Emmett would see to that.

Christopher obviously relayed this – or as much as he wished the staff to know – to the general workforce. Their requests would be passed back to Emmett. It seemed quite a satisfactory method of keeping in close touch with each other without actually being on a one to one basis.

Gilbert came onto the veranda whilst Emmett was breakfasting one morning;

"I have just heard that the County Commissioner (CC) is in the district and would like to call in here to meet you later today."

"Well that's fine by me. What can you tell me about him Gilbert?"

"He's on the President's Council but it is said he doesn't agree with a lot of the President's ideas. He is well educated. – overseas – is very sociable. We like him. He tries to make a lot of improvements in the Province. He is a Tukulu."

"Where is he stationed?"

"In Urukan, fendi."

"And how often does he tour this region?"

"About every six to eight weeks – unless there is trouble, then more often."

"How did you hear about the visit, Gilbert?"

"From the Ratilli men. They know everything."

"That's what's called bush telegraph I understand – yes?"

"Correct, fendi."

"OK. Tell everyone in the compound to clean up the place and I'll get Christopher to prepare some food. Thanks Gilbert. His visit will make a change. Thanks."

Three landrovers drove into the farm at 12.30pm that day. A cloud of dust hung over the entire length of the avenue. Emmett moved off his veranda to meet them calling for Gilbert as he passed through his garden gate.

A lean sprightly-limbed man burst from the front passenger seat and introduced himself.

"Hi, I'm Jeri Ntsemo, good to meet you."

After reciprocal introductions his entourage gathered around whilst Gilbert shook hands with most of them. Jeri then introduced Emmett to his two children who were travelling in the second vehicle accompanied by their nanny.

"This is Zimba Charles and this is Edith. They are both madly keen on riding. I hope you are going to have some horses here before too long."

"I would love too," Emmett replied.

"And this is Anna, their nanny."

Emmett's breath was taken from him as he shook hands with quite the most beautiful black person he had ever seen. Her eyes never left his – they sparkled and seemed quizzical.

"Come on in. Follow me please. Gilbert, will you please see to the rest of the group. Thank you."

Christopher had organised some homemade lemonade and he had half a dozen cool beers on the sideboard.

For the next hour histories on both sides were discussed in great detail. Emmett had not quite got around the culture and colour factors experienced since arriving in the country. But with Jeri there was a big difference – they could converse on the same waveband – discuss universal problems, talk sport, politics and religion. Something Emmett hadn't done since leaving Ireland. This meeting was a revelation.

Christopher announced lunch was served. He had decided on a chicken and ham salad meal with fresh fruit salad and coffee to follow.

They sat on the veranda and discussion centred around Jeri's family. His son was twelve and daughter nine. They were really well mannered and only talked when spoken to.

Anna was a trained nurse and had a teaching diploma. She was dressed in an immaculate white dress, belted at her waist, emphasising an hourglass figure. She wore white court shoes which didn't seem to make her feet large in comparison to the rest of her figure. This was something Emmett had noticed in both male and female Africans – their feet seemed too big for their bodies. Anna's looked groomed and to the right size. Her hair was short but thick with a parting either side of her head. The hair was trained backwards. She smelt of musk. The children obviously adored her and Jeri never seemed to interfere with the trio.

His wife was also in the nursing profession, he explained, and was head theatre sister at Urukan Mission Hospital. She had been trained in London during the same period as Jeri was at the London School of Economics. He had a Master's Degree in Business. He was quite open about his hatred of the corruption in the country and did everything he could to stop it within his jurisdiction, he said.

He warned Emmett about some likely scams operating in the transportation of grain from farm to the co-op.

The talk returned to horses as Jeri showed his utter love for the sport. Emmett was questioned on Ireland's place in world equestrianism and the pros and cons of fox hunting. His children had been taught to ride from an early age and they went twice weekly to a riding school in Urukan.

Emmett was very obviously being coerced into having horses and ponies on the farm and not only for his own use? He took the hint.

After lunch Jeri wanted to see the contour work – he had been well briefed on progress - decided to drive, inviting Emmett to jump in beside him in his Government vehicle. They toured the whole of Section 3 and then continued on around Section 2 before returning to the homestead. This was a one on one tour with Jeri pumping questions on Emmett's ambitions, his impressions so far and his hopes for the next three years. No one else overheard their discussion. Emmett got the feeling there would be many more of these. They had a certain rapport which literally spelt friendship.

He would have to check up with Ian on how well Jeri was respected in the district. Perhaps it was all on the surface – but somehow Emmett didn't think so.

On departing, Jeri invited him to visit whenever in town. He would show him the lights of Urukan including polo and gymkhana races.

"Thanks a ton and I'll keep you to it."

Anna's eyes bore into Emmett's as she shook his hand in gratitude for their meeting and excellent meal. The children reiterated their father's request – especially the riding bit.

That evening Emmett had a lot to think about. Troubling him most were Anna's piercing glances. Those slightly slanted eyes, almost oriental, deep pools of ebony in off-white ivory surrounds following him everywhere he went. Was there a message somewhere within their spheres? Time surely would tell.

Was Jeri as English, or Colonial, as he seemed to portray? Or was that all a façade? Was he after some information that Emmett would, in time, perhaps be able to supply – unwittingly or in factual comment? These were the thoughts that eventually sent him to sleep. Tomorrow was another day.

Next morning at breakfast Christopher was all agog at yesterday's visit. Obviously lots had been discussed in the compound that night and now he was bursting to comment.

"That was first time such a big official was on the farm. Did he enjoy it Master?"

"Yes, I think so – especially your excellent luncheon, Christopher. Did you talk with Anna at all?"

"Oh yes master. She very nice. She ask lots about you."

"Well now, I hope you didn't give all my secrets away."

"Oh no sir. She very nice. She's a Tukulu. They are very smart."

"How did the farm staff take the visit?"

"Well, very well indeed, very proud they are to be visited by big boss in administration. Will he be returning master?"

"Oh yes I expect so, Christopher. He has invited me to visit him when next I go to Urukan."

"Very good sir - that will be nice."

After another long dusty day in Section 2 Emmett decided to pop over to Ian and sound him out on Jeri.

"Oh he's the best thing since biltong[1]. He's one of us and he doesn't hit it off with the President but because he's so well qualified and so astute, the old man has to have him on his Council. You'll find his Province is the best governed and there's very little 'chai' – corruption – around. He's a great sportsman – loves riding and he's a champion clay pigeon shot. Also a fair tennis player. His wife Margaret is also well liked and a great mixer. They are big into the club scene – organising this, that and the other but both are first raters. Really."

Emmett took a little time to reply as Ian was in the midst of changing a blown gasket on one of his tractors. Ian, however, continued,

"Heard you had a visit. What were your impressions?"

"Well I got on well from the start. We talked for hours on everything. He was so interesting and had such a feel for what's going on in the world around us. I showed him the contoured work which, I think, impressed him a lot.

"But the most interesting thing Ian, from my point of view, was the reaction from my staff and farm labour. They thought it really brilliant to have such a big official on the farm. It was the first time they said. Was it?"

"Oh, I should think so. No one visits the Punjabi Plains I'm afraid. The Hindis are not good mixers and certainly not good neighbours. Bhogal with his Landrover agency has the government contracts all tied up and they are beholden to him. Also his transport and haulage business is enormous and very well organised. I'd say that Jeri knows the farm is a tax scam. Perhaps he sees you as someone who is going to turn it around into a real producer. That's what he wants. He needs his Province to be totally self-sufficient with plenty of backup for disastrous times like droughts."

Ian and his mechanics finished the job pretty quickly and then Emmett was invited for a quick drink as Ian said they were going out to a neighbour for dinner.

---

[1] Sliced, wind dried venison meat, a South African/Rhodesian delicacy.

"Just a quickie thanks. I've been in dust all day and the throats a bit parched."

Jan got onto the subject of horses and said she could find Emmett a few in Kenzi if he could arrange transport.

"I'll think about that Jan as I'd have to arrange stabling and paddock first."

"No problem. You tell me when you're ready."

"I would, however, like to get some dogs straight away. Any ideas?"

"What sort? Shepherds any good?"

"You mean Alsatians?"

"Yes. I know of a family returning to England and they can't take theirs. I think they have three. Well trained to farm life."

"Gosh, that would be fantastic. Where are they?"

"About an hour from Urukan up in the coffee country. I'll contact my friends tomorrow and see what's cooking. Okay?"

"Yes indeed. Thanks a span."

4

"Don't trust him further than your arm."

$\mathcal{A}t$ supper Emmett told Christopher about the dogs. He seemed thrilled as he, not only loved them, but used to look after Alsatians and Dobermans for a former employer. Emmett then mentioned horses. Christopher went blank. He knew nothing about horses but said there were a couple of Mandis in the compound and they were the tribe that dealt with horses and ponies in their everyday life back in their reserves. He would enquire if they were interested in working with them.

Christopher was becoming Emmett's confidant in each and everyway. He was a sensitive soul with great depth of feeling. Almost six feet tall he couldn't weigh more than eight stone. His crinkly hair was turning grey. His voice was a deep baritone. He could well be a monk if attired in a habit. A lovely man and one who adored his job. He was a caring person.

Emmett had made two trips to Urukan in his first two months and Jaswant had flown into the farm on three occasions. He seemed to like visiting on a Sunday morning. Sometimes he brought his younger brother Vijay who ran the Landrover side of the business and was also a qualified pilot.

Vijay showed interest in the contouring and told Emmett how spectacular it looked from the air. Jaswant nosed around the mechanical workshops and seemed very friendly with Gilbert – probably extracting all the farm gossip from him, thought Emmett.

It had been arranged, on their first visit that they would bring out grocery and butchery supplies which proved a major factor over the times ahead.

On Emmett's second visit to Urukan he presented himself at the Club. An imposing Colonial cut-stone building with a dozen curved steps leading up to a pillared entrance. Large mahogany doors with highly polished brass knobs and hinges opened into a marble hall with a round table centrepiece. A large glass vase hosted a feast of gladioli entwined with honeysuckle. A long wooden counter ran the length of the left hand wall behind which stood a busy male Asian receptionist. On the wall, also in wood matching the counter, were lines of pigeonholes some oozing with post and parcels. Others strangely empty. Below each opening was an engraved letter of the alphabet.

The secretary had already set the cogs in motion for his membership but Emmett was informed that he may use all its facilities in the meantime. Howard had already proposed him with Ian as seconder. There would be no trouble, but the selection committee only met every eight weeks, which was still two weeks away.

The Club had a very stark 'men only' bar. Some photos of teams with the odd set of antlers adorned timber panelled walls. Chairs and two couches were in real leather, faded brown. Old international magazines – National Geo, Country Life, Homes and Gardens – interspersed with newspapers covered two coffee tables. There was a large fireplace with a pile of logs nearby.

Excellent all-weather tennis courts, a squash court, cricket pitch with nets alongside and a swimming pool were neatly landscaped in the rear of the Clubhouse. Tall blue gum (Eucalyptus) trees acted as a windbreak around much of the perimeter.

Emmett reckoned there was parking for upward of one hundred and fifty vehicles within its surrounds. Obviously functions were a major part of its activity. This interested him greatly. He felt almost at home here – although he had as yet met nobody but Ian, Howard and Jeri, of course.

It was nearly lunchtime so he returned to the bar after his little walkabout and felt well able for a gin or two before having a meal.

There were half a dozen farmer types – bush jackets, shorts and desert boots – at the bar with a couple of well tailored Indians perusing the papers in the large well worn armchairs.

Hugo, the barman – he had his name on a plastic badge on his breast pocket – took his order and on returning with it asked would he like to be introduced to the other Zungus? Emmett replied he would indeed and thanked him.

A minute or so later he was hailed by one of the group along the bar counter "come and join us please. It's good to have some new blood in the place. I'm Charlie Johnson, the local vet and these here are Chris Rutherford, Brian Cunningham and Snobby Wright-Hill. They are all farmers – coffee and tea planters."

"Hi, I'm Emmett Doyle, manager cum partner of the Bhogal wheat farms."

"Oh poor you," remarked Snobby only to be followed in quick succession by "You could have chosen an easier task."

"Oh it won't be that bad. You'll have great neighbours. Ian and Howard are fine chaps," offered one of them almost as an afterthought.

"Hope you have a sound contract drawn up young man. You'll need it," said another.

Emmett looked taken aback. He downed half his glass of G & T before he got his thoughts together. "Well, I've thoroughly enjoyed my first few months here and obviously I'm about to find out how the other half live. Cheers."

They all had ploughman's plates – cheese, pickles and homemade bread- at the bar and Emmett found out that they were in the main, taking the piss out of him. He had to pass their test – it was a sort of initiation process. But they were a grand bunch – all British who had either been in the neighbouring territories when independence was declared, or as in Charlie's case come up from Rhodesia. Ukenza needed medics and vets and he had applied.

Evidently the first President had structured his country on British Colonial lines – he had been educated in England and had gone through Sandhurst. The settlers were devastated when he was killed in a horrific car crash. Victor Ubugu had started off in the same vein but after the first ten years had become very lackadaisical in governance. He was now only looking after number one.

He, however, did have sound financial advisors, so these fellows said, who knew that without the cooperation of the farmers the country would have nil exports. There were good subsidies available but bad farming practise didn't get anything.

"Perhaps that's why Bhogal has brought you out here. Instead of scams he wants subsidies and the ear of the President?!"

"It's not what you know; it's very much who out here, and watch your back at all times."

This piece of advice came from Brian, the quiet one of the group, as Emmett had pigeonholed him.

Emmett had invitations to all their homes. They wanted to see his sporting prowess as soon as possible and he got invited to enter the upcoming tennis championships.

On his drive home, the vehicle loaded with spares, shrubs, seedlings and household provisions Emmett thought deeply about all that had been discussed with the group over lunch.

The Indians certainly did not have a good name in the farming community. They were, however, extremely powerful in the financial structure of the country – so much so that it was generally felt they were keeping Victor Ubugu in power. The Bhogal conglomerate was up in the top six on the power hungry ladder of success.

Anyhow, the good side was that there was a thriving Zungu community who worked hard and played hard – akin to the lifestyle of Kenya before and after the Second World War. A lot of the present farming community had been lured to

Ukenza, on its independence, by offers of cheap lease back land deals. Most of their children went to school in East Africa and a few in Rhodesia.

They kept reiterating to Emmett that he would be experiencing a completely multi-racial society which, back home in rural Ireland, he wouldn't perhaps have come across. That was quite true as he had only ever seen students and a few qualified doctors of other hues. This, however, had never worried him – he wasn't blinkered in any way. Already he had built up such a friendship with Christopher that colour never came into his thoughts.

Perhaps he was a little overawed by the propensity of numbers – pale skins being such a minority. But what the hell – everyone was equal in the eyes of the Lord. In Africa, some, however, were more equal!

Emmett had learnt that Jeri Ntesmo was well liked, was a good administrator and no one could place a finger of suspicion of any corruption within his duress. It was said he was more of a Zungu than some of the Zungus themselves. He promoted every facet of agriculture and exhorted every farmer to produce more. He kept the roads in good order – always had them graded prior to the rains and maintained them through the wet seasons. He was gradually extending the tarmacadam and building new bridges. All in all he was on the farmers' side and cared for them. Or so it seemed?

This was the impression Emmett had gleaned from his visit. He looked forward to embellishing the friendship even more.

Back on the farm the daily routine of contouring continued. Sections 3 and 2 had now been completed. It was time to start ploughing but all that was available were disc harrows and he had been told these were a no-no!

Ian was consulted once again and it turned out to be very fruitful. He had two well used tyne ploughs which he no longer needed. Emmett could borrow them and if he liked the work they did he could then purchase them. Ian promised they would make an enormous difference.

He sent two tractors up to collect them next day. Only his most powerful 150 horse power Steyr could handle these giants once tilling commenced. They were all of twelve feet wide and sporting 13 tynes or teeth. These could be sunk from three to twelve inches into the soil aerating lines along the newly contoured area. Bhogals discs had only broken the top three inches never allowing air or moisture to penetrate deeper. Each season, therefore, saw more of a dust bowl forming. Arid lands produced sparse crops. This had to end if bonuses were to be paid.

It was interesting to hear that both Ian and Howard averaged thirteen to fifteen bags of grain per acre and according to records on Ratilli it never got to more than 7.3 bags. A mighty difference in income. Emmett realised he had to have this out with Jaswant next time they met. He must be left to farm the land his way and hopefully, produce a profitable crop. The breakeven point was seven bags an acre he had worked out. Records showed that as little as three to four bags had been produced on a number of occasions. Was this meant to happen? Emmett had to find out and find out quick.

Jaswant and Vijay flew in the following Sunday and after the customary tour settled down on the veranda for tea, biscuits and samoosas.

It wouldn't be correct to say that a heated discussion took place but Emmett let rip with a volley of facts and figures regarding the crop ahead. If he didn't do this and that then they couldn't expect good returns. And Emmett wanted good profitable figures, otherwise it wasn't worth his time.

He could see what was wrong with the land – over taxed and under fertilized – and he meant to change its structure. Were they prepared to back him in this or was he to be just a puppet with them pulling the strings? In which case he wouldn't be interested in continuing!

Emmett hadn't spoken out like this before and he thought they were a little, if not a lot, taken aback by his forthrightness.

Jaswant was the silent one. Vijay could be volatile Emmett felt.

From under his black turban, with eyes cast down onto the coffee table, Jaswant calmly and bitterly replied:

"I won't stand in your way but watch your expenses. I too want something out of it all. I have put in millions to date for little return. I don't like your attitude regarding 'not interested in continuing'. It sounds as if you want it your way and to hell with everyone else. This has to be a team affair. I will trust you to farm properly – you must trust me to carry out my side of the contract. If not then we are in for a rough ride. I don't need that. Do I make myself clear?"

"Undoubtedly, but why hasn't the farm performed before this. The records are dismal?" replied an agitated Emmett.

"Obviously the correct methods were not used. Perhaps now you will right that wrong. Why do you think I looked for someone from overseas?"

"I respect that. I just want to know that you will back me in my requests and assist me in updating machinery and technology. I am prepared to ferret out all the information and to make a success of the place. That's all."

And with that they rose from the table and walked to their Cessna.

Gilbert had been keeping a close watch on the proceedings and met them at the gate with wage registers and purchase orders, as was the custom.

The silence was broken by Jaswant on the step of the plane.

41

"Come into Kenzi during the week and we will discuss new machinery. Okay?"

Vijay shook Emmett's hand as he was about to step aboard.

"The contours and tilling look superb." He boarded the aircraft and the engine sprung into life.

Emmett slept well that night after spending a few hours mapping out his future strategy for the farm. Perhaps Bhogal was hoping for a return on his investment after all? Might he have had a governmental shove perchance and could Jeri Ntsemo have had something to do with it? It was intriguing whatever way Emmett looked at it.

Ian couldn't believe Emmett's good news but countered with "don't trust him further than your arm. Ever notice how he never will look you straight in the eye, eh? Just beware my mate – but go for it anyway. We will give you every assistance. By the way – I'd better put a price on those rippers and you can now buy them from me, eh?"

He gave Emmett a mighty slap on the back and a peal of laughter erupted from his boots.

"What else do you think I'll need in the immediate future?"

"Oh seeders of course. You need these Aussie air yokes – like that new one of mine I showed you – remember? I think Howard has a couple you could have – going cheap you know. The Hindis like that. They think they are getting a bargain you know. I'll contact him for you."

Jan approached from the house and hailed Emmett as he was getting into his vehicle.

"You can have those three Alsatians by the way. But you have to collect them this week. Could you arrange that?"

"Well yes I suppose so. I'm off to Kenzi tomorrow for a couple of days so I could stop over in Urukan on my return. You'll be able to point me in the right direction?"

"No trouble. Come for a cool drink and I'll draw a map and give you all particulars. You can phone them on your way up. Come in."

Christopher was warned that evening to expect three dogs when Emmett returned from Kenzi.

"No problem, no problem Master. I'll get some planks and make a rest for them on the veranda. Better buy some cheap blankets and some feeding bowls. What kind are they?"

"German Shepherds – Alsatians."

"Oh yes, I know that type. Good watchdogs and very loyal. They will never leave your side Master. That will be good."

"Put dog food and a sack of rice on your kitchen list please."

Emmett had already learnt in these first few months that one must rise before the sparrows and leave for your destination before dawn. It was the coolest time of the day and you got the worst part of the journey over before the main rush of traffic became active.

He made Urukan for breakfast and left off a list of requirements at the office there before setting off for the capital. A mechanic/driver always accompanied Emmett. It was a great 'holiday' for them as they met up with friends at both of Bhogals' offices. The bush telegraph in action. Sometimes Gilbert would also travel so that wages, registers and stock sheets could be audited by head office.

Emmett was checked into the Kenzi Club for two nights by head office. After spending the afternoon in serious talks with Jaswant it was a pleasant surprise to see the old Colonial style building that he was introduced to. Both Bhogals had driven ahead and shown him the way.

The club house was much bigger and more opulent than Urukan's. More tennis courts, larger cricket ground with a smart pavilion and a hockey field. They had two squash courts and a fine swimming pool with diving boards.

There were a lot of Asians present and Emmett guessed that they made up the majority of the members.

Jaswant did not take alcohol but Vijay enjoyed a couple of beers before departing.

Emmett talked to a few Europeans before dinner and afterwards met a family of Shahs who were wealthy merchants with trading stores all over the country. They had seen him with the Bhogals so used that as their introduction.

The bedrooms were large with high ceilings and views over the cricket pitch. Old fashioned electric fans hung from the ceiling and rasped a discordant note when first switched on. A Victorian bath on four legs took pride of place in a spanking all white tiled bathroom. Towels were hard, aged and off white.

When Emmett ran his bath a rusty coloured liquid flowed for the first minute or so. After that clear hot water ran for as long as he wished. He adored a well filled bath.

This item – a bath – was high on his list of priorities for the morrow. He needed his little bit of luxury out 'in the sticks' as he had heard the Zungus call the distant farms.

Something had to have changed, perhaps a 'kick up the arse' from the President or something suchlike, as he found the Bhogals were different people on this visit. They agreed to buying Ian's machinery and anything else Emmett could find out there. New tractors, more powerful than already on the farm, would be forthcoming for the planting season.

Yes, Emmett could make alterations to the house and garden. He was free to get some horses, build stables and make some paddocks near the homestead - Vijay loved riding and so did his two children.

Yes, he could smarten up the labour lines, in fact they would send out two painters to cover the entire camp.

Trees could be planted up the avenue and they would weld together a large water tanker, to be pulled by a tractor, which would irrigate shrubs and trees that Emmett suggested be planted around the camp and other areas on the farm.

By lunchtime on the second day Emmett couldn't believe his luck – but he was now in the mood to request the earth. His house was sparsely furnished so he asked for this, that and the other and was promptly told to go and see three Asian friends who had furniture factories. They would supply all his needs.

What an enjoyable afternoon he had and this lead to him being invited to a Chinese restaurant by one of the factory owners, T.K. Patel.

Emmett felt he had better get to know as many Asians as possible as they held all the aces when it came to commerce. They, very definitely were the power behind the throne. That led him to look for the name given to him by the restaurateur in London. He had learnt from the Patels he had an engineering shop and was well known to the Bhogals. Emmett phoned Rashid and introduced himself. He said he had a letter for him and arranged to meet at the Club later. They both felt the world was indeed a village. At least Emmett had completed his side of the bargain. What would transpire was an enigma?

His stay in Kenzi had been unbelievably successful. Jaswant would send a truck with the items purchased out to the farm the following week. Two tractors would follow and a further two in a month's time.

Emmett made Urukan by noon and went straight to Jeri Ntsemo's office. He had phoned from Bhogal's and Jeri agreed on a meeting with lunch afterwards at the Club. The CC was a very 'available' man, no matter who you were, it seemed.

Their talk produced the answer Emmett had been hoping for. Bhogals farm had not been producing the crops and this brought down the average for the district. He wasn't the only one to blame, however. Evidently the President had put a squib under Jeri and told him to get every farm up to the national crop average. Otherwise action of a giant proportion would be taken. The confiscation of land and valuables. These to be passed along to a closer fendi of 'he who rules'!

Bhogal, despite his cronyness with top dog, was in the firing line. He would lose his government contracts for vehicles and this would prove calamitous.

Emmett was the conduit through which his resuscitation had to take place. It all depended on him. That's why there had been this unlikely surge of energy and agreeableness over the past week.

Over lunch Jeri asked Emmett if he had ever done any clay pigeon shooting.

"I'm afraid negative but I've done a lot of bird shooting so know how to handle a shotgun."

"Great. We have a shoot this Sunday out on Chikurubi farm, the home of a great family, the Edwards; it's only half an hour from here. They are providing lunch and we all chip in with a hundred Dika (the currency of the countrym - £5 in Irish money) to cover clays. It's a great family day and you'll meet lots of people from different walks of life."

"That's a date but I don't have a gun."

"No problem, you can borrow one of mine. Try and get Howard to come – he is one of our best shots and we all love Rachel. Isn't she georgous?"

"Yes indeed. They have been most kind to me as have Ian and Jan. What about them? Not interested in shooting?"

"No. Try them, do. It is the quiet time so both families can get away. They normally like to leave one of them on duty for fires, etc. You will be put on their roster I would think when the crop is planted."

"We haven't got around to plans like that as yet. I've only got the go ahead to change all the machinery and will be buying their seconds for the season."

"I'm so happy that Bhogal has toed the line and is giving you every chance. Don't become too cocky but get all the help from your neighbours. There are four of the highest producers up there near you so others should be able to follow. Yes?"

As they finished their cheese and biscuits Emmett asked about the Ellis's whom he was about to visit and take possession of their three German Shepherds.

"Such a pity they are leaving but age and health has caught up I think. They were the best producers of polo ponies and had a wonderful stud. I think the new people are similarly inclined. Oh, by the way there's a detour on the road out to Urumi so I'd better draw you a map."

"I already have Jan's, on a piece of paper in my briefcase. I'll get it and you can show me the alteration. Won't be a minute, it's in the landrover."

Jeri was in the main hall when Emmett returned so they laid the plan out on the reception desk. He made the alterations and explained some of the pitfalls in the road out that way.

"How long will it take me approximately?"

"Oh about 45 minutes if you don't get lost. Have you a driver with you?"

"Yes."

"Well I'll get my fellow to explain to him and that should do it."

"Thanks a lot Jeri. Am looking forward to Sunday."

"See you then and you'll be meeting my wife this time."

The elderly Ellis's were absolutely charming and showed Emmett their horses, stables and lush green pastures.

The three dogs – Rajah, Rastus and Rani – were never more than two steps behind them as they toured the farm.

Hugh said he and his wife Naomi, should retire inside and leave the dogs with Emmett while he took a further stroll around the place.

Rani – a black spayed bitch – wasn't too keen. She stood by the door and wanted to be inside with her master and mistress. The other two, after quite a bit of cajoling, followed Emmett. Every ten yards or so they stopped to look back but did continue. Emmett threw a stick a couple of times without reaction. Then Rastus, the biggest of the group, decided to retrieve and play a little. Rajah then joined in and within fifteen minutes Emmett had a rapport with them. They answered to 'heel' and were obviously very well trained.

On returning to the house Rani came to join them. Naomi spoke through an open window suggesting Emmett should load them into the back of the landrover. They would then get to know the scent of his driver who should remain with them.

Emmett had tea whilst both Hugh and Naomi told him as much as they could about the dogs. They weren't vicious but were great watchdogs. No one would dare to come near the vehicle they were in. They would lie on the veranda and guard the house growling when someone approached. Hugh had never seen them attack without provocation. Rani was the eldest at five – the boys were a year younger.

Fifteen minutes later they seemed to have settled down on the selection of blankets Emmett had bought. Emmett departed the house and drove directly to the farm. Rastus was the inquisitive one. He found his way over the rear seats and put his head out the window behind Emmett's shoulder whilst he was driving. His driver, Beni, sitting in the passenger seat beside him, was quite apprehensive but got over it when Rastus moved over to his side window and did the same – without biting his head off!

Rajah then explored and followed in his brother's footsteps. Soon two heads were surveying the new surrounds that passed them by. Rani moved to the back seat and found a space beside Emmett's overnight bag. She was more timid but had the most watchful eyes. Emmett adjusted the rear view mirror so that he could see her. With such companions the trip seemed to take no time at all. At the

Ratilli they found Christopher hitching a ride to the homestead. He got in beside Rani who promptly moved to the rear, her eyes never leaving him.

Leads were attached to their collars on arrival. Emmett took Rani and Rajah whilst Christopher led Rastus. They walked and peed them around the compound then brought them onto the veranda where they found two basins of water. They devoured the contents slobbering all over the polished green cement floor.

Emmett then sat down holding the three of them whilst Christopher emptied the vehicle and started preparing supper for all. He was happy to just sit there doing nothing but empathising with his new canine friends.

When he rose from the table after supper the dogs moved to his side with Christopher to the rear. They all moved out into the garden, through the gate and over towards the airstrip. The dogs just followed with their leads still trailing along beside them. They then walked the length of the airstrip and returned without a moment of worry. The pack roamed no more than twenty yards off the strip, nosing the surrounds and then returning to his side.

Thirty minutes later Christopher said goodnight and stroked Rastus. Emmett returned inside where they would all sleep for the first few nights. He placed their blankets along the corridor from sitting room to his bedroom.

Eventually, after half an hour of whimpering and padding about, they settled down. A peaceful night was had by all.

Since arriving in Africa Emmett had become an early riser. The pack were waiting at his door when he opened it. They half jumped up at him in welcome recognition – he could feel their obvious delight. He went straight out, walking at a good pace, through the garden gate and off to the area of the airstrip. He wished them to get a routine and this 50 sq. yds of grass was the obvious place for them to pee and poo! It was the area where the crop spraying planes rested between flights, it was their open air hangar.

This event went without any apprehension and once they finished their toileting they returned to Emmett's side. He sensed they knew this was their new home and he was their master now.

From that day and the next and so on they hardly ever left Emmett's side. They also became great friends with Christopher. He fed them each evening and they would accompany him on walkabouts. The veranda became their bastion and woe be the person who tried to scale it.

Contouring continued for another month. On one of Jaswant's visits he took Emmett up in the Cessna to view the handy work. It really did look spectacular and the ripping of the land had put a different complexion on the farm. Now all they wished for was good rains.

The clay pigeon shoot was a smashing party. At least thirty farmers, friends and some of Jeri's cronies spent an exhilarating afternoon banging away at the illusive discs.

It took Emmett six attempts to get his rhythm synchronised but then his hits became one hundred percent. This was noted by a number of people including Anna Ngare. She came over to Emmett to invite him back to Jeri's vehicle where his wife and family had set up their picnic table and umbrella.

On the walk over Anna praised him on his marksmanship and quite pointedly asked him if he had ever shot someone.

"Good heavens no. Why should you ask such a question?"

"Oh, I don't really know. You just looked so at ease with your gun. You took to it so quickly and after all you are from Ireland, aren't you?"

"Where I come from Anna has none of that IRA business going on. Don't believe everything you hear or read about the Irish – especially that terrorist organisation. Anyway how are you and the children? Jeri's wife is Margaret isn't she?"

"Yes, she's very sweet and a hard worker. A lovely lady. Come, lets meet her."

Emmett offered his hand. "Hello Margaret, I'm Emmett Doyle. Good to finally meet you."

"Likewise Emmett. Come, sit and have a drink. What would you like, beer or a gin with something? Anna will get it for you."

"A gin and tonic with lots of ice please."

Whilst they talked for the next twenty minutes or so Emmett could feel Anna's eyes on him. She was in the background but her presence was formidable.

Jeri joined them after completing his latest shoot. Anna had his drink ready as he sat down.

"That looks an interesting concoction, Jeri," remarked Emmett.

"Its something I've grown a lunchtime addiction to. Gin, dash of lime, a sprinkle of Angostura bitters, water and lots of ice. I've found I couldn't take the Quinine in tonic so experimented until I found this pleased my taste. Try one next time. Anna is a super bar tender."

"Sounds good and yes please."

His mix was indeed different and as Emmett had always loved Roses lime this concoction relaxed satisfyingly on his palette.

Margaret told Emmett all about the children's riding exploits and how much of a passion it was for them. She said that Emmett had to get some polo ponies.

"Wouldn't they be useful for getting you around the farm?"

There was definitely an ulterior motive behind these hints Emmett thought. Jeri was a regular polo player and the Imuru Club where he played, was the strongest in the country.

Anna kept plying the pink gin and limes into them until the Edwards family announced tea and scones to all. It was 4.15pm.

Emmett found himself the centre of attraction at tea as a number of the farmers wished to acquaint themselves with his background and reasons for being in Ukenza. A lot of them knew the Bhogals as most drove landrovers. The majority were either into tea or coffee but two were big diary farmers outside Urukan. One of them also produced cheese – a cheddar type and a brie. Emmett could buy direct from their farm stall on passing they told him.

More invitations came his way which he found gratifying.

This was the first time Emmett had left the dogs with Christopher for such a long period and he wondered how they had reacted in his absence.

He needn't have worried as when he approached the house those three anxious faces, behind the garden gate, turned to smiles, barks and yelps when they realised it was him. Christopher was standing on the veranda, a relieved man.

Emmett took the pack for a quick walk and all again seemed normal. They were part of the farm now and understood the routine. Their confidence was high. Their love for both Emmett and Christopher was real.

5

Dogs, Ponies and Plants

Agricultural and real farming activity suddenly moved up a gear, almost to fever pitch. Between the initial ripping of the earth, allowing for aeration, and the actual planting date, could be anything up to two months. In that time it was hoped that a little rain would fall to moisten the land. Then it was time for weeds to appear and that was when the first crop spraying exercise took place.

Jaswant flew in with one Ethiopian pilot following in his tiny yellow plane, known affectionately as Wasp (a Boeing 'Stearman'). Emmett had been warned to expect them and that the pilot would stay in the house for the week or so that it took to finish the weed killing operation.

Mustafa was a Christian and a very easy going fellow who blended with Emmett's lifestyle. He had no especial dietary requests and in fact taught Christopher some superb new methods of cooking goat meat, an Ethiopian delicacy. Up to then Emmett had only tasted it in a curry dish. With the propensity of goats in the land this was the cheapest meat on offer.

A team of four arrived from Kenzi to act as flagmen under an overall operator, George. He organised the fuel refilling and the mixing of various weed killers. The operator also canvassed the local farms for spraying business. A tight well organised team got on with their work without worrying anyone. They set up two tents to sleep in beside the plane next to Emmett's house. The area had been cleared of all canine deposits prior to their arrival!

Crop spraying is a dangerous activity as one can get the angle of descent wrong and what with ever changing up and down draughts, the pilot really earns his wage. Emmett was itching to fly but not crop spraying. This was too dicey from what he had heard.

By the time Mustafa had completed his stint he had painted such an exotic picture of his country, Ethiopia – although war torn in parts – that Emmett reasoned he should holiday there sometime. He was a superb guest and was welcome to return for a longer stay in the pre-harvest season. The Bhogals had told Emmett that if it didn't work out they would give Mustafa a decent tent for his next job. What a come down that would have been!

The next big job on the farm was the preparation of the lands for planting which had to be completed by March 17 or thereabouts. This was an absolute must as the crop was geared to be ready in four months. Any later and the period of germination might be harmed by the rainy season.

To Emmett it sounded an annual gamble which over a period of five or six seasons could average out to the farmer's benefit. Ian worked on three good crops in five and hoped that the other two would be above the make or break line. With excellent management and a lot of luck he could maintain a profitable margin each year.

Emmett obviously must attempt the same – perhaps his Irishness would bring him luck?

Jan and her syce, Chengi, rode over to Emmett's compound one morning. Mounted on a lovely thoroughbred type grey gelding, the one that Emmett had seen on one of his recent visits. She looked a mighty pretty picture as she dismounted near his garden gate and took off her helmet. Chengi took the two horses over to one of the grain sheds to be out of the hot sun.

Christopher had cold lemonade ready on the veranda as Emmett, who had been in the workshops, joined her for a refreshing drink.

Jan asked if she could wash her hands and was shown the way.

Emmett suddenly realised that she was the first women to have visited him since his arrival. A wee bit strange he thought.

When she returned to the veranda Emmett was struck, yet again, by her elegance and beauty. He had always loved auburn hair but never had had a girlfriend so bestowed. Here now, miles out in the bush on the Punjabi Plains, was someone literally out of Vogue magazine. She was as tall as Emmett with the figure to compliment her height. Both she and her sister-in-law, Rachel, could grace the boardwalks of any international couture house. How fortunate were their respective husbands, he thought.

Jan had come about two things. Firstly, she wanted to set a Saturday or Sunday date for his plant party and secondly, she had found someone with a couple of 'not too fast' polo ponies to give away. Both were sound of wind and limb but just not up to competitive match competition.

Emmett could hardly believe his good fortune and without a thought leaned over and kissed her on the cheek in gratitude. She responded by offering her other cheek.

They set a Sunday three weeks ahead for the plant party. Emmett would therefore have plenty of time to prepare the area. Jan offered to supply the manure, both horse and cow for fertilization. He got the impression that she wanted an ongoing interest in this project.

"You'd better get your staff to fit sides to your truck for carrying the ponies. Oh, and you'd better have an offloading ramp built. Your grader driver will see to that, just chose a suitable place. Well that's about it then. Say thanks to Christopher for his excellent lemonade – it's the best in the district. I'll tell you when you can collect the ponies. Come up and have supper later in the week – any evening is okay – we are in every night."

Chengi had been watching the house and as they left the veranda he brought the horses over to meet them.

Emmett was quite troubled after her visit. He started trawling through his four months of African residency and the realisation became a fact. He had not met any single females of his age – white, black or Eurasian. Was there a problem there? Were all white females sent away to get married off perhaps – he'd have to ask his neighbours about this?

The beautiful Anna was the only one who had set his pulse a thumping. But she was probably married, had children at home with her mother in their homeland, and could well be 'out of bounds' for various reasons both ethnic and status wise.

Emmett would have to spend more weekends at the club in Urukan, play sport and mix with more farmers. He might then get lucky. After all he was a young virile Irishman who needed to sow his wild oats. He'd be planting plenty of the wheaten variety mighty soon but what about his natural passionate needs and ability? They too should be serviced before too long! A pity Jan didn't have a younger sister – or perhaps she did? He would have to find out.

Ratilli farm had its second visit from Jeri Ntsemo. This time he brought a lady agronomist and a male hydro engineer from the main government department of agriculture.

Emmett toured the four sections this time with stoppages taking place every so often on instructions from the two civil servants.

They were impressed with the contouring and the preparation of seed beds which pleased him immensely.

The engineer wondered if he couldn't sink a few bore holes. This might give Emmett the chance to put in some irrigation if the water was strong enough.

Wind breaks of blue gum trees would be an advantage in certain areas, they said. This, however, would be a long term project but it could be started next year.

They had been in the district for two days and were on their way back to Urukan so Emmett thought tea would be a nice refreshment.

Jeri was thrilled to hear about Emmett's two intended polo ponies and could he invite himself and family to the plant party? They would donate generously.

"I'll bring you six well grown bottle brushes. They will make a lovely shaded area for you and they are so colourful when in bloom. Will that do?"

"Gosh, thanks and of course do come. I might have the ponies here by then."

In parting Jeri remarked on the dogs – "nice one", he said, "a good investment," and he winked.

Christopher got a gang of labourers to dig up the garden. They then took off on the back of a trailer and tractor to collect a load of the promised manure. They were a happy lot singing all the way. It was like an outing for them but it was in work time.

Emmett decided to go 'the whole hog' in designing his first landscaped garden. He called for the stonemason and showed him where he wanted his barbecue and how he wanted it to look. He drew him a rough outline.

"Oh yes sir, I know the type. I built Mr. Beaton's some years ago. Just leave it to me. I'll collect stones from the dry river bed."

"Are there any flat stones anywhere around? I'd like you to pave some paths through this intended garden – cement in between, you know the type?"

"Yes sir."

Ali was an aged man, very courteous and wore a white muslin hat on his head. Wisps of grey curly hair peeped out from beneath it. His eyes spent more time downwards than up. He breathed confidence and honesty despite this.

"By the way, Ali, have you built many fireplaces and chimneys?"

"Oh yes sir, many."

"That's my next request then, after the garden. I want one before winter. Ok?"

"Yes, indeed sir."

Emmett could see Ali was thrilled to be involved in the creation of something new. He was a true craftsman as Emmett found out to his utter delight. In fact he kept him employed with little and large projects over the next few years.

Christopher took the end of a length of twine whilst Emmett outlined the flower beds, borders, and paths. They then staked out the positions for shrubs and trees. The entire area was 60 sq. yds. There would be lots of lawn for the dogs to romp and laze on. Garden furniture had been ordered and would arrive with the next truck load of goodies from Kenzi.

A home to Emmett was not a home without a garden and animals. It was almost there. Only one thing was missing. It was still worrying him?

Christopher brought two of his friends, of the Mandi tribe, from the labour lines who knew something, or so they said, about horses. They were interested in working with the intended new comers. They said they rode and knew all the work of a groom (syce).

Emmett, therefore, decided to change their work routine and after measuring out two 12ft. x 12ft. stalls in the back of the grain store, told them to get on with it. Upright and horizontal poles were located in another shed. He only had to pop in now and then to see how they were progressing. They finished them off within two hours then went off to the workshops and had two feed buckets welded. These would be clipped to the top pole and could be taken away for filling and washing out between feeds.

His grader driver, once shown the place for the loading ramp, got stuck in and had it completed in virtually no time at all. He also enjoyed this change of work – his contouring had been a long session away from the compound. This was at his front door.

The farm truck set off to collect the ponies a week later. Jan arranged the entire operation as she was visiting Kenzi and could see to the loading at her friend's farm. Emmett remained at home to offload and welcome them to Ratilli.

Two almost identical bay ponies arrived late at night. Lights were put on all over the compound and very fortunately the offloading and bedding down in their new quarters went without any difficulties. Polo ponies are well used to strange hours of arrival and departure at and from tournaments all over the country as many miles had to be travelled from farms to events. This, therefore, was nothing out of the ordinary for them. The cherry on the top of this deal was the fact that both ponies came with saddles, bridles and grooming kit. What a bonus.

When Emmett turned in for the night he thought of names for them. It kept him awake for hours. Next morning he announced to Christopher that they would be called Corrib and Mask and had to explain this to the two grooms. He told Christopher that he named them after two famous fishing lakes near his home in the west of Ireland.

He allowed the syces to take them for a long walk on lead reins before their morning feed and then turned them out into one of the two newly created paddocks at the rear of his house. This would allow them to 'get the feel' of their new home. On seeing them running free Emmett realised he had to now construct a sunshade for them out there. Not a tree was in sight!

A much appreciated three days of rain showers moistened the farms acres just prior to planting.

Emmett found it so easy to manage this exacting facet on horse back. It was essential to govern the correct distribution of seed to the planters. That they had to complete the task in so many days was absolutely essential.

Many overtime hours were worked by the labour force but they seemed to appreciate the hands on management that Emmett was showing.

Christopher told him at supper each evening how the staff were enjoying this season's planting. They sensed an urgency in his methods – something no one before had achieved.

Emmett had told his entire staff, at a meeting prior to planting, that they would be on a bonus percentage of the crop. He set a figure of 8.5 bags an acre which would guarantee a double cheque. They were vociferous, above all Emmett's expectations at this announcement. From then on they worked like an army of ants. Everyone was happy.

In discussing his incentive carrot with Ian one evening Emmett learned something that guided him through the rest of his years in Africa.

"Don't ever give them some job that you yourself are not capable of doing. Show the way and they will respect you at all times. That's why they hate the Hindi's – they'll work for them okay but they will have no loyalty and that's something you must have."

"I take your point. I've noticed this over the past few months when I've actually got down and carried out the job myself – got my hands dirty and been prepared for any eventuality."

"That's it. You've hit the nail on the head. The other thing to remember is be fair at all times. Hit them hard when they make a cock up and praise them when they achieve. They are human after all. I give my labour force a crop bonus. I tell them my target and when achieved they are all as happy as Larry – and so am I."

"Well I hope we exceed my target of 8.5 bags then all of us will be happy on the Punjabi Plains. I might even get a smile out of old Bhogal!"

"God, you'd be lucky," they both laughed and drank another beer.

Jan, Rachel and Christopher were the 'toast' of the plant party. What they managed to produce in culinary delights was staggering.

For the barbecue Emmett had venison, mutton, pork and beef. The cooks from Jan and Rachel's kitchens assisted. Christopher was in his element. Never had there been such a party before on Ratilli. And the big surprise was that Jaswant and Vijay flew in unannounced to find upward of thirty Zungus and six Hindis all enjoying themselves. To put it into the Irish vernacular 'they was gob smacked'!

Emmett couldn't believe his eyes at the quality, quantity and variety of the herbaceous gifts. His staff, for once, were speechless – until they realised what it was all about and then the women folk ululated for a good fifteen minutes.

Everyone offered to help in the planting but Emmett very wisely refused this outburst of affection. He preferred to do it all himself in the coming week, with Christopher and Maju as assistants.

"You are here to enjoy yourselves – so lets get on with the party."

It went on until well after dark – an excellent gathering of people made for an interesting eight hours.

They had all heard about Emmett from either Jan or Rachel and were therefore mad keen to explore his background and find out what he was made of.

At least six women made advances – others were less blatant.   All of them, however, were married and this in Emmett's eyes was danger with a capital Dee.

During the mid afternoon period Jeri Nsemo stood up and made a speech of welcome and praised Emmett on his progress and wished him a successful harvest.   Emmett felt this must have touched a nerve within the two turbaned visitors?   Jeri then asked quietly could he see the ponies and could the children have a ride?

Sometime later the ponies were made ready and Emmett slid away from the party with Jeri, his two children and the ever attendant Anna.   Margaret said she would follow later; she was enjoying herself so much.   Vijay was also interested and followed them.

Jeri accompanied the children into the paddock and stood in the middle whilst they walked, trotted and cantered around quite merrily.

Anna talked freely to Emmett asking quite pertinent questions.   It was almost a 'come on' and he found himself enjoying this little sojourn away from the crowd.   She wanted to know when next he was coming to town and could they meet?   Was he worried about being seen with a black girl and questions along these lines?

"Not if it doesn't compromise your position with Jeri and Margaret.   I'm not au fait with such a mixed setup here – in this farming community – if you get my meaning."

"Oh it won't cause a problem at my end – in fact it might be a good move on your behalf."   She smiled demurely, questions sparkling from her bright active eyes.

At that she suddenly stopped mid sentence – as Margaret came up to join them.

"You two seem to be getting on well, I'm so pleased.   How are the children?"

"Doing brilliantly as you can see and there's a proud papa out in the middle directing tactics," smiled Emmett.

"How wonderful! They so love their riding, don't they Anna, and I never seem to have the time to give them my attention."

After a few minutes Emmett said he should return to his guests and Margaret said she too would like to return to her drink.

"Maybe you would allow the children to visit you. Perhaps you could give them some instruction?" questioned a proud mother.   "Anna would accompany them with a driver if you weren't too busy and of course you wouldn't mind?"

"That would be fine – only problem is I don't have a phone here. But I could probably arrange something with the daily bus driver. He brings messages all the time."

"Oh that would be easy then. I'll talk to you again before we leave and make an arrangement. Okay?"

With that little topic discussed and finalised by quite an aggressive Margaret – perhaps it was the drink talking – Emmett pondered the thought of having Anna here without her bosses. Could well prove to be a tasty morsel?

Most of the women who pandered after him showed a fascination in his pony tail – something that goes unnoticed back home. They wanted to touch it, unravel it and guess its length. Emmett found it hard to decide whether they were genuine in their interest or whether it was a giant Mickey take? He played along with them for now. One day he would call someone's bluff – and then what? He would chose the theatrical one he mused.

Next morning Christopher was exhausted. He could hardly put one foot ahead of the other. The one enormous point in his favour was the fact he didn't drink – not a sip of alcohol had ever passed his lips, he had told Emmett. He was, however, quite old and had worked like a Trojan all day long.

A great party had taken place in the labour lines when Emmett brought much of the leftovers down to Christopher's room after clearing up had taken place. Emmett had allowed a few dozen beers to accompany the njama (meat).

Next day was spent placing all the trees, shrubs and plants into their respective places. The dogs had a great time christening, with lifted legs, all the bigger items. Soon the lawn would be planted and in a few months everything would be lush, green and blooming. This was Africa.

It had been a lovely idea of Jan's and Emmett now felt he must get something really special for her as a token of his gratitude and appreciation. When next in Kenzi he would see to that, he noted in his diary.

Emmett had met so many people and although he prided himself on remembering names and faces this would prove a mammoth task to categorise. He sat with his diary for at least thirty minutes that night and managed to write down most of their names. He added pen pictures of each and wondered how accurate they would turn out to be.

Wheat planting went to schedule. No one got as much as an hour off during the twenty-five days it took to plant the entire acreage. Very little time was spent on repairs – all the machinery performed with exemplary behaviour. He had to thank Ian and Howard, in the main, for that success. He learnt that their respective planting had gone, as usual, with routine expertise. Now all that had to happen was hope. Emmett prayed hard that night. This was an enormous undertaking for him. Something that no one 'back home' would easily comprehend.

In the four months ahead spraying played a major part in the nursing of the crop.

One item Emmett hadn't been told about was an invasion by the Quelea bird. Evidently they flew in from North African countries searching for 'about to be harvested' cornfields. This time they luckily were first spotted in their millions in the more northern areas from the Punjabi Plains. A visitation was therefore only from their outriders.

A sparrow like bird they rest after dark in scrubland. When this area is located the crop spraying units are sent in with a highly toxic liquid which eliminates most of the flock. This purge is relentless until the last flight is decimated. A 'them or us' battle to the end.

Emmett had heard about locusts and the damage they could reap on a wide area. The Quelea was even more dangerous. What with beetles, bugs, aphids, rust and mildew the crop was prone to attack from all fronts. It had to be protected at any cost.

Weekends could be spent away from the farm as the spray unit had its own management team with two highly proficient pilots, which was an added bonus.

His stonemason, Ali, now had the task of building a fireplace and chimney in the sitting room. It had to be in by July, the start of the cold winter months, Emmett requested.

Various farmers had offered timber and stone so Emmett visited a few of them. He got a lovely cedar block which he would fashion into a mantelpiece. Some Imbuia wood blocks which would be ideal stools or side tables and as much bamboo as he wanted, for whatever, were among the trophies he collected. He had read somewhere that bamboo brought luck – an Eastern superstition he remembered.

Another farm produced the most lovely quartz stone of varying colours. This would be used to face certain areas of the overall stone fronted fireplace, he thought. They were all so generous and so eager for Emmett to be happy in his homestead. He was to drop in anytime.

Emmett was becoming quite blasé about distances – having a near neighbour who was seventeen miles away was a mere nothing! To travel forty miles to a cocktail party was normal. He'd be almost across the next county back home!

The tennis tournament was great craic[2]. Emmett found out that plenty of gin prior to a match made the ball seem as large as a football. This was Shirra's theory and he marvelled at her tenacity and strength of purpose. They became a strong team but got wiped off the court in the quarter finals after winning three matches.

Emmett got beaten early on in the singles – he just wasn't fit enough. His doubles partner – a young black civil servant – was a brilliant retriever as Emmett held the net. They also won three matches but no cups. Emerson worked in Jeri's department of social services. He had been educated in Kampala and was obviously going places within the civil service.

The Club was Emmett's address but he didn't sleep there. The flat offered up a cornucopia of exotic delights. Shirra had a voracious sexual appetite which left Emmett shagged out each morning. His gin intake brought him back to life and they were both well pleased with their tennis exploits.

He was happy to be back on the farm thoroughly exhausted but satisfied. His ponies and dogs took up all of his free hours. He constructed jumps and began teaching himself polo. Both ponies were well schooled but his timing and stick work was way off. Perhaps the bumpy terrain had something to do with his constant and exasperating misses. However, practise did make perfect, at least passable for him to play a few chukkas when he was invited to an afternoon at Imuru. Think of it as 'hurling on horseback' Emmett kept saying to himself.

He played on borrowed ponies who were a lot faster than his. At the end of the session he was complimented on his prowess.

"You must become a regular" said Jeri who showed his expertise in one chukka against Emmett.

"Don't think I can afford the game and my two ponies, as you know, are not really up to it. We'll see at the end of the harvest how things work out."

"Good – remain positive. Oh by the way, the children have a mid-term break soon – could you possibly stomach them for an overnight? I know they would love it."

A message from the Ratilli operator said the Commissioner's party would be arriving in two days time.

It probably meant that a driver and Anna had to be accommodated as well as the children. Their driver would be housed in the guest room down near Christopher. Anna and the children would stay in the house with Emmett. Just as well he had three bedrooms and that the pilots were living further into the plains with the Gill family over that period. Singh Gill had the largest spread this side of

---

[2] An Irishism for fun

the road. The old man was a splendid turbaned Sikh originally from north India, who just adored living out in the bush away from all the hurly burly of city life. He was reported to be one of the wealthiest men in the country. His sons ran the various family consortiums whilst 'himself' languished in a simple existence out on the plains. He was a most humble man and impressed Emmett every time they met on the road, at the Ratilli or in the local village. He hadn't yet called on Emmett but promised he would after the harvest.

The grooms were told to be available at all times once the children arrived. Emmett was going to put them through a rigorous routine he remembered from his Irish Pony Club days. Those were memorable camps up on the Burren, West Clare. He wondered if a pony club existed out here.

The party arrived mid morning so a riding lesson was arranged prior to lunch. After showing Anna their rooms she proceeded to carry in what seemed like freight loads of luggage. Were they here for more than a couple of days wondered Emmett?

He needn't have worried. Two large boxes were packed with all sorts of food and drink. Best of all was a crate of fresh fruit and vegetables.

"Make yourselves at home – look on me as Uncle Emmett – one of the family. Christopher will get whatever you want whenever you want and Anna is next to you here in this room. Bathroom is here but separate loo there. Okay? Just relax and enjoy it all. We'll ride in half an hour."

He left them to get on with whatever. He had checked Christopher's menus earlier that morning.

Emmett decided to make the children work for their lessons. They would groom, saddle up and cool down the ponies afterwards. They should learn to do it all the correct Irish way. This proved no barrier with Edith, the more active of the two. Both had all the basics and seemed full of confidence. For an hour he put them through the alphabet of riding. Posture, hands, legs, toes up, seat, then the walk, trot and canter. They took to the ponies as butter to bread. Emmett was thrilled with this as there could have been a problem.

He noticed Anna watching from a distance. All would be reported back to Margaret and Jeri, of that he had no doubt.

Edith and Zimba walked the ponies down to the end of the runway and back. By then all of them had cooled down and were totally relaxed.

Emmett called to let their legs hang loose but keep in touch with their hands. The ponies must learn to 'let down' and totally switch off prior to stabling. The children unsaddled and then rubbed down the area under the saddle and over their respective loins.

Emmett showed them how to make a straw swatch – a figure of eight – which then acted as a drying-down brush. The children took a keen interest in everything horsey. It was a joy to have such students. They were also well mannered.

"How about some cool drinks before lunch and a quick change of clothes. There is plenty of hot water if you would like a shower. Just be yourselves."

Over lunch Anna remarked how easy it looked when instructed by someone who knew what they were talking about.

"Why not try, Anna?" asked Edith.

"Yes I'm sure Uncle Emmett will teach you too," commented Zimba Charles.

"We'll see," Anna replied with pleading eyes focused on Emmett.

"It would give me great pleasure. Just say when."

"That will be when, Anna? We'd love to watch. In fact reverse the roles for a change," interjected a lively Zimba.

The afternoon was spent touring the farm and looking at the crop. Anna was up front beside Emmett with the children and dogs in the back of the open landrover. Anna was meticulous in her choice of clothes for them – they were now in shorts and shirts. She remained in virginal white dust coat. Emmett had never seen her in any other outfit or colour.

After tea Edith asked if they could have another lesson. Emmett agreed. The youngsters raced off the veranda to change back into riding gear. They then ran across the compound to saddle up. The dogs didn't know who to follow or stay with – dividing their loyalty – Rastus and Raj with the children, Rani kept to Emmett's side.

"They are loving every moment here as I am. Thanks so much."

"It's my pleasure Anna. You must come often."

"I'll stay with Christopher and assist him in preparing the barbecue. I notice the fire is already lit. Go and enjoy yourself. You are good with children."

This time the lesson was over cavelettis[3], the children riding without stirrups. They weren't used to this but their obvious determination won out. They then progressed to 'look ma no reins either'!" Emmett had them holding the pommel first but then told them to fold their arms.

"Head up, heels down. Keep your balance and look straight ahead."

Emmett kept repeating this, time and time, again until he was satisfied with their progress. Their cherry on the top was when he asked the syces to arrange two little jumps and sent both of them at a trot – then at a canter, over the obstacles.

"That's it for the day. Well done you two – I'll make champions out of both of you. Take the ponies off and dry yourselves down. See you back at the stables."

---

[3] A line of poles on the ground at equal distance

Emmett was exhausted. He needed a drink and as he would have expected back home in the west 'the bauld Anna' had it waiting for him. A cold lager.

"They did brilliantly. I wish I could tell Jeri and Margaret. I have to get some telegraphic or wireless equipment here pronto. Thanks a ton for this – it won't touch sides. How about yourself?"

"I've a glass of lemonade over there, thanks."

The talk at supper was all riding, riding, riding. Emmett wasn't used to this constant prittle prattle and was totally knocked out, shagged out in fact. If this was what having a family of youngsters was like, every day, then he would postpone it for quite sometime he thought with resolute determination. Or was he really kidding himself? He remembered what Anna had said to him earlier and frowned.

6

Anna – an Enigma

Was it the musk or the presence which woke him? He pulled himself out of deep sleep to find a ghost-like figure observing him in repose. A finger pursed her lips whispering "keep quiet. We mustn't wake the children."

Was this a dream? He remembered Shakespeare all of a sudden. "is this a dagger I see before me?" This was no dagger but it was some apparition. He was stunned, amused and desirous all in one. It was ethereal.

Anna gently pulled down his single sheet and straddled him. Her white shift softly touched his naked body.

"I wanted to see if you let your ponytail down at night," she gurgled into his face as she bent forward nose touching nose. Her hands stroked his mane, spread out on unruffled pillows, either side of his face.

"It's so soft," she whispered into his left ear nibbling and then thrusting her tongue in and around it.

Emmett wanted to scream but she put a cupped hand over his mouth just in time.

"Remember the children – shush, please. I want to enjoy this." She was the cat, he the mouse.

She stretched her arms up above her head and then dropped them to pick off her shift, letting it fall leaf like to the floor. In that very special African half light, through half-curtained windows, he gazed up at a goddess – an ebony figure sculpted to perfection.

His hands were drawn to her breasts, rock-like with nipples reaching for the stars. He pinched each one, but tenderly, rather caressingly rubbing them 'till her head bent backwards in response. Her own hands clutched her ankles in rapturous recognition of a profound desire.

She felt him rise up beneath her. She rocked slowly in answer to his arousal, her thighs tightening on his prone form.

Her nipples were now sore. She pushed them down one at a time, onto his lips. They needed cooling and his inviting mouth offered salvation.

She was becoming wet. Her grip eased on his legs as his pulsating rod sought for space. Her movements matched his every vibrant touch. Longing lips fiercely split his, their tongues entwined python like as he penetrated into

Neferthitis tomb. He went up and up and up again until he reached the zenith of his fortunes. She was his celestial body and he had captured it.

Climax after climax followed in quick pursuit of total perfection. Sobs and gasps were the only symphony sounded that endless night.

When finally her knees could take it no longer her ebony body subsided into the hollow of his mattress. They lay in silence save for Emmett's deep breathing, her right hand stroking a limp missile now expended. It had done its job crossing far reaching unexplored regions before exploding in victorious passion.

Anna crept out of Emmett's bed returning to hers before first light. He never heard or felt a movement.

For the first time in seven months Christopher had to awaken Emmett with his morning mug of Black Mountain tea. The dogs were bemused and padded around his room questioning why they hadn't had their walkies.

Once showered and out on the runway with his rampant canine pack Emmett felt almost human. Never mind the dogs, he was bemused at what had gone on through the night. Perhaps it was a dream – a very active one, nightmarish in proportion but fantasia like in reality.

On returning to his garden he was greeted by a boisterous Edith bursting to tell him something, "guess what we've done Uncle Emmett?"

"I couldn't possibly – its too early. Tell me."

Turning to his front door she called out "come out please" and with that command a vision appeared. Emmett's mouth hung open.

Proceeding in slow motion was a designer clad Anna in figure hugging faded jeans, wide belt and pale blue blouse. This couldn't be the virginal white uniformed lady of everyday or could it?

"We've got her to agree to a riding lesson. How about that Uncle Emmett?"

"I think its brilliant. So this is how you look when you are off duty is it Anna?"

"I love clothes. I spend all my money on them," she bashfully replied.

She had a new confidence about her – she was radiant and the children obviously adored her. This was a triumph for them – in riding they were the masters, she now would be the student.

Breakfast was a bubble of verbal activity, bursting here and there into gurgles of mirth as both children quizzed Emmett as to how he would tackle Anna's first lesson.

"Are you all right with this Anna? I wouldn't want to pressure you in any way."

"Oh yes, I'm greatly looking forward to it. You'll have no worries there. Just please be gentle with me."

Her curled lip smile got the message through to him – above the children's' heads. Eyes sparkled as in a throwaway cutting edge line.

Emmett allowed the children to toss a coin for who could ride whilst Anna was given her lesson. Zimba won and elected to go first. This pleased Edith as she showed such an interest and devotion to Anna's progress.

Corrib was the pony chosen for the lesson. Anna's remarkable ability in mounting and sitting straight in the saddle amazed Emmett. Her constant observance of the children's various equestrian exploits had obviously become engrained in a very educated and active mind.

Emmett led the pony around the immediate homestead area drawing much amusement from the staff in sight of this unusual treat. An African lady on a horse?

They then ventured onto the side of the runway watching Zimba performing his warm up exercises in the adjoining paddock. Langat, the syce, was present in the centre of the field keeping close watch over him.

Anna couldn't seem to keep her hands down just above the pommel. This was a real novice trait as Emmett had often seen in beginners. On their return trip he trotted beside Corrib making him do the same. Anna rocked around on the saddle until she realised that by holding the pommel she got her balance. Her bottom kept banging the saddle until she pleaded for a halt. She was confident, not at all afraid, but her loins were most probably tired and hurting after the night's activity?

Edith, who was on the opposite side of the pony, thought she was doing really well.

"You'll be able to ride out with us very soon, Anna. That will be great fun, won't it?"

After twenty-five minutes in the saddle, Anna had had enough and Edith took over. She joined Zimba in the paddock and Emmett gave them some jumping practise. He then sent them off on an outride in Section 1 with Langat accompanying on a bicycle.

Emmett and Anna returned to the house. He advised her to have a bath and he would put some mustard powder in it. An old wives tale that really worked, he told her. A good soaking in hot water seemed to take all stiffness away. It was a remedy used by many in the hunting fields of Ireland he added. She dutifully obeyed – only if he were to dry her down afterwards! Very cheeky, he thought but a nice thought anyway. He would consider it. He slapped her bottom in jovial mood. He noticed it had a certain African roundness about it.

This was the first time Emmett had seen a black woman – a beauty – in the raw. He didn't consider the night light of some hours previous would have done justice to her form.

She had three marks – about an inch long – one above the other – above each breast with something similar higher up on each shoulder. Anna noticed his questioning stare.

"They are made at birth, it's a tribal thing, registering the fact that I'm Tukulu and from a high family."

"I wish I'd seen them last night – I'd have kissed them then – like now."

Her breasts were well formed and sturdy. Not a sag and not a stretch mark on her body. He towelled her down not missing an inch anywhere. Her body was a dark chocolate brown, the colour reminded him of Bournville dark cooking chocolate. Her pubic hair a definite black vee of tiny curls contrasted well with her skin. The soles of her feet and palms of her hands were pink in hue with the former hard as concrete.

"You are only the second man to have me – the first was a tribal thing again – to break my virginity, many moons ago. A nasty episode best forgotten. You were beautiful. I knew you would be. I longed for you since first we saw each other."

"That's been the same with me too. But it has been a bit difficult if you can understand what I mean."

"Oh yes, don't worry, I appreciate your position. We'll just have to play, a how you say, cagey game."

She smiled and hugged him as she wrapped herself in two towels and departed to dress.

Just as well as Emmett was becoming greatly aroused by her presence. He departed to the kitchen and drank a pint of cool water. He was suddenly very dry.

At lunch Anna decided they must leave by 4.30pm to be home well before Margaret and before dark.

Emmett proposed to take them all up to Ian and Jan's and then perhaps, time permitting, over to Howard and Rachel's. Both had horses and ponies and it was an idea of Emmett's that he might persuade either family to lend him a horse when next the children visited him.

Emmett demanded that Anna dress out of uniform – she wasn't on duty – and she was too beautiful not to be appreciated.

Both families knew the children, having met them at many functions with their parents, but Anna had always been in the background – a servant.

With Emmett everyone was on the same plain and this was readily appreciated.

"All three of them are having riding lessons with me and so far everything is hunky dorey. Anna is the beginner – but she didn't fall off and she loves it," prompted Emmett.

"You'll be needing more ponies if this continues then," said Jan with a questioning look.

"I suppose so but God knows how Bhogal will take it."

"Don't bother about him Emmett – he has to pander to your every whim once you've got this crop in. And well done. It looks prime so far. We'll cross legs, fingers, everything for you." That was Ian at his very best thought Emmett.

"Thanks a million, guys. I couldn't have done it without your help. I have been telling them all about the farm before, now, and what I eventually want. But all these three are interested in is riding – isn't that so?"

Anna replied for the three of them.

"Yes, but we never realised what went on, on a wheat farm – the size, the amount of machinery and the good fortune, luck I suppose, that is necessary to achieve anything. We are in awe and Emmett tells us that you are even bigger than him. It must be quite terrifying at times."

"You can say that again, Anna," sneaked in Jan before adding "one only sees a fifth of the worries. We have many sleepless nights I promise you."

"Uncle Emmett says you have some horses. May we see them please?" piped up Edith who was obviously getting bored with grownups talk.

"Of course you may. Lets go then."

Jan took the three off whilst Ian collared Emmett and guided him to his office to discuss the crop spraying and how effective certain products had been.

The gang returned about an hour later and Jan called for tea. Emmett noticed that she and Anna had hit if off and were obviously enjoying each other's company. They were equals now.

Ian took the children to see his monster tractor and let them climb up into its cab.

"Gosh. This is like nothing I've ever seen," remarked Zimba Charles. Edith was dumb struck and that's saying something.

They heard shouts of "come and get it" so they headed off for tea. Jan had raided her larder – she produced scones and jam tarts, cool drink and Lapsang tea. A mighty feast and it would be their last as there wouldn't now be time to visit Howard.

"You know Emmett, you can always borrow my old grey and the other two are only used in school holidays and very seldom too – if you would like to?"

"That would be marvellous Jan. Thanks."

"And then we could all ride together," interjected a joyful Edith.

They had obviously been talking twenty to the dozen out with Jan and she had got into the rhythm of the children's enthusiasm. She probably missed her own two who were away at boarding school, and appreciated the company.

As they departed Emmett was quick to remember her offer.

"Don't forget you promised me the grey," he said with a wink and a hug.

His brood followed suit well mannered as they were.

"Thanks a lot Mr. and Mrs. Poultney. We'll see you again soon hopefully," came from Zimba.

"Likewise," from Edith "it's been a real pleasure and thank you both for your hospitality," from Anna.

"Bye the way gang – we are Ian and Jan. None of this Mr. and Mrs. – it makes us sound so old. Safe trip. And Anna give our best regards to Margaret and Jeri. Bye."

That night, sitting alone with only his dogs as company, Emmett thought back over those two unbelievable days. He smoked his cheroot – a Rietmeester – with passion, blowing smoke rings out over a still garden. He was becoming quite expert at this. His brandy and ginger ale began to look pale as the ice melted and weakened the alcoholic content. He would pour himself another. He felt he had achieved something special with the children. He enjoyed their company and they were no trouble at all. They got on with the dogs, ate what was offered, went to bed when told and showed such enthusiasm for riding that the time flew by. They could come again. He must be mellowing, he thought?

Anna, however, was an enigma. He had wanted it to happen but didn't expect it that way. He should have been the wooer, she the recipient. It turned out to be the other way around. She was the aggressor, he the recipient. She therefore was one up on him.

Everything had been so special, the act, the company, rapport, ambience. She appreciated and understood their positions. He certainly wouldn't compromise anything and felt that it wasn't in her interest to do other than proceed along those same lines.

There was something, however, that worried Emmett. Why was such a well educated girl in such a menial position? It couldn't be just for the love of the children. That didn't ring true. He felt there had to be something deeper.

After mulling this over and over he decided to take it all on face value and not look below the surface.

"If you have it, flaunt it," was a phrase he remembered from varsity days. One well endowed Scottish lass had used it as her password to fame!

It felt like all holidays wrapped into one. More than Emmett could ever have dreamed of. Both Bhogals flew in with a great present for the farm. Emmett was over the moon.

A shortwave radio set with additional CB advantages would be installed with a tall aerial within the next few days. They had brought the set and a team would follow from Kenzi to erect the aerial and install it. It would be able to communicate with their offices in Kenzi and Urukan, their Cessna and all neighbouring farms.

They seemed surprised that their licence application had suddenly been granted. For the past five years it had been refused. Why the change of direction they questioned?

"I'm just overjoyed Jaswant. Don't worry about the past, think positive, think the future."

"The crop looks good from the air, very even," pronounced Jaswant, "there are just a few places where growth hasn't been as good as the rest. I'll take you up for a spin if you like".

"Yes Sir. Lets go. Vijay you can have a look at the ponies and have a ride if you like."

"Thanks. I'll think about it."

Emmett knew Vijay would want to ferret around and hear all the gossip first and he didn't somehow think he was pro the equestrian intrusion anyway, but Emmett felt he must show willing.

From the air, lime green tinged acres looked fantastic. The few problem areas were the result of former erosion and the lightness of topsoil doing its best to hold the plants together. Not enough moisture and good soil were available so nothing had a chance.

Jaswant seemed happy enough and then he dropped a bombshell as he flew off to the north of the farm over the main road and the forest next to Ian's spread.

"That's Melelo down there and we've just leased six thousand acres of it. I'm going to send you two D8's to clear it – not all of course – we'll leave windbreaks which should help a new crop. The soil should be rich. We will get the surveyors out to define the boundaries for you and then its go, go, go."

When there was no reply Jaswant continued "I detect you are not happy?"

"No, it's not that. I'm sad at having to destroy beautiful forest. I've actually driven in there and know that there are lots of hardwoods and wonderful birdlife."

"You will have lots of forest left – I expect only two to three thousand acres or so for planting. That's the government estimate – our lease price is centred around that figure. I don't expect all of it to be finished – cleared I mean –

in one season. But two big dozers (D8 Caterpillar) will clear a lot in six months. It should be a very nice block and its next to your good friend Poultney."

With that he banked the Cessna and returned via Ian's farm homestead where he dipped his wings in recognition and then home to Ratilli.

After more discussion about Melelo and proposed guideline dates over a pot of coffee they departed for Kenzi.

Wednesday saw the arrival of the aerial. The team had it erected by the weekend with Emmett making his first call to Ian at Saturday breakfast. The set had been placed in a corner of Gilbert's office. He would be able to listen out for incoming calls. At night the watchman would be based near at hand and would call Emmett if any emergency call came through.

Jaswant promised to install a CB set in Emmett's landrover next time he came to the city. Things indeed were looking up. Emmett now prayed for a successful harvest. All his daylight hours were focused on trawling the sections on horseback keeping an eye on his ever blossoming golden crop. He rode, most times, with an old polo stick practising his movements in the saddle and getting his right wrist and arm muscled up for future games.

The dogs were well exercised – every now and then running in hot pursuit after a little duiker – one of the smallest antelopes. The pack, however, were left far behind in its wake.

When contouring, Emmett had placed earthen dams in strategic places throughout each section. These would hopefully fill up in the rains assisting and maintaining the water table and moisture content of the soil. He also wanted to draw birdlife to the farm. Willows would be planted in the rainy season. A few of the holes held a little water from the recent showers, and these the dogs adored romping in getting thoroughly muddy.

Harvesting in Africa was a completely new experience for Emmett. He was getting anxious as the time approached. He now realised he had taken an enormous gamble when accepting this job. Only Shirra's occasional visits managed to soothe him. Her unannounced arrivals caused problems at times as she caught him way out in the distant sections on a couple of occasions. A message from the office would call him home. Shirra, however, made it well worthwhile.

There was no time for leaving the farm. He was confined to barracks. His mechanics had managed to service five of the farm's own combines. They robbed Peter to pay Paul. At least four harvesters were now on the scrapheap. Various parts could still be rescued from them and these would be stored away.

It meant that ten combines would have to be hired from the contractor who moved from farm to farm until every crop in the district had been harvested.

Emmett had seen photographs of harvesting in the USA where ten or more machines would work one ahead of the other, each one on a route parallel to the other. To get his crop completed meant that over three hundred and fifty acres a day had to be harvested. Massive trucks – twenty to thirty tonners – would ferry the grain to the silos in Koram or Urukan. They would be weighed at the Ratilli, given a docket, and then again on arrival at the silos. This should tally but, as Emmett had been warned, sometimes it didn't. There were a myriad of scams along the way.

His dividing roads along the contours and criss crossing the sections had to be tip top for these monster carriers. Farm tractors and trailers also ferried loads from the fields to the compound thence transferring to the carriers. Some of the grain would have to be retained as next season's seed and this would be stored in the enormous sheds along the north side of the compound, next to the horse stalls.

Harvesting could not start before 11.00am or thereabouts because of the amazing amount of morning dew that settled on ear and leaf. This was winter – very cold at night and it took 'till mid morning for the sun – if it appeared – to warm up. Emmett could only liken this excessive dew crop to spring on the Burren back home. There, one couldn't walk without wellies 'till the sun had reached noontime and had burnt it all away.

The dew returned again at 9.00pm in the evening so that's when one had to call it a day. Then the combines were brought back to base for a night shift of mechanics who serviced and repaired them for the next day.

If the moisture level of the crop was higher than allowed for storage it then had to be put through the dryers on the farm. Precision farming was the form. On hand management had to be strict, accurate and unending.

Meals and liquid refreshments were supplied regularly to the men in the field and those loyal workers riding shotgun on trailers and lorries.

Gilbert and his supplemented team of spotters and counters had the unenviable task of getting a tally of tonnage to acreage. Emmett required this figure at the end of each day. He had drawn up a graph on the end wall of his veranda.

10,900 acres had been planted. His target was 92,650 bags. That would be a record tonnage but more important it would bring a big bonus to all.

Emmett was worried about Section 3. It, from the ground and the air, looked to be patchy and wouldn't crop out a heavy tonnage. This could bring the average hurtling down.

As that section was planted immediately after Section 2 it would be harvested in the same order. He would therefore be able to compare the first forty percent of the crop before going on to count the final six thousand acres.

Section 2 yielded 27,900 bags. Then came 18,000 from Section 3. If this held up then Emmett's figure could well be achieved. Staff felt things were going well. Their effort became greater but this was when mistakes could take place – over exuberance could lead to tractor drivers making mistakes.

Emmett had to be very hard on a few whom he caught speeding up 'the home straight', as it were, with three to five tonnes of grain for the dryer. If a few of those overturned then disaster would be splashed all over the crop. It was hard for them to understand that 'more speed less results' could happen.

However, all was well. Almost! A couple of crippled axels made for unloading and reloading of trailers, punctures on the main road to Koram allowed pilfering to take place and the dryer engine blew up after working flat out for a week. Luckily a spare was on hand.

"Very run of the mill occurrences," was the remark from his neighbours which comforted Emmett.

A wondrous 24,800 bags were reaped from No. 4 Section which showed 9.3 bags per acre. Surely the last Section wouldn't let Emmett down? He had four sleepless nights. He even allowed the dogs into his bedroom as they became upset with his midnight wanderings. Rani found his bed to her liking and guarded it from the other two. Great pushing and scrimmaging ensued. As it was winter she acted as a hot water bottle!

Emmett needn't have worried so much as by the time the first fifty percent of the last section had been reaped his target was reached. The rest would be the Devonshire Cream on Christopher's hot scones!

Emmett's own bonus was worked on 'so much on so many bags' and that figure had been surpassed before the final week started. He was thrilled for his staff 's sake as they had put up with a complete novice and outsider with some, quite strange, ideas.

The final total was 96,803 bags averaging 8.8 bags to the acre. A highly satisfactory ending to his first season.

This would be nowhere near that of his immediate neighbours but he was dying to tell them his good news. Howard averaged 12.3 and Ian 13.4. That was Emmett's target for next year then – all being well. They congratulated him.

Not everyone used the same variety of seed. In the three different types sown on Ratilli only one, No52D, matched those of Ian and Howard's. Emmett must therefore change to their recommendations next planting season. He had already retained enough of his three types to do swaps for others in the months to come.

All lands remained fallow for three months after harvesting. This allowed the local native cattle herds, sheep and goats, to graze the 'Volunteer' wheat that would spring up all over farmer's lands. It also assisted in the natural fertilization of the lands.

Good relations must be maintained between the tribesmen and farmers – Zungus and Hindis were only leasing their land through government, from the locals. One day it would be returned to them. But right now, it was balancing the books – a most necessary fiscal requirement. By and large the tribes accepted this but every now and then they felt government was not giving them enough for their leases and trouble, in the form of protests and riots, would break out. It was volatile anywhere on this continent - some places more so than others and especially this one, Ukenza.

Emmett reflected now on all he had been told and gleaned in the ten months of his first year's contract. Almost one down and two to go with three more years after that. At least that was what ran through his thoughts as he lazed nonchalantly on his recliner with cheroot, brandy and dogs as his companions.

Evidently it was routine for most farmers to holiday overseas or in other parts of Africa once the books had been balanced and the bank managers had a smile on their faces again.

Ian, Jan and kids were journeying to South Africa. Howard, Rachel and their youngsters were off to the Kenyan coast and Zanzibar. Emmett hadn't thought about it at all. If he did take time off he would like to explore the country. He had heard about how lovely Lake Nduga was and how lush and different the tea and coffee regions were. Perhaps he would jump into his jeep and just take off – he had no ties. But he certainly wanted a rest and let his mind wander away from Ratilli.

Jaswant flew in the Sunday after the harvest was completed. He brought two Kikoos of fresh meat, fruit and vegetables. He quietly complimented Emmett on his achievement – no gushing fireworks mind you – and wondered could that figure be beaten in the future?

"I certainly intend it to be," replied Emmett in confident tone. "You've now seen what a little cooperation and help from ones neighbours can do – so bring on next season – the sooner the better say I. Come on Jaswant, have a drink – I'll make a cocktail of delight for you and I promise it will be non alcoholic. Okay?"

"Very well and thank you. Your dogs are really superb and they have settled in so well." He had become quite friendly with them and they, in turn, much appreciated this by keeping close to and lying down beside his chair.

Emmett mixed a Grenadine, lime, Campari and soda with a slice of lemon in a long glass. It looked exotic.

"Tastes very good. Thank you."

Emmett was into his pink gin and limes which he called a 'Jeri' after the C.C. himself. All he had to say to Christopher was one, two or more Jeris and out they came. A magical drink.

"You call yours a Jeri don't you?"

"Yes, that's right. I could get addicted."

"No don't – its not good for you, you know," he said rather worriedly.

"Oh I was only joking Jaswant. I'm almost teetotal out here. But today we should celebrate and I must thank you for giving me such great backup. I knew I could do it but you had your reservations. Not so? It's worked out well. I'm so chuffed for the staff – they performed really well. Cheers to us!"

"Cheers too."

Christopher brought out the now routine plate of Samoosas – a delicacy enjoyed by the Bhogals. And Christopher had learnt to cook them to perfection, either meat or vegetarian. Emmett had become addicted to spicy food, African and Indian.

"Do you wish time off now or later?" came the question from Jaswant and anticipated by Emmett.

"Well now, what's on your mind first?" he countered with.

"I would like to see a start on Melelo. That will need your undivided attention as many things can go wrong."

"Yes, I agree with you there. The boundaries are marked and the dozers are progressing well with the firebreaks. I'm happy so far."

"Good. I flew over just now. The work does look well advanced but now you have to map out sections leaving all the best trees in place. This needs you."

"I understand. I would like to relax for say five days away from here and then take a couple of weeks later on if that's agreed by you?"

"Fine. You could map out enough work for them before leaving and let Limani (the head man) take charge in your absence. Okay by you?"

"No problem at all. I'll work something out and let you know, over the air."

When Jaswant departed Emmett wondered whether he'd ever know what made his boss tick. What went on inside that turban?

7

Melelo – his forest hideaway

During the harvest Anna and the children had visited on one weekend. It had been a needful and welcome two day intermission. Although with little time to attend to them his head syce, Langat, had handled their equestrian needs with aplomb.

Emmett had received another late night call to duty! This time it was far more loving than raw lust. They whispered for long periods between interplay and intercourse. They became real lovers enjoying every little nuance, every exploratory touch and every climax.

At breakfast they discussed the best place to visit in the country. Edith said she loved going to the lake – there was so much to do. Zimba Charles agreed and let slip that his parents had a cabin there "perhaps Uncle Emmett you could use it sometime. There was a riding school nearby too?"

This got Emmett thinking about his holiday. He discussed it with Ian and Jan. They both loved the lake and they too had a house down there. Emmett was free to use it whenever he wanted! They had a speedboat and all the gear for skiing but Emmett didn't know anything about that sport. He wondered who could teach him? He was a crafty fly fisherman and could cast a line anywhere onto a 'sixpenny bit'. Perhaps he could trade expertise? Worth looking into he thought to himself.

But wow, he had a place to go to on holiday – a freebee and whenever he wanted to creep off and away from the farm. He had worked out that it was a three hour drive from Ratilli, a mere nothing in largest Africa. Life was on the up and up.

Meantime Melelo was the card on the table.

Emmett decided to call in a forestry guru to show him the best trees on the farm. He would then paint a dot on each of them marking where the thinning out process could take place.

The land was quite hilly so clearing would have to take place on a contoured progression. Ian's lands, next door, were cut in corridors and for the past three seasons had yielded excellent tonnage.

The theodolite had to be borrowed once again and Emmett decided to give this a three week burst. He would have enough area mapped out for the bulldozing team to follow on with whilst he took off for his well earned break.

Lake Nduga measured fifty miles long by ten miles wide, approximately. It housed a tourist prize. And that was fishing. The amazing Tiger Fish – the continent's most ferocious fighter, blessed with teeth that the Zambezi crocodile would be envious of, combined with a tenacity that tested every fisherman's strength. Consequently there were many little charter companies offering their professional services. Zanzi was the town on the eastern shoreline and closest to the farm, with the most services. Opposite it was Ncema, the lakes largest settlement.

Ian had told Emmett who to contact and get the key from. This done he opened up the chalet. It was a simple clapboard built three bedroom house on stilts. It had a veranda that extended twelve feet out and ran the entire way around. He had been informed that this enabled the kids to have mega sleepovers! The lake's water lapped a few feet away from the stilts. A pleasing sound to Emmett's ears. He realised how he missed having water around him. He had loved looking out onto Galway Bay and simply adored being in a little boat on Lough Corrib. These had been available to him in all his growing up stages. Now he was landlocked with only Lake Nduga as a respite.

The Mandi people – those of this district – always seemed to have a smile on their faces and were ever present to assist. They seemed blacker than other tribes. It could be an illusion? He noticed the propensity of ponies, of all shapes, colour and size, in the countryside.

Emmett spent four wonderful relaxing days in and around Zanzi. He got out onto the lake with a wizened old local called Shadrak. No Tigers – it was too cold he was informed – but he did land a sizeable Carp while trolling back on the second evening.

The Club was a conglomerate of clapboard houses, shingled roofs and luxuriant gardens with lawns sweeping down to the water's edge. There were four tennis courts, a nine hole golf course, a croquet lawn, squash court and a well worn and used billiard/snooker room. Their menu was basic European with local fish, in many guises, as their speciality.

One evening he was introduced to a well jewelled aged Belgian lady – Madam Francoise Henin – who reigned supreme over staff and guests. Her silent ambience held sway in the dining room. She was a doyenne of the last remaining Colonial family.

Over coffee after dinner they talked for a good hour about times past, her family's history, their mining and farming background and how today her grandson

– the only one – was pioneering flori culture. He was the largest rose producer in the country.

"Very tiny by East African standards, but nevertheless, profitable. I live on the farm which is five kilometres from here. You must visit me on your next stay."

The hall porter came to tell Madam that her chauffeur had arrived.

Emmett kissed her hand after accompanying her to her car.

"Merci Monsieur. You are well mannered. Au revoir."

He wrote about her in his diary that night. A most gracious dowager of another era. He would visit the farm next time he was sure.

Something that pleased and relieved Emmett came into prominence on this trip. He encountered many couples of mixed nationalities and races. It was obviously becoming acceptable. This could make his friendship with Anna far more agreeable and easy to live with.

Zanzi had a smashing little hotel, The Grand, whose long bar resembled something out of a Hollywood western. Waitresses were Dolly Parton look-alikes, but of course of a different ethnic hue. Stetsons were worn by barmen et al. A real buzz prevailed. Their steakhouse – the Golden Spur – was really excellent and was packed on the two occasions Emmett visited it. This reminded him of the saloon bar of the Ambassador Hotel in Kenzi. Perhaps they were of the same ownership?

The Club, on the other hand, was very much the quiet elder brother – far more conservative in its décor and ambience. It did, however, have excellent facilities.

It was no wonder that the up-country folk flocked here. He would return and that was no idle promise.

Back on Ratilli the work had gone on at a hectic pace. Harvest machinery was being serviced and stored away for next season. Grain drying, then bagging before storage in vermin protected cages within the sheds, had all but been completed.

A shift roster had been put into operation for the teams in Melelo. Their tented camp had to be serviced daily. Limani and Gilbert had obviously got on top of that job pretty quickly. He complimented them in glowing tribute.

"When is the bonus and wage cheque due Gilbert?" He asked in conclusion.

"Next Thursday, Sir. It will be flown in."

"Great. I think we should buy a big bullock and have a mighty party for one and all that evening. What do you say?"

"A good idea. Thank you sir. I'll see to the purchase."

"Great Gilbert. By the way Limani have you seen a good site at Melelo for a log cabin for me? I'll want to stay there during planting and harvesting."

"I'll look fendi. Should be easy to find."

That had been a spur of the moment thought but one, on reflection, that conjured up erotic images. His forest hideaway, a lovely idea. He would keep it quiet until completed.

Pencil was put to paper that evening and very amateurish sketches were drawn. But Emmett knew what he wanted, something simple, away from it all. This gave him a personal project which could run hand in hand with the opening up of Melelo farm itself. Two for the price of one. He liked the idea.

There was an air of expectancy as the Cessna landed. Out popped Vijay carrying a large briefcase. Gilbert was there to meet him and then accompany him to the office where Emmett was already seated behind the desk with the large wage ledger open in front of him.

Two ink pads were wet with anticipation for the tens of thumbs waiting to be printed on spaces opposite their owner's name. Some of the recipients would sign their names, others would offer a simple 'X'.

This was the first time such a bonus had been paid. It was also the first time a Zungu was in charge of them and to a man, women and child, they appreciated his leadership and trust in them. He had lead. They had followed. The team had won.

The party at the labour lines later that evening was the highlight of Emmett's year. He enjoyed every part of it from assisting in the turning of the spit, the cutting up of the beef, to the desperately tiring arm stirring of the ever thickening sadza (maize meal) in vast black iron cooking pots.

All the women folk were attired in their colourful 'best' and kept up an ongoing chorus whilst preparing and distributing the spread. All the men kept to themselves on one side of the fire with the women facing them.

After about an hour various players on drums with others on strange looking string and wooden instruments struck a sometime melodious but always deafening sound. It carried into the small hours when Emmett retreated to his bed.

After bonuses had been paid staff were let go on their annual holidays of three weeks paid leave. They had to accept the regulatory design of who and when to be absent. A skeleton staff had to remain on the farm at all times. This, therefore, was the quiet period on the farm save of course for the work at Melelo.

For a six week period Emmett managed to spend lots of weekend and midweek breaks away from the farm.

He concentrated on polo and clay pigeon shoots. A very gracious tea planter – Tinus Cloete – offered his sons' string of ponies to play on whilst they were away at Varsity in South Africa. An offer too good to be refused.

Jeri was now President of the shooting club and almost demanded Emmett's presence at every single outing.

After one of these shoots he collared Emmett and moved him to a corner in the club house and started plying him with drink.

"The children love being with you Emmett. You have made them so confident. They tell me how strict you are too. Good thing I said – a bit of discipline never did anyone any harm."

"They're easy to work with Jeri – so enthusiastic – I like them a lot."

"They also tell me how you bring Anna along to their lessons. I must say I find her a new person, whatever you have done to her? It's for the best you know. She leads a very confined life with us."

"I find her a joy to be with – she is so well educated and certainly knows what's going on in the world. And she adores riding now. I hope I did the right thing – I mean, in teaching her as well as your children."

"Oh Lord yes. I must tell you something and perhaps you will understand more easily. You see she is a relative of Margaret's. Anna is from a very good family, both of her parents are doctors – of medicine – and she herself, as I think you know, is highly intelligent. She is a qualified teaching nursing sister."

"Wow – nice to know."

"You see it doesn't end there. She is quite shy and is very against tribal custom, etc. She is of the modern era. She hasn't found her route yet – doesn't know which way to turn and I think personally, is just biding her time with us. We, of course, treat her as family but she wants to do it her way. The children are a job to her and she works at that night and day. They love each other which of course is a blessing – what with both of us working and me away a lot of the time. She is not just their nanny cum nurse, she is their auntie too. And in African terms that's a high place of responsibility. Each, therefore, respects the other." There was a short silence as he downed another gulp of his drink.

"We can get on with our own lives and yet have the family aura all around us. Can you understand that Emmett?"

It took a couple of moments and a swig of his brandy and ginger before he replied.

"I can indeed understand. It's not dissimilar to our Irish family culture – but modern times seem to have erased a lot of that rather special personal feeling and heritage. Parents, and in fact, the extended family, are not much appreciated by the young of the modern day world. It is surely wonderful that these inbred feelings are not lost out here."

"You are right. I even noticed that when I was studying in the UK. Grannies were baby sitters – no?"

"Yes, quite right."

"Here the family unit still holds a strong bond. Long may it be so."

"Absolutely. You didn't mind then my taking Anna under my wing?"

"Good heavens no. As much as you wish. But be careful – she is a strong character – has a mind of her own.

"Which leads me to a rather awkward and personal question, I hope you don't mind."

"Fire away."

"How wrong would it be for us to be seen together – like out riding – shopping or dining together for instance?"

"Good heavens man – it would be marvellous – there's no stigma in this country and we would be delighted for both of you. I've often thought it must be lonely out there on Ratilli."

"Well, 'that's mighty' as we say back in the west of Ireland. I was just afraid there might be comebacks on both sides – although I've no ties whatsoever here or back home, for that matter."

"You have our blessing. But be careful. Remember what I said. Cheers."

That was a weight off Emmett's mind, shoulders, heart. Mind you he had to discuss it all with the lady in question first. She might have other ideas?

During the course of that conversation Jeri had also discussed the harvest and congratulated Emmett on his success. He suggested that the Bhogals would be taking due cognisance of the result and he, Emmett, should strike while the iron was hot. Any request or suggestion should be aired immediately and that he now held the ace in the pack for what he had achieved.

Emmett told him about Melelo and the hard graft it would entail over the coming six months. Jeri feigned knowledge of the lease but Emmett felt he knew more than he was committing to. That short phrase 'watch your back' kept recurring in his thoughts on Emmett's drive home.

His dogs and ponies took up a lot of his undivided attention in those next few months. The neighbours were off on faraway holidays on sun drenched beaches and vineyards.

Jan had very kindly sent a message to say he could use her horses whilst they were away. This proved a godsend as Anna and the children were on school vacation and they managed to spend two stays of three days each during that time.

It was quite plain for everyone to see that Anna and Emmett were on equal terms – an item – and even the children understood.

Christopher was slightly worried that he might loose out in Emmett's affections but was quickly put right when told that she was only trying to help, as with three extra people to feed, serve and house it was also partly her responsibility. He understood and smiled.

During their first stay two of the fencing gang, who patrol the boundary fence and mend the wires and gates when broken or left open, brought in two baby duiker, a very small species of deer. They had either got caught up in the fence somehow or were being chased by native dogs and became exhausted. According to the two men they were very young and needed nursing. One of the duikers had quite bad scratch marks on his back and hind legs which needed dressing.

These two became little jewels on the farm, with the children attending them as if they were their own babies.

A mad rush to Koram saw Emmett purchase feeding bottles, teats and Nestum. Also cod liver oil was bought for both them and the dogs. Whilst Emmett was away for that hour Christopher had got a chicken wire enclosure erected at the rear of the house and beneath the bedroom occupied by the children. He was finishing off the gate as Emmett returned.

A brew of warm Nestum was fed to them which seemed well received. They had the most spindly needle like legs which if free could cut you with their razor sharp hooves into very sore pieces. The children were well warned and towels were used to enwrap them when being held.

A large cardboard box was the next requirement for their overnight shelter – and they must sleep 'indoors ' – the children demanded so!

Anna said they should be fed little and often so a two hourly shift was put in place. One of the adults would have to oversee the operation as it was tricky to catch, wrap, hold and then feed.

It was quite ridiculous really but very sweet in reflection that they were all – including Christopher – one happy family looking after twins, newly born.

Anna suggested the last feed should be 9.00pm but that she and Uncle Emmett would look in on the babes throughout the night. Once morning arrived the children would be back on duty. All agreed to her proposal.

That was a magical evening as after the children went to bed Anna and Emmett relaxed on the veranda, Emmett with a cheroot and both of them with glasses of red wine. Anna wished to learn the delights of Bacchus – she didn't appreciate the taste of spirits. A cold beer or two was also to her liking.

They had time to discuss many things, both wide and intimate. Their lovemaking had become a time of beauty – soft amorous foreplay leading onto passionate scenes of climactic proportions. They had started with whisper, continued along a serene mode with occasional volatile undertones.

Anna adored being the aggressor. She didn't want it 'mission' fashion. She had to see into Emmett's eyes, his very being, his inner soul. He must remain still, only rising majestically to her call. She arranged his recently shampooed hair out across his pillows as she knelt in homage to his body. Her grip was vice-like until she felt his volcano about to erupt. She wanted to cry out but restrained herself for another time. Her body arching backwards as she thrust her cavernous mound into his pillar of life.

Her muscles gripped him, up within her. They twitched in recognition of his victory. Once again his lava oozed in readiness for the escape route.

Sometimes she would ease herself back down his legs so that she could suck him and keep him alive for yet a second or third performance.

All this time he would clutch the sheets with agonising strength straining his body to marry with every movement she made. His head veering from side to side resisting the pain and fire of his motive climax. Many a time he bit his lip to restrain an outcry. Theirs, indeed, was something very special.

Emmett, when riding horseback with her, found it difficult to cool his ardour. He always rode in shorts, his legs having become so tanned and hard that no sores or bruising took place. It was, however, awkward restraining a curled up cobra within his loins from bursting forth through a Y-front and buttons!

How embarrassed he would have felt in front of the children. And they, vice versa. At times when only the two of them managed a ride on their own, children wanting to jump in the paddock or mind the duiker – then when the urge came upon them they would find the nearest fence post, tie the ponies to the wire and let their passions 'all hang out'.

It was a matter of who got their privates exposed first. He or she then got the fencepost. He, to use it as a back rest, as she pressed down and onto him. She to push her outstretched arms against it as he took her from the rear.

It was very much spur of the moment orgasmic stuff but it wasn't lust. It was with feeling, something deeper on every occasion. The act became more rounded, wholesome and heartfelt each time. They both needed each other and felt 'as one' in each other's company.

Her fulfilment and self-confidence had been noticed by Jeri and Margaret who both were overjoyed at the relationship. It was for now. God only knew what the future held for them? Anna and Emmett made this their philosophy and wanted nothing more.

During this period of time it was fortunate for Emmett that Shirra and husband Buster were away on overseas vacation. There would be no meeting of the waters, er warriors! That would have been something Emmett couldn't have handled. Shirra was far too much of an extrovert to hold back on what she was thinking or feeling. She would come out with whatever she wanted to. He could hear it now.

"Darling, how are you today? Oh my, I see you have a readymade family with a nanny too. Just tell them please to take a walk for an hour or so. We have business to see to. My darling, the nanny doesn't look too happy with my suggestion. Tell her to bog off won't you. I need you now sweetie – and I haven't got all day, much to my chagrin."

How on earth could Emmett have kept them both happy or apart!

There was only one thing to do he felt and that was to come clean with Anna. Reveal all so that she would be one up on Shirra.

Anna took it remarkably well. She understood his original need for sex and who better than a nympho to supply it. No hold on either side.

Emmett reiterated it was purely an animal instinct thing – there were no feelings attached – a case of 'wham, bam, how're yer mam' relief - like a Schweppes tonic when the cap is taken off.

"I believe you but I don't like it. I'll make a bargain with you. You have a saying in the west I believe. Its 'what the eye don't see my heart won't grieve for' – or something like that. But beware if she should happen on you if I'm here – or anywhere else we may be – you won't believe its your beloved Anna you'll be watching. Okay? Bargain then."

"I'm with you, I promise."

The subject ended there. They kissed, hugged each other and the juices ran stronger than ever. They certainly shared something. They then made love.

This revelation spurred Anna into a remarkable metamorphosis. She bought a second hand Landrover, joined a rifle club and visited Emmett on a regular basis with or without the children. She became a better than average rider and caught up to where the children were in show jumping prowess.

She let her hair grow and had it plaited. Her confidence ran riot. Emmett thought she looked scintillating – he couldn't believe he was the catalyst in this transformation of personage. She continued whispering into his 'craving for her touch' ear lobes that it must be him and only him who injected her with the adrenalin of life. A life to succeed.

At times Emmett pondered long and hard on what that goal might be. But inevitably came up with a blank. There was, however, a shadow lingering in the background. Of that he was positive.

8

She knew who the *Makinto* were. But - - -

Melelo looked like something of a building site with bulldozers cutting swathes through virginal forest. Emmett had decided to follow along the lines Ian had taken, and that was corridors of one hundred to one hundred and fifty yards wide running on the contour and between areas of mature trees that wouldn't be touched. Some of these corridors ran to a mile and longer in length. This would also allow for safe aerial crop spraying.

The fencing team completed their boundaries after two and a half months hard graft. Evidently there was quite a population of smaller deer in the forest. These had to be fenced outside the new farm's limits. They would have thousands of acres of virgin lands to still roam in. Monkeys, hundreds of them, ran and swung from treetops using the leafy canopy as their camouflage and playground. They could be a major problem once the corn ears started to ripen, Emmett was warned.

Ian employed a team of guards with shotguns to patrol his lands. Their cartridges were loaded with coarse salt. At least a couple of monkeys would be shot dead and left hanging on poles just inside his lands. This evidently helped to frighten the other monkeys away.

According to Limani they could have almost two thousand acres ready for planting in the first season. The remainder, another two thousand acres, would be in service for the second or third season. It meant that four thousand out of six thousand would be cropped, the remainder would continue as forest. An amount well ahead of Bhogal's estimate!

He had also found a couple of sites for Emmett to view. They were both ideal with vistas to die for. But rather a rough route would have to be hewn through forest, valley and rocky incline to one of them. Perhaps, in the rainy season, it would be impossible to reach? It was ideal but, prudently, Emmett chose the other. Limani then pointed out some elegant cedars which could be felled for off-cuts (planks). The two of them walked through the forest aligning a track which a bulldozer could follow and 'blade' a route for tractor and trailer and Emmett's landrover to use.

Set beneath a large wild fig tree Emmett marked out the foundation area. Limani seemed all jazzed up with this 'sideshow' as he called it. He was given charge of the project.

It was a dream of Emmett's to have his bedroom upstairs with a balcony. To this end he sketched out a very simple plan based on a square of 20ft. Downstairs would be an open plan sitting cum dining area to the front. Leading off this would be two little rooms housing kitchen in one and shower with loo in the other. A stairway running up one side of the main room would lead into the bedroom which would take up the entire area save for a 6ft. balcony running along the frontside?

Emmett explained to Limani that he wished it built in their own ethnic fashion – mud and wattle with a thatched roof. He would mark out the inside walls, doors and windows. The floor would be concrete polished smooth and then painted. Everything must be rustic and Limani was to find a local carpenter who could work with the farm's timber, fashioning tables, chairs and shutters for the windows. No glass would be used but the whole unit must be able to be shut and locked up when not in occupancy.

A nearby camp – but not in view – would be built for the farm watchmen. They would act as security guards at all times. The main camp, once ploughing, planting and harvesting respectively got underway, would also, most probably be sited there.

Emmett was already getting excited and the building had hardly started. He supposed it was the fact that this would be his own little venture, a home away from home. He was beginning to conjure up fantasises of great magnitude. Why not dream, it's free. He questioned?

Limani requested a trailer load of small stones that could be taken from the adjoining river.

"Whatever for, might I ask?"

"This has upstairs, so better we make walls stronger. We place stones in with the mud so they dry hard and give great strength."

"Very well thought out Limani and thank you. No problem. I'll send a gang up in the morning. Thanks again."

Limani already had a couple of people splitting the trees once felled to the ground. They had measured the height that was required – approximately 20ft with at least 3ft or 4ft sunk into the ground. These were hardwood so termite resistant. They just needed cementing into the ground.

Building work gives the farm women – wives, sisters of the staff – the chance to earn some wages out of season. One group had been despatched to cut and bundle thatching grass – from where Emmett didn't know or ask! He would just pay them. It was a happy time as the women sang in harmony when at work. Melodious tones came wafting through the forest on the winds scented by pine needles and newly turned red earth.

Limani said the house would only take a couple of weeks to build and roof with the thatch. Allow another couple of weeks for the walls to dry out and set. It would then be time for the carpenter to get working on his part of the contract.

Emmett let them all get on with it, only keeping a watching brief. Once the basics were complete he could then get down to the nitty gritty. He already had sited the hole to be dug for the septic tank. The trailer had to go again for a load, this time, of larger rocks to line its lower regions.

One afternoon while Emmett was shopping in Koram a member of his party pointed out the President's son to him. Jan had mentioned that he had a holding some six farms away from Ratilli, he remembered. His place was evidently enclosed by a number of Hindi farmers – some twenty miles away – a mechanic said. Emmett, waiting in his vehicle, studied this man as he strolled from shop to shop. He was tall, lean and athletic – probably the same sort of age as himself. He had two very light skinned over made up females with him. Their lips were plastered red and shone like traffic lights. Big breasted, big bottomed, their clothes were worn a size or two too tight. High heels clipped clopped along the bits of pavement and broken steps as large coloured bags swung from their ample shoulders. Their escort wore cowboy boots and was swathed in tight faded denim. A NY baseball cap was cockily tilted to one side. He looked a dude – all that was missing were shades!

On the return drive Emmett asked his staff what was his name? But no one seemed confident enough to answer.

"John something" they agreed on. They somehow seemed reluctant to discuss the President's son. Was there a reason Emmett wondered?

At supper that night he broached Christopher on the subject.

"He is Jonathan Sir. Not well liked. A bit of playboy we are told. That's why he is here. Too much trouble in Kenzi for his father to cope with. He's been in this district for five years now. Doesn't mix much we are told."

"Saw him in Koram with a couple of floozies – that's fast women Christopher. The guys with me couldn't give any info on him. Either didn't know or wouldn't tell sort of situation."

"Not much is said Sir. Everybody has ears so we keep quiet. Best policy Sir."

"Yea, I agree. Thanks anyhow. Lovely meal by the way. How were the duiker and horses today – no trouble I hope?"

"Everything is fine Sir. The boys rode the horses out down the runway this afternoon. All seemed fine. I watered the garden just before you returned."

As he turned to leave the kitchen he remembered something, "by the way Sir. Could I have my leave now? I have a long way to go – up north you know, to my home. I'll go when you say its okay by you. I'll find you someone to stand in my place."

"No problem Christopher. Make plans and if it's this weekend I can give you a lift to Urukan. Okay? Work it out with Gilbert and let me know. Thanks."

Emmett's weekend in Urukan was spent at the Club. He expended lots of relaxing energy on the tennis courts, found a superb Indian restaurant, and drove up into the tea and coffee estates on Sunday with Anna.

Once within the area Emmett rather fancied himself as either a tea or coffee baron. The estates were well manicured, especially tea. Their homes and farm buildings were all so clean, uniform and orderly. They were in the high rain belt and on the foothills of a beautiful mountain range. It all seemed so civilised.

This was the region of polo and cricket. The two clubs that serviced the district were opulent, overflowing with members and offered a wide variety of sporting and social facilities. Their culinary 'tables' were renowned. Emmett and Anna sampled one at luncheon. They needn't have eaten for another week, such a variety of delicacies was on offer – and sampled by them.

They joined the Edwards family and another two tea planting couples for a hilariously funny two hours of repast and repartee. One of the planters knew Anna's father for years which made her feel at home with the company and ambience around them. She was the only black lady. There were three very 'with it' black gentlemen also dining. Anna, however, brought a sort of radiance and allure to the room. Emmett was so thrilled and proud of her. Many, many people craved her company and conversation at coffee time. She carried it off without a blush. At least Emmett didn't notice one.

Most of the main conversation was on harvests and pickings. These green leaf and red berry barons were tickled pink with Emmett's description of life on the Punjabi Plains. There wasn't a Hindi in sight up here. A lot of the planters knew the Bhogals – some had dealt with them for years – but never realised they had large tracts of wheat lands.

"So that's where they lose their millions for tax purposes. Sorry Emmett, we've known them for longer than you," as they smiled to each other.

Surfing on the fringes of repartee was a political nuance. It was kept away from Emmett but he, after various obvious putdowns, became a secret listener. He feigned being in romantic one on one with Anna to overhear the other side of the table. She sensed his inquisitiveness. She too wanted to listen in.

Every so often they heard '*Makinto*' being used, referred to. Emmett had never heard of it before – hadn't a clue as to what it was. He had not become interested in local politics, purposefully. This was not his country – he was a guest here and he had been brought up to be well mannered, well behaved and mind his own business.

Anna cuddled up close on their trip back to town. Many things were fighting for recognition within her soul. She knew who the *Makinto* were. She also knew what they were capable of. She must not get her lover involved. It would not be wise.

"They are a secret society, an elite, acting under Presidential instruction. That's all you need to know now, my darling. Keep to your farming and life on the land. I'll be with you. Please." That's all she would say. Subject closed.

9

Victor Ubugu - "el Presidente"

With his first full calendar year now completed, Emmett looked back at his roller coaster progression from simple Irish agricultural graduate to the windswept, tanned man of Africa. He had certainly learnt many things, scaled new heights and achieved, in his own estimation, quite a range of firsts.

Emmett had a variety of tasks to manage on Ratilli. Some of the contours needed upgrading and he wished to make half a dozen more mini dams or waterholes.

The forestry department had offered trees – eucalyptus, or blue gums as they were commonly known – and he needed to site positions for windbreaks. They were quick growers – 60ft in twelve years! Weeping Willows were also offered.

Now was also the time to swap and purchase seed for the new season's planting. His cache of 1,000 bags, all neatly filled, treated and labelled by the women of the work force had to be moved on. Others had to be bought in.

Emmett decided he would put pen to paper and update the other 'four'. Two of them had replied to his earlier communiqué so he hoped for a full response this time.

It took him the week, of an hour or so each evening, to complete his essays. Some were better than others but they all gave an illuminating account of life out in the African bush, or so he hoped?

He realised he had suddenly grown up into a mature thinking adult. Gone were the soft centred scholastic years, the home for supper boy, the dreamer, the ideal lad from next door whose athletic figure and prowess turned many a girl's eye.

If only the 'fractious five' could see each other now they would surely realise that their tenet for life was being fully exploited. Who would envy the other most? How much of a change had taken place in all their lives in one year? Emmett was happy with himself, his confidence was high, he had projects in the pipeline, he had a healthy bonus in his offshore account. And a wonderful girl friend, with sunshine above them, they gleamed with vitality and happiness. It was a solid union of differences – but it worked.

Anna, every time she visited Ratilli now, wanted to practise her riding and shooting skills. She had bought a point two-two with a telescopic sight and silencer. Off they would drive into the middle of one of the sections and expend hundreds of rounds on target practise. She was a better shot than Emmett on her point two-two but he out shot her with the shotgun.

Later, on some evenings, they would roam the boundary tracts hoping to espy a Jack Rabbit or as they were known here, a Sunguru. These are much taller than an ordinary bunny; in fact look much like the Irish hare. They were excellent eating, especially casseroled in red wine and herbs. Anna shot whilst Emmett drove. He was amazed at her determination and her will to succeed.

"Don't get into her bad books," kept recurring in Emmett's brain. She could be lethal he felt. Her zeal and quest for perfection, at times, was frightening.

On his last trip to town Emmett had updated his tape collection – music was his world and his little Sony shortwave radio, his link to that world far away. Every night, when on his own, he would fall asleep with it lying on his chest connecting him via BBC World Service, Radio Moscow, ABC, Radio Brazzaville and South African Broadcasting Corporation (English service) with the wide wide world beyond the Punjabi Plains.

His music was very much Sinatra, Ella, the Big Bands and country and western stars, Cash, Wilson, Kenny Rogers, Parton and then of course he loved Barbra Striesand. He had another musical side too – Vivaldi, Bach and Beethoven. His ghetto blaster would do just that whenever the mood took him. The Four Seasons was conducted with artistic verve on his veranda as if he was Barbirolli himself!

The children's riding had progressed so favourably that they were now competing in the local shows around Urukan. The 'school ponies' they had to ride made them work hard in their endeavours to 'go clear'. Emmett felt it was very good training for them. They had to ride different ponies on almost each occasion.

Out on Ratilli Anna was galloping about the farm with great gusto – she was afraid of nothing. Her wardrobe on the farm had grown considerably through the year. She seemed to have an outfit for every occasion – no matter how spur of the moment any invite cropped up.

The coming Christmas and New Year period came up for discussion one evening and Anna was quick to invite him to her home for part of the time. Emmett had not yet met her parents or sisters. She had no brothers. He accepted willingly.

The piece of news that gripped the area was the forthcoming visit to Koram by the President.

Christopher brought the item to Emmett's ear at breakfast. He had heard it from a bus driver at the Ratilli the night before. Who knows where the bus driver first heard it or from whom?

This would be quite a Maraza – meeting – as it was only the second time the President had been to the district. Would he be touring the wheat lands? Surely he might visit his son Jonathan and that would bring the entourage past the gates of Ratilli. There were so many permutations. Soon the itinerary would be published and all would be revealed.

Farm radios ran hot that day. Emmett decided it wasn't a subject he would get involved or caught up in. It was a month away, at any rate.

To finish Melelo Lodge was much more a priority. Everything external was now completed. The thatch looked magnificent, was 8ins thick, and would have graced any show cottage in his native west of Ireland. Bord Failte[4] would have been proud of it he reckoned.

The carpenter had fitted a bench running the long side of the downstairs room and across under the front window. Doors, window shutters and the upstairs balcony rail were also completed. Emmett had now to take measurements for cushions and curtains. They would be made in Koram by some wonderful crafts women recommended by Jan.

He had ordered an Mbuia wood double bed he had seen and fallen in love with, on display, in a shop window in Urukan. The shop would also supply all the linen, and etceteras. The whole concept had been kept secret from Anna so he had to guess all the little toilet things and kitchen utensils she would need. Most of the basics could be bought in Koram so his weekly sorties there covered all necessities.

Ian arrived at sundowner time – 6pm - to tell Emmett all the gossip about 'the visit'. His farm had been chosen to host the entourage because the Agricultural Department had voted him the best producer in the district. And Mr. President wished to meet and discuss why he was the best.

Ian said he didn't mind the visit but it would put a big burden on Jan's shoulders as she would have to feed upwards of fifty hangers on.

"Could she borrow Christopher for the day?" he asked.

"Of course. I'll help if it is a barbecue and with anything else you think I would be any good at."

"Super Emmett and thanks. We'll have Howard and Rachel and the Beatons as close liaison too. It should be fine. Just a bit nerve racking – not like one of our own parties, totally informal and everyone mucking in. There will be security everywhere and no doubt his elite squad will accompany him. He isn't popular in the district and the local tribe despise him, as you may have heard."

"Actually I've tried to keep out of any political stuff but yes I have heard. I think I have but one Barsoi on the farm. I hope I don't have to employ more after the visit?"

---

[4] Irish Tourist Board

"I beat you by two – as with you, mine do the fences. That's about all they are good for."

"I suppose I better get the Ratilli painted up. I imagine a lot of the locals will congregate there to watch the spectacle."

"Not a bad idea – and keep your main gates closed – you never know who might try what!"

"I'll remember that. Have you been told to invite anyone? "

"Not really. Jeri said 'close neighbours', so that includes you. Okay?"

"Yes, super."

After Ian departed and while Christopher was preparing his evening meal Emmett wandered into the kitchen and told him about Ian's request. He was happy to oblige as long as he didn't have to mix with any of 'that load of gangsters'. They had done terrible things in his reserve and were despised by his tribe. He mustn't be seen to be fraternizing with the enemy. That message came across loud and clear.

Emmett wondered was this the general feeling amongst his staff? God he hoped there wouldn't be a scene up here – protesters and riots or the like. But no, he thought, that would occur in Koram if anywhere.

The President was being choppered into Koram where he would be met by his motor cavalcade. They would drive out to Ian's and return to Koram the same day. After that the Maraza would take place and then he would fly out again. A quick daytrip – but why?

Just prior to the 'big day' Emmett rushed into Koram to collect the items he had ordered for Melelo. The little town was a buzz of activity. A lot of whitewash was being splashed about. Flags and posters of 'himself' were adorning every street corner. The show grounds (football pitch) was being tarted up for the Maraza. A crowd of ten thousand was expected. Emmett thought about the 'rent-a-crowds' back home and expected this one to be quite similar.

Some of his shop owner friends pulled his leg about the visit saying "he'd have to dress smartly for once if he was meeting the boss." No one in Koram had ever seen Emmett in anything but working shorts, t-shirt and desert boots. Most Zungu farmers were attired like this – it was an everyday occurrence.

He collected just about everything, which made him happy. Melelo would now be almost fully kitted out and ready for bedclothes and soft furnishings. A little bit of plumbing, the water tank to be lifted onto its lofty platform and the remaining pieces of furniture would finalise his own first home. It made him extremely proud of his venture and he had managed to keep it a secret from all his friends. Sometime he would have a big party to wet its roof.

The Bhogals were intrigued with it and flew over Melelo each time they visited. They fortunately saw the definite advantages of Emmett being able to be on hand during the various essential times. They said they would be too frightened to spend a night out there. Emmett wondered why?

'Pee Day' (President's Day) the 17th November arrived as any other on Ratilli, save for the fact that Christopher left early morning for Jan's – but after he had prepared Emmett's breakfast. His second in command, Anderson Mukwa, was au fait with dogs, garden, animals and the household so nothing would be left unattended.

The motorcade would be arriving at 11.30am and returning to Koram at 2.30pm. The Maraza was scheduled for 4.00pm. That's what the gossip was.

Emmett decided to watch the 'circus' pass by from his Ratilli building which did look very impressive in its new coats of green and red – colours that Emmett was very fond of. His entire staff had been given 'off' for the day and could line up along the road and cheer if they so wished?

From early morning bus loads of chanting school children had sped by on their way to Koram. Every school in the district was also 'off' for the day. This was how the numbers were inflated.

Landrover after landrover lead the escort. Six trucks loaded with military personnel were followed by three large black Mercedes and finally the rear guard of three more military trucks and six motor cyclists swept up the dusty road, past the Ratilli and then turned right handed onto the Poultney Farm.

Emmett decided to only drive up Ian's road thirty minutes later. Let the dust settle and let Ian show the old man around his castle. He was the man of the moment, let him revel in it. He deserved it – in tonnes!

All Ian's tractors, planters and harvesters were lined up in his yard as if on display at a major plant and machinery show. A most impressive guard of honour, thought Emmett on his late arrival.

Hundreds of militia were rambling around the place, eyeing everything that moved.

Emmett was flagged into a parking area by Ian's headman whom he knew well.

"How's it going?"

"Okay boss Emmett. Too many army everywhere. Not nice."

"Yea, and thanks. Don't take any notice of them. Its just a party" as he smiled to him.

Emmett walked over to the house and found himself ahead of the posse – they were still out on inspection and farm duty.

Ian had evidently met 'himself' in the yard and had whisked him and a platoon of body guards on a walkabout. They would return any minute now.

The barbecue was roasting away – a sheep and a pig on spits. This was for the intimate Presidential party and guests. A bullock was on offer for the militia and camp followers at the back of the barn. Loads of chickens (kukoos) had been roasted.

Emmett met up with Howard at the fire and they decided to plonk themselves there until they were called for. They watched the party converge on the veranda from the yard.

Victor Ubugu was a tall elegant man with a shining almost shaven head. Wisps of close cropped grey curls emerged from behind his ears and continued down the back of his neck. He was dressed in civilian khaki tailored bush jacket and longs. He carried a fly wisp made from Kolobus monkey hair (black and white) on an ebony handle.

His stride was aggressive and athletic for his seventy odd years? No one dared call his age.

A semi-circle of chairs had been arranged on the lawn below the veranda steps. A long coffee table adorned with flowers and fruit was laid out in front of them.

Ian escorted the President to the centre chair, an enormous cane creation bigger than anything on display. A couple of his top ranking militia together with Jeri Ntsemo settled either side of him as Ian gestured for his neighbours and guests to come forward for presentation. They were assembled on the veranda in anticipation of this act. Howard and Emmett moved away from the fire to join up with the line.

Jeri joined Ian in presenting each farmer giving a potted version of their background, size of farm and output over the past three years.

The President looked each person straight in the eye never taking his away from their faces. He asked sensible questions, all centred around the district and its potential. Had its maximum been achieved yet? Could other crops be introduced? Was there a future in irrigation?

When Jeri introduced Emmett they were both taken aback by the President's question "oh yes, I've heard about you. Why do you wear your hair in such a style? I've never seen it before – anywhere."

"It goes back a number or years, Mr. President, when I was at university. I saw the film 'Tom Jones' with Alan Bates in the lead. It's an English historical saga. I empathised with Tom Jones, I enjoyed his character and lifestyle. And you know Sir, I'm sure that at university one is prepared to do anything. I chose the ponytail."

"A great story Mr. Doyle. We will talk again over the meal. Nice to have met you."

Ian was grinning ear to ear:

"He asked the question we have all been dying to put to you but haven't dared. Funny, isn't it. Anyhow, seems you've made a hit. Follow it up."

The President moved around during the meal collaring various locals with continuing agricultural questions. He certainly wasn't a womanizer as he never seemed to hone in on any wife in the gathering. Shirra tried her best to get his individual attention but failed miserably. Jan and Rachel were in charge of the salads and desserts and he talked with both of them obviously showing his gratitude for the spread.

"I am informed, on good authority, Mr. Doyle that you have really put a firework under my friends, the Bhogals. How did you manage that then?" prompted the President when he walked into Emmett on his rounds.

"Well Sir, it was quite easy once I had seen what the other farmers – the good ones I hasten to add – were doing and comparing their husbandry to that on Ratilli. Either they wanted to progress or didn't and I wouldn't stay if it was the latter.

"Did you have a lot of assistance?"

"Only verbal Sir but I did need to update the machinery if results were to follow."

"And they agreed?"

"Yes Sir they did. I'm happy to tell you we had the best crop ever and perhaps, God willing, and if it is not a drought year, next season's will be even better."

"That's excellent news altogether. I wish my son Jonathan would do the same and have some success. Have you met him by any chance?"

"No Sir. I've seen him in Koram but haven't talked with him yet."

"I gather you are keen on riding and are a very good shot?"

"You've done your homework Sir," and he laughed.

"Jeri here keeps me up to date. Nice meeting you. I hope it's not too long before we can do this again. I thank you for coming."

"Sir" said Emmett in acknowledgement and farewell.

He was most astute and well spoken, was the President, thought an intrigued Emmett.

The entourage departed on time and as everyone watched the dust settle Jan invited them all to sit, relax and carry on drinking.

"Did you notice the orange berets Emmett?" asked Ian.

"Could I not!"

"Well they are the notorious elite squad and within their ranks ranges the *Makinto*. Don't ever get on the wrong side of them," and he characterised the slitting of ones throat.

Howard added "they are ruthless and I've heard of incidents that are blood curdling. Anything you've read or seen overseas – no matter how ghastly – these chaps are twice as bad."

"What do they do and when?" questioned Emmett now really interested in the subject.

"Coming up to elections – any kind of elections – they are sent out into the tribal lands and reap havoc on the population – rape, pillage, arson, etc.- just to get the vote for number one. This has made his regime stink amongst the majority of the tribes but they can't vote him out. He has rigged constituencies and boundaries and he has split the vote beautifully."

"How is it so quiet here? I mean there hasn't been any riots or protests since I'm here – that's over a year now?"

"No one dares," came from a handful of those still remaining, in response.

Emmett stayed quiet whilst another topic was outlined.

Buster, Shirra's husband, another good producer brought up subsidies and how he had a word in the President's ear about increasing them. He got a favourable response especially as Jeri was present at the conversation.

"I get the impression," said Emmett, "that Jeri is highly influential in his ear. But how is that? He's an opposition tribe isn't he?"

"Yes, that's true," responded Ian, "but the Cabinet and main Commissioners are from all the tribes. That's how he has managed to keep on top of them. He is in power and no one grouping is big enough to oppose him."

"In the meantime," butted in Howard," they all look after each other's backsides and promote their own wherever and whenever possible."

"Crafty old bugger he is," was Buster's parting shot as he rose to leave.

They all then paid their respects to the ladies and collected up their various goods and chattels including staff lent for the occasion.

Christopher was bursting to find out what Emmett thought of the whole business but he kept him in suspense until supper. Emmett needed time to reflect on everything he had heard that day.

After the fantastic meal and a good few drinks – Emmett stayed on Pims No. 1 – he decided he needed a long walk with the dogs. At this time of year you can see for miles over the lands as nothing – not even a weed – is growing 'till the short rains arrive.

If the dogs could see as well as he could then they would be greyhound in proportion – not the well fed, well covered Shepherds at his side. They never roamed further than fifty yards away from him and only chased butterflies or locusts if within that range.

Jack rabbits and deer were as safe as the clouds above as long as they didn't move off close by.

The home raised duiker had been released back into the wild as soon as they had recovered and were strong enough to fend for themselves. This 'pet's corner' of Emmett's was kept pretty well stocked with waifs and strays of all kinds since the first two inmates had made such an impression.

One of the strangest patients was a Scandinavian stork who had a broken wing. These birds migrate from up north and arrive for the ploughing season. They spiral in their hundreds on thermals above the wheat lands of the district, landing in a line, which at times stretches for a mile or more, behind the tractors devouring all earthworms, slugs and grubs that may be uncovered by the tilling.

This fellow, Emmett named him Sven, was found flapping around on his own out on the newly ploughed lands. Brought back by one of the tractor drivers Emmett found the fracture and with a piece of bamboo made a splint and then bandaged it. Christopher sent some workers off to find worms, etc.

Emmett had a great 'get well quick' remedy. A swig of brandy in hot milk – down the animal's throat a.s.a.p after finding it seemed to assist in the shock therapy system?

Sven stayed for two months before flying off again to, hopefully, catch up with his flock wherever they might have migrated to.

The pet pen hardly ever was vacant. Christopher was a natural carer and would have been a wonderful vet. That was a profession Emmett wished he had graduated into. He adored animals and they, in turn, seemed to empathise with him. The one exception was snakes. He understood their good points but just didn't need to confront them.

Bush babies or night apes were 'the' most beautiful of the tiny cuddly items that had been brought to him. They are only seen after dark in scrub land within small but thickly branched trees. In some ways they reminded Emmett of miniature Koala bears.

One baby, not more than a couple of weeks old when brought in, became the household pet. Christopher called it Tippy and it terrorised the dogs, liked olives, tore up any paper left about the place, and slept in a box on top of the wardrobe in Emmett's bedroom.

When finally seated on the veranda for a fruit, cheese and biscuit supper, Emmett opened with:

"A strange man, the President. So nice on the outside but obviously an odious cretin within. He gave me quite an audience asking all about the farm and it's potential. Mr. Jeri had given him a good report on everything and quite a lot about me personally too. I suppose very little goes on in the country without the big boss knowing?"

"That's true, Sir, Anyoka – snake – Sir, that's what he is. You saw all his special guards around him? He is very fearful for his life. There have been a few attempts on him. His *Makinto* are ruthless. They will have had a close look at you Sir. You are the new Zungu in the district. Please watch your back Sir. They will have one of them on this farm you can be certain." On leaving he turned and asked:

"Anything else Sir?"

"No thanks Christopher and I'll take your sound advice. Don't worry. You can go now. I'll put these away. Thanks a lot for helping out. It went well. I wonder how the Maraza went? We'll hear tomorrow, no doubt. Goodnight and thanks again."

Left alone with his own private thoughts Emmett wondered about the future of the white man and, for that matter, the Indian population within this country ruled by such a tyrant. Surely there had to be an uprising and attempt at dethroning him in the not too distant future. Were his militia too strong for the masses? Or would they betray him when numbers became too weighty against his regime? What would follow and what changes would ensue?

Africa was a volatile continent – a spark anywhere could ignite a heat of volcanic proportion.

Emmett was enjoying the experience but didn't fancy being caught up in someone else's war. This President was looking after agriculture and commerce. He was obviously milking the country but was he milking it dry? Surely his financial 'think tank' wouldn't let that happen?

Keep to your farming and enjoy your social life Mr. Doyle, he told himself as he switched off his little radio. It was late.

10

"Clouds" – A mystical home

Melelo Lodge came into use on the first Saturday in December. Anna arrived the night before at Ratilli for a usual weekend. Little did she know what was in store?

After a long ride out with the dogs, an hour of gardening and attending to the pets in the enclosure, followed by a brunch, Emmett announced that they were going on a picnic. He had primed Christopher into packing the cool boxes with food and wine and had placed them in the landrover secretly.

"What do I need to bring? Where are we going and will we be late returning? I'll need a jumper I suppose? Oh you are a beast! Why not tell me where we are going?" She stamped her feet in female friendly anger when Emmett remained silent.

"It's a surprise – that's why. Trust me. It'll be fun. And all I need is you – oh, and the dogs. Come on then – ups," and the pack jumped into the open back of the vehicle. "I'm going to show you our new farm. You will see all the work we've done over the past five months. Just sit back – no better still – cuddle up here close to me and relax. Some of the roads are only tracks. You will need to hold onto – whatever you can get a grip of" – wink, wink, - smile, smile.

She leaned across and kissed him hard on the lips.

After viewing an hour long trip of contoured forest glades Emmett slowed the vehicle to idling.

"Close your eyes – tight now. No peeping 'till I tell you. Promise me."

"I promise. Kiss me and I'll close them."

He moved off slowly around a corner which brought into view his masterpiece. He shut off the engine.

"Okay. Open up."

"Oh my god, darling. What have you built? It's beautiful."

She opened her side door and stood statuesquely gazing at the house and setting. One hand held across her mouth as if to halt any outburst. Then she started to run, increasing her pace as she neared the front veranda and door.

Her amazement was etched on her face, tears appeared at the corners of her eyes. She looked back at Emmett pleadingly:

"Come quickly and show me inside. Please darling."

He restarted the engine and drove up to the side of the house. He let the dogs jump down and investigate their new holiday home.

Emmett took keys from his shorts pocket and opened the front door. He then picked Anna up and carried her across the threshold. She was crying with joy.

"It's the most beautiful place I've ever seen. Oh my darling, you are so brilliant and such a surprise."

They clung together in a symphonic embrace. The dogs were whimpering – they didn't understand what was going on.

"Well, this is the lounge/dining room. Here in this corner is your kitchen – ha, ha, and here is the bathroom and loo. I'll open up the shutters now and you will really see what it is like. My carpenter made all the furniture, by the way."

Once the shutters were opened the western setting sun burst through the windows enlivening the colours of curtains and cushions. Anna looked longingly and slowly at almost every square foot of the room and then her eyes turned to the stairs.

"And what's up there?" Anna asked more with eyes than arms.

"That's for you to find out and me to follow you."

With that she rushed up the wooden stairs and let out a shriek as she reached the top "Oh Emmett, I just don't believe this – it's beyond words."

She touched the bed, running her fingers along the side of the eiderdown as she walked over to the open balcony enclosed then by a massive mosquito net which ran from side to side and eight foot up into the thatch.

Opening the centre fold she moved gracefully onto the balcony and put her hands on the rail. Emmett joined her. They gazed out in awe at the serenity of it all.

The house was sited beneath an enormous Acacia thorn looking down a valley. In front and running across from east to west were corridors of plough. Little and large trees remained on the contours. There was a mist rising from the valley floor miles and miles away. The odd bird moved but not a breath of wind had a leaf stirring. They turned into each other and in a fond embrace felt as if they were one. This was theirs, their own private nest away from the world of reality. Their little Eden.

"Make yourself at home, my love. I've got to get the provisions in."

An hour later they witnessed a golden sunset whilst strolling around the immediate area and checking out the farm guards who were housed in a camp some two hundred yards away from the house.

The kitchen was Anna's. Food was simple. Wine was cool. The bed luxuriant.

That night of nights their cries were heard deep down in the valley. Even the dogs were alarmed. Guy Fawkes night had never seen the like. All their pent up passion from months of whispers with lips on lips avoiding speech were now in release. An explosion of emotion this time reached seismic proportion. The dogs howled in unison.

Emmett awoke and immediately smelt a fry. An empty space beside him told the story of an early riser. She wouldn't change her daily habits. Emmett too was that way inclined but last night had left him a spent force. He didn't need to rise early – today was a day of rest.

Anna was in her element, something Christopher never allowed her on Ratilli. Between sizzles and ordinary kitchen noises he heard her humming, at times actually breaking into song. Someone downstairs seemed more than happy – another body upstairs lay limp in ecstatic limbo. He rose to view his kingdom from the balcony. His perspective had been correct. This haven had all his desires knitted into one favourite sweater. The one he felt like wearing in a myriad of guises and emotions – the one that felt comfortable, warm and secure.

It was only 07.30 and the sun was already warm. Not a breath of wind moved a leaf in any of the hardwoods. A group of mossies – sparrows – scratched the remaining seeds in a recently sewn lawn below him. Starlings sang in the flattop above. Wood Pigeons coo cooed in the distance and a creaking board made him turn. Anna was padding across the room with a laden tray held in outstretched arms.

"Morning my lover, please draw the netting across for me and I'll place the tray on the table for us."

"Anything you wish my angel is your command."

They were both wrapped in colourful lungis – sarongs - that Emmett had purchased on his last trip to Kenzi. These were placed on the linen chest at the foot of the bed when required for wearing. Both of them slept naked as was the custom in the summer months.

They embraced and kissed salutations of the morning prior to 'brekker'. An appetite was upon them – they devoured in silence.

That morning they walked for miles, through untouched forest, over newly opened lands recently tilled until they reached a stream that acted as the western boundary between Melelo and Ian's land. The dogs had the time of their lives putting up Guinea Fowl, Francolin (little partridge) and covies of pigeons. Monkeys followed in the canopies above. Every now and then they saw a grey Lourie flying from tree to tree. These all grey cockatoo look-alikes are known as the 'go away' birds for that is their cry as they fly, disturbed from whatever slumber.

Every now and then they came upon beehives high up in cedar trees. The African version is a pipe like creation of a hollowed out tree trunk with wooden ends. Emmett had always been a honey addict and in these woods he could have his fill. All he had to do was locate the owners of these hives. Something for the future, he noted.

The Shepherd pack never really left their sides until they reached the stream. Off they then went to cool down. They found some pools which quickly became muddy with their playful intrusion. This stream would become a raging torrent in the rains. Emmett decided he would walk its length one day and see if it was feasible to put a couple of small dams across it. He had this 'thing' about conservation and water was the subject closest to his heart in agricultural terms.

Anna decided she wanted another night at Melelo and she would leave for Urukan very early next morning This was 'honey' to Emmett's ears. Luckily he had pre-empted that desire and had packed food enough for them and the dogs.

He wished to try out his barbecue so they lit the fire at 5.00pm, ate at 6.30pm and turned in at 9.00pm.

"A magical day my darling, I hope the first of many. I love your house and the setting is just perfect. May I do things with the garden please?"

"Be my guest and by the way how did the kitchen utensils work out? What have I forgotten?"

"Only a colander I think – I had to wash the salad leaves with my hands. Everything else seems to be in place. Well done."

"I want Melelo kept for us Anna, so please don't mention it to Jeri or anyone for that matter. When the time is right and we have made great use of it I might let the secret out."

"Understood fully, I agree. Let's keep it as ours."

Christmas was just around the corner and Emmett had to make arrangements for certain staff to be on duty at both farms. Christopher had returned from his leave so all would be under control at the homestead. Animals would be under his care.

Emmett managed to get all the routine farm chores finished before the week of the festival so that as many of the local tribesmen and women could return to their homes for a couple of days. Most of the staff had already taken home leave and had completed their shambas (little farms) work so they were happy enough being employed and having very little to do. The busy months were just around the corner.

Emmett's first Christmas had been spent with Ian and Jan, a lovely family celebration. Their children were home and they hosted Christmas with Howard and Rachel taking over the New Year celebrations.

This year Emmett was moving on to completely new territory – staying with Anna's parents. He was slightly apprehensive. Anna had tried her best to allay any fears he might have but he still felt it would be quite strange living under the roof of another ethnic culture.

He bought a range of presents for the family whilst in Urukan before driving onto Kambu the town where they lived. Anna was to meet him at Shahs, an enormous rambling general store on the main street. No one had accompanied him on this trip after Urukan where he had left a driver whose home was there.

Her landrover was parked across from the store with a vacant place two away from it where he parked and stretched his limbs. Kambu was sixty miles east of Kenzi, in the foothills, and was one of the biggest towns in the Tukulu tribal lands. He was in the opposition's heartland. All along the entrance to the town and especially here in the main street were posters of Lelonge for No. 1. This was Patrick Lelonge, leader of the Tukulu, a cabinet member and now seeking re-election as the Mayor of Kambu.

Anna had spoken a little about Patrick as she explained to Emmett about tribal affairs. He was charismatic, a lawyer who had travelled extensively overseas. She emphasised he was not, in any way, corrupt. He was a close friend of her father's.

The image which appeared on the sidewalk in front of the store was of an African queen in full dress regalia. It couldn't be his Anna – the prim nanny on the one hand and the jeans and t-shirt equestrienne on the other?

Emmett had seen plenty of women dressed like this in Kenzi but very few in Urukan. He was dumbstruck.

She called to him to move quickly from the centre of the street where he stood spellbound, oblivious of the passing traffic.

Green, blue and white material enveloped her from wide shoulder pads to full length dress. Her head was encased in a turbanesque design of the same cloth. Her arms were bare save for hundreds of gold bangles on and above each wrist.

She flowed down the steps to greet him with a slight curtsey, holding out her right hand for Emmett to kiss.

This was something out of an MGM African epic. He got into step with the scene and followed her back into the store where he was introduced to the entire Shah family whose ladies were equally impressively attired in Indian saris. Two young sons carried enormous boxes full of goods out to his vehicle. This family were cousins of the Shahs Emmett had met in Kenzi some months before.

"We are about five miles out of town so follow my directions kind sir," as she leaned across to kiss him full on the lips. "You should have seen your face when you spotted me. I've never seen such surprise on anyone. I should have warned you. Poor sweet thing. Anyway, you like it – yes, no? It's called a Kanga in tribal custom and its worn on special occasions. Today is special for me. You, my Irishman, are to be a guest in our house."

"It's beautiful, you are beautiful. What more can I say?"

The streets became smaller and more cluttered with children, dogs, broken down cars and shabby once painted dwellings. Then all of a sudden the road rose steeply up a winding hill with impressive views all around. The houses became bigger, were better maintained, some with ornate gates, some with extensive treed gardens. Fortunately, Anna's vehicle was being driven by a member of their household and was already well ahead so she was beside her man.

"Up here a bit we turn off to the left and its only another mile or so. Are you tired from your drive?"

"No, not really – certainly not now after seeing that vision. Its bucked me up no end."

His left hand felt her thigh and kept it there 'till he had to make a right turn up another incline onto a shrub lined gravel driveway.

A Mercedes and a Peugeot car were parked beside Anna's landrover. Two boisterous Dobermans romped over to greet, or devour, the newly arrived.

"Friend or foe?" Emmett enquired as he withdrew the ignition keys.

"Friends when we are around but after dark – Atari, danger. Beware, " she smiled.

A fat nanny in pink uniform with white apron appeared and welcomed Missies return.

"This is Mr. Emmett, Mumbi. His case can be taken to the blue room please."

"Yes, Missie. Abuni Master," and she busied herself with the various boxes, packages and cases.

"Thank you Mumbi. These here can go with my case."

Emmett grabbed a quick glance at the view out over tanned lands with few trees to a forest on the right with a lake peeping through.

"I'll explain it all to you tomorrow. Come on in now and meet my family." At that she climbed the stone steps leading up on to a wide veranda. Anna stripped off her headgear and rubbed her forehead.

They walked down a central passageway towards daylight and a glass panelled door, through which they entered an atrium full of wondrous plants. At its end, her father and mother sat at a round ceramic tiled table reading newspapers. They rose when they heard Anna's approach.

"Welcome, welcome, Emmett. Sorry but we didn't hear you arrive. This is my wife, Mimi and I am George. Come sit down. Everything all right Anna, you purchased what was needed?"

"Yes father," as she kissed him on the cheek and "hi Mum" and kissed her too. Emmett shook hands with both and then took a seat between them as Anna made her excuses and departed.

"My, what a view," were Emmett's first words. They looked out and up at the mountain straight ahead. It must have been due west as the sun was just dropping over a forest peak. Its large golden rays piercing strips of sunlight through tall timbers.

"It is quite special. We love it, don't we Mims?"

"How could you not?" butted in Emmett before she could respond.

"Good trip? No problems?"

"None what so ever, thanks."

"Sometimes as you turn off the Kenzi road onto our Kambu highway, as we call it, there can be protestors and hold-ups of many kinds. You were fortunate then. Anyway, nice to have you with us. We have heard so much about you from Anna and also funnily enough from Jeri. He thinks highly of you."

"That's nice to hear. They are a fine family and I adore their children."

"Yes, we hear they are riding now with great confidence, thanks to you."

"Wouldn't you like to change and take a shower? I'll show you your room. It too has a special view. Follow me if you will." George lead Emmett away from that quiet haven to an airy corner room with two splendid views, totally different.

Out one window was an enclosed rose garden. Out the other was a similar mountainous landscape to previously commented on. Emmett couldn't believe his luck – looking out onto green pine forests instead of sandy sunburnt clay devoid of anything at this time of the year. The Punjabi Plains.

This was a beautifully proportioned Franco Colonial house. Space was the defining factor. High ceilings made the rooms cool. The use of natural stone, timber and glass in the structural design blended with surroundings.

It had that 'well lived in and well loved' feel about it. Not a show house but a home.

When Emmett emerged showered, shampooed and reeking of an overdose of Aramis (accidental) he was greeted in the living room by the whole family.

Anna moved to introduce her two sisters, Catherine and Sarah, who were almost identical in face and figure. Taller than Anna they were lean and very like their father. Both were westernized and spoke good English. They were studying at Kenzi International Technical College.

George offered drinks all round after which they settled into a comfortable double suite of armchairs and settees. Topics discussed in jovial mood were as different as Guinness and Lager ranging from sport to science, farming to pharmacology. The latter was the subject being studied by Sarah. She had one year to go for her degree. Her sister Catherine had just completed her degree in law.

Mimi was a G.P. and ran a large clinic for the treatment of malnutrition. George was a surgeon and held a lectureship at the University in Kenzi. A highly motivated scientific family who lived as westerners was therefore not difficult for Emmett to empathise with and become part of. Although the atmosphere was informal throughout there was a definite feel of discipline and respect for the parents.

Probably the best roast leg of lamb or mutton since he had left Ireland was the highlight of a sumptuous dinner.

Emmett offered to show them how to make an Irish coffee – admittedly with Scotch whisky – which they all participated in and were avaricious for seconds (repeats). It had been a joyous family gathering and Emmett was proud to have been party to it.

Prior to turning in he asked if he could stroll in the garden – something he did each night at Ratilli with the dogs. Anna offered to accompany him as she wouldn't trust their dogs with a white stranger.

"The air up here is so much nicer than on the farm," he remarked as she linked her arm into his.

"Did you notice the name on the gateposts?!

"No – what it is?"

"Clouds. Sometimes you can't see five yards from the house – especially early mornings."

"That must be marvellous, but cold in winter I should imagine."

"Yes, very. We have log fires in most rooms."

"It really is a beautiful place, Anna. You must be proud to call it home."

"I love it here. It's so peaceful. It's great for Mum and Dad as they lead hectic lives – their workloads are incredible."

"You are gifted my lovely one – such divine parents, great sisters, marvellous home – what else could one want? Come close and let me show my appreciation, Anna. And thank you."

They embraced long and hard. No more was needed. Their bodies could feel their passion.

They slept peacefully that night – each in their own room.

Christmas Eve was a mix of parties and meeting family and friends. No one looked sideways at Emmett, he was accepted everywhere he went.

They all crammed into George's Mercedes, Emmett and the three sisters in the back seat. He was as chuffed as a teenager off to his first debs ball.

Holding hands is a lovely African tradition and everyone does it. Even men. Emmett found himself lead by Catherine here, Sarah there and Mimi whenever she got a look-in. Anna was playing it cool and attending to father. She was enjoying seeing her family cosseting her man. They were all one happy group of people.

Back at Clouds that evening Mimi told Emmett she had prepared a traditional turkey dinner for the morrow. It would, however, go hand in hand with their traditional dishes of maize meal and stewed mutton with lots of vegetables.

"Great. I love mealie meal, especially yellow maize. My man Christopher prepares it for me at least twice a week. Heaven knows where we will put it all though?"

"We will go to Church at 9.00am – I gather you are Catholic like us?"

"Yes indeed but out on the farm I don't often get the chance for Mass."

"That's very true. I'm sure the good fellow upstairs doesn't mind that as long as he keeps you in his army." Her smile lit up her entire face and Emmett saw the joy and strength within that façade.

Mimi was much smaller and rounder than her family. But Emmett could see all her good points shinning through. She showered them with affection and love but let them show their independence. Her daughters were certainly not wrapped in cotton wool. The unit was built on strength.

That's where Anna got hers from. She had shown that will to succeed on many occasions. She was dogged in her ambitions. Emmett was sure she would achieve them. Whatever they were. They had not delved that deeply into the future.

Just as Emmett had kept Melelo a surprise for Anna she, this time, was not saying a word about Christmas Day.

"Let it happen darling," was all she replied when Emmett pressed her on the etiquette and protocol on the day.

His one and only suit was duly paraded. Anna told him he looked like a movie star. She had never – nor had anyone else in Africa – seen him dressed as a 'city man' as she put it.

Prior to leaving Ireland Emmett had the family tailor in Galway make him a grey flannel suit of the softest and lightest material on the market. It was single breasted and slightly flared at the waist. Pockets were on a slant.

A blue shirt with a woollen tie of red, blue and white stripes complimented and highlighted the blue of his eyes. He had been told by his mother to always wear something blue 'to match your eyes'. He always respected his mother's wishes. His hair was almost blond with bleaching from the sun. He felt good, taller than usual, but wondered how his feet would handle a day of being confined in tight leather shoes?

The four ladies dressed traditionally in Kangas of differing hues. They were so elegant – even regal.

George was dapper in a tan suit, cream silk shirt and a chocolate and cream silk tie. He looked even taller than his six foot two. A very fine looking man.

"Wow," thought Emmett, "this was pure theatre and these were the principle players. Nobody could match them."

The service was a joyous occasion with a choir the likes of which Emmett had only heard on the radio back home. Then the congregation joined in clapping and dancing on the spot. No wonder these people had faith, it being such a happy ongoing celebration.

After shaking hands with hundreds of well wishers they moved on to George's recently widowed sister and her four childrens' home. Everyone drank coffee and ate biscuits. Presents were extricated from the boot and duly distributed.

Next stop was at another of George's family. This time his brother, Raphael, and family of five. Here they drank cool beer and nibbled spicy hot samoosas. Emmett noticed a tremendous bond between the cousins as off they went to bedrooms to open each other's gifts.

Prior to leaving for Church Emmett had cornered Mumbi and asked her when the meal was being served and for how many?

"At 6.00pm tonight Sir and we lay for twelve. Happy day Sir."

That gave Emmett an idea of how to coast along without too much imbibing and guzzling that was obviously going to be on offer along the way. He certainly was not used to this.

Mimi's mother and father were next on the list. They were aged and not in the best of health. Their little home was immaculate with a pretty garden out front. They lived on the other side of Kambu and were close to a welfare centre whose staff kept a close eye on them. Obviously Mimi had their care organised to the nth degree. They were sweet but didn't have much English so Emmett found it difficult to communicate.

Cloud's welcoming gates ushered them home at tea time.

"There's nothing quite like a 'cuppa' to relax tired bodies," was Emmett's sage remark as they flopped down into comfortable armchairs and noticed the tea tray already laid.

"Now tonight Emmett you don't have to be formal in a suit. Just something comfortable – its only family. And by the way – you look terrific," said an excited, yet exhausted, Mimi

Emmett needed to get out of 'those shoes', his feet were killing him. He sported shorts, t-shirt and bare feet when he walked the soft green lawn. This was relaxation for him. The sisters joined him, having already shed their Kangas for shorts and shirts too.

"We have an hour to let ourselves down and make ready for the feast. You must be full of our family by now," queried Sarah.

"No, not at all. Nice to meet them. We do the same thing back in Ireland. It can be a little taxing when you don't know each family inside out. Who is coming for dinner?"

"Oh so you've been peeking have you," goaded Anna with the most mischievous smile of the day so far.

"No, not really. I got it from Mumbi this morning."

"Crafty one you've got here Anna," said Catherine with a nudge to her elder sister.

"That I'm well aware of – aren't I my sweet? – but to return to the subject in question, our very favourite Aunt Ngugi, mum's sister, who is a widow, and her two gorgeous sons Edison and Doctor. They chaperon us everywhere. One is in computers and the other is a medical man, as his name suggests." All three siblings giggled at this.

"The other three you should really enjoy are Paul and Pauline Moffet and her sister who is visiting from South Africa. Zungus darling – you won't be the only piece of white meat on the table," and with that they all roared with laughter.

"Oh Anna you are so bad," interrupted Catherine, "poor Emmett, he must be embarrassed," added Sarah.

"Not a bit of it. He gets far worse from me on a regular basis. Don't you?"

"I suppose so. It was all quite strange and frightening to start with this mixing together of the races, but now I find it plain sailing. Who is Paul Moffet and what does he do?"

Anna was first to speak, "he is a visiting professor at the University here on a five year contract. He is a scientist and is a close friend of father's. They are a very sweet couple."

"Well thanks a lot for filling me in. I'm greatly looking forward to the evening. And thanks for the day so far. It's been fun."

They then strolled around the garden pointing out different landmarks in the countryside below them. The lake was a dam – the main reservoir for Kenzi. Excellent fishing with lovely walks and picnic spots. All the land around and as far as the eye could see was Tukulu tribal reserve. It evidently stretched for hundreds of square miles and was the largest in the country.

"But," very pointedly cut in Sarah, "we do not have the President and that's a real bugbear."

Presents were to be distributed before the meal and all had been placed under and around the tree which was a real one from the forest next door. It was decorated as if in Ireland.

The Moffets arrived first and Emmett looked after their drinks. He found it quite difficult to understand Patricia's accent, it was so guttural. Her sister Pauline's wasn't nearly as strong and Paul's quite refined in comparison. This was the Afrikaans accent of South Africa which Emmett had heard Ian talk about up on the farm. The sisters were balls of fire and would liven up any graveyard.

When Ngugi and her sons joined in, the success of the evening was assured. The buzz that rang around the walls of the living room even had Mumbi dancing with delight. It would certainly be a festive occasion if the pre-meal repartee was anything to go by.

Emmett had chosen scarves for the girls, a tie for George, a Gucci style leather bag for Mimi and a Lalique statuette of a nymph for his precious Anna. He had noticed her eyeing the nymph in a store one night when they went window shopping in Urukan. The other items were not very special but were the best he could think of in the circumstances. Anyhow Emmett didn't live in opulence – the thought was the thing, not the expense, in his book.

Kitty Kallen used to sing a song called "Little things mean a lot" and that melody wove a web of mystique through Emmett's mind that night.

His objets d'art included a gold neck chain with matching Taurean bull from Anna. Two elephant hair bangles – for luck – from her sisters. From their parents he received a silver clip for bank notes. Embossed on it in gold was an interesting tribal symbol. Emmett had seen it that first night with Anna. Three parallel cuts above her breast. A symbol of the Tukulu, a very intimate gift.

This treasure trove was something far beyond his wildest dreams. His gifts palled into insignificance he realised but then it was the thought that counted – 'wasn't it Emmett' kept ringing in his head. No matter, he was a very lucky boy.

He spent two more days with the family, one of which they motored over to the reservoir, walked and picnicked. The entire festival event was a resounding success. He jelled well with the family, and they seemed to look on him as the son they never achieved.

11

A "loaded" driving licence?

Early into the New Year was crop spraying time again. The Ethiopians arrived and departed three weeks later.

This time, however, Emmett had a mission in mind. He wanted to pinch a ride on one or more of their sorties. They used these tiny little machines and the only place for him was to lie down in the nose cone. He wanted to experience the thrill of zooming down onto a carpet of wheat (when the time came). Now it would be down onto weeds.

The pilots showed him how to fly the baby – taking off and landing. They called it circles and bumps. It didn't seem too difficult but of course the actual spraying process was exceedingly difficult and dangerous. They suggested he have Howard teach him in a 'proper plane'.

This was to be Emmett's next project. Learn to become a pilot. There was an instructor in Urukan who had a Piper Cub and a Cessna 79. The Ethiopians predicted he would go 'solo' in four to five hours if he got plenty of dummy flights out over the Plains with Howard.

Ian was about to buy his own plane and had already cut a runway next to his homestead. He had gone solo after five hours.

It wasn't so much that Emmett would buy his own plane in the few years he was planning on remaining but more the joy of having flying lessons. Then he could hire a plane anywhere he went once he had his licence.

"What a pleasure" he thought.

The other interest in Emmett's life at that moment was gymkhana racing. He had heard about this from the polo crowd. Evidently there was a circuit of five different tracks in the farming areas. It was an idea that originally came from the Raj days in India – had crossed the ocean to East Africa and was now active throughout East and Central African countries.

It was really the poor man's answer to full blooded rich thoroughbred racing on large city courses. For 'poor' read fulltime farmers who just loved to utilise their polo ponies out of season. These gymkhana races took place over three months at the end of the polo playing season when the ponies were fully fit.

Only amateur gentlemen (or ladies) riders could take part. It was run by a committee of stewards on immaculately prepared courses, usually around the perimeters of the country club polo fields.

They were, in fact, mini race meetings with a tote for betting. Some events were held over two days, Saturday and Sunday. Large crowds would attend and as they say back home "the craic would be mighty". They would be counted as 'flapper' meetings in Ireland – unlicensed by the Irish Jockey Club.

Emmett had been a horseman all his life and had ridden in 'bumper'[5] races in Ireland. He used to ride out with a local trainer, Tim O'Sullivan, in all his school holidays and graduated up the ladder from there. He could weigh in at eleven stone which was ideal.

In this country he could be less, ten stone seven, as he was much fitter and leaner. Most of the meetings were held either in or bordering on the tea and coffee regions. These ranged in distances of one hundred to one hundred and seventy miles from Ratilli.

His two ponies were not fast enough to race but gave Emmett all the practise he needed on the farm for polo.

Once he got his first invitation and showed that he could race ride, others flowed in. He even got invitations for Anna to compete. She was the first African lady to ride in a race. All her family came to watch. The meeting was at Kitos, in the heart of the tea country, probably the neatest and wealthiest club in the country.

Emmett had four rides on a card of eight races. There was a lady's only race in which Anna rode. She didn't win but she didn't fall off either!

In the unsaddling enclosure after she had dismounted she whispered in Emmett's ear "that was almost better than sex." Her parents, thankfully, were out of earshot!

Emmett was well pleased with the day. He rode a winner, two thirds and was unplaced in his other race. That evening there was a dance in the clubhouse which fortunately was only a mile or so away from The Tea hotel where most of the punters were staying.

On their return drive the next afternoon, to Urukan where he would drop off Anna at Jeri and Margaret's house, they met their first 'holdup' or road block. Emmett had not experienced one so far but was quite apprehensive when he started to slow down.

Anna was cool and said to act normally. One didn't know whether these uniformed people were actual government police, militia or just a rag tag group of mercenaries making a quick buck or a hundred? Sometimes, he had heard, they became quite vicious especially if drink had been taken.

Emmett had been warned to always have a big money note enclosed within his driving licence. If and when they asked to see it the officer would discover and deftly palm the note while deeply inspecting the photo and particulars. He was most probably illiterate anyway but a 'show' had to be made.

---

[5] Races for amateur riders only

They proceeded along these lines – one officer at Emmett's window, another giving Anna the once over and two more having a good look in the back of the vehicle. Many questions such as "where are you going – where have you come from – what were you doing – what are you carrying?" came in stuttered tones. Eyes sought out every little item of value.

Emmett had buttoned up his bush shirt as high as possible not to have his new chain on show.

Anna fortunately wasn't wearing any jewellery – she knew the rules of the road. Emmett's watch was cheap and its band looked dirty and well worn. His elephant hair bangles wouldn't be worth anything to them.

Five cars were backing up behind him and plenty were oncoming in the other lane.

Oil drums were placed in a slalom style hindrance. Idle trigger happy louts lounged around the area. A couple of greenish painted trucks were parked off the road and beneath Acacia thorns. His note had vanished as his licence was returned. They waved him on.

"So tell me now. Who were they?"

Anna kept looking ahead. After a long silence she explained:

"Those were government all right. They were on the make. Their own group will benefit from the day's takings. They probably haven't been paid on time so off they go and make up for it this way. By the way who told you about the licence scam?"

"Oh, Ian of course. It seems to work."

"Yea, it's a good ploy – but sometimes it can go the opposite way. A bastard officer can pin you down for bribery – and then demand much more."

"It sounds as if you can't win then."

"Just play it their way. Cooperate with whatever they demand."

"As we are on the subject – tell me about *Makinto*."

She turned her face to him and stared in a strange faraway fashion – but one that went straight through him, as he glanced over at her.

"They are something you really don't want to know about. I promise you. They are evil, bestial, brutal – all the descriptive rotten words one can think of rolled into one sick group. And controlled by the President. *Makinto* keep him in power and for that they are allowed run riot throughout the country. My tribe fight back and that is why we are hated by them. We lead the opposition – the other tribes follow us but some are bullied into voting his way. He has the voters roll totally rigged and starts off every election with forty percent of the seats his. No one else has a chance, except us the biggest tribe in numbers, but he has even managed to divide us by offering plumb positions and riches beyond one's dreams to certain Tukulu gentlemen who actually have a say and hold sway within sections of our people. But that will end soon. We have had enough. We are going to fight."

There was silence for at least ten miles and only at the outskirts of Urukan did either of them feel the urge to break that silence.

"I don't want you involved," Anna finally said "and I don't wish you to know anything more about *Makinto*. Listen and learn. Don't ask questions except of me. Promise me, please Emmett."

She sounded so worried, intense as if a heavy cloud was overhanging the situation.

"I promise, my darling." Emmett squeezed her hand into her thigh.

Jeri and Margaret invited Emmett to stay for supper which he gratefully accepted.

"Your little nanny rode in a race yesterday and she acquitted herself magnificently," Emmett opened with "and she will ride a winner before too long and that's for sure."

The children were wide eyed at Anna's description of her latest experience.

"I want to ride too, Uncle Emmett. Oh please may I?" Edith pleaded gripping his hands.

"Not yet my sweet. You are underage – both of you," looking at Zimba Charles and anticipating his question, "sometime there well may be a children's' race but until then eighteen is the age. So you have a few years to go, the both of you."

"Not fair," rebuffed Edith. Then Anna explained to them both the rules of gymkhana racing and likened it to driving a car. They sort of understood. The looks on their faces remained quizzical.

"There is a school long weekend coming up in a week or two, isn't there children?"

"Yes, Dad," they replied in unison.

"Any chance you might be on the farm for it, Emmett?"

"Don't see why not. Let me know nearer the time and I'll make arrangements. How about all of you coming to spend a night? I'll make a plan on sleeping arrangements."

"Great idea. We'd love to," replied Margaret as she passed a Spanish omelette with salad to Emmett. Jeri brought another glass of wine.

Cunningly Emmett had prearranged to pick up one of his drivers outside Bhogal's office for the return trip to the farm. The driver was having a weekend off. Their journey went without a hitch. His dogs careered across the compound

114

to meet his vehicle as it slowly manoeuvred its way through machinery which had been paraded for inspection on the morrow.

Christopher met Emmett at the gate and brought in all the tack and bags he had taken for the weekend.

Everything was ok.

"Only Miss Shirra called this morning, Sir. I told her you were away."

"Thanks, Christopher and good night."

Planting in his second season was a lot more hectic than the first. Emmett now had to factor in Melelo, an extra few thousand acres. Both farms had to be completed in the window of opportunity which lasted less than a month.

Logistically it wasn't too much of nightmare but mechanically it was. Trailers laden with seed could break down – punctures and broken axles being the main problems.

Although he had arranged what he thought was the top team of mechanics with all tools and spares on hand, inevitably something broke or became bent or the oxygen cylinder for welding ran out. The law of Murphy was activated to a great extent.

Rain clouds built up in the late afternoons as the final ten days of mayhem approached. The odd showers that fell on Melelo made some of the newly cut tracks almost impossible to traverse. Time was of the essence and little pinpricks made the deadline more difficult to achieve.

In the end the operation finished five days over what Emmett had predicted. And the first heavy rains followed three days later. A sigh of relief was exhaled as in a burst football.

It was quite amazing to learn, from members of his staff, that all Ratilli's neighbours, on both sides of the road, completed their planting within a week of each other.

The farms new dams started to fill up in the third week of the rains. The stream below Melelo Lodge became a river washing away one of the newly dammed walls. Emmett now saw the torrent of water for the first time so knew the exact places to dam up for next season. Two walls held so he did manage to conserve a certain amount.

The thatch was waterproof on the new house and everything remained nice and dry within. Thank goodness for four wheel drive. What on earth did farmers do twenty years ago when most areas would be quagmires after the first rains," he thought.

His dogs loved the lurching about in the back of the vehicle, sliding from side to side, and got onto the roof when wheels became entombed in a rutted grove eight to twelve inches deep.

They had become well disciplined and remained in the vehicle until told to jump down. Farm staff could quite readily jump aboard without any canine complaints. But let a foreigner try to cadge a lift - oh boy, teeth would be bared with growls aplenty forthcoming. They knew who was who.

Horseback riding in the rains was a dicey business although lovely and fresh in the atmosphere. The slimy slippery soil was deadly underfoot for unshod (as these were) ponies. How they never did the splits Emmett wondered on every occasion? He realised how important iron horseshoes were and likened their unshod state to being barefoot in similar conditions. Only mountain goats and Connemara ponies could handle this situation.

Howard touched down, literally out of the blue, and taxied back up to beside Emmett's house, who was in the office with Gilbert when they heard the plane approaching.

"Come on up for a spin, I have to go to Urukan for some spares," shouted Howard as he approached the house on foot.

"Give me five and I'm with you. Okay?"

"Fine. I'll wait in the plane."

His Cessna 387 was really a motor car with wings. That's how he described it and "all you've got to do is remember the basics. It's a routine. Every single time you want to take off or land. The bit in the middle is common sense. Just watch me, everything I do, and watch the control panel. Right. Here goes."

Lots of switches on, revs up and down, ailerons checked and he was down the runway.

Emmett tried to estimate the point of takeoff and wasn't far off the target. One obviously got to know ones own engine sounds, just like ones own motor vehicle.

Once in flight he climbed to a certain altitude which was obligatory on long journeys. The wireless crackled into life and Howard gave his flight path and estimated time of arrival (E.T.A.) at Urukan.

He gave Emmett an aerial view of his crop before setting off for town. Every so often, whether with Bhogal or Howard, Emmett felt queasy when the plane went into a tight turn, descending or ascending, to look at certain items. His tummy had not become accustomed to 'being in space'. The crop looked healthy, there were still some wet clay patches, but on the whole Howard said he should be satisfied with it.

Emmett found the hardest part was gauging the distance and height, even with instruments, on the approach to landing. Rattles and shudders made Emmett realise how frail the little craft really was.

It was interesting to note that Howard kept the plane about ten feet above the landing strip for a good hundred yards before touching down. The nose had to

116

be kept up all this time while, hopefully, the wheels below hadn't fallen off on the way, were ready for a soft touchdown.

Wind velocity obviously plays a major role in the art of flying. Something only experience and hundreds of hours in the log book can handle.

The John Deere agent was there to meet and take them into town. Whilst Howard went collecting spares, etc. Emmett went across to the Club to check if there were any messages for him. People left them in pigeon holes, alphabetically arranged, behind the reception area. A sensible foolproof method of communication.

One wedding invite, the clay pigeon calendar of shoots for the next three months, a tennis club coming events list and a bill for items he had bought the last time he was in Urukan were accredited to him.

Over a cold beer Emmett wrote two messages, one to the Chairman of the Gymkhana racing committee about the rest of the season and the other was for Anna. This he placed in Jeri's pigeon hole. Then he went to settle his account with the hardware store.

Ahmeds was the biggest and best store in town. They stocked everything from camping and sports equipment to household linens, furniture and then a separate section for groceries and liquor. The family were part of an East and Central African dynasty with stores in all the main cities and towns. Emmett was amazed at their powers of recognition – every client was personally known to them, their fads, delicacies and dislikes.

"Oh Mr. Emmett we have a consignment of excellent French cheeses and your favourite Mango chutney is back in stock again." Little touches like that and probably the best of all,

"How have you come to town? We will deliver to the Club, Bhogals or airstrip or wherever. Just tell us what time you will be leaving." A wonderful service that couldn't be bettered. And they never let you down.

Emmett loved walking through the streets of Urukan. They were wide, the main three were tarmacadamed and ran north/south with eight murram streets cutting across from east to west.

Indian dukas brushed shoulders with African shops, some no bigger than two Husquvarna sewing machines wide and a ten foot wall of materials for suiting.

Then there was the market square on the west side, about seven minutes walk from the Club. There you bought kikoos full of vegies and fruit freshly displayed on slanting stands beneath ceilings of thatch. Plenty of active flies of all hues and sizes made meals of the produce and hawkers on display?

Donkeys, goats, chickens and ducks jostled for recognition – the latter two in open wooden crates, the former roaming and making a general nuisance of themselves.

Everything was for sale and they expected you to barter for it. A job that became second nature to Emmett. He loved it – such a buzz it gave him.

There was a group of brightly clad women who would latch onto the Zungu shoppers. Each lady would meet you on arrival, commandeer your kikoo and yourself, accompany you throughout your half hour or whatever, suggest certain stalls with better offers and then carry your goods back to wherever you were parked or wanted them delivered.

For this, of course, one paid a fee. And that was up to you.

Mary had grabbed Emmett on his first sortie and remained his 'bearer' for his entire tour of duty. She was a tall regal lady of light brown complexion who spoke good English. She carried one full kikoo on her head and another at her side. She always wore a chiffon type of material wrapped around her well proportioned figure, almost as a sari, but it wasn't one. Her ancestry must have some Arab in it Emmett thought. She told him she had been doing this for fifteen years and had educated five children from the proceeds!

Normally it would be like looking for a needle in the proverbial knitting basket to find a policeman on duty in the town. Yes, they were on traffic duty, standing in the centre of the main crossroads when the coloured lights didn't work (sometimes for weeks) – but patrolling or driving around in cars was a definite no no.

This time, however, Emmett noticed quite a number of militia on foot and in strange vehicles. Not police, but these uniformed types seemed half army, half thug. They weren't actually doing anything but observing and perhaps listening. They did, however, succeed in creating an odious feeling amongst the locals.

Mary had remarked on them when accompanying him back to the Club.

"They are too cruel looking, Master. They are here to frighten the people. It is not nice, believe me. There will be trouble soon."

So this undercurrent that Anna had explained to him was rife and obviously spreading.

The flight back to the farm went without any trouble with Emmett pretending to do everything, from his seat, mimicking Howard. That prompted Howard to think about fitting a joint control stick so that Emmett could really get the feel of the plane in flight.

"Next time I'm in Kenzi I'll have one fitted, then you'll be flying young man," and he dipped his left wing and went down in a curve to see something he had spotted in the bush below.

"Oops," here goes his tummy again!

It was a roadblock on their road, like the ones Anna had been caught up in. Emmett explained her story of the recent encounters which made Howard furious.

"What the hell are they playing at? We keep this country going. Without our agricultural input the place would be down the swanee. God how I hate this corruption. He's getting worse you know. I dread to think what the place will be like in three years time when the next election is due. It's this bloody *Makinto* that's the trouble. The President's cold blooded murder gang."

Emmett kept quiet taking it all in. He could hear the fear and dread in Howard's tone. They were all worried but didn't want to show it.

"I think you had better get your licence quickly so that you can fly away if the going gets tough. Swipe one of Bhogal's kites and say bye bye." He was laughing now in jocular mood, but Emmett felt a word or two of warning was etched within that remark.

Bhogal flew in that Sunday. Emmett noticed he was decidedly pallid in his countenance. After coffee he explained.

"We have had four trucks and their loads destroyed over the past week. All on the main north road. Gangs, well armed and organised, put up roadblocks, get the drivers out, beat them up – some fatally – and then drive the trucks off the road, taking from them what they want, then setting them alight."

"Oh my God, Jaswant. What a tragedy. You must be devastated. I'm so sorry."

"For what I ask? What good is it doing anyone?" His eyes never leaving the floor.

"We are now having roadblocks on our road from Urukan. So far only money and food taken but what next? Not a nice prospect for the future," said Emmett.

"I'm worried, Emmett, about the grain trucks when we start harvesting." His eyes, never wide at the best of times, now narrowed into troubled trenches of deep remorse. It is so difficult to read a non European face. Colour definitely clouds the clarity of thought but Emmett knew the man was indeed desperately troubled.

"I think a meeting of all the farmers up here must be called and a security plan put in place. Will you discuss this with your neighbours please?" he asked with quite a pleading tone of voice.

That was the first time Emmett had ever heard him use the 'p' word. Jaswant was a very worried man no doubt.

"No problem. I'll call on the nearest dozen over the next few days and gauge the temperature."

Jaswant took Emmett   up and flew over the crops on both farms. He then flew along the road to Koram and then to Urukan and its outskirts.

There were no roadblocks but they both looked at likely spots where trucks could be taken off the road by high jackers.

Emmett felt the old (well established) farmers would come up with a plan as they knew this road like the back of their hands.

His crop looked good. The colour was strong and even. Perhaps it would be better than last year? Both Howard and Ian's crops looked magnificent and dwarfed Ratillis in extent.

Some of those further down the Punjabi plains looked a bit sick, thin and rusty in colour. Probably poorer soil Emmett thought and maybe less rainfall.

Jaswant departed again once he touched down and deposited Emmett back on Ratilli. Not much was communicated in the air on that return trip. It had taken almost forty-five minutes.

Ian was as worried as Jaswant and decided to call the initial meeting at his within the week.

"Not before its time," he said, "but I had hoped it wouldn't come down to riding shotgun so soon."

Twenty-seven Zungus and Indians attended – an almost ninety percent turnout of the local farming community. The others were either away, in ill health, or just didn't bother?

Ian chaired the meeting and asked for an update of what everyone had heard on things subversive in the recent weeks.

Emmett was astounded at the variety and amount of highjacks, beatings, arson and robberies that gushed forth from this community. They had family and friends all over the country and consequently their networking, once collated into one large database, was quite horrendous. Emmett only listened to his overseas radio programmes and other than Anna had no reason to be in constant contact with outsiders.

By the end of the two hour meeting it was established that for the protection of their district, families and farms, they would pool their resources.

That meant there became available: 8 planes, 10 pilots; 41 landrovers or similar 4x4's; 20 light trucks (3/5 tonnes), 16 heavy trucks (10 tonnes plus); 150 tractors, 90 trailers and 40 horses/ponies. Each farmer pledged 10 security guards which meant that at a given time there could be 300 plus personnel available.

Six Zungus had army training, two police training and two Indians had been policemen.

Buster was elected Commander-in-Chief (C in C) and it was his responsibility to assemble this rag tag bunch, get a strategy formulated, and by the

120

next meeting, in ten days time, come up with a plan for the immediate harvest and its safety.

Emmett was delegated the job of bringing Jeri Ntsemo under their wing and finding out just what action government was prepared to offer to tackle the looming crisis.

A very positive attitude and feeling ran throughout the group. Emmett got the impression that they were actually all prepared for the inevitable.

This sort of disruption had beset virtually every independent African country, so forewarned was forearmed. It was just the speed of the latest outbreak of violence that had taken them all by surprise.

The mass of the trouble was happening up country from them but as a cancer it was obviously spreading.

One noticeable absentee from the meeting was Jonathan, the President's son. Did they have the proverbial 'nigger in the woodpile' amongst them? His Indian neighbours had been present and opted to keep an eye 'on goings on' down on his farm. The pilots agreed to be extra vigilant on their flights. This would be a decisive factor in the district's favour. All agreed air power would be the trump card.

At the next meeting the subject of arms, ammunition and the training of a special convoy guard would be discussed in detail.

121

12

GSU, WB, FRO and DMU all aiming for WERU

"Luckily", commented a really worried Jeri Ntsemo about the extent of recent disturbances, "they haven't infiltrated my district in any force yet but that could change any day." He continued in a mood quite foreign for him, with head and eyes down on his desk top, quietly spoken and with little bon hommé evident.

"My police chief is one of us – Tukulu – and he has a lot of fellow tribesmen in commanding positions. He respects the needs of the farmers to have security so you can tell your next meeting that whatever your lot offer in convoy guards, the police force will back them up. The harvest must get to the silos no matter what it takes. You can quote me on that."

"Are these activists being run by anyone in particular?" asked Emmett.

"Yes, we know of the leader. He is known as Naded Itamik and is the President's number one hit man. He lives in the mountains mostly, has many disguises and hops over the borders at will. He was well trained in the military, a sergeant major and an excellent shot. Let me put it this way. Unless he is caught in a crossfire situation the present army will not pull him in. Not that they are likely to come across him, or his own henchmen, as they are rarely seen. He operates a strike and retreat strategy. Very effective. Within these four walls, there are only a select few of us – people not in union with the President – who are actively interested in getting rid of him and his regime. We do have a grass roots following, however, which is increasing in number daily. That is where the uprising will start. But we don't know when. Not for sometime in my opinion. But, it will come."

Silence reigned for a good few moments. Emmett found it hard to take in all this subversive talk. It was surely very, very dangerous to be so involved? Even more so for Jeri – all his walls could have ears. Life out on Ratilli, and even more so on Melelo, was so serene. His thoughts immediately switched to Anna and her involvement. *Emmett felt she hadn't been totally open with him.* She had to be more up to her pretty neck in the subterfuge than she let on. She had to be careful. He didn't want to lose her so soon. They had more landscapes to investigate, interpret, and colour before the final frame was fitted.

She was Emmett's next stop. He found her ironing, being wholly domestic. She liked to do her own clothes and uniforms. She was proud of her appearance. She was a very proud person. After kisses of welcome,

"Can I ask a big favour," she said with eyes downcast, concentrating on the job at hand

"Anything my darling."

"Will you please take my rifle out to the farm with you and keep it safe for me. I don't dare carry it in the landrover anymore when I'm driving out to you." Then looking at him eyeball to eyeball she added "I might use it on someone."

"Of course. You can practise up in Melelo. That will be nice and secretive. What about your .32? Happy to carry it?"

"Yes. I'll take my chances with that one just in case I'm attacked. Anyhow I carry it in a place only you know about."

"I'm not so pleased you are taking this all so lightly – for God sake don't let your defences down. You warned me, long ago, to watch 'my back'. Please, please beware. Is Jaci armed?" Anna had recently taken on a female driver and companion. Jaci had been a police woman for ten years and had been highly recommended by Jeri. He was worried about Anna's lone trips to the farm.

"Yes, she can well look after herself. She is also a champion in close quarter combat. The pair of us can look after ourselves."

"I'm pleased to hear that. Tell me, are you well in with the local police?"

"Fairly well in. I know a lot of the higher ups and of course Jaci is really well in with them. We act as eyes and ears for them."

With that piece of rewarding information up his belt, Emmett then lead off on more intimate items of conversation. The prospect of living up in Melelo during harvesting was topmost in Anna's mind. She would spend each weekend if not required by Margaret. Having the ponies there would be a big bonus.

They talked about a holiday together after harvesting and then looked ahead to next Christmas. Her parents didn't mind not having all the girls present so perhaps they could travel to a neighbouring country to see how the other half lived!

Suddenly the children arrived home from school and the talk was all centred around horses. They commandeered Emmett and sat on his two knees. They told him they had competed in two local events – both winning rosettes and they looked forward to the round of agricultural shows where they would be jumping.

Anna had them well disciplined as off they scurried to finish their homework and change into sports gear. Zimba had hockey practise and Edith netball. Anna would take them and stay with Edith for her session.

Neither parent would be home before 7.30pm. Emmett was staying the night at the Club so he and Anna made arrangements to meet up later and have a Chinese.

The Peking Restaurant was a jewel, with lovely well travelled owners producing superb dishes. Every farmer made it a must whether for lunch or dinner. The Club's 'table' was very basic and bland but its amenities made up for any shortcomings on the culinary side. And the price was ridiculously low.

Emmett woke up to the fact that he could have the country's English daily paper "The Standard" delivered to the Ratilli by the daily bus service. This supposedly arrived from Urukan via Koram every morning at 10.00am, give or take an hour or so! By passing a 'note' to the driver he would see to this little extra delivery. It had taken Emmett almost twelve months to wake up to this luxury? He hadn't needed to know what was going on within the country up until now. But with disruption and violence taking place on an ever increasing frequency it was probably prudent to learn about and keep up with the local news. Back home he had been an avid "Irish Times" reader and crossword fanatic.

The paper would be somewhat biased towards government but he had heard that it was equally controversial on primary matters. The editor was Indian, very powerful and well versed in economic policies so was quite prepared to speak out against scams, or corruption that might upset the fiscal strategy of the country.

Their agricultural section was edited by a European and he had stringers all over the country giving weekly reports on the state of the land. It also had an excellent meteorological column which gave a five day forward forecast, district by district.

The only 'down' about the rag was its doom and gloom headlines and acres of column inches on the three Dee's. – death, destruction, desolation.

The worrying inches, however, were those that described the beatings, the bestialities, the crass cruelties that were being perpetrated by an ever increasing band of thugs. These gangs were popping up here, there and everywhere like slices of toast from a commercial gismo on the breakfast buffets of top hotels.

Official government forces – army and police – never seemed to be around when assaults took place? But, the interesting facts that were emerging concerned the pockets of resistance that suddenly offered hope for the populous. Pitched battles were taking place and the thugs were alarmed. Emmett feared reprisals of a massive kind.

The second meeting of the district's farmers brought forth strategies covering the movement in convoy of grain trucks from the Ratilli to silos.

4 x 4's would be used to lead and cover the rear of the convoys. Farmers would be armed. If any untoward activity occurred they would fight it off. Open warfare would be declared. Their futures were ever dependent on these harvests. Any disruption to their safe delivery would be resisted.

Buster came into his own as the man in charge. Emmett visualised him in full military combat gear commanding his troops. He was very precise in his manner, dogmatic when needed, light and easy when required. His dark well groomed moustache became prominent on a weather-beaten face, tram lined on his brow with smiling crows feet on each flank. Close cropped waves of greying brown hair kept his military allure very much alive. Shirra must have been bowled over by his dapper bearing all those years ago when he was serving in the Far East. She loved playing the officer's wife. "All those parties darling," she told Emmett between bouts of pent up passion with perspiration oozing out of every pore of their bodies.

Buster was a singular man, a good communicator with his troops but very much one to himself elsewhere. And that evidently included home. Hence her wandering eye and body.

Her ongoing affair with Emmett was purely animal – explosive, momentary and unlasting. It proved a perfect relationship. She was the predator, he the victim – but a wily one. She gobbled him up, each time it being a wonderful release. No strings were attached.

Farm radios became an active network as rosters and timetables for duties were worked out.

Jeri was brought into their confidence and he approved of the initiative.

"But please don't give anyone the chance of blaming you for starting a fracas. That could become dirty with 'you know who' having to use his muscle – his official one." He virtually guaranteed the cooperation and assistance of his police force and the general service units (GSU), but they couldn't be totally involved with the security of the wheat harvest.

"They will be there in backup format. Take that as confirmed."

Emmett had requested from Bhogal some arms and ammunition: a repeating Greener 12 bore shot gun with 20 boxes of cartridges; a magnum .22 and a .38 colt revolver. He had constructed a metal gun lockup in his bedroom. It already housed Anna's rifle which he used most evenings on his dog walks. Jackrabbits were the target; they were extremely tasty when casseroled. Emmett reckoned he was becoming quite a tidy marksman. Certainly a lot more proficient than when he first arrived.

Emmett's sitting room fireplace was a great success. The previous winter had seen its baptism of fire but funnily enough it wasn't used that much. This year was different. It had been bitterly cold each evening since the outset of winter and last season's blocks of wood were being devoured by a gargantuan appetite.

All his visitors and guests had made requests for Ali to visit them – he was quite a personality and moved from farm to farm but did return.

The dogs adored the heat. They became patterned rugs laid out in a semi-circle between the two Sanderson print armchairs. Discipline forbade them from getting up on the furniture. Rani did sneak onto his bed at times but not as a regular happening. It could definitely get too crowded!

They had become marvellous watchdogs, vociferous and formidable when neither Christopher nor Emmett were immediately available to meet the visitor. Their frontline was the garden gate. Their fallback line, the veranda. No one, as yet, had dared invade their territory.

Not a soul ever approached the landrover when occupied by them – usually standing free in the open space behind the cab. They simply lived for a trip and would race well ahead of Emmett leaping into the back like gazelles. Rani was definitely Emmett's shadow and being black all over was very akin to a panther in form and demeanour. Raj had latched onto Anna which was a good thing as he was the largest and most lion like. Rastus was Christopher's. He would lie in the doorway between kitchen and sitting room and let no person or beast pass until Christopher had filled their three bowls for evening feed. This took place on the veranda, each with its own placemat.

Emmett had impressed on Christopher that they needed vegetables just like we did, so he mixed them in with gravy meat on top of the maize meal.

During the winter months Christopher would prepare yellow maize, as porridge, for Emmett's breakfast. Brown sugar or honey and cream made a most energising feed for the start to his day. Emmett only allowed himself an F.I.B. (full Irish breakfast) once a week – usually on the weekend.

With the tremendous amount of daily activity Emmett managed to keep his weight at 11st., the same as when he boxed at public school. For his 5ft. 10ins. it was a well distributed load. He had big bones so a lot of strength was in his thigh region.

Anna used to mock him when showering together as his body was a chequerboard of suntanned skin. Feet and ankles pale, legs to half thighs tanned, crotch and surrounds pale, waist to neck tanned (lightly), hands to shoulders deep brown as that of a conker, face a polished brown as that of a new pair of brogues. It did look comical. Even Anna's body had shades of browns and black blending to fine ebony glistening under droplets of water. Only the pink of her tongue, palms of her hands and soles of her feet made a contrast to her overall dusky hue.

Emmett adored the intimacy of drying each other after bathing or showering. Then the powdering, the dusting down of warm wanton bodies ready and willing for the freeway ahead. That was erotic.

"A bath, a bath, my fiefdom for a bath," was Emmett's nightly signature tune. He had never been a shower man back home. To soak, for as long as hot water kept flowing from the tap, was his nirvana. He was a believer in lanolin products and kept his body refreshed and moisturised. It needed this ongoing attention after being exposed to the elements for a daily ten to twelve hours under African conditions.

Only since Anna came into his life had he appreciated the pleasures of sensual showering. It was the singular unit in the house on his arrival. This changed when he found an antique Victorian bath in a second hand shop in Urukan. Its depth and six foot length made it into a mini pool. The dogs found an amusing game, dipping their heads over the side, attempting to lick a submerged body and getting only oily or soapy water for their adventurous attempts. Then suddenly being surprised by a rising knee with an accompanying splash and wetting of outstretched nostrils. They would sneeze and shake dry their bodies.

They would then find his shoulders and lick like active windscreen wipers until he disappeared once again below the high waterline. Their questioning eyes showed intense chagrin at the unexplained. He had to be stern with them when it came to towelling down as they then attacked as a pack of lick soldiers. Each evening Emmett would then don his Elvery's of Dublin tracksuit and sit on his veranda contemplating the stars, attempting to blow rings of perfection from an ever diminishing cheroot.

The dogs would decide when it was time for their walk by waking and fretting around his chair or swing, 'till he got the message.

"I think it's the treats you want, not the walking," he would say to them on occasion.

On returning to the veranda each would sit on its own sheepskin in pleading anticipation of their biscuit treat. After that it was bedtime for all.

A happy conclusion to each day.

Isolated farm attacks and hamstringing of cattle became more frequent in the areas north-east of Urukan. Many worried farmers met in huddles when visiting the town and Club. Most had heard of the Wheatlands Brigade (WB), as the Koram and Punjabi Plains crowd were named.

The first season of escorting their crop had been such a success that a number of 'up country farmers', as the tea and coffee planters were called, requested a meeting with their committee. Tony Pope's farm east of Timuru was the chosen venue. It had a superb airstrip and commanded a panoramic view of the Mandaras.

Howard flew Ian, Emmett and Buster with Ann Purdon piloting David, Fred and Bill in her newer Cessna.

Emmett had not seen the Mandaras from the air before so Howard gave everyone a tour along the plateau on the top pointing out the well known fishing streams, stocked with rainbow trout. To the north lay Mount Amma peeping above the clouds and to the south Mount Oga, this day completely cloud bound.

Howard also pointed out the bamboo line which defined the altitude (approximately 8,000 ft.); these tropical grass trees grew to enormous heights. Either side of them were hardwoods and then tall grassland all along the narrow plateau. Three quite different types of terrain. Ravines, some really deep, ran east to west down to Kitos and Timuru.

"We haven't time to see the other side of the mountain on this jaunt, Emmett, so that's another surprise in store for you."

He then descended into the closest ravine leaving Emmett's stomach some hundreds of yards above him, breaking through the low clouds at approximately seven thousand feet above sea level and headed for Pope's farm.

This was also on a narrow plateau but this time highly cultivated. Mixed farming, of crops and stock, would best describe the area. Lower (approximately four thousand feet) than that for tea and coffee but not quite the altitude of Koram which would be much warmer.

Tony Pope was a stocky little Cockney fella, one that would never lose the Bow Bells accent. A chain smoker with an active mind matching flashing blue eyes and broad smile. He had been in the area for twenty years and combined farming with a timber sawmill business in the forest region ten miles from the farm. He had been a pilot in the RAF. His wife, Patricia, was also a Londoner but a more refined one. They had two sons, one in the USA and the other, Patrick, ran the sawmill.

Tony had assembled a dozen farmers from the western region covering Shamwani to Kitos. At the end of a hard talking two hour session it was agreed to form an association which would be known as the Farmers Resistance Organisation (FRO).

The eastern side of the mountain would be brought into the structure and Tony would coordinate that. A retired Guard's colonel living in Urukan was elected coordinator and he was delegated to find a similar person to fill the post in Kenzi.

Emmett had met the majority of those present at either the Club, polo or gymkhana race meetings. A few of them offered him rides in the upcoming season which thrilled him no end.

A most enjoyable barbecue rounded off the meeting.

Flying home brought the necessity of such an organisation to the fore as they counted three roadblocks on the Urukan/Koram road – "our lifeline" as Buster put it in a damning tone. A meeting of the WB was called for the following week and Buster's farm would host it.

Widespread human rights violations were creeping into the local news bulletins and press. No one would put a name on the organisation behind the violence and atrocities. No one came forward to publicise or claim responsibility.

This lasted six months with most occurrences taking place in the north of the country, an area deprived of new schools, hospitals and any services. An area and people – the Tukulu – who were anti government. They were paying for their honest desires and beliefs in human relations, with their lives.

Every time the public called meetings to express their feelings they were disrupted and the speakers taken away by the *Makinto*. The police force just looked on, helpless.

Urgent representations were made to the President but deaf ears greeted them.

The opposition then went underground. A party, consisting of all the tribes, the DMU (Democratic Movement for Unity) was formed and a nationwide drive for membership and funds put into motion.

It spread like a 'bushfire', fanned by a strident wind. First they covered the rural settlement areas, then the farming communities. Grass roots was where it started and only ended when the tallest timbers of the forests had been scaled. No one was left out. Democracy or WERU – freedom – was the cry of the people. Waving arms above the head, with hands clenching and unclenching, was the signal.

Labour lines on each and every farm were canvassed and the Barsoi, the President's tribe, were shown the hatred felt by the others.

Emmett was fortunate to have but a few and they actually pledged allegiance to fight terrorism and 'all that the evil President stood for'. One, Emmett felt, did not altogether trust them. Wary eyes plotted their every move.

It became common knowledge that Naded was the leader of the terror groups. He had been two I/C *Makinto* and had branched out and away from Kenzi and their urban HQ to concentrate on the rural areas. First in line would be the tribesfolk in open opposition to *Makinto*. This purge had gone on relentlessly for over twelve months. It became quite clear that Naded was operating from the forest regions. He had based his entire structure on terrorising the outlying tribespeople by arson, torture, ravaging and plundering their crops. These would be transported up into the forest and stashed away in a series of hideouts. Cattle, sheep and goats would be slaughtered – some driven – and they also treasured away, as meat (salted), into pits beneath the ground.

This information became available from members of the group, now known as UMA (Death) – who had deserted back to normal life. They then became marked men and feared for their lives and those of their families. The DMU spirited them away to 'safe' locations using their information as a basis for covert operations when the time presented itself.

Francois Cuvet was the man chosen to be Kenzi coordinator by Col. Stapleton. He was an ex pilot in the Belgian Air Force and had settled in the Congo after the Second World War. He was an accountant and had moved to Kenzi when the Republic of Ukenza was created. He had been a confidante to the founding father of the nation and was therefore extremely well connected.

Francois feared for the country under Victor Ubugus reign so was happy to assist in any way that would lead to democracy. The FRO was creating a step in that direction. Now that the opposition had been officially formed he felt it would be difficult for the ruling party to turn a blind eye any longer.

He came to Urukan for a meeting with the FRO of the district.

It was agreed that the FRO would organise a strategy for the entire country and only when this was up and running would they think of offering themselves to the DMU as an overall operation. Most of the farmers had seen some kind of military service and would therefore be more adaptable to whatever operation lay ahead. They also had arms and ammunition.

Geoff Bamber ran a wireless and electronics business in Urukan. He was British and had also been in the RAF during the War. No repair job was too much for him, whether it be the lowly local band radio that almost every African loved to carry around, with music blaring into an already jingle jangle sounding atmosphere, or the VHF sets used throughout the farming districts and installed in Jeeps and homes.

He joined the Central Committee with his prime job to set up a communications network throughout the country. Geoff flew his own Piper Comanche so could deliver and repair at the turn of a knob.

It was pointed out to Emmett by Howard one day, the method of distinguishing an Englishman in Africa.

"He will be wearing socks with sandals, a sure sign! The other way of course was to see red sunburnt necks on Englishmen and women. They never learn to take it easy with the sunning when first they arrive." After a moment's reflection he added, "they are called rooineks (red necks) in South Africa and Rhodesia you know. Geoff is the one exception to the rule."

Emmett had never worn socks since arriving and only donned long stockings when in smart bush jacket and shorts, on formal occasions. He had never been burnt by the sun and had sported a fine mahogany tan after his first three months. His pony tail was now plaited (originally by Anna one sultry night) and was bleached golden by the climate. As he wore a floppy cotton hat by day his crown was slightly darker than his tail.

"The two tone Irish", as he was frequently referred to!!

Anna's part in the Resistance Movement was intensifying too. She and another lady, Emelia Mtuku had organised a women's association in Urukan – the Wazuri - which not only disseminated information but offered backup to families who were violated by thuggery. Their committee had members from all walks of life and were a highly educated band of women. They had a charity number and collected dry food, clothes and blankets with every shilling donated.

Emmett was waiting outside a church hall one evening to collect Anna when he was grasped by a sense of fear and trembling as the audience within started to ululate - a sound that emanates from the mouth when the tongue is flipped up and down through intakes of air.

In the still of the night this sound really made the hairs on ones neck stand to attention, explained Anna. It was also used as a rallying call from one African village to another. "Much better than a telephone line which can be cut," said she with a wily smirk across a hot face.

"It was a good meeting. We now wish to take lessons in arms training. Can you help Emmett darling?" said she with a slithering across the front seat and almost onto his lap type of plea. "I thought we could use Melelo as a training camp. Lovely and private and no one need know our intent." Her right hand gripped his crotch and kneaded it. She got her reaction with immediacy.

"Oh so you've worked out a whole plan of action have you and what's in it for me then?"

"Need you ask and need I answer. Drive on – if you can concentrate on the road," as she gave his projectile a lasting tug.

Anna and the children came to the farm that weekend. They went riding for hours on the Saturday, taking a packed picnic with them. At a shady turn in the river, now flowing, they dismounted and ate. A lovely sandy spot offered a splendid rolling surface for the ponies who also loved just standing in the shallow moving water, pawing at imaginary images. The aromas of Acacia thorn, splashing water now muddied, and lush undergrowth made for a heady elixir of nature's best ingredients.

The children had essays to write so in late afternoon Emmett took Anna off to Melelo. It was still unknown to Zimba and Edith.

Only three farm guards lived up there so it would be easy for Emmett to square them when an intrusion of women took place. Also, the guards were anti government which made the idea doubly easy. All Anna wanted was an area for target practice, hand gun and rifle.

This was easily located at the nearest clearing to the house. A row of tall Cedars stood like a platoon of troops on one side of the contour. Any distance, up to a hundred yards, could be measured off. There was only forest behind so no one should get shot, except perhaps trespassers?

Anna couldn't let the chance pass? Once they outlined the area which Emmett would have his guards clear away, she enticed him back into the house and upstairs to the balcony

There, like the female praying mantis, she devoured her lover. Magic and myrrh was in the air. Birds sang, guinea fowl cackled and grey louries exclaimed the world to 'go aw-a-y'. The lovers totally concurred. This was the Melelo mood, an experience for two. Something to savour.

13

Medieval Fortresses in Twentieth Century?

Buster Thompson found a new lease of life. He rode chariot, Ben Hur like, into the regimental routine of warfare. Rosters were drawn up, strategies analysed and discussed, plans of action put down on battle boards.

An unused space just off their veranda became 'ops room'. One of his farm workers showed unbelievable artistic talent in making a three-dimensional tabletop map of the region. Each farm with buildings, dams, rivers, bridges and forest areas was neatly displayed.

Shirra then used her unusual talent and grasp of scriptology to illustrate and itemise each and every name and detail of the district. Emmett had only ever seen such a display in war movies and was enwrapped in amazement at such a fine scale model.

"Next time I'm in Urukan I'll buy some Dinky toys of cars, trucks and the like. Perhaps Buster can use them to some advantage?" Emmett said as he also praised her artistic talents obviously unknown to most people. They were as two friendly neighbours working to one objective. No side issues were evident.

Shirra was becoming a great sergeant major in that she was in charge of supplies and collating information. Having been an officer's wife for twenty odd years she knew the military routines and parameters and seemed thoroughly disciplined in them.

Emmett realised she needed this adrenalin rush at home where something passionate may have been missing. She wasn't a humdrum housewife to be stashed away on a God forsaken farm. She needed that certain special extra item to maintain a balance. Now that she was actively employed in a meaningful project, her undoubted energies would be fully utilised.

Another large map, this time of the entire country hung from the adjoining wall. Here Buster devoted his planning skills to the FRO air wing. Every plane, its make, capacity with distance and load capability, was pin pointed. Respective pilots names flew on flags alongside.

"Not all information from the eastern highlands had come to hand," Buster explained but an entire network there would also soon be in place.

Flying instructors and their 'kites' from both Kenzi and Urukan had volunteered to join the organisation. It was looking like a quite formidable air wing and one that could offer backup to any given region within a very short time.

Farmers now thought in security terms and along military lines. The younger set, of which Emmett was one, looked on it as a rare challenge. Perhaps, if things did deteriorate into riots and mass murders, as in neighbouring countries, it would be their introduction to a kind of military service. Not on the schedules of many western peoples, he ventured. Once again the fantasy world of the movies came into his images of what the future could bring. Certainly security on the farms was stepped up.

Emmett placed a guard on the main entrance and everyone had to sign in and out of the farm. A further guard he now placed on the compound entrance who would also have sight of any movement into or out of the farm's staff lines. Guards had to check whatever baggage was being brought in or out. Machetes or knives of any kind could easily be stockpiled. Not to mention arms and ammunition.

There was a radical change taking place. One that could well govern the future path all would have to take.

Life on Ratilli proceeded in the well oiled fashion that Emmett had put into operation. There was a certain 'aroma' of success about the way the staff set about their designated chores. The bonus received from the first completed harvest, under Emmett's tenure, had given everyone confidence to proceed with high hopes for the coming season.

Each sector now had its own headman who answered only to Emmett. They felt important and took on the responsibility with zest.

Bhogal's visits were now monthly or whenever he wanted to impress a visitor from overseas or a new client. A curtain of trust had been erected around the Bhogal -Doyle partnership which obviously worked admirably for both sides.

Rains had fallen in their virtually correct proportions at just the right time. The Ethiopians taught Emmett how to pilot their 'wasps' but not to swoop low and maintain altitude. That was too dangerous and only hours of flight experience qualified one to partake in such an exercise.

He was happy to know how to take off and land, the in between flight was an easy enough task to master. Howard had told him he was ready to go solo and would contact a great instructor, Boris Wanko, in Urukan to take him through his qualifying hours. After that he was on his own.

Each night Emmett thanked his God for the pleasures he had experienced since arriving in Africa. Brought up a Roman Catholic his discipline in things 'religious' had been blown out the side door since university days. Here on the

Punjabi Plains the nearest RC Church was in Koram and there was no way that he could guarantee a weekly or even monthly visitation. His thoughts and prayers, however, were never far away. A St. Christopher medal on a gold chain around his neck was his constant companion. In his wallet was a little prayer 'This is what the Lord asks of you: only this, to act justly, to love tenderly, and to walk humbly with you God." Micha 6:8. His mother had given this to him on his departure to the 'dark continent', as she had so sweetly put it. Packed next to his driving licence it was a comforting thought each time he dipped for some money. She had also packed, in newsprint and cotton, wool a statue of the Child of Prague which virtually every Catholic home in Ireland had on display in either the garden, for fine weather, or inside for safe health and happiness.

The tradition back home in the west of Ireland was for the 'Child' to be placed outside for the wish of good weather. Often used for an upcoming wedding in the family or for their horse to run well at the local point-to-point or Galway festival, the 'Good Child' had plenty of uses!

He followed the hardened Irish tradition of putting it out prior to the rainy season, hoping it would act in the reverse situation. His stone mason, Ali, had very proudly made a stone grotto for the statue, without being asked. A lovely and rewarding thought, much praised by Emmett, Anna, the children and Christopher. It would then return to its shelf on the veranda when the wish had been granted.

Africans, he learnt, were dreadfully superstitious and were ruled by their Ngangas – witch doctors – no matter what faith they believed in. Anna had great fun describing initiation ceremonies within the tribes and the variety of rites that existed within their ethnic bounds.

Circumcision was still rampant throughout central Africa no matter how missionaries tried to plead for its eradication. Tribal lore was proving too strong a bastion to conquer.

Bestiality, violence and extraordinary acts of brutality were, seemingly, an everyday occurrence in cultures completely foreign to European upbringing and beliefs. Even the everyday treatment, or lack of, towards animals, domestic or commercial, brought frowns to Emmett's bronzed forehead. Christopher and the syces, however, provided the exception to the rule.

Emmett had many a swearing session with the syces when first employed, but then they realised it was easiest and best to do it his way. It only then needed the occasional shout from him to bring them back to earth and the job at hand. Praise followed when the task was satisfactorily completed. This was evidently something lacking in their previous employers repertoire. Emmett traded on building loyalty and trust, and felt he never really knew when he needed to call it in, but hoped it would be available in an emergency.

Activists did manage to set up a roadblock early on in the harvest but once the FRO landrover arrived ahead of the convoy they backed down and let it through. They were then intent on harassing their own kind who travelled that road. Somehow it was felt that the thugs wouldn't back away for good and some of them would one day dare to tackle a lone truck or even a convoy.

Jonathan, the President's son, wasn't too keen on towing the FRO line about convoys and every now and then would send a couple of his loads ahead on their own. He probably thought he was above 'all this regimentation and security business' and with his name would sail through. The thugs, however, thought differently and plundered where possible. He soon realised it was best to be 'within the group' than out on a limb.

Once the harvesting got underway farm radio links sprang into action. Duty rosters were adhered to and trucks, once weighed at the Ratilli, lined the lay-by beyond the building awaiting the armed vehicles and personnel to move into place.

Twelve to sixteen trucks made up each convoy to Koram. Once inside the silo area the FRO vehicles returned to the Ratilli to escort the next contingent. Sometimes the weighing and offloading at Koram took hours and the backup became prodigious. The police force was in control of proceedings within the town. They were 'well rewarded' for their vigilance by the FRO and instructions from the CC at Urukan – the farmers' friend Jeri Ntsemo.

A few half hearted attempts were made to disrupt the smoothness of the convoys, perhaps as a tease. It was the thugs way of defining their strength and to what lengths they would go if pushed, they were a raggle taggled force who obviously played on the unprepared sector of the tribal public, an inert population who hadn't yet learnt to fight back.

The DMU opposition was gradually rallying the masses to offer resistance and was instructing them in the best ways to combat thuggery.

More consistent raids were being made on tribes provoked by the insurgents operating from forest areas north of Kenzi. They obviously needed more food, whether for storage, or for ongoing appetites. This was their method of supply. Stealing down from the wooded areas during the night, raid the villages and isolated homesteads, cause a bit of mayhem, and make off with maize meal, chickens, vegetables and the odd sheep, goat or bullock, they then hightailed it back into their hideout areas knowing that their victims would not dare to follow.

No one really knew how many of these bastards were already resident on the mountain range and what their final intent would be aimed at.

The FRO groups of Shamwani and Maru got together with the DMU opposition and worked out a strategy which might assist the tribes people in combating the enemy, their own people. This was what made the situation so unusual. Everyone understood that cities and some towns had gangland goings on but why was this group – UMA - intent on harassing and violating its own kind? Humble peasant folk just could not understand why they should be attacked and targeted? There had to be a deeper motive.

European farmers thought they knew just what that might be, having seen what went on in Kenya in the fifties, when a certain sector of the black population drummed up enough support from the majority to try and oust Europeans, they now feared that something similar might be on the agenda here.

Was the President playing a two handed game or was his authority being usurped by a section of his *Makinto* who were taking things into their own hands? He might not be able to quench the thirst of Naded and his cronies. Then what?

Dickie Barker was the man in charge of Shamwani FRO and he'd got together with Patrice Kalumba, Chairman of DMU opposition. They, with various other members of both parties, met at the Shamwani Club one afternoon and drew up a plan to combat the frequent terrorist incursions into the tribal trust lands.

African farmers, up to two miles from the edge of the forest, would be moved to a central fortified village, their stock housed within the confines of the fort and let out daily to graze. Farmers would work in their fields during daylight hours, returning to the stockade before dark. These stockades were medieval in design, rather like fortresses of old. Timber was supplied by local mills and barricades, of fifty to a hundred yards in length by ten feet high, constructed on a square. Raised lookouts were built in each corner.

Only one single, extremely strong, gateway allowed access above which was a walkway with armed sentries.

The villagers built their own temporary accommodation in lines within the stockade and ate from a communal galley. Latrines were dug in one corner. Only at night time did the population return for food and sleep. Guards would be mingling with them during the day and would alert the local FRO if any disturbance or infiltration took place.

Security and the saving of lives was the prime aim of constructing these fortresses. The locals were against it at first but were quick to realise the advantages.

The CC of the district was totally behind this concerted effort. Evidently the President was growing increasingly concerned with the Uma Group and saw it as a definite thorn in his side. He therefore gave his commissioners the powers to assist in whatever way was possible.

He followed this up with a 'decree' outlawing the terrorist organisation known as UMA and any other similar grouping with intent on destabilising the country. The Shamwani and Maru districts put the 'stockade strategy' into operation immediately. Other areas looked on nervously hoping that it would

137

work. They made plans for following Dickie Barker's lead and awaited results. The tribesfolk did not like the concentration camp style of security but were prepared to put up with the inconvenience if it stopped plundering and violations of their people.

"It's only for a short time, until these thugs learn a lesson," said Patrice during his speech to the second stockade members on its completion.

In the first three months no daylight attacks were made on the Shamwani tribespeople or their livestock. Nights were quiet and one felt that UMA was pondering its next move. The FRO agreed that the strategy was working so a blanket operation was put into effect encompassing all tribal areas on both sides of the Mandaras.

A scorched earth policy or a no-go zone would make it terribly difficult for the mountain movement to feed themselves.

To set it up was proving a gigantic problem, however, as there were pockets of resistance to the plan in every tribal area.

The general public were confused. They couldn't work out who was who and who was fighting whom. It wasn't a matter of colour or religion. Politics, up to this moment was of one hue. Pleas to their President had not earned a response. Now an opposition – political, in the form of the DMU – was offering a rainbow with purported treasure at its end. However, a third group in the guise of UMA, were evidently opposed to everyone, everything. And were let get away with it. They were mainly of the Tukulu Tribe – a breakaway section with radical ideas.

FRO's policy was to assist the tribes people wherever and whenever possible. They felt that their own farm, whether tea, coffee, dairy, beef or grain would be next on the terrorists shopping list. They made their labour lines more secure and moved livestock well away from the foothills. Constant radio contact was in operation and the eastern districts was monitored by their western counterparts and visa versa

When Emmett saw the first two stockades he likened them to the forts he had seen in western movies, built to house the troops in preparation for attacks on or by Cochise and his renegade Red Indian tribes, but these, however, had a dry moat all around some thirty yards from the barbed wire fence enclosing the people. On the bottom of the moat were bamboo spikes known as pungees. If any marauder fell into them he was a 'goner'. Evidently this was a method used in wars in the Far East and was most effective. A type of drawbridge was pulled erect when all tribe's people were returned for the night. On each corner was built an elevated watchtower which gradually became armed and therefore fortified. Lovely newly built mud-hut homes with corrugated sheet roofing housed the villagers in lines. The confined life gradually honed a new spirit of united strength with young men and women volunteering for security and policing duties. A camaraderie was built up with tribal law very much to the front.

Tribal chiefs and elders ruled supreme and sat in on all FRO meetings. A Home Guard (HG) was formed and all ex-police or army personnel assisted with basic training. It was amazing to see what came out of the woodwork and what pride was created in each encampment.

Recreation in the form of football and netball became of prime importance. So much so that after twelve months of living under these conditions an inter-camp championship was set up with sponsorship coming from Central African Breweries.

Delegates from all the farming areas were taken on tours of these anti-terrorist camps, which helped in promoting the Home Guard (HG) within their own districts and farms.

Emmett called a meeting of all his staff immediately after his second harvest. He outlined the policy adopted in the tribal areas near the foothills of the Mandaras, the stockades, the Home Guard and how successful their combined methods had been. He wished to form a voluntary HG on the farm so that it would be able to act on any emergency both here and when they returned to their homes.

A lot of them had already heard from relatives and friends and were quite up to date with what was going on elsewhere. There was an immediate response for HG duties which pleased him no end.

This was the reaction on all the wheat farms and Buster set about coordinating a basic training programme.

Emmett, having not had any military training, was included in this initial stage which he took to without a problem. He rather appreciated discipline and in fact had once thought about a career in the British Army. But university, a time away spreading his oats, and then Africa had put an end to that idea.

He had always been a good shot with a .22 and 12 bore, for his father had taken him out from an early age. This aptitude was now a definite requisite and was being well utilised in various formats.

For the pot he kept Christopher busy with Impala, Guinea Fowl, Francolin (African species of Partridge), Jackrabbit and the occasional wild pig. He continued to turn out for the monthly clay shoot and what with Anna and her gang, his right shoulder was kept busy. Emmett now owned a pair of Colt .38 revolvers but he was nowhere near as accurate with them. Over close quarters yes, but not past twenty yards. He continued to practise with them up at Melelo but never would be a John Wayne or Wyatt Earp!

His second harvest showed an increased total overall but that of Melelo was not as good as he had hoped for, dropping the average of the two farms down a fraction but luckily not enough to stop a second substantial bonus – for him and all his staff.

Teething problems at Melelo, like poor results from crop spraying thereby allowing a lot of rust to stunt its growth; battalions of monkeys racing through at ground level causing 'lodging', after they had eaten their fill; and not a good enough seed bed preparation in certain areas due to the unevenness of the ground caused the tonnage to drop. Also the tracks out of the farm caused a deal of spillage from the trailers. They would have to be a lot smoother for next season.

As Ian reiterated "they're teething problems young man, don't fret over it. My first year wasn't great either."

That was great comfort coming from such a complete farmer and general nice guy. Emmett kept reminding himself of what good neighbours he had, and how they had been there for any emergency or whenever he needed help.

Tribal troubles had abated over the winter months with only the occasional arson attack on outlying holdings and some stock being driven off from unprotected herds.

It was the custom of the pastoral tribes, the Wasti, Kipsis and Sintu to have their cattle, sheep and goat herds minded by young men (children in most cases) of the tribe during daytime grazing hours, allowing the men and women folk to work for wages. However, it was inevitable that some bully gangs would easily outwit and overpower these infant herdsmen and make off with whatever they needed.

As time went on, and grazing grounds on the plateau became eaten down, the herds would be moved closer to the foothills. It was then that Home Guard would be employed to bolster the herd boys. They had 'walkie-talkies' and would be in communication with their nearest stockade, who in turn, would be linked to the local FRO branch.

Backup patrols could then be dispatched to the area, the theft followed up, with hopefully, contact made with the gang and a prisoner or two taken. They would be brought to FRO HQ and grilled for information before being handed on to the police.

From these infrequent arrests a quantum of intelligence was built up on the daily routines of UMA and those living in the forests.

Most of those arrested were small fry and didn't know a lot about numbers and gang hideouts, and actually seemed happy to have been taken into custody. Perhaps things were not 'too kosher' as Emmett's Jewish friends used to describe a certain similar situation.

14

Corrib, Mask and Geronimo

The polo season started up a month after the grain harvest finished. Emmett had been keeping his stick arm in practise by carrying one and using it on imaginary white missiles as he rode around the farm.

About halfway through the season, and leading up to Christmas, gymkhana racing started and continued for three months.

Rachel and Howard's pony, Geronimo, was coming on in leaps and bounds under his guidance and training. When it first arrived on Ratilli it ran away with Emmett and both his syces respectively. Its mouth was granite hard. Nothing anyone could do, by pulling reins or changing bits, would stop him.

He remembered a friend of his father's who trained point-to-pointers near Craughwell, Co. Galway, telling him how to put manners on any horse, mule or donkey, that had this problem.

"Take the animal into a ploughed field and ride him round and round in ever decreasing circles at full tilt. Grab the left or right rein and tuck it under your leg pulling the animal's head hard to that side. Drive him on when you feel he is getting tired. Bring him to his knees when he's exhausted. He'll never do it again boyo," were the words that rang in Emmett's head. And that's exactly what he did. The nearest hundred acres to the compound was chosen to set about proving this.

It did take three different attempts over three days but Geronimo was cured of his hard mouth. He did, however, take a fair 'hold' but never again took off to scare the living daylights out of whoever was onboard. He calmed down and started cooperating and indeed enjoying his daily work routines.

Emmett had one of his tractor drivers harrow a circular mile long track. He marked out the eight separate furlong posts around the track and painted a red circle on a white background atop the final one. The winning post.

Just to the east side of the winning post he walked the ponies in a circle each time they prepared to do some work. This would get Geronimo accustomed to parading in the paddock prior to a race. He brought out his ghetto blaster and had speech and music blaring as they exercised.

As Geronimo would not be playing polo he had no knowledge of an audience or the noise created on such an occasion.

He certainly was fast and after three months of walking, trotting and finally cantering, a preparation to harden the muscles and gradually bring the body to complete fitness, Emmett rode him in a small, but fast trial against Corrib and Mask. They managed to stay with him for the first one hundred yards but then toiled in his wake.

Geronimo was indeed a speed machine. Emmett would now have to concentrate on building up his stamina for the hurdle races which would be over two miles. The longest gymkhana race (flat) was one and a half miles, usually two of them on a card, with four to seven furlongs making up the other races.

He would perhaps try Geronimo over a sprint distance, five or six furlongs, in his first race and see how that panned out?

It was an amateur sport and anything could happen on the day. Emmett was not going to be unprepared. He wanted everything to be correct. He was a perfectionist. A well fed, prepared Geronimo, would be the 'wheatlands' trail blazer and one that the district would be proud of. Why do things in halves when the whole is just as easy?

At the first polo weekend, up in Timuru, he learnt that two hurdle races had been agreed on and would be held at the end of the season. Chuffed to bits with this, he was then asked to design the hurdles and be on the race committee. Even better he thought.

Now he set about schooling – training to jump – Geronimo who wasn't too keen on the idea in the initial stages. He didn't take to discipline but once he realised these funny coloured poles were not a challenge he settled to the job with zest.

Corrib and Mask acted as 'school ponies' leading him over cavelettis, single poles, spreads and finally forty-four gallon drums on their sides.

Geronimo was a proud horse, his thoroughbred genes came through like cream to the top of a milk bottle. You could literally hear him saying "I am better than these other ponies, they are in a class below me and I will show them." Arrogance would have been a suitable name for him. But once he realised that TLC was a real bonus he settled down and became a pet. Both the children rode him in the jumping paddock but not out on farm rides. Anna got on well with him and Emmett allowed her to canter him around the track. No one had yet put Geronimo into a full blooded gallop. That would only happen a couple of weeks prior to his first race.

Emmett had persuaded Bhogal to give the farm a two ton truck with high sides. It would be ideal for transporting the staff to Koram and for collecting small loads from Urukan and cheaper to run. It was also ideal as a horsebox! With a wooden addition to the tailgate the ponies loaded and unloaded easily. Geronimo took a bit more time to come to terms with this but once he saw Corrib and Mask walk in and out without any trouble he too complied.

Geronimo travelled over to his old home and unloaded without a worry to the joy of Rachel who was present when Emmett drove in, and invited her to put on some jeans and have a ride.

"See what you think now. Have we a winner or what?" he chided her.

After a twenty minute workout she returned flushed and triumphant.

"Incredible Emmett. He is a joy to ride. Such graceful movement, not like the short choppy strides of the polo ponies. Well done. I think you have a star."

Over some chilled lemon juice he discussed his plans for Geronimo. Rachel said they would fly up for the hurdle races if all went to plan, and maybe even for the others too.

"My darling daughter will be thrilled to hear that you have tamed him."

There were going to be six race meetings over the four month period, two of which would be in the Shamwani district. Two each were allotted to Urukan, Kitos and Timuru. The hurdles were scheduled for Urukan and Kitos. These would be easiest to travel to. They had the widest running tracks and their bends, although sharp, maintained the width around them.

Geronimo's first run was at Kitos. The race was over one and a half miles and Emmett didn't think he had a chance. 'Out for the spin' would have been the description back in Ireland.

He wrestled with whether to run him in a sprint, over five or six furlongs, which he thought he would most probably win or at least run into a place. He was like lightening over sprint distances. That would expose him, however, and so a decision to give him a slow baptism to the hurley-burley of racing was chosen.

Ridden by Emmett from the back of the field for the first mile he then allowed him to extend, but kept him tight and 'still on the bridle', as his stamina came into play. Geronimo finished a strong fifth in a field of twelve, full of running and evidently relaxed having enjoyed the experience. He was highly impressed and told Howard and Rachel as much once they were well away from the 'eyes and ears' of those who thought they knew the whole game inside out.

The connections wanted to win the hurdles, nothing more, nothing less. It wasn't for the money or the gamble, just the pride that a horse from the Punjabi Plains could outrun and confound the experts. Both Howard and Rachel had full confidence in Emmett and he in turn was adamant that, barring accidents, the duo could 'bring back the bacon'.

He was happy with Geronimo's stamina but kept his work rate high on pace strategy. His two polo ponies were now well used to joining in these routines,

143

giving their all in short spurts and just happy to keep their more illustrious – yet to be proved – stable star as company. They had been adept on the polo field. He now had to make a name for himself in hurdling. Both syces, Langat and Sunguru, yearned for these workouts as they felt they too were jockeys.

Schooling over fences was a bit hairy as he not only took a real hard hold of the bit but he was also prone to taking off a full stride ahead of where Emmett wished him to. This was quite scary and Emmett wondered what trouble he would get into in a race when there would be horses all around him? Only time will tell he silently mused, as in every other way Geronimo was the ideal ride.

It was a pleasure to have these weekend interludes interspersed with the ongoing and ever increasing home guard duties that the farming community was experiencing.

The latest string to their bow was the covert operation that was being used all around the boundaries of the Mandaras.

The immediate response unit was proving a thorn in the sides of the bush terrorists. More and more Zungus, however, were needed to monitor and lead the sorties which meant that every district was constantly supplying manpower to assist in this sector of combat.

Emmett, with other Plainsmen, would be called away for five or six days at a time to bolster the ground forces of various regions. During the non-harvest periods this didn't create a problem but his absence from Ratilli and Melelo at actual planting and spraying times could well be.

A backup farm relief service was put into operation which maintained strict management criteria and was much appreciated by all farmers.

Emmett noticed that Bhogal was ageing appreciably with all the troubles his haulier business was experiencing. At times he was so down and depressed when he flew in that Emmett wondered if one day soon he might decide to give up the farming venture. Only one of his sons, Vijay, showed any interest in its future. Emmett felt he had better be prepared, with options, in the event of this catastrophe occurring.

He discussed it with Ian who blandly said "rubbish, absolute balls. Bhogal's pride would never allow that to happen. What a cave-in it would be within his community. No young man, there's no chance of that happening. Trust me."

Having fallen in love with the life he would not want to leave it so soon. He felt he belonged in Africa and Ukenza was as good as anywhere. He would, however, keep eyes and ears open for other positions that might crop up.

Anna also felt as Ian and she certainly didn't want him to have to pull out altogether. They had something special going between them, something they both intended to be lasting.

Her trips to Ratilli were at least twice a month now and her ladies' group outings once a month to Melelo. These followed a regular format. A mini bus with sixteen ladies would arrive at 8.00am which meant they had risen and met at 5.00am in Urukan! On de-busing, the kitchen unit of two got cracking on brewing tea and cutting 'doorsteps' of bread which were liberally covered with plum jamb.

The group meanwhile was being put through weapons training by a retired police sergeant. This included small arms and rifle training. They were then given 'bush craft' and ambush practise in the forest close to the lodge.

After breakfast all of them went onto the rifle range where six cedar trees sported targets. These rose majestically from the fringe of a ploughed area about a half mile from the lodge. Distances of twenty-five, fifty and one hundred yards were marked out in front of the targets. The group fired standing upright, kneeling on one leg and lying down. They were becoming sharp shooters. Dedicated killers, assassins, if and when they were called upon.

Emmett, at times, was worried about the consequences if *Makinto* learned of these outings. He didn't think that the C.C., Jeri, would be able to assist in his defence if he was taken away for questioning.

He had therefore registered a gun club for Ratilli/Melelo, in clay shooting, so the noise heard could be allied to that sport. A membership list had been drawn up, rules and regulations adhered to, so, on the surface it was all 'above board'.

The group found that 'shooting clays' was even more of a challenge and all of them wanted to outscore Anna who remained their champion. She was one of the best shots at the Urukan Club and represented them in league matches.

On other weekends Melelo hosted local farmers in regular shoots, hence marking it as a known and active club. One could never be too careful or fastidious. Too many avaricious eyes and ears, eager for cash rewards, were roaming the countryside these days. Emmett had been warned of this by Buster.

Anna and Jaci were ever on the go, after hours and on days off. Their group now numbered hundreds with active pockets establishing themselves in outer regions. She however, spent as much time as possible with Emmett on both farms and became a more than capable rider picking up spare mounts at each gymkhana race meeting. He felt it wouldn't be long before she recorded her first winner. That would be an enormous day for racing relations and a massive step for feminism. And Emmett Doyle would have been a major part of that stride into the future. Perhaps this would be a breakthrough for the forces of democracy?

15

"Don't shoot the lot, we need some alive."

Emmett was called for his first tour of duty, on May 12, his birthday, a date he wasn't likely to forget.

He was to be away ten days and had to travel to the east side of the Mandaras. There he would meet up with Bobby Barker, son of Dickie, at Tembu and then both would travel north to Dashu. This was the HQ of the local Farmers Reserve and looked up at the peak of Mount Amma. They would be on forest patrol.

A lot of activity had been reported with gangs raiding labour lines and grain sheds. This was one of the best tea producing areas with miles and miles of shimmering green tabletop acres of pristine cropped tea bushes laid out on an undulating canvass.

Tall clumps of Bluegum and Mountain Oak defined the homestead's whereabouts, usually halfway up a hillside. All farm buildings were whitewashed with roofs of cedar shingle. A lot used off-cuts of hardwood timber as walls above three foot of natural stone. Gardens were extensive with magnificent rolling lawns, beds of roses, Agapantus and Cannas interspersed with shrubs of 'Yesterday Today Tomorrow' (Brunfelzia) and Pride of India. Usually a copse or two of Frangipane was strategically placed near bedroom wings allowing their pungent but decorous scent to infiltrate inside and out of the area.

His patrol was issued rations for seventy-two hours – a three day hike into the forest. Radios, stenguns and hand grenades made up their pack They then travelled in convoy up to Nimmers Farm which was literally on the forest edge. Tall hardwoods presented a backdrop of mystery, intrigue and violence some few hundred yards from the homestead.

Johnny Nimmer had been an RAF pilot in the Second World War, then learnt tea planting in Ceylon before being enticed to Ukenza. He was regarded as one of the leading producers of this liquid gold and his farm was immaculate, almost clinical in upkeep and appearance. Johnny had lost his wife, an Irish girl, in a car accident whilst holidaying in South Africa. Some years later he had married Albertina, a tall lissom Tukulu from near Kenzi. They had two children, a son and daughter, to add to Johnny's first son, William, who was now managing the farm.

He had been educated in England and completed an agricultural degree at Cirencester.

The farm had a pedigree herd of Jersey cattle which Emmett had noticed as he followed Bobby into the depths of the farm. Its name was Karirana.

Johnny was the local C-in-C as Buster was on the Punjabi Plains. The house was like a beehive. It was command HQ and reservists were coming and going all the time.

As Emmett parked his landrover next to Bobby's he heard a colossal noise which made him duck down for a moment or two.

"Don't worry, its only a plane landing. The strip is right here beside the house and these guys come in really low."

He was relieved and joked with Bobby as they walked up to the house.

After an hour of introductions and extensive map reading they were shown to their sleeping quarters where other bedrolls were lined up like slabs of chocolate on a shop counter.

Their patrol was to set out at first light next morning with five African trackers, two of which were repatriated terrorists who knew the terrain like the backs of their hands. Another hour was spent getting to know them. Bobby spoke fluent Tukulu and had a good spattering of Wasti which one of the group acknowledged with great happiness. Emmett was completely out on a wing and prayer in this sector but hoped that his fitness and gun slinging expertise would make up for his linguistic shortcomings.

Bobby recognised quite a few of the other Zungu farmers and lots of them knew his father so the evening was like a grand dinner party. Stories of ambushes, attacks, hidden caches of arms and food stuffs and the art of bush craft ran around the large oblong table like a ball just launched in its pinball machine.

Repartee bounced back and forth with such levity that no one realised it was past eleven and time for the 'troops of the morrow' to be tucked up and asleep.

Sleeping feet were kicked by the orderly sergeant on duty at 04.30 hours.

They needn't shave as their faces were to be made up by the Officer in Charge, they were told. This was the first time Emmett had seen facial camouflage being used. Their faces, necks and hands were covered in a blackish brown greasepaint. Certain areas of the face were highlighted with stronger lines and the grease was rubbed back beyond hairlines so that no whiteness could be seen. Only the whites of their eyes were evident when they looked into the mirror.

Tattered and very smelly old clothes were given to them to overdress their essential undergarments, shirts, shorts and pullovers.

By the time they were passed fit for duty they almost looked like Africans and definitely, from a distance and within the light and shade and leafiness of the forest, would pass for anything but heavily armed Zungus.

Both Emmett and Bobby had to carry parcels wrapped in gunny bags (Hessian) which observers might think contained food and meat. Meantime they contained their loaded stenguns and ammo.

Clipped onto their waist belts each had four grenades with extra clips of ammunition held in long strong pockets especially sewn inside the clothing.

Instead of setting out from the farm they were transported to an old sawmill some three miles north and inside the actual forest. They set out on foot immediately on arrival as the vehicle returned to base.

From recently captured terrorists it was learnt that an enormous cave on the slopes of Mount Amma had the largest store of arms and foodstuffs in the district. It was to be their objective. Quite a daunting task.

Bobby had been on many such patrols so Emmett took heed of every little thing he offered along the way.

Ambushes could be expected so each step was a silent and vigilant one. Not a crack from a trodden twig should be offered as a warning of intruders.

Within half an hours' stealthful stepping they had entered the bamboo belt which continued upward for a thousand or so feet.

Emmett had been warned not to let anything hard hit against any of these towering stems as the reverberations would be heard miles away.

Their eyes were peering into a pillared abyss, their heads very slowly rotating from left to right. Out ahead of them were the trackers, one ex terrorist and one reservist, whose ethnic expertise was being pitted against that of the resident gangsters. The other three followed behind. All of the patrol was in single file and slightly crouched in position.

They were climbing ever skywards and breathing was becoming more stressful with each hundred yards achieved. Only Bobby and Emmett were experiencing this and halts were called every twenty minutes or so.

The silence of the forest was overpowering. A musty aroma permeated the air and succeeded in penetrating their Zungu lungs, unaccustomed to such levels of organic decay. Elephants and certain buck (deer) inhabited these slopes. Bamboo shoots were culinary delicacy's for these incredible beasts of the forest. With such extensive gang movement both species had evidently migrated southwards, to the top most plains, where sparkling trout filled streams trickled through bog-like terrain. This area had been viewed by Emmett when accompanying Howard on one of his flights some months before this. He thought of the inconvenience this protracted terrorist campaign had been to the routine Zungu farming tradition of camping out 'en famile' during the fishing season! Now, it seemed, nowhere was safe around the Mandaras. Hopefully such a situation would not occur on the Punjabi Plains?

148

Suddenly, Simeon the lead tracker, signalled for them to leave the path and fall flat in whatever cover was available. As if by telepathy he had heard something up ahead.

The patrol secreted itself some yards off the track. Bobby and Emmett had stens (guns) at the ready. Machetes were held tightly by the others as all lay deathlike in readiness.

Perhaps, thought Emmett, this could be a group setting out for a foraging attack and were not too disciplined in military tactics up here close to their base camp.

It was a tricky situation as Bobby did not wish to openly come into contact with them. Having to use fire power, at this critical time, would signal their arrival.

The cave dwellers would then be alerted and all chance of a surprise negated. This was certainly not what was needed.

Lying so close to the ground with face and right cheek buried in leaf mulch Emmett now, for the first time, understood the magnitude of this undertaking. His life was in the firing line of survival and the latter he wished to achieve.

Noises could now be heard, faint murmurings above the odd bamboo being brushed against. In an amphitheatre of silence Emmett then realised why silent movement was such a necessity.

The noise was sporadic but definitely getting closer.

Four 'Beebees' (females) leaned forward into large baskets upon their backs. These were fastened around their foreheads by thongs made of dry cattle hide. Probably empty now these would, on the return trip, carry food, arms and ammunition. And on that trip they would be escorted by an armed guard of two or three. Presently this quartet was on its own.

They passed along beside the group of prostrate explorers never altering their rhythm one step. Eyes firmly fixed on the path ahead they were not interested in what lay within the adjoining undergrowth. An odd piece of dialogue breaking the silence.

Emmett had always wondered about firing off a barrage of bullets when inside these pillars of bamboo. Not a lot of shots would reach their objective he reckoned. But it would be the same for the opposition. A lottery of survival he wagered.

Bobby kept his patrol in their unsavoury positions until his trackers could hear the 'Beebees' no more. He then signalled them to continue their way forward along the track.

In whispered consultation with Bobby, Emmett learnt that they might be within an hour of their objective. It would be a hard climb up the final mile with the bamboo giving way to scattered hardwoods and various pockets of scrubland.

Bobby wanted to arrive under the cover of the forest trees just before dark so that he could survey the ground around the cave.

They had had a pretty exact briefing at Karirana before setting out and the two of them carried a vivid picture of their goal.

All five of the trackers knew the layout from previous hunting trips in peaceful times with the two ex terrorists having recent knowledge of it.

Lookouts and sentry guards would probably be posted above the cave affording them an eagle's eye view of any approach. It was Bobby's strategy not to use these routes and not to advance in single line ahead.

He had, in his mind's eye, positioned his patrol in line abreast formation with Emmett on the right flank. He would be in the centre of the line.

After dark the two ex-terrorists would crawl to the entrance and attempt to enter or infiltrate the surrounds or barricades. It wasn't necessarily known by the gang that these two had been captured, interrogated and then debriefed. They had been away from this camp for only forty-eight hours. They therefore could possibly arrive and talk themselves into the confidence of the gang members present at this time. They would present 'made up' stories of goings on in their respective villages. If this happened and things seemed quite normal they were then to give a signal and part two of the attack could commence.

If, however, they were sussed or immediately taken captive Bobby was to wait a certain amount of time before putting his Plan B into operation. All the patrol were fully conversant with Plans A and B.

It took an interminable age to finally crawl into position. Not a shot or shout was heard so hopefully everything was looking rosey for their mission to proceed to conclusion.

Once the tablecloth of darkness covered the surrounds Emmett became aware of the tightening of his intestinal regions. His heartbeat would have increased fifty fold. He sensed the nearness of 'them or us', which was the vital factor. And the meaning of it.

No stray bullets, no stepping out of synchronized advance line, no chance of being caught in crossfire, no indiscipline. It had all been well rehearsed. Now, like a first night, let the play commence. Those in the wings must take centre stage. It was 'curtain up' time.

Hand signals proceeded along the line and everyone 'leopard-crawled' the final hundred yards.

Voices and dry wood crackling on an open fire could be heard as the entrance came ever closer. That beautiful scented aroma of wood fire spiralled into the night air. Not a guard was insight. The patrol had to await the signal before any further advance.

It finally came, the resonant call of the grey lourie bird 'go away, go away' from one of their ex-terrorists as he ambled out of the quite well concealed entrance. He pretended to have a pee near a large shadowy tree as Simeon, one of their trackers, sidled up to him at the other side of the tree. They talked hurriedly for a few minutes and then both returned to their respective previous positions.

Simeon reported to Bobby with the other two reservists listening attentively. Emmett was on guard and would be briefed in turn.

If there were many people, terrorists, within the cave then immediate plans of attack might have to be rearranged he thought. Bobby would have to work that one out and relay his plans pronto.

Emmett was now getting really anxious. It was almost 'shoot out' time and this would be a big moment in his young life.

In short sharp whispers Bobby laid his plan of attack. He called everyone around him: "Now listen up. From what I can understand there are women cooking over an open fire. That's in a corner to the left. Next to them are food baskets stacked up against the cave wall.

"Now, just inside the entrance and to the right is a cache of arms, rifles, and ammo boxes."

Simeon then prompted: "There are two men sleeping close by, fendi."

Bobby continued: "There are four terrs talking to our two and trying to establish whether their stories are true. Okay?

"Now we don't move 'till we see our guys causing a commotion and being followed out of the cave by the terrs. That's when we take them out with one burst or two from you Emmett."

"I will then rush in and lob a couple of eggs (grenades) into the rear of the cave and get back out. Whoever else is in there will be exiting at the same time or else it will be too bad for them. Understood so far?

"Simeon I want you to take prisoners with Mr. Emmett. Don't shoot more than is necessary. Keep your eyes open everyone and watch your backs." He then changed to an ethnic language and was cut short for within thirty seconds of outlining his plan their fellows rushed out with the terrorists firing after them.

Bullets sprayed over the patrol's heads in the onrush. Bobby held his fire 'till literally the last ten yards of their advance. A well directed burst of 9mm ripped into the two leading the rush. They dropped in drunken strides as Emmett pressed the trigger of his stengun hopefully aiming at the figure who was running off to his right, firing aimlessly into the night. Emmett kept his finger tightly on the tiny cold curved sliver of steel spraying his allotted area. The first figure had eventually fallen into bushes about twenty yards from him. Another was moaning, but hidden, seemingly quite close to him. Emmett was now upright looking for any movement. His nearest tracker had located the injured man and was about to chop him with his machete when Emmett stopped him.

"No, no. no," he yelled, "we need him alive.

"Have you seen where the others went?"

151

"Over that way, fendi. Atari."

Emmett was warned. Be careful.

His trigger finger itched to press once more. In the momentary silence he heard stumbling steps brushing through the undergrowth behind him. One or two of the gang could have got past and were escaping. He had been told not to follow on his own. At that moment the explosion took place, two muffled eruptions increased to a rocking blast of cacophonous proportion.

Scarlet and yellow flames broke out of the cave followed by a series of minor explosions.

Emmett could feel the ground shudder beneath him as he lay behind a large tree trunk They had been instructed to 'fall flat' when they heard the first bang, no matter where they were.

Had there been terrorists trapped within the cave he wondered as he kept his hands cushioning his ears? Explosions kept repeating over the next five minutes, obviously the arms cache was now obliterated. Whether the entrance was walled off would only be known when Bobby gave the signal to re-group. Provided Bobby was okay? This suddenly struck home as Emmett tried to gather his senses together again.

The smell of cordite hung heavy over the area. Shrieks of human agony emanated from somewhere to his right. He would investigate immediately.

Now was a dangerous time he had been warned. Wounded terrorists could be armed and like a caged lion or cornered cobra would be at their most ferocious.

Simeon suddenly appeared at Emmett's side with another tracker. They indicated their wish to survey the area where the intermittent cries came from.

He lead them in arrow formation, his sten duly refitted with a new magazine of 9mm bullets, his finger twitching with anxiety, eyes, peering like owls, now well used to the darkness ever alert for strange shadows or movement.

Simeon pointed to their left where an outcrop of rock rose above a clump of scrub bushes. They halted for a moment or so and heard sobbing from that area.

Emmett lead on in short silent steps, eyes covering the hundred and eighty degrees before him. The others, on either side, doing likewise. Their machetes were raised in striking position.

A single shot rang out. The whirr of the bullet was heard above their heads as they dropped to crouch positions.

"Hold your fire," he hear Bobby's words in his bemused brain. He would, for the moment, at any rate. Waving his two companions to move away in a flanking direction he inched forward towards the bushes, now only about ten paces away.

Moans and intermittent movement became more evident from the dim and dense beyond. Emmett decided to give the bush a burst of 9mm. Short, sharp, followed by a series of howls and cries from within the area was the result.

Both of his companions rushed the clump at the same time and within a minute shouted back that they had one wounded terrorist under their control.

Out came the wretched sight of a bloody body being dragged along by the two. It was alive and complaining. Simeon had a rifle in his other hand alongside his faithful machete.

Emmett turned to where they had set out from and saw Bobby with two of the patrol looking down at what looked like a couple of dead bodies. These had obviously been dragged from where they fell, found by the trackers.

He joined Bobby and they discussed the operation briefly before realising that their patrol was one short.

"Where's Gitau?" questioned Bobby of Simeon firstly and then all the other faces. None could give an explanation. He had been positioned to the side of Emmett at the advance. Where was he now? Emmett proffered a snippet.

"I let loose at one terrorist who was breaking away over that direction," pointing to their right and quite near the outcrop from where they had just brought the wounded one.

"Perhaps there was another wounded and Gitau maybe chased after him?" Or as Bobby suddenly said "maybe he's decided to do a bunk and return to his bed fellows?

"Oh my god I'd never thought of that," said a perplexed Emmett.

Bobby then took command and ordered the prisoners' arms to be tied behind their backs. He checked the wounds and told Simeon to "do what you think best".

With that Bobby took Emmett to look at what remained of the cave and its entrance. Two reservists were left on guard and to listen out for any non forest noises.

There had been a thundering rock fall and most of the entrance was now blocked. High up they could see a gap between the original and rubble. Perhaps one could climb through it? Their rubber bound torches came into prominence for the first time. Nothing could be heard from within but the pungent smell of cordite exuded from the crevice.

Bobby offered Emmett the dubious choice of climbing up and through the gap.

"You are younger than me so have a crack at it. No one can be alive in there I bet."

He handed his sten to Bobby and climbed up for about ten feet before reaching the gaping hole. Inside he could see some smouldering pieces of wood with embers, every now and again, being fanned into action by a passing draft.

There was a lot of rubble ahead of him and he didn't know whether he would be able to reach the bottom where the grenades would have landed. The only sounds were of moving and falling stones disturbed by him as he climbed in and over the fallen rocks.

Bobby was to call him through their walkie-talkies to ascertain the damage and his findings. There would be little to report as very little space remained. There had been a monster cave-in and whatever escaped the explosion was now buried twelve foot deep under rubble. Emmett didn't think the cave could be used again save for the odd 'sleeper' perhaps.

He was on his way back when Bobby came alive on the radio. He told him he would report on his emergence back into decent mountain air as he was finding it difficult to breathe within the acrid smell and taste of spent explosive.

It had obviously been a successful action, an entire wipe out of the cave, a few dead 'terrs', and one wounded prisoner for further interrogation once returned to Karirana.

After about thirty minutes on their return trail down the mountain their lead tracker signalled a halt.

They listened. Faint voices became louder. The patrol sidled into the undergrowth beside the track and waited.

Simeon nudged Bobby and whispered "its Gitau, I know his voice." With that the two of them moved back onto the track.

A couple of minutes later two figures emerged through the gloom, the one in front had hands tied behind his back and was half stumbling on each stride as Gitau pushed him along with the point of his machete.

"Good work Gitau," or something like that would be the welcome given to him by Bobby in his own language.

Both eyes of the prisoner seemed exaggerated in their size and stared as they surveyed the patrol now encircling him. The prisoner had a ripped thigh with blood congealing around a gaping wound. Most probably a couple of rounds of 9mm from Emmett's first barrage had caught him in his flight of escape.

When, doubly checked by Simeon and Bobby, the two 'terrs' were strung together by a long length of tree bark with hands tied to ankles. They would walk in the line, one behind the other, and if the patrol should meet with enemy opposition it would be difficult for them to escape as they were now well hobbled.

It reminded Emmett of seeing calves being loaded off the Aran Islands onto hookers and then being transported to the Galway or Clare mainland. Once hobbled in this fashion they were prevented from movement onboard the boat.

The return trip took another two hours to reach the farmlands below where Bobby had radioed through to Karirana for transport to pick them up. When back on Zungu land they relaxed beside a farm track awaiting the dawn.

At base they were debriefed in the ops room. Their route and the map position of the cave were marked on the vast handmade plan of the Mount Amma region. A large cross in red felt pen now covered the cave – OOU, 'out of use' pencilled in beside it.

That hot bath was the best thing in Emmett's world an hour later followed by a right regal full Irish breakfast (without the puddings but double eggs, sausages and rashers). The jackpot was the two pieces of fried bread atop his immense plate.

He had always, since childhood, loved his fried bread with runny orange yoked free range eggs atop the crisp slices, preferably brown and homemade. This however, was just as good. He wasn't at all tired and supposed the adrenalin was still pumping.

Asking if he could borrow a horse as he wished to ride over the farm and this was duly granted. On that ride he thought back on the happenings of the previous twenty-four hours. How fortunate he was to be alive. How lucky he had been in his first burst of gunfire against the enemy and fearful he had been on hearing that single shot that whizzed above his head. He was intact and relished the idea of another encounter and questioned what it would be like to be wounded?

Emmett didn't feel a thing, good, bad or indifferent, about shooting at someone. It was them or him he argued. The answer was simple. After all, this was a sort of war, killing would happen at anytime, any day, anywhere. He wondered what his parents and family back home would think of all this? He wouldn't tell them, not until much, much later.

That night he slept a deep sleep. Nothing emerged from dreamland.

16

Hurling "eggs" from above

Through an interpreter, Kosmos Ibunya explained it thus:
  "I was taken by force when herding cattle and goats. A group of people moved from the foothills spreading across a wide area. They rushed in grabbing whoever was near them. I was one. I tried to fight back but with only a little stick I had no chance. It all happened quickly. Our arms were tied behind our backs. We were herded like animals, into a gully and made to follow in single line behind two armed men. There were also armed men behind us. After a walk of one hour we were rested and made to squat in the undergrowth. I noticed two guards climbed trees to survey the area behind us. We were given a short rest and then made to follow on again. All the time we were climbing higher into the mountains. I counted nine of us who had been taken. We arrived at a clearing in the forest with a little river flowing beside a rock. We were made to squat again in three lines of three and told to keep our heads down. I was very thirsty. I was too frightened to ask for a drink. We were pushed into a dirty hut. The door was bolted. It was dark. Slowly we started to talk to each other. I knew most of the others. We come from nearby villages. We ask each other's age. One was sixteen, the rest under fourteen. We were frightened and didn't know what to do. We were all of the same tribe.
  Sometime, I don't know how many hours later, but it was nearly dark outside, we were allowed out to toilet in the bush. We then got a bowl of mealiemeal and our hands were untied. The hut door was bolted from the outside. The floor was damp so we sat and lay down beside each other to keep warm. Next morning we were brought outside and given a lesson on why we were here, why our help was needed and what we had to do to keep the country for ourselves – not the white man. We were all too frightened to ask questions. We noticed armed guards all round the camp. They had no need to tie us up. We were too scared to try to escape. Clearing up jobs like collecting firewood and carrying water were given us. A large opening into the mountain could be seen near some rocks. On top of these sat three armed men. There were women cooking and making clothes, uniforms of some kind. A couple of army types, like soldiers, with military styled clothes swaggered around the camp. They were obviously in charge and shouted orders. This daily routine carried on for two weeks or thereabouts. Our group of

kids became a unit with a wish for escape. We made many plans but never attempted one of them. Too many eyes were watching.

Four of us were chosen to become food carriers one day. We went with a group who would raid the village's stock driving off whatever they could into the forest where we and others would catch and slaughter them. We cut them up and on dried hide stretchers carried the food up to the camp. That evening we discussed this trip. It was felt we had a chance of escape when waiting for the others to return with the cattle. Only two armed guards had accompanied us and they were keeping their eyes on the group below them. Five of us wanted to try and escape the very next time but were dissuaded by the others who felt it better to wait and get it right. Then all could benefit in one move. I noticed we were part of sixty or seventy youngsters who had been detained. Some were now carrying guns with others like our group the camp labourers. Perhaps we were all to be trained fighters. But some of us didn't want this and were prepared to fight only for our freedom from this group who were UMA. One morning four of us were told to clean the cave. I had heard some talk about what was in there and was looking forward to finding out for myself. It was a Seebu (hole) with a tall narrow entrance, a split of two big rocks which opened up into a large underground room. Outside light came through the entrance to see what was going on inside. It was quite clean. Some senior uniformed people lived here. In one corner there were small wooden boxes piled on top of each other, eight or ten high and stretching along a wall of overhanging rock. Next to these were rifles standing along the wall as if ready to be grabbed up and put straight to use. There were sleeping bunks with some grey blankets all over the floor, probably twelve or so. Near the entrance was a fire. Various gang members kept warming themselves. They were returning from sentry duty. A number of young women brought food from the main kitchen outside. They were also seen cleaning rifles and machetes. In another corner was a large table and on it were maps. A pile of paraffin lamps were nearby with cans alongside. Stacks of dry wood were piled near the entrance. This was the HQ of the gang, one of UMA's. We wondered how many they had?

One of my friends had a small knife which he managed to keep hidden. He suggested, on our next trip out into the forest, he would mark certain trees on the way down and on the return journey. This would leave a trail, only known to him and those who wanted to escape with him, when the time came. His little group had only one thought and that was to escape to their families. They would succeed in their wish. It must have been in the third month of camp life when the chance to do so came. We were on another daylight stock theft when the gangsters were ambushed as they were driving their animals back to the foothills. There was lots of shooting and shouting. We were hidden in the forest awaiting the stock. The guards became worried by the shootings. They didn't seem to know what to do, and climbed up trees to get a better look onto the ground below. We, on the *signal of a bird call, took to the forest, all in different directions and ran like the wind for a good five minutes. Not a shot was fired after us. We had planned it well. To lie up until nightfall then using various birdcalls meet up at a certain giant wild fig tree. From there we had to travel quietly through the barren area to the nearest HG post and village. Knowing it would be dangerous when we saw there was security ready to fight the forest gangs, even if we were taken prisoner by them, we were happy we could prove our innocence."*

Such a statement was instrumental in bringing Uma's movements to a standstill. As it transpired this brave little troop of cattle kids slept that night in a gulley near to their village and Home Guard post. They waited for the cattle, sheep and goats to be driven out to their grazing and the farm workers walked to their prospective lands before intermingling and integrating with them.

The kids were immediately taken inside the village fortress and handed over to the Home Guard who then proceeded to grill them on their escape and internment. Radio contact was made with district HQ where a GSU was immediately despatched to their village outpost.

Once again they were questioned, this time more thoroughly by the two Zungus In charge.

After another three hours a plan of attack was formulated with Kosmos and two other kids agreeing to return with the GSU into the forest and 'take out' the gang and weapons at their hideout.

The very fact that trees had been marked made it easy for the unit to follow at speed and set up their ambush and assault positions without being noticed. The gang were too arrogant and confident that no one would follow them up into their forest domain. They, of course, had not counted on the guile of the escapees who would eventually lead to their downfall and utter defeat.

This was part of a new strategy known as CDD – capture, disseminate, defeat - which evidently had been carried out with great effect in Kenya during the Mau Mau days. Dickie Barker had brought the idea forward at an FRO meeting and it was gradually being put into operation all along the foothills of the Mandaras. The initial success rate was high.

With escapees, such as these young kids, it was easy for the authorities to ascertain all information relevant to that particular situation and camp. They had been willing informants.

What the FRO needed most were captured terrorists who, once put through the 'griller' would offer information of a much more rewarding kind. The FRO needed to get into the psyche of the gang, learn their strategies, movements, numbers and most importantly their next or upcoming attacks.

Later on the FRO, Home Guard and General Service Units merged to form a covert group who would respond immediately and infiltrate the gangs hideouts. This actually proved the turning point in the war against terror. But this wasn't for a further twelve months.

Emmett was asked if he would accompany Ray Marsh, their leading pilot, who would fly a recce along the Mandaras.

Every couple of days Ray would survey the region looking for gang movement, stray cattle, sheep and goats, and fires above and within the forest line. All 'spottings' were chronicled on the ops map and interesting info was built on these findings.

They flew off in his Cessna and expected to be up for a couple of hours.

Ray had been in the South African air force seconded overseas in the '39/45 world war. He was regarded as one of the best pilots in Ukenza. He now ran an export/import business in Kenzi and offered his services to the FRO at the outbreak of violence. He loved flying and knew every nook and cranny of the country. This would be some experience thought Emmett.

After an hour of crisscrossing the entire region he asked Ray to fly up near Mount Amma. He wanted to see if they could identify the cave and surrounds of his recent patrol.

Ray decided to fly from the opposite side of the peak and circle down from west to east via the north side. Emmett sat on the mountain side peering out at the peak from a few hundred feet above. It was quite steep and jagged near the top and although not snow clad at this time of the year, must be highly impressive when covered.

Ray banked the Cessna the opposite way and spiralled down a gully almost at tree tops height. Emmett's stomach was left some hundreds of feet above him and he felt suddenly nauseous. The plane evened out as they sped down the mountainside. They then shot upwards and banked to the right and ran up the centre of a parallel gully. Emmett was now almost in touching distance of the trees when a line of tracer bullets zoomed past their right wing not too far from Emmett's window seat.

Ray immediately took the kite into a steep climb getting out of range of whoever had opened fire on them.

"Two can play that game my friends," said he.

"Emmett see that box behind my seat? Lean over, open it and take out a couple of eggs (grenades). We will show them just who they are dealing with. Okay?"

Emmett did what he was told and placed two of these cold ribbed 'eggs' on his lap.

"Good. Now the procedure is as follows. Listen up. You must pull the pin with your right hand and keep holding the clasp down tightly in your left hand whilst I line up our approach. You must then open your door with your right hand

and strong arm it out keeping it open wide enough for you to lean out bringing your left hand over your lap and out through the door. Okay so far?"

"Yes, I'm with you, just."

"Then wait for my signal to throw it downwards through the opening. Okay?"

"Yes."

"Right then. Get ready and be prepared for an immediate upward climb. It will leave your guts in your garters. Right. Okay?"

"Fine. Yes."

"Here goes then."

Emmett could see the leaves of the trees as clearly as if walking beside them. He could even see the ground below when all of a sudden he spotted a group of terrorists looking up at them.

"One, two, three, throw."

Emmett conjured up all his strength and let the grenade fly downwards on top of the now scattering gang. The instant climb had commenced and he had automatically closed the door when he heard the bang of the explosion which slightly rocked the plane. It took him a good few seconds before he felt he was back in the living world once again.

"Be ready for the next sortie. We will scare the shit out of those bastards. There are plenty more eggs in the basket. I'll come from a different angle this time but just be ready for my count. Okay?"

"Yes, I'm fine now. This is quite fun, isn't it?"

"It won't be if we catch a stray tracer."

He banked away from the gulley and crossed over the adjoining spur before banking left again. This time Emmett realised Ray was coming back over them from sideways on which would make the terrorists' angle of fire rather acute as these were large trees below. Their line of sight would be difficult.

"I don't expect to do much damage you know," he said leaning over to Emmett, "but it will scatter and give them the fright of their lives. Get ready. Here we go. One, two, three, go for it!"

This time he didn't immediately climb but increased his speed and was long gone over the hill before they spotted another trail of tracer emerging from the dense forest. This time it was nowhere near them.

"I'm going to circle a few more times and radio their position back to base. Just keep an eye out for any sightings."

Back at Karirana Emmett battled a myriad of feelings as he showered for what seemed an hour. Exhilaration and wonderment would have been topmost. He thought back to the unusual method of combat he had been involved in. Never once had he feared for his life. He supposed he never had time to think about such things.

These had been an eye opener of a few days. He wondered how many more such 'breaks from farming' would be in the offing. He would be willing to serve at any time anywhere. His adrenaline was pumping.

His next few days were spent in an admin capacity and learning the ropes of the operations room. He would be filling in for others who would be returning to their farms, like him the following week – he hoped.

17

A Castle in the Bush

Christopher noticed a difference in his master. He didn't dare ask where he had been or what he had got up to but there was something 'changed' about him. He didn't seem to be as exuberant as before, the dogs even picked it up and kept very quiet some two steps behind him.

Emmett didn't shout as much as usual and Christopher detected a sadness in his eyes. Only when Anna arrived for the weekend did his former self assert itself even though they kept very much to themselves and were off in Melelo for most of it. Christopher knew he had experienced something quite unusual. Perhaps one day his master would tell him all?

The only people Emmett talked to about his mountain sojourn were Ian and Jan whom he visited the second day after returning.

"He's the most amazing pilot," said Ian on hearing of Ray Marsh's exploits.

"I've known him for ten years or so. He's been up here on many occasions and he has assisted me on many of my early car rallies in Uganda and Kenya. Hasn't an ounce of fear and his timing is knife edge. Grand fellow altogether."

Emmett suddenly realised he had never spoken to Ray about where he was farming or where he came from. He had been solely interested in the job at hand.

"Enjoy it then?" smiled Ian as he said he was finished with the task at hand, "let's have a drink to welcome you back in one piece. Jan will love hearing about your exploits."

Her emerald eyes widened immeasurably as he recounted his stay at Karirana.

"I sincerely hope we don't have to get to these extremes up here if trouble should ever break out in the district," she pointedly passed her remark at her husband about to be pilot!

"We have it all sussed out my darling and we are ready for anything and everything. Buster and his crew are doing a sterling job, aren't they Emmett?"

"Well I think so. I'm having a 'report back' session with them tomorrow. That should be of interest. Perhaps we can go together Ian?"

"Fine by me. I'll pick you up at the Ratilli."

There was a full compliment of farming personnel at the meeting. Firstly Emmett had to pinpoint the cave on Mount Amma and the gullies up and down which they travelled. Then the position of the grenade attack. This episode tickled their fancy and lots of them wanted to try the tactic in the forests to the west of their own region. Not much happened, as far as they knew, within them other than honey hunters and game poachers. Ideal they all agreed.

Buster then presented a sitrep (situation report) of the ongoing action taken by all the pockets of FRO around the country. Emmett thought him very thorough and up to date with their own group right in the forefront of information. A satisfying position and as all agreed, when at his conclusion, he received a rapturous round of applause.

Shirra and her team of farm ladies (wives) laid on a sumptuous spread and many drinks were taken by one and all.

"I'll have to call on you to hear more of the intimate details," she whispered on passing close by. Their eyes met for that moment of yearning which inevitably occurs when magnetic forces are at work.

Emmett hoped her visit wouldn't coincide with Anna's weekend. But then he dismissed the thought. He and Anna would spend all of it up in their love nest, Melelo, away from the world and its wicked witches!

Ian, on their return trip, mapped out his thoughts on security measures. It looked as if just about every angle had been covered with a countermeasure planned on Buster's drawing board.

"We must protect our staff and make it impossible for any subversive infiltration to our labour lines. You must have informants well disguised within your ranks. I suggest Christopher as an ideal one and choose one other; a 'Tuk' would be preferable. They seem to know everything first. I've already put my plan in operation. Here we are then and well done on your trip, a bloody fine presentation too might I say. You are certainly one of us now. Cheers."

Emmett pondered his words as he collected his vehicle at the Ratilli and drove the final mile to his homestead. He was already sketching in his mind a security fence with a watch tower overlooking the labour lines and entrance to the farm compound.

Christopher had waited up with the dogs on the veranda. He went inside and Emmett knew that meant a hot mug of tea prior to turning in.

His dogs were so disciplined he thought as they stayed within his garden and behind the gate over which they could easily jump. Emmett revelled in their welcome and let them run ahead as he set out for a short 'pee run'. It was a starlit night with the air scented by the lone moon flower growing at the end of his house, a legacy of some errant bird who dropped the seed many years ago. The shrubs long ivory lily-like funnel flowers exuded the most pungent sweet scent, but only after darkness had fallen. At dawn they lay limp and scentless, probably cringing at the oncoming heat of the day. It was necessary to have but one, two would make it overpowering.

"Well done lovely bird whoever you were," he would call out each time his nostrils thrilled at the aroma offered to the night!

Two overseas letters arrived in the same post, ferried out by Jaswant, one Sunday morning. Emmett left them unopened until the plane took off on its return flight to Kenzi. An extensive 'drive around' had taken place. Bhogal seemed happy with what he saw.

The letter from home was the first opened. Its contents were not pleasant reading. His father was not at all well, in fact was in hospital in Galway. It was prostrate trouble and Emmett was being warned. His sister Sinead had been the scribe and she told of how badly Mam was taking it. "Be prepared to fly home if things get worse." Emmett was stunned. His eyes glassed over as he sat on the veranda not able to reread the scant two pages of immaculate script. He knew his mother would be devastated. She had relied on her beloved Patrick for everything throughout their life. Sinead, who was ten years older than Emmett, was a teacher, unmarried and would now have to take time off to look after their mother.

He wondered whether he should fly home straight away or await further news. It was a quiet time on the farm so he could get away. Perhaps he should wait, however, as things could get better? He would hold fire for the next few days and then decide. He realised the umbilical cord was very much in place. His natural love of family was deep.

The second letter was full of fun, interest and ambitious plans. But Justin's energetic prose passed swiftly overhead obliterated by the trauma of his sister's revelation. He would put Justin's letter aside and reread it thoroughly when his head became less confused.

He needed to clear his mind.

"Christopher tell the syces to saddle up the ponies please." He would gallop his 'blues' away and hopefully return clear headed. It was obvious his father was terminally ill. He could do nothing about that but comforting his mother would surely be a rewarding prize for all? In his contract he had insisted on a 'compassionate' clause for return airfare at full wages if and when absent. Emmett couldn't help reminding himself of his good fortune in meeting up with genuine ex-pats prior to his African venture and for taking their advice. The Bhogals hadn't liked some of these clauses but had included them in his final written contract nevertheless.

He drove his ponies Corrib and Mask to the ultimate that afternoon. He made Langat ride upsides him until the ponies started to tire. Emmett felt much better on the walk home. His mind was clear. He would await a further bulletin and then fly out immediately for however long was necessary.

On returning to the homestead he got on the wireless to Kenzi and explained his problem to Vijay who took the call. He understood and agreed to put a plan in place and would alert their travel agent. Emmett hoped it would not be soon – better later, when he could arrange everything for his departure.

He put a message through to Jeri to ask Anna to make contact A.S.A.P.

That evening he visited Ian and Jan to tell them his unfortunate news. They would keep a close eye on things when he decided to depart they said.

"Not to worry old man. You're one of us, one of the family."

"I agree," said Jan "especially with your choice of staying until you hear the dreaded news which sounds inevitable. We both understand. My mother died of big 'C' so we know the feelings aligned with the curse. Chin up and we'll all cover for you."

How confident he felt on his drive home accompanied by a fresh soda loaf and six jars of marmalade and jam. After supper he sat on his veranda and opened Justin's letter. From Perth, Western Australia, it painted a vivid picture of spectacular success. After nine months of internship in the Colman Swift Memorial Hospital he was in the right place at the right time and got an offer he couldn't refuse.

Since then he had been the junior surgeon in a partnership of three, regarded as the most prominent practice in the State.

He had bought a small but beautifully sited bungalow overlooking the sea north of Perth. Girlfriends were plentiful and he had taken up golf with a passion. He was happy to remain 'down under' but would return to Ireland next year for two months. He hoped the others would follow suit and they could all meet up again as originally planned.

Emmett had written to all four of the gang. His letters went through an intermediary in Dublin who then forwarded them to their respective continents. He wasn't the greatest letter writer but did manage to get one out to each of his friends annually. Justin's was the sole reply. He pondered on this lack of communication and felt unhappy and a little lost by their silence. He vowed he would continue to make contact whatever the outcome. Living out here in the 'sticks' was quite lonely. And one needed friends, all over the place.

His family back home burdened his mind and even with Sinatra in the background he found it difficult to relax.

Geronimo's second race was the coming weekend. He was in superb form as witnessed by his gallop that morning. Langat had done a grand job whilst he was away in the mountains. Emmett didn't expect him to win as, once again, he was entered in a mile and a half race. Experience and atmosphere were the factors he wished Geronimo to comprehend. A good run would be a bonus. The objective, the Spencer Trimon Hurdle at Kitos in a month's time was foremost in his mind. Geronimo was on a learning curve.

Emmett spent the weekend in the Club at Urukan. The gymkhana meeting was held on Tom Stafford's farm just five miles out of town. Anna met up with him for lunch on the Saturday. They then went out to walk the course and see that Geronimo had settled in satisfactorily. Anna had two rides so was keen to 'feel' the track and listen to any advice Emmett could offer.

It was a very tight circular track whose bends, although wide, would not be easy to ride. He had heard back home that on such a track you must get to the front from the break and try to let no one pass. "Keep tight to the rail and get your horse onto the correct leg from the off," were his words of wisdom to his eager Anna.

Emmett decided that he would hang back at the start and let Geronimo come wide around the field of runners over the final two furlongs. It would be a good 'blow out'. He wanted to get a decent price about him for the hurdle. Howard and Rachel would then be able to get something back for their faith in him. He, himself, would love a little 'punt' too. Anna would place the bet.

That night she remarked on how much weight he had lost. She lay in his arms as he recounted every minute of his 'dice with death'. He had been lucky, he knew that. Next time it might be very different. She told him that her group would be called on to do exactly what Emmett had just done. They were to work with the FRO in a covert operation right along the front. Her ladies would act as food carriers and would return with ex terrorists into their hideouts. On their next food or wood carrying journey they would pass back whatever information was possible. That too would be highly dangerous but their hatred of things corrupt; UMA and *Makinto,* outweighed their desire for safety. The FRO gratefully accepted their voluntary entry into the fight for freedom.

"Will you be going on any of these safaris?" he questioned as she moved on top of him.

"No. Jeri will not allow me to be away from the children. No, I'm going to be kept in the background and hopefully unexposed – not like I am at this moment." She gurgled with glee as she teased his ears with snake like strikes from her rapier tongue.

Emmett felt really good to have her body next to him once again. Three weeks had been too long an absence he decided.

Their lovemaking was long, gentle, embracing every facet of emotion, every little nuance of body and mind. In finality they slithered into 'spoon positions' and slept the sleep of spent lovers.

They awoke at first light with an obvious lust for love. This time Anna joined Emmett in the shower. They washed each other down with his Lentheric gel. Suds and fingers finding crevices yet undiscovered at this hour of a morning.

He pressed her body into the corner of the shower. Her arms encircled his neck as he lifted her legs to straddle him above his waist.

Hot spray cascaded down his shoulders and back as his pillar glided into her soapy cavern. Anna gripped tighter and tighter as he discovered yet again, her most sacred place. Lips bit and drew blood while limbs pumped gently in an exotic rhythm. All the time the warmth of the water produced a steam that enveloped everything. It was dense and divine. Emmett never wished it to end but the water was cooling down and soon a cold shower would sort them out.

"Bring them back to reality," he tempted to say but Anna's lips wouldn't let him out of her grip. Her legs started to slip down over his hips, her strength on the wane.

Suddenly it was a cold shower.

"God almighty its cold Emmett. Let me out of here," as she pushed past his still rigid frame and out the curtain grabbing a large towel from the rail.

"Chicken," Emmett cried after her as once again he soaped himself down. His manliness subsiding.

After a flurry of washing off suds he shut off the taps and found Anna at the ready with an outstretched towel.

"Welcome back lover boy. Hope you didn't do any damage to yourself?" as she touched him up, finding nothing in response.

"Now for a big breakfast with lots of energy replacements."

They did just that as it would be their only meal 'till after the races. "Perhaps we will find a tuna sandwich and a glass of milk on the course somewhere," he quipped.

Anna rode a blinder to finish second in the third race. She would have won in another stride. She came a close fourth in the fifth race. Another polished performance and he praised her highly, as did the owners she rode for.

Emmett had a bad day, no winners but Geronimo ran exactly as he wished and finished mid field of twelve. Nothing impressive for public viewing but Emmett felt the power between his knees, a power that only needed to be tapped. He felt the horse was just right for the hurdle. Now he needed to school him attentively 'till the race. Langat had seen to his stamina needs by relentless cantering over miles of open country on Ratilli. These bursts of racing speed would now have put his breathing right. All he had to do was get him to the meeting, well schooled over hurdles, in sound condition.

The Staffords held a barbecue in their extensive garden afterwards which everyone was invited to. A really smashing Afro-Cuban band kept a tiny slate floor packed all evening. It ended with a Conga around the outskirts of garden, shrubbery and outbuildings where various couples took the opportunity to vanish!

Love making somehow wasn't necessary after all the spent energies of the day. Emmett and Anna lay as one in total abandon later that night. Their reunion weekend a total success.

A European farmstead was burnt to the ground whilst the owners were on a trip to Kenzi.

This caused an outcry in the papers with blame being evenly distributed between Uma and *Makinto*. The President had to come down strongly on his elite guard and the security forces had to tackle the ever increasing strength of Uma. These were the thoughts on everyone's mind – black and white. Opposition parties launched into tirades against Victor Ubugu. He wasn't able to handle his forces they kept reiterating. Demonstrations down the streets of Kenzi and Urukan were taking place with regularity now. These were passive and were fronted by hundreds of women clad in white and red robes.

Security forces, including police, just stood by. Obviously the multitudes were not prepared to trade violence with violence so peaceful displays accompanied their voices, raised at times, in condemnation of the government.

Emmett wondered whether Victor Ubugu could withstand this ground swell of criticism. He feared one day it would erupt and bloodshed, on a massive scale, would be witnessed. "Please God" he prayed in momentary thought "it should not happen when he was near or party to it." He was quite prepared to fight a straight war but not an onslaught of bestial brutality when minds were far from thinking logically. Emmett had seen on British Movietone news scenes of mass demonstrations that had got out of hand when a single shot had been fired. What happened then did not bear thinking about.

"The African, once motivated, was a volatile person, too easy it would be to set the fuse that sparked a volcanic eruption," so said Buster at one of his meetings.

At least, Emmett thought to himself, out here on the plains he could see them coming. Or was that also wishful thinking?

Anna asked a favour of him. "Next time my group come to Melelo would you please address them on your recent trips up the Mandaras? They would like to know what to expect."

"Yes of course I will but mums the word. Okay? By the way, how do you know that you haven't got an informer within your ranks?"

168

"We don't, is the plain answer, but we do have a fairly intensive screening before someone is invited to join. We are wary of volunteers."

"Keep it that way for heavens sake. Trust me."

"There will be a group next weekend and they want to camp out this time. They feel they are a bit soft and might not be able to handle the mountains."

"That's fine by me. I will drill a bit of military discipline into them, like I saw on my trip, if you would like?"

"Yes, that's a good idea. It will put them more on a war footing, I think you guys call it, eh?"

"Yea, that's it all right. Fine I'll put some ideas down on paper. In the meantime what are you going to do this weekend?"

"Sleep – and I mean sleep, good clean 'la la' master, if you don't mind. It's been a hard week for me and I feel drained. Know what I mean?"

She got up off the veranda, with a lingering smile, and asked Christopher for some tea.

Emmett had heard from Howard about a castle that had been built by an eccentric Belgian scientist fifty or sixty years ago. It was on the border of Ukenza and the Congo some thirty miles south of Lake Nduga. Travelling across country and on back roads he estimated it was a two hour drive away. It was evidently now owned by a wild life photographer who had enclosed it by ring fencing the estate and was rearing indigenous wild animals. He was American and married a Congolese lady of wealth.

Anna agreed to the idea of a visit. It would be fascinating to see up close such an enterprise she said. And it would be a lovely change – a holiday!

Emmett asked the workshop to check out his landrover and he put out the word, through Christopher, for anyone interested in visiting this quite remote area. They would set out next morning after a lazy breakfast.

Two volunteers emerged for the safari, both from reserves near Fuda the border town. One was a junior mechanic, the other a labourer. Emmett agreed to both of them accompanying him. Christopher packed a picnic lunch and added a tin of Sadsa (mealie meal) and vegetables for the extra passengers.

Roads were rough, river crossings deep and rocky, the countryside uninteresting in the main. It was mostly bush scrubland (very thorny) where only the shy Francolin and Guinea Fowl mixed with lizards and snakes. The odd hill raised its head with a dozen or so indigenous trees, like the wild fig and marula popping up in a fifty mile drive.

Nearing the outskirts of Fuda he noticed a very battered and broken sign heralding Mandalay Sanctuary, twenty miles. Proprietors: Jay and Jasmine Freedo.

That was the objective, so off he turned to the right and headed up a really badly corrugated murrum road. It was noon so he asked Anna to pick a place for their picnic. Like a homing pigeon she smelt the water well before they came upon a stream which crossed the road.

"This is from the lake," said one of his passengers.

They found a pleasant spot just upstream from a drift (cemented causeway) next to an over hanging Acacia tree whose lowest branches were tightly packed with a multitude of weaverbird nests.

It was a local folk law tale that nests close to water meant a drought. Nests high up meant a monsoon. Emmett had learnt this from Christopher on one of their trips out and about together. These nests were on the bottommost tips of spindly twigs so he feared for the worst in the upcoming rainy season. He remarked on this to Anna who was busy laying out the groundsheet and unpacking the picnic.

Both of his staff took themselves off into the bush to most probably relieve themselves. Emmett lobbed a couple of rocks into the pool testing its depth. It was shallow so probably no crocodiles would be in residence!

An hour later they arrived over a narrow cattle grid between stone walls onto Mandalay. Emmett drove very slowly up the narrow track so that he didn't raise dust and he was also on the lookout for game. He wondered what they stocked in their sanctuary?

A very fancy stone built arch with the Mandalay sign hanging in central position welcomed one to a wild but well maintained garden landscape. Two bougainvilleas, an orange on the left and a purple on the right, had climbed up the arch and met in colourful profusion above the sign. All natural vegetation interspersed with wild flowers and shrubs fitted the ambience of the thatched haven that suddenly came into view as they rounded a bend which curved to the right of a large outcrop of rock.

The track then divided around another outcrop, but a much lower one, which formed the centrepiece of a well filled rock garden.

A golden retriever bounced ahead of its companion a black Labrador to meet the visitors.

Emmett drew to a halt just short of a crazy paved patio that lead up to the front door which was set well back under the overhanging thatch.

As he walked with the dogs towards the door it opened and a tall lean man with spectacles wedged above his forehead, on a mop of grey hair, made his appearance.

"My apologies for just dropping in. My name is Emmett Doyle and I farm in the Punjabi Plains near Koram," burst out Emmett embarrassed at their arrival.

"No apologies needed young man, come right in. Are you alone?"

"No, my friend Anna is with me and I have two farm staff." Jay walked on past Emmett and opened the landrover door for Anna, taking her hand and introducing himself. He then told the two staff members where to go to find the kitchen and his staff.

"By the way Emmett, I'm Jay and welcome to Mandalay. Come on in and meet the family." His accent had a lovely lilt of the southern twang which branded him American.

They followed him into a high ceilinged hall with immaculately polished pieces of furniture suitably positioned to highlight their taste. Then on down a corridor to an enormous veranda where the family was seated.

"Emmett and Anna, right here is my wife Jasmine and our teenage kids Jason, Tinki and Buster. Come seat yourselves and cool off a while. Its great to have visitors. How long have you come for?"

Emmett and Anna looked stunned, not quite believing what they had just heard.

"Well, eh, we wanted to see the castle we've heard about and then would be moving on to wherever for the night."

"Now look you here. You are staying with us, the castle's ours, we'll show you that and then I 'd like to take you around the sanctuary. Do you ride horses by any chance?"

"Yes indeed we do."

"Great. We'll have an early morning ride," and looking at Jasmine as he sidled over to behind the well cushioned bamboo chair she sat in "we'll party tonight. How about that my darling?" smiling at his wife and questioning Emmett.

"I'm lost for words and that's not easy for an Irishman," he replied as he looked for and found Anna's hand on the sofa where they were seated.

Jasmine hadn't said a word and the kids kept their eyes pinned on their father's every word and move. Anna, too, was gob smacked to use a descriptive Irishism. She clung to Emmett as if she was afraid of Jay's next suggestion. This quick fire hospitality was all too gushing from what they were used to.

Things quietened down to a normal pace with Jasmine taking up the questioning. Jay left the veranda with one of his sons following him. Jasmine had a strange accent, a mixture of French and American. She was smaller than Anna and plumper. Rows of gold chains nestled on her ample bosom with arms heavily bangled. She was dressed in a red blouse over a green ankle length skirt. All the family wore flip-flops (sandals).

"Would you like to spend the night, really?" she asked "Jay is so quick with invites that it is hard to refuse."

"No, it would be grand, wouldn't it Anna, if its not too much trouble. We would have gone to Fuda and looked for something there."

"That's settled then. No problems, we have many guest rooms and Jay would adore showing you his pride and joy, the sanctuary. I see it everyday, if you know what I mean?"

Tinki was busy at an easel in the corner of the room. Jasmine explained that she showed a talent for wildlife portraits and was taking after her father who was a well respected international wildlife photographer. This, Emmett had already heard from Howard who had evidently been over to visit on a number of occasions.

They had been left with Jasmine for half an hour or so before Jay returned, once again full of energy and his exuberant self.

"I've been talking with your two farm boys. One has a relation on the farm here believe it or not. Also, if it is okay with you, I have organised my driver to take them to their reserve which is quite close by. You've just got to tell me when you will be leaving tomorrow and I'll have them meet you at our turnoff. Is that okay with you?"

"That's fine Jay and very kind of you. They will be thrilled."

"Fine. Let me arrange it then. Say you depart after lunch tomorrow. They can then wait for you around 3.00pm. Suit?"

"Great," was all Emmett could muster as a reply.

"Oh, I'll be back in a little while and I'll take you to the castle. Mims will show you to your suite. Bye now."

They sat for sometime, Emmett admiring the landscape, Anna talking to Jasmine. They seemed to have a lot in common.

For him it was paradise to look out onto trees and shrubs running far into the distant west. The sun was now losing its searing heat and afternoon warmth took its place.

Every now and then a small buck - a duiker – would saunter onto the lawns, that covered a distance of perhaps a hundred yards, unafraid of the two dogs who lay under a Pride of India shrub some way off the veranda.

Birds aplenty, finches of different hue, weavers and starlings made themselves known by mustering on the nearest shrubs and trees. A feeding table stood erect close by. It was a piece of heaven. Emmett was very envious. He remarked as much to Jasmine who totally agreed.

"I was originally a townie and I was afraid of the bush. Our family were mixed up in mining. Then I ventured abroad – the USA to do a PhD and that's where I met Jay who was on a lecture tour. He came to our college to show his wildlife photographic portfolio and lectured on conservation. He gave three lectures. I attended all of them. We talked and he learnt of my background and from whence I came.

"We met up five years later in Brazzaville. The rest is Mandalay."

"Oh how romantic. Don't you think so Emmett?" said a wide eyed Anna.

"I do indeed," he replied "and did you easily overcome your fear of the bush?"

"Oh with Jay around you just have to," laughingly she added "but his project was so full of interest that we both fell into it with a gusto seen to be believed."

"Jasmine, you sounded then as if I had been describing Emmett. He is exactly the same. Give him a challenge and wow-wee he goes to it."

"That's very flattering my darling but I think theirs is far more interesting and fulfilling than mine. But it gives me hope for the future."

Jasmine then showed them around the house which had a guest wing of four doubles en suite. "You can choose whichever. I'd recommend the end one, it has the best view and gets the earliest sun in the morning."

Emmett returned to the vehicle and collected their overnight grip. The two ladies were once again deep in conversation, this time, seated on the bay window seat overlooking a different part of the garden and terrain.

"Don't dress for supper, we are very casual here and I would think Jay will take you down to the castle before sundowners. Have a rest now. We'll call you later."

After her flip flopping sound had disappeared out of earshot Emmett threw himself on the inviting double bed and let out a roar "Wow, wow and more wow. Unbelievable my love, don't you think – they and the place? Are we going to enjoy this little break! Come here you sexy sensuous black beauty you."

Anna collapsed into his arms. They rested for two hours in a fantasy dreamland.

The family were seated on the veranda when they eventually rejoined them, refreshed after snoozing and showering.

"I guess we ought to take a walk down to the castle now. Its best to see it in the dusk, the amber shades are very special. Let's mosey down there; okay with you folks?"

"Sure thing," Emmett replied for both of them.

Jasmine and the two boys stayed behind. Tinki accompanied her dad. The kids had lovely milk chocolate complexions and were wiry in build like their father. Emmett felt they were a close knit unit with love permeating throughout.

After about five minutes of a walk the land suddenly dropped into a gully – a donga – and there on the other side and on top of a rise, was the castle.

Emmett noticed it wasn't like the one at Kinvara or even like the 'keep' at Thor Ballylee down near Gort, but it certainly was styled on small castles he remembered seeing in the film Camelot and such like. Not something tall and grand but rather more conservative and manageable.

173

As they approached he could see it was built on a square, its exterior walls perhaps twelve to fifteen feet high with castellated turrets on each corner. The main building within was only two-storeys high with a central tower rising another twenty feet above the building.

Everything was made of local stone and he supposed the doors of the best Congo hardwoods.

"It was originally built by Etienne du Bois in 1933. He had mining interests and loved the bush. He was 'stinking rich' I think you'd say. In UK it would be known as a 'folly'. Out here it is ridiculous! Someone told me about it in Brazzaville and it somehow intrigued me. I found it, fell in love with it and bought it and two thousand acres." Jay almost said all this as an afterthought. But Emmett noted the passion in his tone.

Whilst Jay was recounting this piece of pure mystery he had led them through the open archway into a quadrangle which had a peek-a-boo covered well in the centre. Both Emmett and Anna held back in amazement as the other two sauntered on.

"In the middle of Africa a medieval castle Anna – and its ancient well. Look here, turn the handle and a bucket will bring up water. Quite amazing."

She didn't reply. She was struck dumb. Her hand gripped Emmett's with the power of awe. Anna would not have seen anything as beautifully constructed as this before. He took her in his arms and held her ever so fondly.

"Come on you two lovebirds. Lets see what's inside."

They joined Jay at what was obviously the main entrance door which Tinki had opened and proceeded inside ahead of them. An enormous high ceilinged hall, all walls painted white, with a giant of a hand hewn wooden table as centrepiece. An array of heavy high backed matching chairs were set in place. The floor was square tiled in black and white checkerboard design.

Very obviously, Emmett thought, this was a gallery for Jay's photographic work. Pictures great and small, mostly in black and white, were tastefully sighted on all walls with a couple placed on triangular easels. There was a gallery overhead which ran the full extent of the room.

This would take hours to fully appreciate so another trip would be inevitable, ran through Emmett's mind. Now they would give it all a perfunctory glance and he would be content to get an invitation to return.

That evening at Jay's party, where roast wild pig was served, they learnt, in detail, everything about Mandalay. Two other couples were invited – local ranchers, who knew some of Emmett's neighbours.

He felt that loneliness and lack of regular visitations was the reason these few families longed for a chance to meet, greet and party. Emmett would have to invite them over to his neck of the woods to reciprocate their kindness.

Anna looked completely unfazed by their exuberant personalities and slotted into all discussions which went on 'till the small hours of the morning. Both couples also over-nighted which seemed taken as natural.

This revelry did not, however, stop Jay from waking them for their early morning ride. Perhaps he had been a little lenient as it was 07.00 hours and not 0600 hours as suggested originally.

The next two hours were exhilarating. Jay had no 'cats' (lions, cheetahs, leopards). "Too difficult to maintain," he explained. Zebra, buffalo, wildebeest, giraffe and twelve species of buck, from the tiniest and timid dik dik to the graceful trotting antelope, the eland, four of which he had domesticated and trained to harness.

Jay was still wary of his buffalo herd of seventeen "one just never knows with them" he said as they kept their distance in front of the herd.

The farm had a magnificent river running through it which provided ample water for the animals and from which he irrigated ten acres of Lucerne or as Jay called it, Alf-Alfa. This he baled and stored in case of drought.

"We found a lone hippo once but he moved out after finding it too lonely. Guess he's moved upstream and is in the lake with his harem. Lucky guy!"

Emmett felt so at home in this environment. His dreams of being a game ranger came flooding back. What better way of living he considered to himself as he mentally counted every animal they came upon and transplanted them, perhaps multiplied, into an area of his keeping.

"Better make pots of money in wheat," he thought and then he'd be able to move on. One may dream – it was no harm.

Then back to reality with a bump as Jay spotted a black-backed jackal with cubs so off he galloped with the two of them in hot pursuit. They didn't go near the cubs but kept at a reasonable distance not to frighten them in any way. This reminded Emmett of cub hunting days in September/October back home. He always loved the sight of spotting a red 'Charlie fox' on a grey lichen covered County Clare wall. His feelings towards wildlife had been protective from his earliest days and nothing had changed during his African safari.

After a gargantuan breakfast which was full of Irish craic – good humoured banter – Emmett took Anna off to study Jay's photographs. They spent all of two hours within the castle. Both of them returned time and time again to their favourite black and white. It was enlarged to life size and depicted a lioness landing onto the back of a wildebeest. The detail was enormous, the moment tragic, an awesome shot.

18

Experiencing an Irish Wake

Back in the real world their drive home was spent remembering points discovered and experienced during their 'stay in heaven' for that was what Mandalay felt like. Such immediate warmth, depth of hospitality and kindness had never before been felt by either of them. What a memorable moment in time. And, perhaps best of all, Jay had presented them with two signed pictures each as mementos. Emmett knew exactly where he would hang his. One on each side of his fireplace. Their colour would blend with the stonework which wound its way to the ceiling above that unique wooden mantelpiece.

"Funny he hadn't filled those spaces before," he thought to himself. Spooky perhaps?

Anna said she felt so at home with Jasmine and they promised to keep in touch.

"Let me arrange the weekend when you invite them back – please?" Her plea did not fall on deaf ears. Far from it. In fact he was already planning that outing. The amazing thing was that the two farms could now be kept in contact as Mandalay was within range of Ratilli's radio and vice versa – now that they knew each other.

A very distraught Christopher hurried to the vehicle as they arrived.

"Rani is very ill fendi. I call Misses Jan and she give injection. Wont eat or drink since you left. Just lies down in corner – there," pointing to the far end of his veranda.

She didn't rise up when Emmett approached her. She was listless. He checked her gums - they were plainly anaemic, her nose dry. Her paws cold. He immediately feared poison but what and from where? The other two were worried but seemed alright and full of spirit on welcoming them home.

"Anna, please get me some brandy and Christopher some hot milk. I'll dose her with that. Sure remedy – for anything! Its worth trying anyway," as he looked at Anna whose quizzical frown etched a worried countenance.

Emmett then went to the office and called up Ian on the radio. They were over at Howard's he was informed. So he called Howard's sign. Five minutes later Ian came on the line and explained just what Jan had administered. She also thought of poison but why only one of them?

"Howard is flying to Urukan tomorrow. He will bring you and the dog to the vet if she is no better. Okay? Keep in touch. Good luck."

That was a splendid idea and if Rani was no better he would take up the offer. Meantime he carried her inside and covered her with blankets. Like a human she might sweat it out, whatever it was.

All that night Emmett administered t.l.c. to her. He force fed her hot milk every couple of hours and kept her warm. It was the first time anything had gone wrong with his animals. He supposed he had been very fortunate so far? Rani had been his shadow from day one. She must come through it, no matter what it took.

In the morning she attempted to get up but she couldn't move, the blankets were too tightly folded about her. He undid them and she sat up. Her eyes were not focusing as they should. Perhaps she was pissed thought Emmett as he had given her too much brandy perhaps? But she was attempting to move and that was a plus.

During breakfast they noticed her peering out onto the veranda, longingly.

"Perhaps she wants a pee?" said Emmett through a mouthful of toast and marmalade.

"Christopher, come please. Lets carry her out onto the lawn." This they did much to the amusement of Raj and Rastus. They sniffed and sniffed 'till shooed away by Christopher.

Rani, after a few moments, sat up in a wobbly sort of way. She then pulled herself up and off the blanket gracefully collapsing onto the fresh grass which she licked with a couple of strokes of her tongue.

The humans returned to the house and left her alone. She might be embarrassed if she relieved herself out on the lawn – not allowed in normal circumstances.

Emmett took his half empty tea mug and stood looking out the window at her. His commentary kept Anna in fits as she finished off her breakfast. She then joined him in their stakeout of one sick pooch.

Somehow Emmett felt a lot easier and made light of the situation, although it was still grave. During the night he had wondered how he would take her death if such a tragedy should occur. He was desperately attached to his pets – they were his family. It would be like losing a sister. Strange but true.

The call of nature took him hurriedly to the loo. It was a long one and he browsed the National Geographic that was top of the pile.

An ecstatic cry from the front room brought him back to reality: "She's walking – staggering away from the blanket. Oh darling come quick I 'm sure she is better." The excitement in Anna's voice was heart warming.

"She's squatting or trying to. Yes, she's weeing. Oh come, come quickly or you'll miss it."

Emmett joined her at the window and held her close to him. Christopher was right beside them with a smile that would outshine the brightest African sun.

"Oh Master she is better. Thank the Lord. I prayed all night."

They didn't wish to frighten or upset her and he called the other two dogs to come inside. They had been sitting on the top step watching Rani's every movement. Their tails were active once again and their eyes brighter.

Rani was by no means over the problem – whatever it was, but she was certainly on the mend.

Emmett and Christopher got hold of her and once again carried her inside and placed her among the blankets. She was very weak.

"Do we have any liver Christopher?

"Yes Master."

"Cut some up into small pieces please and bring it with some more hot milk. I'll make her better, believe me."

"Yes Master – our prayers will be answered then."

"You are something else my Irish," said Anna grabbing him into her arms and smothering him with kisses.

"Woah, woah, my love. We haven't won yet, the finishing post is still out there. But don't stop your loving – especially after such a disturbed night. I adore it," and he clasped her into his eager body.

Two hours later, after being force fed and keeping it down, Rani made another effort to move outside. All assistance was afforded with recovery definitely on the agenda.

Emmett had earlier radioed Howard and declined his offer but asked him to please phone the vet, explaining everything, and return with any medication recommended. Howard answered "Roger. Wilco. Out."

"Understood, will cooperate, bye!"

That evening Howard flew in with tablets and injections for the patient. Her recovery was slow but sure. She actually ate some liver and mince and did have a drink.

Emmett thought about what his friend James (the Irish vet) had said in a flash of inspiration many moons ago.

"Animals are really very like humans so treat them as such. I always like a shot of brandy or whiskey with hot milk if a dog or cat is very poorly. It usually works."

Well this time, many thousands of miles from the west of Ireland, it looked as if it had worked again. Emmett, however, could not rule out the shot of penicillin given by Jan. But let the myth role on he thought. A good few pints of the 'black stuff' would be drained with this story on his return!

It took another three days before Rani returned to her normal self. He felt it had to be something 'off' or 'bad' that had done the damage. But what he wondered?

The first public murder or assassination of a prominent person took place the following week. A Catholic bishop, returning from visits to mission stations up in the foothills of the Mandaras, was gunned down together with members of his entourage. It was a massive ambush with the three vehicles totally burnt out. The scene was one of carnage. Dying bodies were slaughtered leaving no survivors. No one could tell a tale.

Total outrage gripped the country with, for the first time, international bodies fuelling their anger. Questions were voiced at the United Nations but few knew the actual locality of Ukenza. Those with shortwave radios kept ears focused on world opinion.

The Vatican took up their attack on the limp administration and the President in particular.

Demonstrations took place all over the country. This time they were of a magnitude never before witnessed. The 'Wabeebee' – women folk – made up the majority of each meeting. In these numbers the administration had to take heed of the outrage and failure of the government.

Who had perpetrated this scandalous act? Opinion became divided between two old faithfuls – *Makinto* and Uma. But why? That was the question on everybody's lips.

For once it seemed that all the tribes were in unison but didn't know how to proceed from here.

In stepped the FRO and their associates. Personnel were galvanized into countrywide action. Leaders of all action groups were welcomed to join the Zungu Farmers Reserve. A combined opposition front had to be organised with immediacy.

Buster called a meeting at which everyone was issued with black berets. A very descriptive brass badge fronted these military-style head pieces. It had been designed by Shirra and accepted by their GHQ. It was now the officially accepted logo of the force. One up to the wheat farmers they all chanted in the drinks party that followed the intensive meeting. The logo was simple. Three sheafs of wheat in front of a setting sun.

Emmett was asked to bring Anna and the leader of her Wazuri group to a meeting at Ratilli the coming weekend. Buster and a couple of his committee would address them.

Things seemed to be moving fast and all plans were designed to prevent an escalation of terrorism around the country.

179

He hoped he wouldn't be needed fulltime, there were murmurings that the under thirties might be called up for ongoing active service. But only if terrorism looked like getting out of control.

It became obvious at the FRO meeting that there was no way they could rely on the army, no matter how much of a raggle taggle group they were. The President would hold them close to his control for personal safety. The police, however, might well be able to assist but their support seemed reliant on the CC (County Commissioner) in control of respective areas. Jeri Ntsemo was completely on the Zungu side and would detail support whenever possible. His area, however, was quite extensive and deploying his police force would be problematic. The FRO ideals were well founded on experiences from Malaya and Kenya. They were not armed with modern weapons but did have substantial fire power and were a well disciplined and fit group. Their brain tank was substantial. They were confident of taking on any terrorist group and, indeed, looked forward to all encounters.

Input from Zungu wives was on the increase with a WR (Women's Reserve) now working alongside their 'partners in war'. It was quite obvious that the senior strategists were putting all their knowledge and aged experience into the formation of a private army. And to hell with government, to hell with authority. They were happy to take on the main role of governance with security, law and order their prime objective.

"The situation must not get out of hand. Anarchy must not rear its head and we, the farmers of Ukenza, must unite with all like minded peoples to maintain honest and God-fearing beliefs in our country, our future." Stirring words from Buster at the conclusion of his well attended meeting.

Emmett pondered on all that was said and now finally realised he was caught up in an ongoing revolution. This was not what he had come to Africa for. None of this had been remotely thought of or discussed in the lead up to his filling the vacancy of farm manager.

He was now surrounded by the forces of good and evil. Good being the FRO and Wabeebee. Evil by the terrorist gangs of Uma and the President's elite corps, the *Makinto*.

If the FRO could get the backing of all opposition groups there was an outside chance they would succeed. But at what price wondered Emmett? Would his lifestyle remain? Would it be safe to travel around the country without guards and backup? What about sport? A multitude of questions kept appearing on the panoramic screen that had become his mind. Answers were impossible to find. Hope, yes. Optimism, also a yes. Faith, everyone had to have otherwise one best pack up and return home.

Emmett certainly didn't wish that on his worst enemy. He would resist all intrusion into his idyllic world. He had fallen in love with Africa and in his mind that meant for life. For better, for worse.

He also had a 'love' in his life. Someone so full of mystery and intrigue that Anna made his cup runeth over. Together they wished to conquer Africa and make a part of it their very own. Whether it be in Ukenza or wherever they wanted a part of it. Their desire was burning a hole in his thoughts. Nothing must hinder their ambition.

But something very nearly did. Another message from Ballyvaughan via Bhogals head office had hasty arrangements for his immediate return to Ireland put in place.

"His father was much worse and wasn't expected to hang on much longer. Come home," was how the message was transmitted via the farm radio.

Vijay took on the responsibility of arranging his tickets and flew out to Ratilli to collect Emmett the following morning. In the meantime Emmett made arrangements with Ian to keep an eye on things with Jan promising to monitor dogs and horses.

Luckily he had feared this inevitability and had drawn up plans for every little last item to do with the farm. His bag was packed and all that had to be added was his wash things.

Christopher promised to sleep in the house. Jan would see that Geronimo's training schedule was adhered to. Anna would come out each weekend. It was November and not much work was needed except for routine chores and continual contouring. The team were now on the fourth and final section. Ian would throw his eye over their progress.

The FRO wished him a safe trip and 'hurry home' please, to us!

Anna was distraught and drove out with Jaci, her driver, for his final night.

"You are coming back aren't you?" she kept asking with tears in her beautiful twin pools of liquid ebony.

"Of course, I promise, what do you want me to say," as they cradled into a closeness not experienced previously. Hers was a yearning for him not to leave. His for the strength and reassurance of his love for her.

"I would take you with me if it was a joyous occasion. But this is not. Next time I promise."

That night they felt closer than ever before. Their love making was joyful tinged with sadness. They didn't sleep very much.

Emmett made it to Galway hospital a day before his father passed away. His entire family, it seemed like hundreds of them, arrived from the four corners of Ireland. Cousins, uncles and aunts not seen since childhood kept shaking his hand. Questions on Africa only surfaced at the wake which lasted four long and harrowing days.

He had totally lost contact with this pure Irish tradition and he felt very out on a limb until his old friends James and Simon urged him out of his depression and into the arms of Bacchus in the surrounds of Mullins' pub.

Three nights of African exploits ran off his gradually inebriated tongue. More ears of the parish came and went with minds now befuddled by the rashness and daredevil acts being retold by one, so young, of their own.

Many mission fathers and sisters had returned from Africa, down the years, but their tales were of hunger and deprivation. Emmett's were immeasurably more colourful.

He spent a week with his mother and close family members before taking off for Dublin. His duty had been performed.

"No, he wasn't returning to Ireland. Yes he had a job to complete in Ukenza and yes he loved Africa and everything about it. No he wasn't getting married. Yes he had a girl friend. No she wasn't Irish. Yes, believe it or not, she was black and very beautiful."

That usually concluded the questioning with eyebrows raised and eyes not strong enough to look straight into his.

His school and university friends, whom he managed to locate, were a different bag of maize, as the saying was in Ukenza. They, to a man, were envious of his exploits. Things were not good economically in Ireland and emigration was still rife. A few had heard from the other four of the original adventurous team. Like Emmett they were not good correspondents. He was happy, however, to know that they were all progressing favourably in their new habitats. He hoped that their lives were as full and loving as his.

Explaining what was happening in Ukenza was not easy but during his stay in Ireland the 'troubles' in the North posted killings on a daily basis. At least that wasn't taking place in Ukenza. Not for ever he hoped.

Emmett invited many of his friends to visit him.

"Just fly out, that's all the cost for you. The rest will be on me."

Both James and Simon showed interest but the latter was married with young children and had a farm to run. If he could get a locum, as James would have to for his practice, then he was 'A for away and lookout Ukenza'. That was the attitude Emmett wished to hear. But would it happen? He somehow didn't think so.

He flew back to Nairobi seven days later. It had been a culture shock, returning home. Even in those couple of years he had matured beyond belief. He was an African now loving the smell, heat, filth and feel of that vibrant continent. Nothing would change it.

Emmett had cabled Jeri asking his permission for Anna to fly up to Kampala to meet him. This was granted by return. He would spend a day in Nairobi then three days in Uganda before returning to Kenzi.

A number of his fellow farmers had given him contacts in Kenya. Some were near to Nairobi and a couple of these met him in the New Stanley Hotel. Comparisons of the two countries were debated in the Long Bar and then a magnificent meal was taken in the Lobster Pot, the best restaurant Emmett had been into since arriving in Africa.

He was invited to holiday back in this pearl of East Africa. Colin Dymott, one of the two farmers he met, had a house at Malindi - on the coast north of Mombasa – and it was Emmett's whenever he could get away. That was a treasure he would keep for a special occasion in the future.

It was a heart-stopping ten minutes prior to landing at Entebbe Airport outside Kampala. The East African Airways pilot gave his passengers a view of Lake Victoria only ever experienced by clear weather tourists. One never knew just when the plane would touch down on the tarmac as they cruised close to the water. Emmett had heard about the sensation and had now experienced it. Quite exhilarating. But there was a group of Muslim women who commenced chanting some way out, heads bowed and enveloped in black cloth. Emmett thought he heard a fair quantity of snivels emanating from within those tented Burkah ladies.

What a joy it was to see Anna waving from the balcony. His emotions welled up from within his loins. These spelt out his homecoming feelings – Africa and Anna meant more than Ireland and his family. He was definitely smitten.

Anna had booked them two nights at the Imperial overlooking the lake. Five star luxury prior to returning to basics.

He had never slept under a mosquito net and always fantasised about the experience.

Here, their en-suite offered such luxury, in the form of a four poster bed with the finest netting encasing it. Heaven, absolute bliss. The view was breathtaking, the breeze sylvan, the ambience luxuriant. A honeymoon environment if ever there was one. They took the opportunity to renew all the previously experienced nuances of passion and perhaps a few new ones along the orgasmic way.

By day they shopped and took a boat trip up the Nile. Emmett needed sun on his body so a couple of hours a day was spent poolside. He taught Anna the crawl. She looked sensational in a new peacock blue one-piece swim suit he had espied in Tanzi, a petite boutique down some side street in Kampala. They were very obviously madly in love with no inhibitions.

The small plane which flew them – twelve passengers – onto Kenzi met turbulence and rocked, bucked and kicked them all into reality. Kenzi arrived just in time. There was a majority of pale green faces on arrival.

Anna went off to meet her parents at the university while he visited Bhogals head office. Everyone was very respectful and couldn't be more helpful. His landrover had been given a complete service and makeover with extra lockers welded into the rear sides. The driver who had brought it to Kenzi would be collected at Urukan and Gilbert would also be a passenger. All was well on Ratilli. That's what Emmett needed to hear. Thank God he muttered to himself.

19

"We should have known – a Bloody Irishman on a Roughie"

After lunch he collected Anna, shopped for farm provisions and set off for Urukan. He dropped her off at Jeri's, had tea and cake, collected the driver and some spares for the workshop, making Ratilli at 7.30pm. Many hours of varying hues had passed since departing Kampala and arrival at his Ratilli homestead.

Oh how good it all felt. The dogs bounding out to meet his vehicle, the sound of which had been alien to them for three weeks. The ever smiling Christopher at the garden gate, the cheers and waving arms from his labour lines, his garden and homestead exactly as he had left it. Emmett even managed a quick glance into the stables as he passed by. Three inquisitive heads peered out wondering what the commotion was all about.

He felt so at ease here. It was much, much better than his first arrival. And it would get better each time from now on he promised himself.

It wasn't all roses though in the district which he heard from Ian once he radioed him of his return.

"You had better come up for lunch tomorrow and I can tell you all. The farm and animals are fine so that's a bonus. Welcome back."

Emmett slept a full eight hours that night. His amorous exploits over the past few days coupled with a lot of driving had exhausted his body and mind. Not a semblance of a dream. Pure silence, unsaturated slumber filled his night.

Funny how his early wakeful hours had not ceased in the three weeks away. How great it was to be surrounded by Rani, Rajah and Rastus on opening the veranda door. Their whimpers came through loud and strong from the minute he flushed the toilet.

"Master was home. Now he would take us walkies."

They pre-empted his every movement and responded to each noise within the house. Following him into the kitchen while he made his mug of tea, they sat in line abreast looking at the 'bickie' tin high up on the second shelf. Treat time was first thing in the morning and last thing at night. Christopher had obviously maintained the routine.

185

Sitting out on the veranda and watching the labour lines come alive, the dogs also watched and waited for their friendly soul mate Christopher.

Just by watching their ears and tails could Emmett gauge the distant appearance of his lone matchstick like figure moving up the centre of the compound. As he approached, the dogs left the veranda and rushed to await him at the gate. Emmett was forgotten now, Christopher was foremost in their minds. It was truly remarkable to see the joyful companionship now experienced by Christopher and the pack.

His caring ways had taken up many minutes of rapturous conversation and explanation with James and Simon. Each time Emmett would remember another anecdote and the one that tickled their fancy most was about William.

Within a week of the first duikers release, one of his fencing gang brought in a very distraught baby warthog (wild pig). It had been savaged by something, and must have either feigned death or managed to drag itself into a hole. Besides nasty deep cuts on its back it was found to have a cleft foot. Its little left front hoof was doubled back. His rate of progress through the bush must have been severely curtailed. Perhaps the runt of the litter?

Comparing its size to an Irish bonham Emmett put it at about ten to twelve weeks old and probably just weaned.

Once again the stable was used as a stopgap pen. The carpenter put together two old machinery packing cases which approximately gave the porker a 12ft x 6ft house and run.

Having learnt by experience at home and then at university that pigs are quite the cleanest of farm animals, only manuring in one area away from their bed and food trough, it would be interesting to note this wild one's inherent breeding and etiquette.

After treating its wounds in the same way as the other waifs but giving it a reduced dose of antibiotic it was transferred to its new pen at the back door of Emmett's kitchen. Feeding was easy. Anything and everything made into a warm gruel (to start with) with plenty of vegetables and mealie meal.

It thrived and became a pet within no time at all. William Warthog was christened when Jan paid a visit soon after its arrival.

"He should have an aristocratic name, he's such a charmer. How about Willie, no - William, it sounds very grand don't you think?"

"That's it then. Christopher, his name is William and he must be called that by everyone. In fact I'll paint a sign on his pen. How about that?"

Everyone seemed amused and pleased, it evidently was a lucky omen to befriend a warthog.

No way could this little fellow every be released back into the wild as he would be scoffed (eaten) by hyenas within no time.

186

William, within six months, ruled the compound. He was lord of the patch, court jester to all.

The dogs took to him quite readily and as he grew they became very aware of his gleaming ivory tusks that started to curve outward and upwards from just behind his ever active snout.

Christopher, once again, was brilliant and taught him his name. He had a natural affinity with animals. He was blessed with that wonderful gift.

The weekend after William appeared Emmett and his equine team had luck bestowed on them.

It was the inaugural hurdle race at Kitos and Geronimo was tuned to the minute. Whilst Emmett was in Ireland, the strict daily routine had been adhered to with Jan and Rachel overseeing the gallops. Anna had spent every weekend on Ratilli and had ridden him out on long walks and trots, up and down riverbeds, through the little dams, in fact anything to take his mind off the routine stamina workouts.

Emmett had four rides, Anna two. Best of all was Anna's win in the Lady's Mile – the third race of the afternoon. What a thrill for everyone and quite historical. The first African female to ever ride a winner in Ukenza. The jubilation had hardly died when Emmett won the Open Derby (one and a half miles) for his friend the South African   Tinus Cloete. He also managed to finish in the placings on his other two rides.

All eyes were on the 'last' – the Kitos Novice Hurdle of two miles. Hurdles were placed on the track after the last flat race and every single person crowded around the paddock to see the twelve intrepid history making steeds as they paraded.

A number were well tried and trusted performers on the flat. A few were definitely not thoroughbred and then there was Geronimo.

Both syces had travelled with him and in the parade he was the only horse to have two attendants leading him around.

Rachel, Howard and Anna were in the paddock when the jockeys arrived. Emmett was thrilled to hear Rachel remark that "no doubt about it, he looks the fittest."

Geronimo was very much on his toes with neck arched so that his head was literally tucked between his legs as he danced around the ring. His number was '5'.

Emmett noticed that the majority of horses were bandaged on fore and hind legs. Their owners were obviously worried about knocking hurdles. He mounted and paraded in position in front of the big stand. He was quite worried about the bandages as he thought not a lot of schooling (jumping) preparation had

187

gone into these entrants and that could mean anything from refusals to pileups on the agenda?

He didn't wish Geronimo to get into any trouble that might sour his zest for competition. Also Emmett must look after his own hide, it was the only one he possessed for God sakes!

The original strategy was to hold Geronimo up, coax him along with the others jumping upsides him, increasing his confidence and speed once he settled and had a good rhythm moving, then finish wherever possible. A typical waiting race in Irish racing parlance.

He had insisted the field be allowed to jump a practise fence on the way to the start which he argued, with the stewards, would allow the horses and riders to settle before the start. Although this did not happen in the UK or Ireland, Emmett and another farmer and committee member felt it a worthy idea and they swayed the others.

Geronimo took a strong hold as Emmett placed him at a hack canter some fifty strides off the fence. They were joined by No.3 who was almost out of control with its head high in the air and fighting the attentions of his jockey.

"Sorry, Emmett, this is a real bastard – no mouth – but come along with me if you like. Woops," and Charlie Perks yawed at his mount in passing.

Emmett squeezed Geronimo up alongside and a little way – about half a length in front of him. He wanted to reach the hurdle first, just in case.

They both fenced it in style with Charlie taking off into the distance attempting to pull his creature up. Geronimo came to the hack canter once again and then to a trot all the way back to the start, almost in front of the stand and just short of the winning post.

Emmett only noticed the size of the crowd in his pre-start walkabout. It was of football mass proportion. The little covered stand stood halfway along a raised grassy bank which ran for upwards of seventy-five yards. There wasn't a place for late comers. It so reminded him of Galway races – only thing missing were the bookies.

"Twice around gentlemen. That means three times past the winning post. All set? Best of luck. Come in on my orders and don't rush the starters flag. Walk around once more then line up. Right-ho. Go."

All this shouted by the starter from his raised rostrum placed twenty yards ahead of them.

The first hurdle, of eight in total, was around the left handed bend past the stand about a furlong from the start. Emmett chose to be near the inside a little off the pace. There were rails all around the inside of the course so horses could only run out to the right.

Charlie and No. 3, Emmett couldn't remember its name, took off like a missile and hit the first hurdle a good ten lengths clear of the rest. He hit it a mighty crack and smashed the top bar. The hurdle then leant almost flat away from the others. It didn't seem to stop the horse in any way as he careered off to the second fence.

Geronimo jumped in about fifth place. He took it in his stride and reacted to Emmett's urges of 'one-two-three' to his strides away from the fence. This was something he had used with great feeling in the training of Geronimo.

He felt the pace was too fast. They would never keep it up over two miles, in fact they were going the speed of the race he had previously won. Ridiculous he thought, unless of course there is something very special in the field that he didn't know about?

Funnily enough there had been 'no talking horse' mentioned in the build up so perhaps Emmett was correct in his feel of the pace being set.

Charlie was almost a hurdle ahead as they came past the stands a second time with Emmett riding cautiously in third place. Geronimo's jumping had been superb.

Half way around the back straight and with two hurdles to go he suddenly found himself only a few lengths behind Charlie who was visibly in trouble. They jumped the second last together but Charlie called across:

"I'm finished, both of us. Go for it Emmett. Good luck."

Approaching the last, Emmett could hear the roar of the crowd, a goodly portion of who were lined up either side of that fence. He couldn't hear any galloping hooves behind him but as taught by a few well heeled punters back home 'never look back'. He just sat and drove Geronimo hands and heels to the line. Passing it he stood up in his irons and glanced behind. There was no one coming up the straight? He gradually let Geronimo pull himself up and turned him back to the stands. Two horses and riders were cantering past the last hurdle and obviously were also rans, not having completed the course.

Incredible, he thought, as his two syces rushed out onto the course to lead him through the crowds into the winner's enclosure.

Just everyone was congratulating them, patting Geronimo and shouting applause at Emmett. Many faces he recognised but the majority was a blur.

When he dismounted he asked:

"Crikey, what happened?"

Rachel and Anna were in tears and only Howard could talk.

"They just crumbled, couldn't keep up and didn't jump. Well done. Brilliant."

In the jockey's room Emmett heard all that went wrong.

"Didn't stay."

"Doesn't like jumping."

"Never again."

"We should have known – a bloody Irishman on a roughie."

Congratulations did go the rounds, however, with 'when's the party?' being the leading question.

"Up in the Club in about an hour, we'll see you all there. Okay?"

"You bet! And by the way – it'll be a double whammy eh Emmett? That girl of yours rode a blinder."

"I agree," responded a happy Emmett, "you'll all have your chance to show her your good wishes. Let's make her the belle of the ball. Right?"

"You bet. See you there," they all hollered back as Emmett left to shower.

Meantime Anna had taken control at the polo stalls where Geronimo was hosed down and walked around to cool off. He had no cuts and seemed in fine order. The farm driver and syces would have their party the next day. Today was Emmett's big moment of success. He had trained his first winner and 'over the sticks' too. Could be back home he thought?

Everyone arrived safely home at Ratilli. The compound and labour lines came alive with hands clapping, shouting and yelling, all dogs going crazy as Emmett drove in through the new security gates.

He had promised the staff a party and that night they had one hell of a bash. His driver had been despatched into Koram to collect the necessary drink and food. Loud music could be heard up at the Ratilli that night as Emmett returned from dinner with his proud owners. Champagne corks popped as Ian and Jan joined in the celebratory meal. Howard enjoyed relating every moment of the race which Emmett could now only start to realise how his father's almost last words rang true.

"Be a perfectionist in all you do. It don't cost any more. Believe me. Trust me."

"Thanks Dad," Emmett had reiterated many times since and this success was truly fashioned on that philosophy. He remembered one well-known Irish trainer stating the obvious:

"Jump races are only won by jumpers," and that's a fact.

20

"God, you're a lucky bastard. It's the Irish I suppose?"

Anna's group of Wazuri arrived out to camp at Melelo on the Friday night. Emmett and Anna collected Jemima Wanju, their leader, on Saturday morning and drove to Buster's. It was decided to meet up at HQ instead of Buster coming to Ratilli, so that both ladies could understand just exactly what went on and what they were letting themselves into.

Jemima was a well-educated wealthy Tukulu lady who owned half a dozen trading stores. She, together with all the others in her troop, could no longer take the corrupt society the President was permitting. She was a political figure and would stand in the upcoming elections.

Both Emmett and Buster agreed they would rather have her and hers on their side than against. She was one tough mama. Although most of her troop came from in and around Urukan they would hopefully be part of this FRO and could be used on any of their operations.

On the return drive he called in to show Jemima his homestead. She had heard all about Anna's equestrian exploits and wished to see Geronimo. They spent a pleasant lunch hour before moving on up to Melelo.

On their approach they heard what sounded like rapid fire – as if a battle was in progress. Jemima, however, explained that 'her ladies' would be practising on the makeshift rifle range.

"They were mad keen for action," she said, and hoped for their inclusion in a forthcoming mountain safari. Buster had said he wished to get them up into the front line a.s.a.p.

To take their minds off the action at hand, Anna gave them a yard by yard account of her racing success and about what goes into training a racehorse. Although Emmett couldn't understand any of it he knew from her eyes and arm movements, in fact her entire body language, exactly what she was recounting. Bully for her he thought. She deserved all praise for her imaginative and dedicated rise to fame.

Melelo was indeed paradise and their large feather bed voluptuous.

Emmett and three others from the Punjabi Plains were 'called up' once again and had to report this time to Popes on the west side of the mountains. He was being driven by Rajeev Patel and sat in the front passenger seat of his landrover with David Purdon and Bob Watson in the back.

There had recently been a spate of arson attacks on schools and labour lines in that district. The FRO needed a concerted effort to flush out these bastards. Hand picked groups were being mustered to lead the Wazuri into the tribal areas surrounding the tea estates and up into the mountains.

They would be stationed at Popes and move out from there for several seventy-two hours periods.

The farm was a virtual military barracks with hundreds of reservists from all over, gathered there. Emmett saw two Cessna aircraft and hoped that he might cadge a few recce flights with their pilots. He was becoming more and more confident of 'going it alone' in the air and taking his licence as Howard took him up quite frequently these days.

Tony was pleased to see them but didn't have a second to discuss the time of day. Off they trooped to TACHQ within the complex to check-in.

There were eight patrols out, four of which would be returning next day. Emmett would be setting out with David and a group of Wazuri immediately the patrols debriefing had finished. Today he was to meet the ladies, the Wazuri, for their briefing, after which they would get to know each other, their strategies and meet the trackers who always accompanied these patrols.

Some of his Melelo group recognised him and came over to talk. Jemima, however, was not on this callout but was on standby.

Emmett asked the CO if this group could accompany him as he knew their capabilities, but unfortunately he was too late. They had already been allotted elsewhere. A great pity he felt but this was no friendly game, this was a serious military operation. Discipline had to be recognised. Orders were orders no matter how trivial or serious.

The Wazuri allotted him were from the Kitos area and knew every track up the mountains. They were mostly Tukulu and half of the ten understood and spoke English. Some of them had already lost relatives and two had seen their houses burnt. They were extremely anxious to get in contact with the gangs.

It had been made specifically and plainly clear by the CO (commanding officer), at the briefing, that prisoners must be taken if contact was made. No patrol was to obliterate everybody, as in revenge, but they needed to realise the importance of securing information from the enemy.

"There would be plenty of chances for you to get your own back during interrogation," he said. This was knowingly taken up by the ladies and they ululated in response. A case, Emmett thought, of what the eye don't see the authorities don't grieve for. Native justice?

Bambi was their leader and she came from a polo playing tea planter's estate. She knew the Zungu scene inside out as her husband travelled to all the

192

games, matches and races. He was Ted Barton's head syce. Bambi often went in the truck with the ponies. She visited family when the others were playing.

They went onto the rifle range in the afternoon and although these Wazuri were unarmed a few of them knew how to use a .303. Their shoulders and arms were mostly immense, from toiling laboriously since early childhood. Their use of the machete was awesome. God help anyone getting into hand to hand combat with them. To round off their prime features and facets was each and everyone's stamina. They moved like a Perkins diesel engine, slow and deliberate, never missing a beat, going on and on relentlessly. Discipline came naturally to them. African mothers, throughout the continent, were renowned for the masterly way of raising children. Here and now they just had to follow their leader and get the task completed in the best possible way. Emmett's patrol had an hour's trip in a lorry which then deposited them on the foothills above a deep gorge. Recent feedback had intimated a large gang was using this area as a 'resting up' venue prior to infiltrating back into the tea estates.

Bob Upton was I/C (in charge) with Bill Mason as his number two. Both of them were hardened campaigners, great shots and were tea planters of the district. Emmett and Patrick Stapleton, eldest son of the Urukan FRO CO were the other two Zungu. Three trackers and ten Wazuri made up their patrol, seventeen in total.

It was structured so as to be divided into two if pincer or flanking movements were to be deployed. It was strong in fire power and it had strength in numbers if hand to hand combat came into force. Also a lot of captives could be taken and escorted out of the forest.

They were offloaded at 06.00 hours and moved into the dense forest immediately, lost to the outside world. Only the diminishing sound of the lorry's diesel engine could be heard as it quickly faded out of earshot, down the hillside.

The enemy certainly didn't make it easy for would be explorers as was only to be expected. It was not easy to follow the tracks that lead down a very steep incline without making some noise. Footholds gave way, slipping and sometimes falling occurred as a consequence. The three trackers moved in arrowhead formation, the two flankers being about ten yards away on either side.

Bob's plan was to approach within one hundred yards of the stream that flowed down the base of the gorge and then proceed, parallel to it, up the south side for an hour or two if no contact was made.

They wished to make a base a half a mile or so away from the head of the gorge where, according to recent information, a well stocked camp had been set up. This was their target. Their information was hot, only twelve hours old. They could be in for a battle no matter what or who they found. Everyone was up for it. Emmett's pulse raced.

The patrol happened on a leafy glade at about noon and decided to call a halt for nourishment. A number of pro-tem hideouts had been rumbled in their upward progress but all were empty, most probably only used for laying up ambushes or accommodating lookouts.

An eerie silence pervaded across the forestscape. Only the odd rippling sound of water over rocks from the stream beneath them could be heard. Most peculiar, however, was the lack of bird song and flight, as if everything had taken fright and vanished. There certainly would be no wild game frequenting these parts with constant movement of humans. During their rest up, for almost two hours, they maintained total silence. Most snoozed with armed guards posted as sentries.

Scouts were then sent ahead, two trackers, Bill Mason and three Wazuri. They were to proceed as close to the end of the gorge as possible without triggering a response.

If all remained silent then the rest of the patrol were to move forward and rendezvous at a certain place at 16.00 hours.

All was quiet so the patrol set off to meet up with the others.

Mason and Stapleton were to lead a splinter patrol up a track which would give them a better view of the area where the camp was thought to be. They set off ahead of Upton, Emmett and the rest.

Within minutes all hell broke lose. A cloudburst of bullets rang out and struck into their patrol. Everyone hit the deck. A few shouts of "aye, aye, aye" meant that one or more of the ladies had been hit.

These had been single shots, quite a few in fact but not automatic fire. They came from across the stream. The 'Terrs' (terrorists) had obviously been watching the patrol and decided to curtail any further advance.

Emmett kept his head down flat to the ground. He could see Upton, also in the same pose, but he had managed to place his patchett gun in a usable position. Emmett's was by his side so he gingerly groped for it and got it up by his head with arms ready to act.

A second burst of fire splintered timber just above them. The 'Terrs' obviously had their measure. Upton whispered to hold hard, not a movement. Not an easy act if one had been wounded, and certainly one or two seemed in that position. Low murmurings emanated from down the line.

Another burst of six to eight shots peppered the ground in front of them.

Just then Mason's patrol opened up on the 'Terrs' with automatic fire.

This gave Upton the chance to get his group into better positions and ascertain his casualties.

Emmett got behind a tree on sentry duty while Upton and Bambi crept down the line. They found two of the Wazuri had been hit, both by single bullets in the arm. One was a graze and not too serious. The other had penetrated a left shoulder and must have lodged there. She could not lift her arm. Both bled profusely but with a bit of bandaging by Sumpi she would be fine. Tough ladies these.

Mason could evidently see the 'Terrs' and had taken them by surprise. They had split, some heading for the camp, others keeping low. Upton sent regular bursts into the enemy area and this certainly curtailed their fire power. Then Upton decided to advance and radioed Mason to keep him covered. Evidently he was twenty feet above and ahead of the patrol.

Emmett's group moved warily through the undergrowth with larger trees being kept close to them. They moved in slow march tempo, heads rotating two hundred and seventy degrees at each step.

A shot, a ping, and Emmett was blown backwards. He awoke moments later with Rob Upton cradling him in a crouched position. Emmett saw light filtering through leaves but from only one eye, his right. The other side of his face felt as if molten chocolate was spreading all down from his forehead above his left eye, cheek and past his mouth. The fluid felt hot.

"Don't move, stay still Emmett. Bambi is getting the first aid kit."

Shortly after this he felt his face and head being swabbed down. Some of the fluid reached into his mouth. He recognised the taste. It was blood. He raised his right hand to his forehead but Rob obviously stopped it there.

"Hold hard young man, this might hurt. Grab my arm if it does."

The swabbing continued and nothing really hurt. His head was throbbing. That was all.

"Well I never," said Rob, "all you've got is two little holes where your badge was rammed into your skull by the force of the bullet."

He leant over Emmett to have a closer look and asked Bambi to apply some antiseptic cream.

"God, you're a lucky bastard. It's the Irish I suppose?"

Kneeling back on his heels he continued:

"The shot must have winged your badge and carried on. Three inches lower and it had you in the eye. How's your head feeling?"

"Singing slightly but I can see perfectly, just a headache now."

Rob got on the radio to Mason and explained the problem:

"Yea, he'll be fine, we'll continue as planned, any sightings?"

While they were continuing radio contact Emmett got gingerly to his feet using Bambi and a tree for support. Someone brought him his beret. He turned it inside out and saw the two pins that had done the damage, they were covered in blood. The badge had probably saved his life, its façade being slightly buckled.

Rob waited a further fifteen minutes.

"Okay Emmett. Ready to roll again?"

"Yea. Fine by me."

195

He moved his beret around his head with the badge now facing the back. Lightening never strikes twice he was once told as a little boy when watching a violent thunderstorm coming in from the sea onto the farmland next to them. He had certainly used one of his seven lives thinking of another superstition as they slowly made their way along the track. He had taken a couple of swigs of water and felt quite ready for action again.

The shooting had ceased. Rob halted his patrol and warned of a possible ambush ahead. They were nearing the camp and "heaven knows what they may do now".

A crackle on Rob's radio, who was three paces ahead of Emmett, brought him to a halt. Up went his hand as all in line followed suit.

"I can see smoke ahead" said Mason "so we are very close. I'm moving up top and will cover you. Best of luck."

Rob signalled the trackers to come back to him. Emmett heard him talking in their language. He ended with "okay?" They nodded and crept back to the front of the patrol.

The plan was to approach the camp site on a wide front with their fire power, Rob, Emmett and Bambi, placed evenly along the line. A full frontal attack, which would be covered by Mason and his group, was about to happen.

Emmett was anxious as he didn't know whether all of his faculties were fully in place. He did, however, feel in a killing mood. They had very nearly got him. Now it was his turn for revenge.

Mason started sporadic firing as Upton's line got within sight of the wooden barricade fencing off the camp. Retaliatory shots were being returned from within. Hopefully the 'Terrs' hadn't realised they were being outflanked and were concentrating on Mason's group.

The sparse barricade was obviously an attempt to keep out small wild animals who might attack their feed store. Where Emmett lay, almost opposite the zigzag style entrance, he could see the area where the gang's firepower was centred. Rob was listening to Mason once again.

"Seems like six or seven males with rifles and half a dozen or so women. When you are ready to storm we will open up and make them respond. That's your signal. Okay?"

"Wilco. Roger. Out."

He put the radio behind his back, checked his ammunition clips, signalling Emmett and Bambi to follow suit. Others had machetes at the ready, some with wooden clubs in their extra hand.

The patrol had trained for this moment. Each knew what was necessary and how to look after their line neighbour. It had to be a quick in and out, obliterate, capture and withdraw.

Mason drew the Terrorists' fire and in advanced Upton's patrol. Once inside and seeing what was where, their automatics blazed into the fortified area. The 'Terrs' were caught reloading their aged Lee Enfield .303s. and down they fell to the combined fire power of Upton and Emmett.

Trackers and Wazuri were already rounding up the various camp followers, who, to a man and woman raised their hands in defeat. There was no fight left in them.

After a few hectic minutes, Rob radioed Mason to say:

"Mission completed. Keep your eyes open. There may be more outside."

"Wilco."

Four males were dead, three wounded. These were collared by the trackers while Bambi and crew were busy rounding up the women followers. Emmett had to find their arms cache, Bambi their food store while Rob planned the next move.

The radio crackled into life:

"Better come down if nothing is in view. We have a lot of mopping up to do."

"Roger. Wilco."

Six boxes of .303 amo, 15 rifles, 2 shotguns, 4 boxes of 12 bore cartridges, machetes, picks, knives, iron bars were part of the inventory Emmett collected.

Eight large bags of mealie meal (maize) with pots of ghee (lard), vegetables and some dried meat were Bambi's haul.

Once Mason and his patrol had met up with Upton's a plan for transporting the majority of the haul was put into operation.

It now became evident why the Wazuri were such an essential ingredient. They were bearers at work. They knew exactly what to do, what to make, like two stretchers filling their head carriers with meal and putting the prisoners to maximum use.

A brew of coffee was served to a satisfied and now relaxed patrol. Bananas and chocolate were eaten with gusto.

Rob radioed base with the result. Transport would be required at approximately three hours from then. A medic should be available to treat the wounded.

Everything that wasn't needed was piled up to make a fire and set ablaze. An area around the fire was cleared to prevent it spreading outwards and the possibility of setting the forest alight.

The patrol moved out an hour later. It was a long line now with the trackers roaming well forward. It was well known that this was a vulnerable time. Counter attacks could take place. This patrol's guard was up, however, and ready for anything.

Transport, two lorries, met them on a deserted forest track and returned the extended group to base. It was a job well done.

Debriefing took an hour and then it was hot shower time. The best part of any engagement. Beers came later.

In discussions with other FRO members each patrol realised how fortunate they were in encountering only gangs with non-automatic weapons. The FRO held the advantage but for how long was the question on everyone's mind? Two other patrols had been successful with similar results. The prisoners would be 'grilled' for information and follow-ups put into operation straight away.

Emmett's head wound healed rapidly as he remained indoors over the remainder of his stint at Pope's. He loved the ops (operations) room duty and being in radio contact with all patrols. His voice was praised as being the most precise. He also managed to get a couple of spotting trips up with the air wing pilots.

21

"So be prepared for any eventuality"

Without mentioning his injury to Anna she noticed it almost immediately he doffed his hat. There were two little marks right on one of his twin partings.

"They stand out," she said.

Emmett had then to relate the story.

"Goodness you were lucky. Have you made a will by any chance?" she said jokingly.

"God no, not yet. I'm going nowhere. Not up there I mean," pointing heavenwards.

They hugged and kissed as if these were their last goodbyes.

"How morbid we are," he said as he broke away and hastened to get drinks for them. Anna had fallen for Cinzano and lemonade. She also appreciated a glass of wine with the odd dinner a deux.

She had come out to Ratilli for the weekend as they had invited Jay and Jasmine over for the night. They had included six local couples for the meal so there was quite a lot of preparation to see to. Emmett had decided on a curry luncheon, three different types: lamb, chicken and fish with a dozen side items. Anna had prepared one such meal at Jeri's house using an old receipe of her Granny's. Christopher had to cut up dozens of different fruits for a gynormous fruit salad, matured in Cointreau.

Anna and Jaci had brought all the ingredients fresh from Urukan. She made up the curry paste on arrival and would cook the three dishes on Saturday, the day before. This was very necessary she told Emmett as curry always tasted better when matured overnight or even for a couple of days. Who was he to argue?

In Ireland all he had ever tasted were curry pies from the local Paki chipper. God only knew what went into them and when!

The Clubs in Ukenza were famous for their Sunday curry lunches. It was impossible to get a table without booking well in advance. The side dishes, Sambals, intrigued Emmett and his plate usually contained more of them than the curry dishes and rice.

He had also fallen for Pims No. 1 as his luncheon tipple so this would be the main item on offer at Ratilli. Lager and wine would also be available.

Emmett appreciated the two girls and the enthusiasm they put into the event. They had it neatly planned, itemized, designated workloads and all he did was pay for it. He owed his neighbours a good party and this would be part of an ongoing tradition.

Anna had very kindly donated to Emmett, for the weekend, the two pictures which Jay had given her. They now graced the long wall behind the red settee in the lounge.

"They are only on loan, you understand. If I leave they come too," she joked and smilingly kicked him in the shins on handing them over.

"Understood, my black beauty," he responded by whacking her sensuous rear end.

The aromas wafting out from the kitchen that evening brought his taste buds to tantalising frustration. Anna allowed him a teaspoonful taste of each.

"My mind is made up. We are off to Kenya on our next holiday, down to the coast and we can eat this sort of thing until we cry. Okay by you?"

"Yes siree. You like eh?" handing him his first teaspoonful.

"Don't tempt me. I might get up in the night and eat it all."

"You wouldn't dare – and I wouldn't let you."

"Take heed Christopher. Learn all about curry from madam. I will try out your attempt in the weeks to come."

"No problem fendi. I learn."

Jaci had decided to stay over, so the three went with the dogs. They drove all over the home sections and gave them a romp in one of the well filled dams. Six mallard duck took off in protest with a single grey heron remaining statuesque against a shimmering unruffled corner of the water fringed with reed.

They dined together on the veranda and then Jaci retired to the guest quarters down beside Christopher's room.

Emmett played Sinatra, Ella and King Cole all evening. Anna was becoming appreciative of his music and especially warmed to the great Ella Fitzgerald, first lady of jazz. They shuffled, nightclub fashion, around the dogs to 'My Funny Valentine' and then retired.

Jay and Jasmine arrived at 11.00am. Coffee was on the go. Emmett then took them on a short tour of the farm showing off his best wheat. They then looked over the horses and compound. Jay was fascinated with the machinery so Emmett told them all about Ian's stable of agricultural monsters and that these were mere infants in comparison.

"I will talk to him about those later on. I couldn't hope to visualise these on my ranch. Saw them in operation in our middle states back home."

Anna met them on the veranda with the first glasses of Pims.

"Wow. I never expected such elegance. Isn't this supposed to be a colonial tipple?"

"It's my favourite. Who cares. Drink up and good luck," responded Emmett offering them seats to relax into.

Soon the dust clouds started rolling down the avenue as his guests arrived.

When every male guest went up for seconds and thirds Emmett drew Anna's attention.

"See that? Your curries are superb, much appreciated, well done."

Their hands touched in an emotional grip. Both sets of eyes said a thousand silent words,

"If this is a sample of life on the Punjabi Plains then Jasmine, you and I must move here pronto. Our gratitude, Anna and Emmett, is abundant beyond boundaries. Thank you. May we come again?" with a big smile all over his face.

Everyone raised their glasses in a toast and response to Jay's emotions.

"Anna and Emmett. Bless you both," prompted Jay and Jasmine.

They had brought, as a present, Jay's latest sighting of a migrant hippo in the river below the castle. He had managed to capture, in stark black and white, the hippo yawning with its mouth wide open in the bottom left corner of the picture. In the top right hand corner was the castle silhouetted against a setting sun.

"Quite magical Jay. How long did it take to capture that precise moment?" asked Rachel.

"About two hours in total. I have about twenty other shots but I love this one the best."

"Lucky you Emmett," cut in Jan, "any chance of a local exhibition Jay? Its about time we all bought your work."

"Hadn't thought about that. Lets put heads together and come up with something. As you probably know I show in the States annually, that's how I keep the ranch and sanctuary going of course."

"How about a big charity do in Urukan with net proceeds to the FRO?" chirped in a slightly inebriated Shirra.

"Great idea. Something for our ladies to tackle," commented Ian.

The last guests departed at 18.30 hours. Obviously it had been a roaring success and Emmett had enough leftovers for another couple of meals for himself.

"A well catered function. Thanks a million girls and Christopher of course. You were stars."

All the clearing and washing up had been completed by Anna and Jaci with Christopher carrying everything and putting away. Emmett kept himself busy clearing up glasses, paper napkins, ash trays and finishing off the last of the Pims and fruit salad.

Dogs didn't get any treats, there had been nothing dropped in the culinary line. They needed a good walk so off he took them enjoying his evening cigar as he strode down the runway accompanied by the Freedos.

The girls had decided to make a 5.00am start on the Monday morning. So a night of reflection with anecdotes from the party had them all asleep in no time at all. It had been a pleasant day and a fine reciprocation of gratitude to all in the area especially those who had shown kindness and assistance towards them. Jay and Jasmine departed mid morning.

"Mandalay is open to you whenever you wish," were Jay's parting words. They were driving over to Ian's before setting off home.

Farm radios went into meltdown. Gilbert ran from his office to tell Emmett to come quickly. He was being called by Buster. The radio in the house had mysteriously broken down and was away for mending.

"Get over here a.s.a.p. Thanks."

That meant the worst. On the drive over he put many scenarios across his mind screen, any of many could be a tragedy. Vehicles of all sizes made their way and the buzz outside the building was electric. Dust clouds shaded the area. It seemed everyone had been fearing such a callout.

"Morning all. I'll get to the nub straightaway. The Luckes, Raymond and Maureen, have been murdered and their little son, Jason, is missing. For those of you who don't know them, they were both medical doctors and farmed up near Popes. They had been in that district for fifteen years. Their large clinic was an icon. People came from all over to receive their free care. They were highly respected and liked by all and sundry."

He continued:

"Tony has got six patrols out already. By the way, this dastardly act occurred during the early hours of this morning when his radio 'call-in' did not take place. A couple of jeeps, heavily armed, found the bodies, bits of them strewn all around their front lawn. Now I know we have had a number of you blokes up there recently but I need to know who will be available within a couple of days. I'm not going to delegate just yet. You must volunteer. Break for ten minutes and a smoke, coffee is on the hob, then lets show how we feel about this tragedy."

Many of the older farmers had known the Lucke family. They were devastated, eyes shrouded in fear, speech not readily forthcoming.

Emmett's age group were vibrant in their desire to volunteer. He had only just returned from a week up in that region so he didn't feel he would be needed again, if there were enough volunteers. It was getting close to harvest and he had to be present, if at all feasible, to achieve the maximum work rate. This was commonly accepted in the area and there were at least a dozen others who had not yet been called up for forest duty.

He would put his hand up for further duty but Ian had said to him in the break that he most probably wouldn't be called, this time.

There was virtually a hundred percent yes to volunteering so Buster expressed his thanks and said once he had been in contact with Pope's and a strategy had been worked out he would contact them all again. He then gave the members a real tough 'pep talk' with complacency being his main theme.

"It could be one of us next. Just think about that. There seems no logic in their road of carnage – no way can we get ahead of their thinking. So be prepared for any eventuality. Return to your farms and thanks for your immediate response. We will win."

A very depressed crowd departed to contemplate their next move. Ian asked Emmett to come up for supper that evening. He wished to put a plan into operation.

Prior to supper Ian, Howard and Emmett sat together working out a strategy, in case of any trouble, covering all three properties. Each would look after the other and collectively be on twenty-four hour call.

A secret call sign known only to them, *Moses in the Bushes*, was to be their 'Mayday' or emergency signal. That meant put everything into action pronto or as Howard put it "get your fucking wings on." Emmett thought long about this and decided to have something similar – some catch phrase or something – with Anna.

"Each farm must strengthen their respective farm guards. Give them training for specific functions. Standardise uniforms and categorise their ethnic plus factors, i.e. who was best for tracking, driving, welding, etc."

Finally, each of them must find out whom and how many were ready for a fight. Literally, who would stand up and be counted in the face of a terrorist attack. Where lay their loyalty?

Over supper they discussed the Lucke murder. The son's body had been found hidden in bushes some way from the house.

"Why pick on them?" asked Jan of no one in particular, "when all their time up there was spent aiding and caring for the sick and malnourished. Is there an answer?"

There wasn't, or not one from around their table at that moment. Everyone was shocked and Emmett felt the ladies were a little scared.

"I suppose we will all have to carry gats (guns) from now on? Proper pistol packin mommas we will be! I'm not looking forward to it I must say," came from a subdued but cynical Rachel.

"Oh now steady on old trout," said Howard in mock reply, "its not the wild west yet and hopefully will never be."

"I'll drink to that. Cheers, once again to all of us," responded Ian, and with that they retired to around the fire for final 'bum warmers' before Howard and Emmett drove home. The conversation lightened up over coffee and the subject was Geronimo. His next race was in three weeks time.

"The others will have done their homework this time but I suppose you will be confident again," said Howard.

"Everything is going great up 'till now," replied Emmett, "but one never knows the outcome until the winning post. I know, I know, sounds corny, but it's true. With no cock ups on either side, his or mine, I would be very confident."

"That's all that's asked for. It gave us such a thrill. You two," looking at Jan and Ian, "must not miss this run."

"We will do our best. It will be the week before harvesting so can we break the bank this time, Emmett?" queried Ian.

"Put your monsters on us," smiled back Emmett. "I'd best be off now and thanks."

Two days later Emmett halted all work on the farm. He called the labour to a meeting in the grain shed. With Gilbert as interpreter he outlined his farm guard strategy.

The day before, with Christopher's help, Emmett had gone through each person by name with him assessing them on a scale of 1-10. From this and from his own knowledgable 'feel' he highlighted six likely leaders. They, if they agreed, would get special training and would come together with the same calibre selected by both Howard and Ian.

Meantime the labour lines would be fortified with rules and regulations drawn up. A very strict visitor count would be put into immediate operation. There would be no outsiders allowed anywhere on the farm and most definitely not near the homestead/compound.

Langat would mount a pony patrol at unspecified times. No daily routines, excepting for start up time in the morning, would be run making it difficult therefore for someone to know exactly when anything definite might happen. Make internal information as difficult as possible to factor into any outside attack or infiltration was Emmett's goal.

Special and increased security would be mounted on all harvest work. This prime product must be protected at all costs.

The local pilots would be giving aerial surveys and backup right along the route.

Security in and around the homestead and compound/labour lines must be tight at all hours as the vulnerable times would be when maximum personnel was out in the field.

The staff seemed up for it and applauded each point stressed by Emmett in emphasising the importance of security.

"The bottom line everyone, is that if we lose the harvest, even a part of it, we all lose our bonus. And I for one don't need that. Agreed?"

They cheered, stamped feet, hit the corrugated sides of the store, and in fact made one hell of a noise. Enough to frighten the ponies and Geronimo in the next shed to them. Langat was standing between both sheds and signalled to Emmett his concern. A blast from his whistle, now carried around his neck at all times, brought order and silence. He thanked the staff and gave them the rest of the day off. A football match had been prearranged against Howard's side.

In the following days barricades and barbed wire entanglements were erected around the entire compound. Bhogal had sent a lorry full of wire, fence posts, strainers and halogen lights on receipt of Emmett's urgent radio message.

There was a hectic sense of urgency in all the work carried out during that period. Both Christopher and Gilbert spoke to Emmett about the feelings of the staff.

"They are sickened by what is going on up country fendi and don't want it to happen here. They are also worried about their families back home. You are our leader. Everyone is happy about that and you are amongst us."

The message was clear. Everything depended on his handling of the situation. That night, puffing a cheroot or two with a lager or two, on his veranda, his pack of canines around him, Emmett realised he was growing up fast. What had been for him, an agricultural dream, was now becoming a military nightmare. He questioned his right to carry such a weight on his youthful and inexperienced shoulders. His hope was that his stolid upbringing would carry him through.

At that moment he craved Anna's arms, a shoulder to lean on, a body so warm and willing to comfort him. He felt lonely that night, for the first time in two years. Was he a little morbid he wondered?

Emmett was not called to go on active duty this time. Four other youngsters headed off to bolster support at Pope's farm. The wheat farmers now had seventeen of their FRO 'blooded' on Uma duties since its formation. Luckily there had been no casualties.

Both syces, Langat and Sunguru were taken out and shown by Emmett what he meant by mounted patrols.

First thing every morning they would trot and canter along the boundary fence looking for any cutting or breaking of it. If an entry had been made they must then follow the tracks of whatever had made it to find out where they or it had proceeded. Langat must report back on his walkie-talkie to Gilbert in the office who would then contact Emmett and various procedures would be put into practise.

Sometimes large antelope, Eland and Kudu, or Zebra and Wildebeest would, by sheer strength and numbers, make the break through for whatever reason. One or two would get entangled in the wire and badly maim themselves. These, if they were mature, would be shot and their meat distributed to the staff. The youngsters would be brought back to Christopher for nursery recuperation. Emmett's back garden seemed to always have a few patients in residence. William, the three-legged warthog, was now the joke of the compound, having full freedom. As tame as the dogs he at times thought he was one?

If, however, the break in was by humans then cautious follow up procedures were to be adhered to with directions coming from Emmett.

Geronimo loved these 06.30am exercises, on the days he wasn't having a preparatory gallop in his tight ongoing training schedule. His second hurdle race was only ten days away.

Emmett taught the two syces to jink at a canter and gallop in case the intruders took a pot shot at them. Both riders and ponies enjoyed these games. It was not only good for fitness but also the morale of the staff. Word got back to the labour lines pretty quickly. The syces saw themselves as the farm's first line of defence. A little 'OTT' (over the top) Emmett thought when Christopher reported back with this finding.

22

"Who won Uncle Emmett?"

With a landrover, jeep and truck, the farm guard could be transported speedily to any part of the farm to intercept any intrusion if and when needed.

Emmett organised mock callouts and even had some staff acting as 'Terrs' hiding in the wheat and being flushed out by the guard, rounded up and captured. He wanted all his staff to know that he had his hand on the pulse of things and no one need forget that or try anything stupid. He let off shots every now and then just to keep everyone on their toes. This part of training was teaching the ponies not to be afraid of shooting. Corrib and Mask couldn't have cared less but Geronimo freaked when he heard the first shot near to where he was standing with Langat holding him by reins and head collar only. He went into reverse, head held high with violent bursts of snorting exhaled from flared nostrils.

This was not what a horse in training for a vital race needed so Emmett sent Geronimo home. No more shooting near his prize athlete. The other two must have either been party to a lot of shooting, perhaps clay pigeon, on their previous farm, or else been actually trained to guns prior to moving to Ratilli. They never moved a muscle or twitched an ear!

With scenes of the Wild West, guns a'blazing from horseback as cowboys and injuns rode madly at each other in his mind, Emmett would test the ponies to this degree in the days ahead.

Morale was high amongst his staff, of this he was left in no doubt. Whenever he called a halt to a training session they asked for more. He noticed they loved being disciplined and they loved to be lead from the front. They were not too keen on taking the initiative, however, but he could trust them in an emergency. They would be loyal.

The barricading and wiring of the compound and labour lines, when finished, looked like something out of a Second World War film of German concentration camps.

An area around the open-air hangars and rear of his house was next to be tackled. This was in his opinion the weak spot in the perimeter security fence. Eight telegraph poles with halogen lights enclosed in wire mesh were positioned throughout the compound area. No shadowy spots remained. Rocket flares were placed outside the office with only Emmett or Gilbert allowed to ignite them. These were in case of the compound being attacked. Their glare would be seen by neighbouring farmguard lookouts and a general emergency situation would then be put into action.

At times Emmett felt he might as well be living up in Northern Ireland where these sorts of security aids were commonplace. Buster had emphasised complacency and slackness being a worrying factor as all the problem areas were far from this region. But one never knew. "Better to be aware and prepared," he kept reiterating.

Bhogal had come up trumps in providing all equipment and with speed. The team he had delegated had worked flat out from arrival. They most probably didn't like being out in the bush for long and wished to return to urban dwelling as soon and safe as possible.

Emmett was becoming a little paranoid with the stress on security and he wondered about the chit chat that would emanate from these town visitors. His farm strategies must not be bandied about the place, especially within town and city folk. One never knew who might be listening? The evil *Makinto* were secretly everywhere, listening, reporting back, and planning. No one was outside their range. Their web was widely cast.

Whether Uma was a part of *Makinto* had not yet been fully established. It was quite probable that the President wished both prongs to be the fork in the side of the settlers. He would sit back, gloat and preach innocence. This holier than thou attitude might well ricochet back and hit him hard in places he wouldn't relish? There was a feeling that infighting was the flavour of the month with a battle royal likely to take place. This could see the ousting of the President.

Opposition parties were gaining momentum countrywide. They were becoming more confident and seemed to have policies that were applauded by the populous.

Emmett awoke with a start. He looked at the travelling clock beside his bed – it read 04.23. He was sweating profusely. The nightmare must have been torrid. He remembered not a single item.

Whimpers from the veranda and the odd scratch on dividing doors meant the pack were awake and worried. After stoking the fire and placing the half filled kettle atop the hob he ventured outside. He had clothed himself in his Irish tracksuit and had given his body a quick top and tail to rid himself of the perspiration then turning cold on his body.

After a delicious mug of honey sweetened Black Mountain tea and two of Jan's rusks he took the pack on a recce of the compound and then down the runway.

Emmett always carried a powerful torch on such nocturnal jaunts and after a couple of minutes caught a pair of glinting eyes about one hundred yards off to the rear of his house. The eyes were close to the ground so it was most probably a black backed jackal that had been sniffing around the henhouse.

The eyes didn't move and Emmett and his pack ventured towards them. Perhaps it had a kill and was loath to leave it. Rastus suddenly saw the 'eyes' and took off with the other two in pursuit. Suddenly 'eyes' took off in retreat. A great chase ensued but of course their quarry, it was a jackal, out sprinted and left them far behind.

Rani stopped first, turned around and nosed her way back scenting to where 'eyes' had been. There, she and Emmett, who had arrived simultaneously, found the remains of a jack rabbit. The pack made light of the scraps. 'Eyes' escaped into the night or what remained of it.

By the time they circled the extremities of the compound, from some hundreds of yards out, the day's dawn was breaking. Cocks started to crow answering each other's calls and the 'pie' dogs started yowling, especially when they saw the pack approaching from outside.

He had been having these shortened nights quite frequently since his last sortie into enemy territory up the mountains. He didn't worry about them and as none of the nightmares could be identified he didn't think they meant much. His sleep pattern was only slightly out, as by then his body would have experienced a sound seven hours.

Geronimo had grown in stature since the hurdle race. He had muscled up and like a modern athlete had 'bulked' up appreciably. He was a long way from the wild little thing that first arrived on Ratilli. Langat was doing a great job and the boiled linseed Geronimo received in his night feed was making his coat glisten. He really looked magnificent.

It was a Wednesday morning and that meant fast work for him. Wednesdays and Fridays fashioned sprints of up to a half a mile in order to keep his wind right. His stamina was excellent and he was eating up like a good'un.

His second hurdle race was the coming Sunday at Timuru. Emmett knew the opposition this time would be strong. They would have done their homework and would be prepared to throw down the gauntlet at the 'Irish'! Geronimo and Emmett must repel all opposition and keep doing so. It was a great game and one he targeted as being champion of.

The Timuru meeting also had a children's race over four furlongs (half a mile) and he had invited Zimba and Edith to ride his ponies in it. The two syces would ride them in the last event on the card, the Grooms' Gallop. Neither pony would be fast enough to win but it would be fun for both sets of riders he thought.

Anna and Jaci brought the kids out on the Friday evening. They would accompany the truck load of three animals, prepare them, race them and cool them down afterwards. The kids would get the feel of a race meeting and the thrill of the contest.

Emmett promised to put them through the entire routine on the Saturday morning so that the actual event would not be too daunting a task. He remembered his first pony race outside Kinvara back home and how he was totally unprepared for it. He got left at the start and only had dust and dirt in his and his pony's face for the length of it.

These two would be fully conversant in the routine and it would then be up to them alone. He liked perfection and accuracy. It had stood him well up to now.

Anna had already been through Emmett's process and it had proved a success for her. Now her wards were in the classroom.

At breakfast Emmett outlined the parade ring, cantering down to the start, circling around and checking their girths, the line up for the start and then the 'off'. The race itself was up to them. After finishing he told them how to pull up to a trot, then walk back to the parade ring. It was their duty to unsaddle and return their silks to the jockey's room. All very adult they thought but he immediately interjected by getting them to agree to the age old maxim 'better to do it right than not at all' – and especially so when dealing with animals. He told them he would ask questions about each step of the race build-up throughout the day. He thought that young minds needed this exact revision of what was their most sensational event in their short life. And nothing must go wrong. They were Emmett's responsibility. Their parents and extended family would be watching.

Both Emmett and Anna were quite astounded by the manner in which both of the children took to the task. The ponies behaved in an exemplary fashion and by lunchtime he was completely satisfied with the results.

"Brilliant you two. I now wish I had better ponies for you to give you more of a chance of getting placed. But never mind, hey? It will be a grand experience."

"Uncle Emmett, it's going to be such fun and thanks for the chance," piped up an ecstatic Edith ahead of her brother who rather mumbled the same thing but was overshadowed by his exuberant little sister.

Anna took them off for cool drinks whilst Emmett discussed plans for boxing and at what time the lorry was to leave in the morning. This would be the first trip with all three equines onboard. Langat asked if they could bring a friend to help out. Emmett agreed.

He had asked Anna to buy the kids coloured polo necks to wear as colours.

"It will look so professional, even if they are warm. Trust me." She had managed to find a lovely light blue and a deep maroon. Edith chose the blue.

He had a hard time getting them to agree to travel with Anna and him in the landrover rather than with the ponies in the lorry. Jaci would travel behind the ponies as far as Urukan. She would then go home but would travel on to Timuru in time for the first race which was the children's big moment.

Jeri and Margaret were already at the Timuru club when they arrived. The lorry had also arrived safe and sound and the ponies, Geronimo included, had been walked and placed in stalls. They looked relaxed.

Emmett asked Jeri and extended family to please stay away from the children in the build up to the race. He needed their undivided attention. Only Anna could be with them. Zimba and Edith had to be focused.

There were twelve runners and in Emmett's view his two ponies were equal to anything in looks, turnout and fitness. He questioned their speed, or lack of it and wondered it there wasn't perhaps a 'springer', a pony from a different grade to that specified in the declaration form, within the group?

Most of the Zungu children, the majority, were sons or daughters of their polo playing fathers and the other African riders would be children of their syces.

One Zungu boy exuded an exterior confidence which made his machoness standout. All the others seemed apprehensive with eyes gazing on the ground as they stood beside their parents in the centre of the parade ring.

Two ponies took off at a lickety spit gallop as they were released in front of the crowd. They sped off down the course where hopefully they would be waved down by the starters and stewards and brought under control?

This was something Emmett had feared and had spent most of his time explaining and practising on the farm. Luckily both of his ponies behaved themselves and their riders kept full control of them.

The start was ragged with the macho boy screaming off ahead of the rest. Corrib and Mask broke well. Emmett had told them to line up side by side and both children could hardly be seen as they crouched low along their ponies necks. Most of the riders were in an upright, polo, position.

At the halfway marker they were second and third and seemed to be galloping well within themselves. With about one hundred yards to go the leading pony veered sharply to the right, catching his rider by surprise. He probably saw the stalls and decided to go home. His rider, however, caught him up in time and kept them within the rails. They had lost a good six lengths which put Corrib and Mask on even terms with fifty yards to go.

It was a sensational driving finish as the three flew past the winning post with two others about two lengths behind.

211

The macho boy had held on Emmett felt in his gut and told Anna as much as he raced from the little stand down onto the course. Hopefully the children had stayed aboard as all the ponies pulled up.

He was so relieved when he saw them both trotting back, confidently sitting high in the saddle, smiling and chatting to each other.

"Who won Uncle Emmett?" blurted the two in unison as they pulled up to a walk beside him. Anna had joined him.

"I think you were second and third but the result hasn't been announced yet. You were brilliant, absolutely fabulous, well done. And you too," patting both ponies, "performed beyond my wildest dreams."

He lead Corrib and Zimba until Langat arrived whilst Sunguru took hold of Mask and Edith. Anna took Emmett's hand as they walked back to an ecstatic crowd full of applause for all the riders who were now collected up by their parents or syces.

The winner was No. 3 – macho boy – by a whisker said the announcer, from the dead heaters Nos 7 and 8 – Zimba and Edith. What a thrill for all thought Emmett as Jeri, Margaret and 'God knows who' thronged around the children as they dismounted.

The parade ring was bedlam as congratulatory screams, pats on back and general relief exuded from every pore for the safe return of their own loved ones.

A great success was the general comment and opinion as the crowd dispersed. Emmett and Anna had taken no outside rides on the card that day as with entries in three races they needed an 'all hands on deck' availability.

The hurdle was over two miles with eight obstacles, as was the first such race. The four of them had walked the course early on noting where the hurdles were placed. Emmett was glad that there was a long run into the first and a short sprint from the last flight to the winning post. This suited him fine.

An entry of fifteen faced the starter. Geronimo was very much on his toes and literally 'champing at the bit'. Unless another or two decided to go to the front from the off Emmett was content to take up the running and see if once again, he could run them off their legs.

Three of them, however, had learnt from that first hurdle race and took up front running tactics. Emmett guided Geronimo into fourth, about five lengths off the pace. This continued for the first circuit when one of them started to fall back and let Geronimo through to third.

On going out for the final circuit Geronimo was cruising in second place and Emmett felt they had the beating of the leader whenever he wished to push the button. He left it late and jumping the final flight upsides the long time leader he asked for Geronimo's effort. The horse flew past the other and put five lengths between them at the winning post.

He had a class act beneath him and was now prepared for all comers in the final race, the Champion Hurdle, in a month's time.

Geronimo was a natural jumper and met his fences on an even stride. He seemed to see his stride even sooner than Emmett. He was, in his minds eye, the Ukenza edition of Ireland's Hatton's Grace. It was a pity there were not more races for him.

His syces had great fun in their 'tiendi', the farewell race, and were thrilled just to have taken part. Both finished out of places as some of the fastest polo ponies of the district were running.

All in all a great day for Ratilli and the lorry set off with extra passengers all singing at the top of their voices. It, luckily, didn't seem to worry the equines.

Jeri and Margaret had invited Emmett and Anna to meet them at the Chinese in Urukan for an evening meal. That was speedily accepted.

The children were still pumped up, their adrenalin was high and even though they had school next morning they were allowed to stay up until 9.30pm. Emmett had booked a room at the Club.

23

Getting too close for comfort

The worst incident in the ongoing terrorist battle for supremacy came early on a Wednesday morning, a week after the start of the harvest. The Gita Massacre, as it became internationally known, was a crime almost too horrific for description.

Hundreds of staff and their families from the saw mills of the same name lived in the supposedly secure village. Rows of thatched houses, twenty-five to a row, with lines of cho's (latrines) between every second row were enclosed by a security fence. This was built as part of the overall plan to secure communities working up near the forest line along the Mandaras.

Gita Saw Mills employed over a thousand labourers who, prior to the troubles, lived in a patchwork of groups in and around the Mills.

From reports coming in over the wires the attack had been a well prepared and planned operation with obvious collusion from within the commune. Most likely traitors were the security guards who manned the two gates and turrets?

It was a masterful plan filled with bestial overtones. At least a dozen of a gang must have taken part.

Once inside the camp, they each went to the head of the rows of houses and set the thatch alight. They had chosen a night when a breeze fanned the flames down the rows with each torched roof blowing sparks onto the next house.

The gang, armed with guns and machetes, stood outside the doors of the houses and as the occupants rushed out, in terror of the burning roofs above them, they were hacked to death, maimed and left to die. Some were shot dead.

It was a chaotic and terror filled hour before the gang withdrew and disappeared into the night and forest. General Service Units arrived from Kenzi within two hours of being informed. The alarm was triggered by an alert farm guard on a neighbouring farm whose Zungu owners were away on business.

Emmett was told that Gita was quite close to Kambu the area he had discovered when visiting Anna's parents over that memorable Christmas. Buster warned him to be ready if the FRO of that region needed supplementing. He personally didn't think they would be called out as the powers that be knew it was harvest time and the other areas could augment the strike force when required.

This was without doubt the most bestial undertaking of the evil Uma or *Makinto*? Talk was that they were getting desperate and the strategy of stockading the local populous was having the required effect, ie the terrorist food supply was drying up. This massacre, however, put a dampener on the entire rural population.

Opposition groups massed and marched on the President's palace in Kenzi. Smaller groups did likewise in Urukan and the other district towns with administrative headquarters.

Their leaders managed to keep the protests peaceful but outbreaks of bullying and retribution were committed by government forces lead by the Orange berets of *Makinto*.

Victor Mbugu took to the airwaves of national radio. Everyone listened but the majority were unimpressed and immediately called for his resignation. This went unheeded like most requests. The tyrant was as a cobra, most fierce when cornered.

It was now reported that two hundred and fifty-seven deaths were recorded at the Gita massacre. Double that figure were allegedly maimed for life with others badly injured. Children had not been saved either with forty-three deaths and over a hundred injured.

This angered the Wazuri more than anything up until then. Volunteers were signing up in their hundreds throughout the country. They wanted their voice heard in Mbugu's marbled halls. And they would get it.

The first few weeks of harvest went according to plan. All the contract combines arrived on time and transporters (hauliers) followed suit.

An interesting visitor, in a really vintage model landrover, arrived into the compound just before lunchtime one day. Out stepped a wizened old man, a Zungu, who stretched his back a few times and moped his brow before heading for the office. He was dressed in khaki bush shirt and longs. The back of his vehicle was packed with African women, mostly in blue and white uniforms with scarves over their heads.

Emmett was inside his house and watched as the visitor met Gilbert and talked with him. He was then lead over to the little garden gate as it became obvious Emmett was the person required.

They met on the steps below the veranda.

"Hello and let me introduce myself," he said in the softest of voices as he wiped his forehead once more, "I'm Father Martin Green from the Parish of Fuda. Your friends Jay and Jasmine told me to call on you when next I passed."

In shaking hands Emmett lead him onto the veranda and sat themselves down at the table. Father Martin was affectionate towards the dogs who crowded him returning his love and attention.

"Something to drink, Father?"

"Oh, very definitely a yes please."

"Soft or beer?"

"Need you ask a fellow Irishman such a question?" came his reply with a Barry Fitzgerald sort of a smile. Christopher was attentive nearby and returned inside to collect refreshment. Emmett opened with "and what part of the old country are you from Father?"

"Castlebar, County Mayo. Do you know it?"

"Afraid not. I have passed through the town on my way to Westport. I'm from Ballyvaughan which you most probably do know."

"Yes indeed I do. I've been in the caves many a time with visitors. Grand place, lovely scenery."

Christopher arrived with cold beers and asked about lunch.

"Of course you'll join me Father? We'll have so much to talk about. Thanks Christopher. Let's eat out here. By the way Father, what shall I do about your jeep load of Wabeebee?"

"Oh they will find themselves something in your camp. They probably have relations here. I never worry about them, they sort themselves out pretty hastily.

"Cheers."

"God bless and good health," responded Father Martin.

Over a succulent piece of roast pork with crisp crackling followed by fruit salad they discussed Ireland, the world and 'the troubles' in Ukenza.

He had been a missionary for thirty-seven years in both the Congo and here. His fluency in language covered French, German, three local dialects and Asgeilge. Emmett invited him to say Grace. His was exactly as Emmett had learnt at school. He felt a lump in his throat.

They didn't move from the table until Christopher asked if they would like tea? It was 3.45pm.

All the time they had sat there Emmett was keeping an eye on proceedings in the compound. Tractor and trailer loads of seed wheat being offloaded into the store. Hauliers arriving and departing up the avenue. The mechanic's jeep rushing here and there. A smoke screen of musty smelling dust hung over the compound and out along the avenue.

It had been a fulfilling few hours. Emmett learnt a lot more of the vagaries of the Kenzi people. Father Martin was a font of knowledge and only the surface had been scratched. He was invited to return whenever passing. On the spur of the moment Emmett asked if he would be party to a blessing of his next season's crop.

"What a grand idea. Of course, wild horses wouldn't stop me. Just tell me a likely date well in advance and I'll do the rest. God bless you."

Christopher, Emmett, Gilbert and the dogs waved then off. Perhaps this visit was a lucky omen?

Luck went straight out the window in double quick time. Emmett was urgently called to his landrover radio by staff who heard his name being repeated over and over. He was at one of the combine harvesters which had a problem some one hundred yards into the field.

"Yes, Emmett here. Go ahead," in breathless syllables.

"Emmett this is Ian. Have just heard that the bus has been ambushed and attacked ten miles this side of Koram. Completely burnt out with dead and dying strewn all over the road. We are halting all transportation and Buster is sending a squad to look see. Two kites are already in the air so listen out for further information. And be prepared to follow up. Have you got all that? Over."

"Roger Ian. Horrible news. Will listen out. Wilco. Out."

He jumped into the landrover and sped back to the office giving instructions to Gilbert to hold all lorries.

"Incoming ones can be loaded and retained here. There's a big problem this side of Koram."

Gilbert butted in before he got another word out.

"I've heard from the Ratilli about the bus. Dreadful and frightening Master. Where next?"

"We must keep calm Gilbert and you must handle the staff – okay? I've to be prepared to be called out on follow up."

With that Emmett went to his house and put all his kit, clothes, boots and guns on his bed ready for a quick getaway.

"Christopher please make me a dozen sandwiches, anything, and put some fruit with them. Two thermos flasks of kawa and half a bottle of whisky. Pack them ready in a kikoo. Okay? Thanks."

He returned to the field and noticed that the combine which had been broken down was now thankfully back in action once more.

All faces looked at him for news and comfort. There very well could have been farm labour and family on that bus. It was 4.30pm and it would have been on its return trip from Urukan, jammed tight with farm families and most probably school children.

He stayed close to his vehicle and listened to Buster's HQ getting in contact with all the FR and rostering them into shifts.

"Come in Emmett. Emmett come in please."

"Emmett here go ahead."

"Will you link up with Ian at the Ratilli at 20.00 hours. Bring four farm guard with you. Prepare for an all nighter. Okay? Over."

"Roger HQ and wilco out."

Emmett toured the area being harvested and instructed his headman in the field to carry on until 8.00pm then all to return to the compound. Gilbert would give them the latest news and instructions.

What worried him most was the fact that a gang was operating in their region and had shown its strength in no uncertain manner. This was what the FRO had feared all along. Hopefully their months of planning would now click into action and a successful result would be achieved, without further bloodshed. It was indeed very close to home, he thought. And where was the gang now?

Road blocks had immediately been set up throughout the district. All farm labour lines had to be screened for visitors, outsiders. No private or public transport was allowed on any district road until the all clear was given.

Harvesting, however, would continue. Stockpiling of grain must, if needs be, fill all suitable areas. This was an emergency.

The two spotter planes, one piloted by Howard with Ian aboard, had sighted three pick-up trucks travelling at great speed through scrubland west of Koram headed for the Klintoo forest reserve. All this information was being monitored in Urukan as well as at Buster's HQ. Two general service units (GSU's) were despatched from Urukan and would rendezvous at the police station in Koram with the wheatlands FR.

Meanwhile three vehicles with a compliment of four Zungu, three Hindi and twelve FG's were already hightailing it to Koram and onto the tracks of the alleged gansters. They would form the immediate follow-up group. The spotters would have to return to their respective airstrips before dark so contact if possible, must be made by then.

When Emmett and his group arrived at Koram and made themselves known to the GSU's it was learnt that contact had already been made with the gang. Evidently one of their vehicles had broken down – a burst radiator reportedly – and the occupants had scattered on foot into the bush.

Some of these had been met head on by the FR; a brief exchange of fire power followed with the terrorists losing one dead, one injured and the other raising his arms in surrender. A few stray bullets had strafed the FR vehicle with, fortunately, no real damage. Half the FR personnel from this vehicle joined up with one of the others whilst the driver and two FG returned with the bodies to Koram police HQ.

Emmett was ordered to oversee the interrogation of the two live prisoners. Questioning would be carried out by a senior GSU officer and one FR – Rod Beaton – who was fluent in two ethnic languages.

Emmett would disseminate any information gained and pass on all relevant items to the chasing FR units. It was the speed in breaking down the prisoners and following up information gained that made arrests in other places such an essential factor. The FR network in conjunction with the police's own urban setup was now really making inroads into the terrorists underground movement. Surprise raids on houses, offices and warehouses were amassing incredible amounts of information and stores.

It was becoming increasingly obvious that a lot of those being arrested were only partially pro terrorist. They were cooperating through fear: fear for their families being targeted by UMA, without recourse.

In interrogation these people unwittingly passed on information which was then matched to previously received titbits from whence a whole new covert operation could be mounted.

Jeri Ntsemo's cooperation and determination to rid his district of UMA and any others attempting to jump on their bandwagon, had cemented relations between the Farmers' Reserve and the Government departments. He regarded the FR as the senior arm of security as their Zungu personnel were far more experienced than their Kenzian – African brothers. Only a few slightly suspect police officers felt put out by the FR presence

"These rats", as Jeri so succinctly put it "are being watched very closely by me and will be replaced when necessary. A lot of them, believe it or not, are afraid of the *Makinto* and need to be seen to be on the right side."

Forty-seven bodies from the bus were being identified by unbelieving family and friends. Twenty-three were injured and being transported to Urukan Mission Hospital. A number of children unfortunately were dead.

The horror of the bus massacre was only now, twenty-four hours later, getting through to the outposts of the district. A curfew had been declared from dusk to dawn. Only FR and GSU's were exempt.

In the follow up of the two pickup vehicles which had gone on relentlessly, the vehicles had been found abandoned deep in the forest.

The local air wing was airborne again at first light and two small groups of insurgents had been sighted about five miles north of their amandoned vehicles heading on foot for a native reserve.

Emmett heard the CO giving instructions for the two GSU's to circumvent the forest and get into the reserve ahead of the gang and set up ambushes there. The air wing would direct operations.

Emmett wished he had been with them and been allowed to lob grenades down on the gang as he had done months before in the Mandaras; perhaps that would happen anyway?

He liked working in the 'ops' – operations – room when not aiding the interrogation. It was the control centre and he felt a hands-on contact with those in the front line. He felt it was the next best thing to being out there in the thick of it.

Contact with Gilbert was being kept and only three, so far, of the bus load were associated with the farm.

By noon of the second day nine of the gang had been taken into custody and one shot dead by the GSU. That part of the chase had been called off and the FR could return to Buster's.

Info taken from the prisoners at Koram showed that the gang had been despatched by Naded of UMA to show the Farmers' Reserve that they could strike any place and at any time. They were striving to instil fear into the farming community as a whole – black and white.

Little did they realise that these sort of incidents would turn the masses against them. And that backlash would prove their eventual downfall.

That afternoon a truckload of orange berets drove into Koram and swanned around the massacre scene trying to make their presence felt at police HQ. The CO would have nothing of their intrusion. It was his patch and his combined forces had it under control.

Emmett noticed how the locals cowered from the *Makinto* presence. They really were a hated bunch and becoming, seemingly, more unanswerable to anyone. Had the President lost his hold of their reins? It was increasingly looking more like it.

All FR and their farm guards were stood down that night and returned to their farms. It was left to the authorities to handle the results of the massacre. Jeri Ntsemo and his entourage arrived shortly after the *Makinto* and were greeted with great warmth and enthusiasm. He addressed a crowd in front of the police station and offered free transportation and food to all who had lost loved ones in the tragedy. He said the hospital was treating, with urgency, those who had been injured. Everything was being done that could be. Prayers were being offered at the local churches. He managed to break away and had a few minutes with Emmett alone over a sweet cup of tea.

"Has your farm lost anybody?"

"I think three but only relatives."

"Well that's something anyway. It won't upset the harvesting?"

"No. Not at all," replied Emmett and then quickly added "I hope."

"I know what you mean. Anyhow tell your staff that the perpetrators of this foul deed will be found and dealt with very quickly. You have my promise on that. We are close to getting Naded and his lieutenants so lets be positive. How is everything otherwise?"

"In great fettle when I left and hopefully when I return later."

"I think I will visit Buster and his crew shortly so will keep you informed.," said Jeri.

With that he returned to his group of civil servants and the police CO. Never once did he bother to contact the *Makinto* or even look at them. He knew he was walking a tightrope but he had self confidence a-plenty and one hell of a backing on his side.

"Blow them," would be the nastiest words he would use!

24

Coral, Makuti and Bare Breasted Beauties

Everyday routines ran a little out of kilter from the next week on most farms in the wheat lands region. Everyone was a little edgy and some were torn with grief, and the overriding question was why?

Emmett tried to explain it to Gilbert as best he could and asked his to convey his feelings to the staff. He himself would have one to ones with his main leaders. He hoped this tragedy would strengthen their resolve to quash the enemy and keep secure their own compound.

The immediate response by the FR had shown everyone in the district that they were prepared to fight for their freedom and to protect their property and personnel.

It now seemed that prevention had been the trump card. A covert operation of spies had to infiltrate UMA and bring forth information prior to any more incidents of such a dastardly and bestial nature. To this end the FR felt they should call on the Wazuri to assist in this strategy.

All of it took time but by the end of the harvest meetings had taken place throughout the country and a national plan put into operation.

Urban members of Wazuri were told to return to their villages and stay with family for a week or two. They were to gather whatever information offered and if possible to become food carriers and go-betweens for the mountain gangs.

It was known that Naded never stayed for more than a day or night in one place. His movements must be mapped and some sort of grid system outlined at command headquarters. All hideouts must be marked, whether already visited, destroyed or yet to be attacked.

It was becoming plainly obvious that the FR movement was in control of all anti-terrorist strategy. They got 'backup' from certain government departments and worked very closely and amiably with the GSU's.

Jeri Ntsemo's individuality and charisma was spreading. Other CC's were coming onboard and assisting the FR in their respective regions. This made the overall operation much easier to coordinate.

The Mandaras was virtually a closed area. Any movement, in or out, was monitored. Regular air wing recces were proving a real thorn in the enemy's side meaning that raiding parties could only operate at night time.

The FR were mounting ambushes right along the forest line with increasing success which meant that food supplies must be dwindling.

Buster called a meeting to relay the facts and figures of the recent carnage and the success of the follow up. It was evident to the rest of the country that the Wheatlands Farmers' Reserve and Home Guard were totally 'on the ball' and prepared.

"The bus massacre, however, does prove that gangs can," and after holding everyone's eyes in his for an endless ten seconds "and will infiltrate our area. We are to be doubly adept as this incident could be the first of many."

He would be visiting each farm to inspect security measures already in place and also wished to address each farm's home guards. He planned to start his rounds straightaway and would like the meetings in the morning prior to harvesting.

Everyone agreed it was a good idea. It would assist the staff in knowing just what they were up against and how best to combat the enemy. Emmett had read how patriotic it felt to 'show the flag' and now was a good time to boost moral.

Harvesting was too important to really let ones mind take on any outside influences. This season was a good one. Heavy crops were reported on each side of the road. Talk at Buster's meeting, once his 'sitrep' had been delivered, centred on everyone's average. Ratilli's was well up on last season's and Melelo should establish a new record high for Bhogal in bags per acre.

Emmett's diligent management wed to his labour forces' outstanding man hours of true grit had combined to prove that the earth was as good as anyone else's in the region. His neighbours must accept a lot of his success as theirs. After all, he could have had a bum steer! They could have been Bhogals or worse? Emmett smiled at this scenario and was grateful that he had been dealt a fine hand.

Both Bhogals, Jaswant and Vijay, flew in to congratulate Emmett and his staff on the crop's results. They had gone past the magical ten bags an acre target finalising on 10.65 bags. Melelo had performed above expectation. It was bonus time and Emmett asked for two weeks leave. It was agreed.

They had discussed their destination many times in their most intimate interludes. Anna had never been to the sea. Emmett had heard so much about Kenya's coast that he felt he could almost taste the salinity of those crystal clear waters of the Indian ocean.

It only took ten days to make contact with his Kenyan friends – a few of whom had offered houses in Malindi and Diani.

They stayed a couple of days in the Urukan Club with Anna shopping for a few last minute items.

Nairobi's Norfolk Hotel accommodated them for three days where they met up with Colin Dymott and John Blay to finalise arrangements for their coastal trip.

A day spent in the Nairobi National Park rewarded them with sights of cheetah, elephant, buffalo and a pride of seven lions. Their guide rattled off the names of all the antelope species, a lot of which were present in Ukenza but never had they seen such multitude at any one time. Emmett's yearning to be amongst these beautiful creatures surfaced yet again.

On their second night they were taken by John Blay to the Equator Club, a nightclub restaurant with a superb live combo playing Afro jazz intermingled with the swing numbers of the era. This was the first time, since leaving Ireland, that Emmett had the opportunity to smooch with Anna on a dance floor. It was postage stamp in size but their square inches of foot shuffle was all that was needed. They were very happy in this environment – it suited them.

Kenya's coastal strip was an eye opener in many ways. Firstly, the local tribe, the Giriama, were a short squat community of happy faces whose women folk all went bare breasted. Their little 'tutu' like skirts were made of copra – the lining of coconut shells and their bodies glistened with cleanliness.

Anna thought it quite stunning. Emmett was a little embarrassed to start with but familiarity brought understanding and kept a smirk on his suntanned face. He had bought Anna the most beautiful bikini in one of Nairobi's elegant boutiques. It was a deep yellow, like the yoke of a free range egg. She had christened it in the Norfolk pool. Now, down here, she could probably go without the top but somehow to both of them, that didn't seem right.

The house they had been directed to in Malindi was three down from Lawford's Hotel. They were all built of white coral blocks, no glass windows, only openings when not shuttered, a large veranda facing the sea and the roofs were of makuti (palm leaves). A servant, Josiah, went with the house. He was a man of all trades and knew the fishermen who hawked their wares each morning, on landing their catch.

Walk five steps off the veranda (stoep) and they were on the whiter than white coral sands of Malindi. High tide would have been another ten strides down the shore. Idyllic, clean and peopleless.

Emmett found he needed the first two days to just relax – laze in the sun, swim and cavort in the aquamarine blue of the sea and eat fresh fish. Ice cold Tusker lager went down well with this diet.

They sauntered, hand in hand, arm in arm, up and down the miles of beach gazing at the rows of houses, some occupied, others shuttered. Every now and then a hotel – Eden Roc, Sinbad – took up a long stretch of the dunes and seashore. Their opulent architecture and outside landscaping was very much in contrast to Lawfords, which was characterised in the old style makuti/coral block design.

During the week they travelled out in an ancient dhow – the Arab world's mode of marine transport. A trip down the coast from Malindi to Blue Lagoon brought them face to face with the mysterious and multi-coloured world of the underwater. Shoals of yellow and black angel fish swam with other pink, blue, green and red species of every size and shape. The first glass bottom boat in the district had recently been launched and was constantly in use.

After five days they moved down the coast south of Mombasa in two bus trips to Diani Beach and met up with Dan Trench who was caretaker to the house they had been loaned. Dan's family was originally from County Mayo. He had a really amusing ramshackled conglomeration of huts and rooms under palm and mango trees which made up his hotel. The atmosphere around the bar at midday and sundowner time was electric. Most of his guests were upcountry farmers.

Emmett and Anna ate there for most of their main meals. Everyone wanted to hear about Ukenza. They were kept in booze virtually all the time and many invitations were proffered.

On their last morning they decided to walk to where they could see a rocky outcrop far down the south end of the beach. It took them almost an hour to reach it.

"But oh my goodness was that worth it," were sentiments echoed in their thoughts. A rock pool all of twenty feet long by about seven wide had about six inches of luke warm water in it. They lay for a full ten minutes before Anna said "lets swim, this is too warm." Off she ran, shedding her bikini on the virginal shore, into the lazy ripples lapping against the sand. Emmett followed suit and disrobed where he found her bikini pants. They romped in the azure waters, playing like children, until Emmett's body felt hers hard up against him. Her arms enwrapped his neck as long ebony legs encircled his waist. They were almost breast high in the serene Indian ocean.

Emmett's arms met and held her just under her buttocks as his wanton Irish rod fished for eternity within her secret cavern.

Anna's head fell backwards almost submerging as they climaxed again and again and again. She let her arms fall either side of her head, now gazing skyward into a canvass blue, with only Emmett's hands holding her buttocks into him. His head also, for a few vivid moments, arched backwards as each cast found its prey. If this was heaven on earth what must life ever after offer to two such sanguine lovebirds.

They slowly slipped apart and floated side by side with finger tips touching until Emmett felt his pulse return to normal. He then lead Anna slowly from the sea to bask in their rock pool not forgetting their cossies on the way.

224

Their return journey was much more a saunter with each admiring the errant array of sea shells scattered before them.

After a chicken kebab and a pint of Pims No.1 each they slept all afternoon.

Next morning they hitched a lift on Dan's truck which was going to Mombasa for supplies. They arrived back in Kenzi two days later and drove up to Clouds to spend the night with Anna's parents.

The time spent with them was heart warming in that they were so thrilled to hear all about their Kenyan holiday. Anna hardly ever stopped to take a breath she was so exhilarated. After dinner they then heard the news that brought it all into perspective.

Whilst away there had been further arson attacks, this time on schools, roadblock confrontations and another massacre of the occupants of a bus outside Kenzi.

Kitos was awash with people of all hues and trades as the day of the races dawned. It was Champion Hurdle time. The card also hosted the Derby (one and a half miles) and the Champion Polo Pony sprint (four furlongs). A sponsor, for the first time, had come on board – a very generous one too. He was P.K. Shah, the biggest tyre and re-thread merchant in the country with enormous holdings in Kenzi and Urukan. His eldest son, Poonie, had become a leading polo player and had even travelled to India and the Argentine for professional tuition. The sponsorship of the hurdle race would be for a three year period. This was a real breakthrough for the Gymkhana Racing Association. And fortunately others were to follow the pioneering Shahs.

Emmett had not brought his two ponies to compete in the children's race as word had gone the rounds that all riders would be on their father's best ponies. Corrib and Mask were just not in that class.

The Champion Hurdle was the second race on the card. Fifteen runners this time with most interest in whether Flyman, who finished second to Geronimo in the last race had improved sufficiently to challenge and even beat the champion.

Emmett decided to run them ragged from the 'off'. He was afraid of such a big field hosting dodgy jumpers and he didn't wish to be involved in any pileups or run outs.

Only at the last hurdle did he hear someone galloping quite close to him. He didn't look behind and on landing he asked Geronimo for his usual surge of energy and sprint finish. It wasn't there as in the other two runs but he nevertheless put his head down and answered Emmett's urgency. He was a battler and though Flyman came up to his shoulder Emmett drove him across the line half a length to the good. They had achieved their objective. Three from three, this was the jackpot.

225

Rachel and Anna rushed onto the course and took a rein on either side as the victors were lead into the unsaddling enclosure. Crowds thronged the area with whoops and ululations of delight amid loud applause accompaning the two horses who had made the finish such a nail biting affair.

Emmett was drained and flopped down on the bench in the changing room. Every rider congratulated him with some emphasising that this was his last. They would give him a real run next season. Emmett knew, full well, that these words would most probably ring true. He had stolen a march on them. Now, every big strong thoroughbred, would be found to battle him for the honours.

"Sure isn't that what its all about – lead in the clowns," he smiled and laughed into his second pint of shandy.

"I'll be ready for ye."

Emmett knew that his fitness or lack of it, had nearly lost it for him. His Kenyan holiday had put pounds on and blunted his usually cutting edge sveltness but wasn't it worth it? He certainly thought so.

25

Makinto – the Evil Spirit

During Emmett's time away on holiday Bhogal had had another radio – a much advanced receiver/transmitter – installed in the passage leading to the bedrooms. The office unit could then be switched across to the house when he settled in for the night. This, he thought, was a grand idea on two counts. Firstly Emmett would have immediate access with listening out facilities and secondly the airwaves would be only for his ears. A definite closing of a security gap, even though Emmett didn't wish to believe his night guards were anything but loyal and honest. One just never knew these days?

Now, instead of falling asleep to BBC et al world programmes his mind had to acclimatise itself to radio procedures. It did, however, give him the added assurance that all farms were being monitored. This time he wasn't lulled into a false sense of security. It only took a couple of nights to get used to this new sound bite.

Emmett found it hard to understand that within five hours flight time from Kenzi he and Anna had been in 'another world' and yet within a neighbouring country. No security fences, burglar bars, farm guards in Jomo Kenyata's new age Kenya. Perhaps his philosophy, and hard won UHURU (freedom), would stamp the blue print for all emerging African states? Emmett certainly hoped for this as he felt a definite magnetic force at work every time he thought of that country, an East African jewel.

"Ratilli, Ratilli, come in please." Emmett awakened with a start and rushed to the wireless.

"Ratilli here. Who is it, over?"

"Emmett, its Jeri. Are you sitting or standing? Over."

"Standing Jeri, with virtually nothing on. Over."

"Bad news I'm afraid. Anna, Jaci and a truck load of Wazuri have been ambushed and badly shot up. Don't know who or how many but bodies are plenty. Over."

"My God!" was all that Emmett could muster.

"Emmett come to the hospital , a.s.a.p. Over."

"My God, Jeri, wilco. Out."

He dragged himself from his shocked state and went out onto the veranda.

"Guards, guards," he shouted with an immediate response coming from one outside the office. He instructed him to call Gilbert and Christopher immediately and then get two of his farm guards ready for an urgent trip.

Whilst putting clothes on and packing a grip he yelled at Christopher to make tea and told him the news. He remained glued to the floor, a grey horror invading his sad countenance.

"Hurry please." Emmett then went onto the network and enquired whether HQ had picked up Jeri's transmission.

He got Buster out of bed and explained his plan. He would travel into Urukan immediately and stay there for x hours, sort the whys and wherefores out and report back. Please could he keep an eye on the farm.

"Good luck, Emmett. I'll say a prayer or three. Over and out."

That was the longest and strangest journey of his short life. He had addressed such a scenario many times in his silent hours before sleep. But here it was, reality in person, the sign of the devil in all its worst trappings. Was it Uma or *Makinto*, he wondered? Where had they been? Exactly what had been going on?

Jeri's wakeup call came at 02.47am. It was now an hour later and he still had another thirty minutes to go before reaching Urukan.

A large vociferous crowd of women blockaded the surrounds of the A & E entrance. Emmett counted four ambulances and six police vehicles as he shouted to two policemen to let him through. They attempted to split the crowd as Emmett crept forward finally achieving success. He parked close to Jeri's landrover and hurried inside.

Total pandemonium was the order of the moment. Emmett was wearing his combat kit and people recognised his beret. Some of the Wazuri knew him and howled anguished laden exclamations as they hugged and clasped him on his advance into the entrails of the hospital.

Margaret beckoned him to head to his right, down a passage where more discipline reigned.

"She hasn't been found yet. She's not amongst the bodies. Jaci is. So far it is a count of thirteen – unlucky for some, eh?" With that Emmett spotted Jeri and went to him.

"Margaret has told me. Anything else?"

"It was *Makinto*, no doubt. The survivors saw them."

"Shit and bloody hell. What's the plan now Jeri?"

"Come into this office and lets pause a moment."

They moved into a cramped room full of files, cabinets, desk and two chairs.

"They were on call out to an arson attack on labour lines – about fifteen miles out of town. They were to comfort the people and arrange a follow up with the local FR. It was a well organised ambush – *Makinto* knew their movements. Inside job I'd say. Jaci was driving and she took the first shots. Anna would have been next to her in the cab with the leader of the Wazuri on her outside. Both of them are missing. The truck went out of control and overturned into a culvert. According to some of the survivors the 'orange berets' opened fire indiscriminately at those they thought had survived the crash. There were two *Makinto* vehicles. They took off in the direction of town. That's all we know – so far."

Silence reigned for a few moments as both men tried to understand.

"Do you realise what this could mean, Jeri. Anna could be their prisoner, hostage, whatever? Oh my God how awful."

Tears welled in his already bloodshot strained eyes.

"What's the plan?"

"Police have put GSU's into the town's locations (African suburbs) to try and find *Makinto's* vehicles and then their occupants. The FR are already out scouring the countryside. At first light it will be easier to coordinate the follow up. Better go over to our house and phone Anna's parents. I've left that for you I'm afraid. I thought they would understand better coming from you. Okay? I'll stay here and keep you informed. The police have their team of interrogators awaiting the survivors willingness to communicate. Nothing you can do here or out there for an hour or two. Better be with the children, they adore you. Good luck."

Emmett was in shock. He felt he was visibly ageing before their very eyes. His movements were slow and exaggerated.

"I must find her," he kept saying, sometimes aloud, sometimes to himself.

Two hours later he was at the crime scene searching for clues. Anything that might connect Anna's disappearance with the wreck of their upturned truck.

Perhaps she too was dead or injured, perhaps having crawled away unnoticed from the carnage? Every foot of the countryside had to be covered for any fragment of hope.

The worst, Emmett felt was the thought she had been carted off, half dead or severely wounded, by *Makinto* as a hostage. She was high profile enough to attract the maximum attention. He could see the headlines "Nanny to CC's children taken hostage;" "CC in the dark over nanny's second life;" "Gang strike close to CC's heart."

A pastiche of script kept appearing and disappearing in his troubled mind. Ugly questions popped up. What would he do without Anna? How would he cope? Perhaps he would return to Ireland? Perhaps, perhaps, perhaps!

Two *Makinto* vehicles were spotted bulleting back to Kenzi. They were just off the main road utilising secondary tiny country passes trying to elude detection. The FR Air Wing once again outwitted the enemy.

Units of the Kenzi police were despatched to block their route, make contact and if possible to take them into custody. When Emmett heard about this he feared the worst. *Makinto* would not surrender – their pride would not allow this. The police could well hold their nerve and take them on head to head in open conflict. They hated *Makinto*.

And then, what if they held Anna prisoner in one of the vehicles? Emmett rushed back to police HQ were Jeri and his advisors were assisting in manning their ops room.

Talk was centred around the word anarchy. This would be the first time two branches of the country's forces had clashed head on.

Which side would the President support? And would he send in his troops to defend his elite corp?

This could be Groundhog day in tiny Ukenza and Anna could be bound up in the midst of it?

"Oh my God," said Emmett to Jeri, "what have I got myself tied up in?"

"Stay calm. I know its not easy for you, for any of us, but we just don't know where she is and we must hope – for the best outcome. Sorry."

The standoff took place at a small bridge over a river called Zuzzi – short for an incredible long ethnic and unpronounceable word.

An extremely bright police commander had split his four vehicle force into two, sending half to the far side of the bridge hiding in the undergrowth. He and the remainder stayed on the north side just off the edge of the road and in some scrubland.

He waited for the two *Makinto* landrovers to get onto the bridge before moving his two vehicles across the road as a block. His other two followed suit. The enemy was trapped in the middle.

They opened fire first which was immediately returned by both sections of the police. The lead *Makinto* driver decided to ram the opposing vehicles until one hail of bullets cut him short with the vehicle careering into the grid iron railing on either side, coming to a standstill just short of the police blockade.

Orange berets appeared from side and rear of both vehicles, some with hands over their heads, others attempting to jump the railings and drop into the waters below. These were picked off by the sharp shooting police squad.

Seven were dead and fifteen taken prisoner. This was the report that echoed over the wires in both HQ's at Kenzi and Urukan. Anna was not amongst the group.

Only when these prisoners reached Kenzi would they be interrogated. Perhaps then some light on Anna's mysterious disappearance would offer a semblance of hope?

Meantime Emmett asked for permission to lead a truckload of Wazuri to comb the area of the ambush.

Urukan's police commander, after much persuasion from Jeri, agreed and offered a GSU as backup. Their leader would have overall command. Emmett readily agreed and within one hour the patrol set out. Emmett travelled with the Wazuri most of whom knew him.

Once at the site he lead the ladies, twenty of them, on a yard by yard search of the area. They set out in a line west of the road and across the ditch into which the truck had overturned. The GSU was to patrol the roads in the area quizzing all and sundry they came across.

Emmett and his line of Wazuri combed every inch westward for a good half mile before sweeping to their south flank doing the same in that area back to the road. These two sweeps took them just over an hour. Every household they came across had seen nothing. Yes they had heard the shooting in the night but no one had passed their way since. Their dogs would have barked if a stranger had come close.

His patrol stopped for water from a farm pump near one of the homesteads. One of the group who was a little away in the field shouted, "dama, dama" – which meant blood. Emmett rushed across to where the woman was crouching and sure enough the smudged stains did resemble blood. Everyone spread out with eyes peering onto grass, weeds and earth.

Another shout and Emmett moved slightly to his left. They were headed towards a corner of an old corn (maize) field with a pile of stalks surrounded by two strands of barbed wire.

Emmett's heart was racing as cautiously, step by step as if in slow motion, he approached the pile. Perhaps it was one of the gang, a *Makinto*, wounded and armed whose blood had been spotted?

"Atari" he shouted the danger warning. Four of the ladies carried shot guns, the rest machetes.

They crept up to the pile with all arms at the ready. Just short of it Emmett noticed soil was disturbed as if something had been dragged over it.

Two of the Wazuri crept on hands and knees to the sides as he watched the front. Others had the rear covered. Nothing moved – all was silent save for some guinea fowl cackling away in the distance.

Emmett bent down and with his left hand started to pull the stalks away from the centre.

"Yeissh" cried the nearest lady "a foot, effendi". Emmett saw it the same moment and recognised the footwear. It was Anna's boot, a soft safari boot they had bought in Nairobi.

He put his revolver back in its holster and grabbed the stalks all around and over her body. There was blood on her face, tunic and arm. He took her left wrist and felt for a pulse. Tempi, one of the Wazuri, had her ear at Anna's mouth.

"There is a pulse, it's very weak. Can we bring the truck nearer? Do it, no negatives. I need clothes to keep her warm. Please hurry," Emmett uttered with a loud pleading screech that made the ladies jump. He wasn't going to move her until the truck arrived. He just got down beside her cold body and held it. What more could he do he asked himself?

"Oh crumbs," more to himself than anyone in particular. "The radio," he pulled it from around his neck and clicked the switch "Urukan HQ, Urukan HQ, come in please."

"Go ahead Patrol One."

"Anna found but in very poor condition. Need ambulance here pronto with a doctor. Pulse very weak. Shot in a few places."

"Roger Emmett." It was Jeri, "and well found. There is one on standby so it will probably be twenty to thirty minutes. Good luck. Out."

It was almost impossible to get the truck within a hundred yards of that corner of the field so Emmett told the Wazuri to return to it and get themselves something to eat and drink. Three of them, Anna's close friends, stayed with Emmett. He also told the truck driver to return to the road to show the ambulance how to get near the body.

They must have broken all land speed records as the crew arrived within twenty minutes. Doctor Khan came running across the field with four stretcher men in pursuit.

After a thorough examination he told them to stretcher her to the ambulance. Drips were put in place and various injections administered.

"The next hour is going to be the crucial one. Who would know her blood type?"

"I do," exclaimed Emmett with joy, "it's the same as mine, O positive."

"That's fine; I have some in the ambulance."

"Can I ride with her," Emmett asked in pleading tones.

"Of course, yes, no problem."

Emmett, at the ambulance, radioed in their progress. Jeri said he and Margaret would be at the hospital. Anna's parents were on their way to his house so he would take them across when they arrived.

Within the hour she responded. Blood pressure and body temperature were almost normal. It was three hours forty-seven minutes since finding her in the maize stalks when her eyes started to flicker and finally opened. Emmett had monitored every second of her rescue: had held her hands through the journey and had talked sweet nothings to her without a break. He had heard somewhere that the subconscious can pick up talk no matter how bad the situation seemed. He was prepared to try everything – even prayer. Perhaps his had been heard?

Once Anna returned to life they whisked her off to x-ray. She had flinched when her mother touched her right arm, her eyes closing in pain.

The x-ray showed she had three fractured ribs, broken collar bone and a fractured right arm high up. Three bullet holes were shown in her left side but only embedded in her left thigh. There was no internal bleeding but bad bruising to her back and shoulders. She was in a very sorry state. But she was alive and would recover fully the doctors said.

All breathed sighs of emotional relief. Emmett suddenly felt very tired, exhausted, drained.

Jeri had booked him into the Club. He needed a hot bath and a bottle of whisky.

26

"Must fly now. Oh! Excuse the Pun."

During his first two years at Ratilli Emmett had one objective, that was to produce record wheat yields and so earn big bonuses. He didn't put any great store in his design and completion of Melelo Lodge or the successes of Geronimo. These were mere passing fancies. But now he was presented with a mountain of Everest proportions to climb. It was simply – revenge on *Makinto*. That they should summarily snatch from everyday freedom the almost last breath of a lovely girl's life – not just any girl's but his – made Emmett feel emotions that had never pumped through the vibrant veins in his twenty-seven year old body.

He had grieved at his father's funeral and felt deep passionate emotion for his beloved mother in her loss. But they were of a different era, generation. The love felt between siblings and parents was one of family devotion and respect.

His love for Anna was of a much deeper and more passionate strata. His venture into that unknown realm. They were as one unit – thinking, working, playing alike – and in their very beings they held a devotion, trust and passion that Emmett now only realised the depth of. They were soul mates. Two vastly different cultures entwined in a vine like grip that welded complexities with an outward vista of life. A life the two of them wished to share no matter what it took or where it lead.

To have it almost stamped out, like the glowing embers of a camp fire, was something neither had planned for.

It was up to him to reek revenge on *Makinto* in no uncertain way. Not only for Anna but for Jaci, Imelda, Joyce and the other dozen casualties in that dastardly deed.

Jeri and Margaret were also amazingly 'shook' by the near fatality of their beloved niece. George and Mims were devastated. They had no idea of Anna's covert operations. Proud on one hand but mightily distressed on the other. They felt she should have trusted them with her secret, then Emmett's phone call would not have been earth shattering.

It was the first time Emmett had seen black faces turn grey. They aged appreciably in those first four days. And that held for Jeri and Margaret too.

Once Anna was out of danger her parents returned to Kenzi. Margaret would give personal and individual attention to her niece. Anna could not be better looked after. She was also a great favourite of the nuns whose hospital she rested in. Recuperation and recovery would be slow but she would be "back to her normal self in no time at all" voiced Sister Stanislaus, the matron.

Many loose ends got tied during the next few weeks. The *Makinto* prisoners spilt the beans on the structure of the organisation with repercussions felt right up the ladder to the President himself.

Some terrorists captured in the Kitos region included a boy of ten years who admitted to the killing of little Jason Lucke (six months previously). He had been the boy's playmate and had been reared as another son by the family who had trusted the child implicitly. He confessed he had been frightened, terrorised into killing his friend because the gang threatened to kill off his family if he didn't comply.

A ring leader of Uma, third in command, had been shot dead in the Mandaras. Information gathered from an increasing number of prisoners taken by the FR showed that food was short in the mountains and for the first time there was a steady stream of departures from the terrorist gangs. These were giving themselves up to whichever farm lay in their path of escape. Some had been badly beaten and severely wounded, mostly machete cuts, and were, from the outset, only there for fear of their families safety. "Made to fight master", was a repeated outburst.

The Uma leader, Naded, was becoming increasingly cruel and bestial with his own troops. It was obvious he was about at his wit's end. All the escapees felt something 'big' was about to happen.

Emmett made a promise with himself that 'till his dying day he would devote all his waking hours to the planning of *Makinto*'s downfall. He had to do it for Anna's sake, and all the other atrocities they had perpetrated. This would be like a boil festering beneath his skin. He would await a ground swell of hatred and cries for revenge from the Wazuri. He would now, in Anna's absence, work closely with her segment of their group. His plan had to be covert from the outset. If other Zungu sympathisers wanted 'in' then he would be happy to accommodate their expertise and enthusiasm. He did have certain personalities in mind and would draw on them when the time came. For now he would test the waters of discontent and evaluate his chances.

Anna's recovery was slow and tedious as broken bones do greatly alter ones everyday routine. Her mental state was more traumatic. She had lost the sparkle in her eyes. She was withdrawing into her inner self. The shock and horror of that attack would bring nightmarish flashbacks.

Emmett thanked the simple farmer who had stacked his pile of maize stalks so neatly in such an available position. It was most probably the difference between survival and death that prompted his continuing red eyes syndrome. Distress brought tears to his usually bright blue eyes.

Emmett rode his ponies on long soul searching journeys around Ratilli. With only his equine and canine companions this helped to clear his mind. Wild birds and game graciously broke his solitude. These were happy interludes. He realised he had become a brooder. Each night he looked at the face in the mirror. It was lined, and it was ageing.

He got knocked out of this depression by Howard asking him to fly to Urukan with him. He was going to introduce Emmett to Boris the leading flying instructor in the country.

"Half a dozen lessons with him and he'll have you going solo. Then it will only be a matter of time before you will be whizzing around the place cock-a-snooping at all of us. Seriously though, he's the best."

"This has come at just the right time, with the harvest completed and Anna in recovery. It will help to get my mind off the horrors of those few days."

"That's what we thought. I've been discussing you with Ian and we're all worried about you. Remember for God's sake you are not alone in this. You have us."

"Thanks a span for those cherished words and thoughts. It has not been easy, believe me. So tell me about Boris?"

"Well, he's the best, ex Polish Second World War pilot, squadron leader to be precise. Has a small holding outside the town and came here from Nairobi ten years ago. Has a good business. He's taught most of us. You will like him."

They were flying over the outskirts of Urukan and Howard took him on a kaleidoscopic tour, one which Emmett was so pleased to be party to. He could now see exactly the size of the African shanty townships which spread, like a cancerous growth, from the north to the south-west of the town. The other sides were occupied by a patchwork of seemingly well organised farms. Herds of cattle grazed on pastures green. Red and green painted roofs glistened on white bungalows and two-storied homesteads. Plenty of trees and large shrubs landscaped their close acreages. Rainbows rose from miles and miles of spray irrigation.

"A totally different world, eh Howard?" as Emmett kept peering out of his tilted window with Howard flying low then high over the entire area.

Then Emmett heard the traffic controller calling them in. It was time to come down to earth once again. He had a much better idea now of the topography of the town and its surrounds. His mind was on a never ending planning mission and every little speck of information was most welcome.

Boris was as tall as he was broad. An almost bald head seemed to be neckless as its moonlike countenance ranged sturdily from equally broad shoulders. Grey eyes sparkled above a grin that reached from ear to ear.

"Another to improve my bank account, eh Howard?" as the three met outside the tiny reception area.

"This is my next door neighbour, Emmett Doyle. Boris you've got to treat him lightly. He has a good stomach, has done some hairy flights with Roy in the Mandaras. Must fly now, - excuse the pun!"

On turning to Emmett he said "will see you at the Club for lunch, right?"

"Please God and with this man's good guidance," Emmett smiled at Boris.

He spent the next two hours in intensive mode, some of it within the confines of a tiny Piper Cub. The kite, as Boris called it, in which he would eventually go solo.

Boris was really generalistic in his comments.

"Same as a car. Learn on one and you'll be able to pilot all the other private craft around. Like riding a bicycle, right?"

Emmett was given a handbook with all rules of the air, regulations and signs. He was told to study it thoroughly, it was his new bible. They took a spin in the Cub which had dual controls.

"You will be doing circles and bumps for hours, once you become au fait with these. Just follow me now."

Off they took circling the airfield a couple of times before landing back on terra firma.

The cost for a two hour session was the equivalent of IR£20. Well worth it thought Emmett. Now for solo and then a licence. He wondered whether any of the other 'four' had progressed along these lines? What a reunion they would have back in Dublin – one day, when?

To kill two birds with one stone was proving really advantageous as Emmett could tell Anna all about his lesson. She was on the road to recovery all right as she sparkled with innuendo on the various snippets of flying jargon he slipped in at every chance he got.

Margaret said she would be out in a week or so, would stay with them as they were close to the hospital for dressings, etc. and then move up to her parents 'till the plaster casts came off.

"She would then be all yours, Emmett. Patience is a virtue, believe me." Margaret had a wry sense of humour and adored being one up on everybody. It was done without any malice. She loved the reactions.

Boris presented Emmett with his log book – a 6 x 4 x 2 ins thick blue hard backed well ruled diary for every flight. This would stay with him until full and then another, etc. would be issued. It had to be guarded with his life he was told. He was extremely proud of this 'passport to paradise' as he named it.

"It's all yours Emmett. You can go solo now." Those were the words he ached to hear. Now they were a reality. It was crunch time.

Boris did not look around as he strode away from the Piper Cub. He had left Emmett in charge. He was confident he could do it. Emmett buckled himself into the pilot seat, attached his headphones and asked permission to take off.

He had done the routine hundreds of times in his head and alongside others. This time, however, he was on his own. The butterflies multiplied as he made ready. His tummy wobbled, just that fraction, igniting a spark of apprehension which made him cross himself as he had been guided to do in his childhood, on passing each and every Roman Catholic church, and in moments prior to any competition. He hoped his maker would be on his side.

Just as in all aspects of life he took the challenge by the scruff of its neck and flew off into the cloudless sky above Urukan. Once up over the tiny airport all his fears vanished in that sweet, sweet air.

He made three circles and then bumped down on the welcome but rough runway. He had to continue this routine for three landings. His confidence grew with each takeoff and the third landing was close to perfect. It had been a magical half hour. One of trial and triumph.

Once taxied back to its parking bay, with chocks in place at each wheel, the Cub got an embrace and kiss on the engine cowling.

Cold beers were awaiting inside the Club's premises. Everyone drank to the Irishman's luck.

"Yes, yes, yes," was all that Emmett could reply to the round of cheers and applause that greeted him. On reflection, when driving back to the Club, he realised he had never appreciated the beauty of the sky and the world below as he normally did as a passenger in someone else's plane. This time his attention was focused totally on the stick and controls. He could not remember whether the sun shone or not. At least he had got himself down to earth safely and in one piece. Next time it would be a lot easier. His confidence was high.

Now he had to put in the solo hours and learn navigation. Then he would earn his licence. What then?

He went solo after five hours and then went on his triangular tests after a further six hours of flying. His navigation needed to be spot on and despite a few wobbles here and there had it all done to a 'T' within the month.

Emmett progressed to flying a Cessna, with Boris as co-pilot, for another five hours before telling him to "bugger off to the farm and take up Bhogal on his next visit to you. That will show him how serious you are about succeeding here.

The Department will contact you about your licence and when the tests will be. Have fun."

He couldn't have had a nicer person as his instructor. And it had only cost Emmett a month's wage.

Ian had already received his licence and had bought a Commanche (Piper) very like Geoff Bamber's. Both Ian and Howard invited Emmett to fly with them as often as he could. Howard praised his 'feel of the 'plane' and especially his landing technique. With their three landing strips in close proximity he could 'circle and bump' to his heart's delight. Sometimes cross winds caused major problems but this, according to Howard and Boris before him, was merely a matter of experience. Emmett would master it in time he felt.

It really was like driving a car when one came down to basics. Perhaps the fear of plummeting to the ground from great heights or having a prang on landing made him even more careful in his handling of the machine. He had already, in his two years of driving on African roads, been involved in a number of ferocious and spine chilling slides in both dry sand and wet slimy conditions. These were ideal precursors for his trips into the blue abyss of his seventh heaven.

Even though he never wished to be a crop spraying pilot Emmett was drawn to these little yellow 'wasps' that were parked next to his house. He was confident he could handle their extremely basic instrument panel within the tiny cockpit. Rather akin to comparing the Ford Model T with the 1966 Morris Oxford at home. At a push or a shove Emmett reckoned he could fly one. When Mustapha next arrived he would try a few circles and bumps he proffered.

More and more Farmers Reserve were being sent up into the Mandaras on five day sorties. Emmett was readily available in this slack period on the farm and completed three of them in a month. He was becoming battle hardened and embittered with each suspense filled episode.

What on earth was Uma trying to achieve? The majority of the population were against them. They didn't have a political wing and Naded, their leader, was obviously losing control of his mob.

It had become noticeable over the last six months that their 'hit and run' tactics were diminishing. In their place came waves of passive resistance, however. The kind where farmers found their tractor tyres slashed, generators misfiring on tainted fuel, cut telephone lines, severed irrigation pipes and the continual hamstringing of cattle. All vile irritants that impeded every day progress on farm or small holding. It meant that Uma did have a network of sympathisers, here, there and everywhere, who were primed to ignite at a moment's notice. The 'bush telegraph' was up and running and very, very demoralising.

It meant that farm staff loyalty was being put to the test. Not an easy enemy to combat.

Fortunately this epidemic had not reached the wheatlands although the odd incident of strange proportion was being chronicled by their local FR group.

Emmett's 'mole' on Ratilli – an insignificant member of his fencing gang, had nothing to report save for the fact he had heard of a few outsiders stopping off at some of the farms in the district.

Emmett reported this to Buster who informed him "he wasn't the first to hear that. We are monitoring all movement in and from the district. Raids would be carried out on random labour lines with the hope of capturing the intruders. Nothing major or nasty has yet occurred but keep vigilant young man and thanks for the information."

Shirra beckoned Emmett to join her for kawa on their veranda. She was gushing towards his and Anna's misfortune.

"Dreadfully hard luck. I hope she recovers quickly for you."

"Thanks. That means a lot to me," he replied hesitantly not quite knowing what she was up to.

"Don't bother about me darling. I won't trouble you in your misery. I understand what she means to you. Honest I do."

Emmett felt better, a lot easier and happier in her company then. It was a weight off his shoulders.

Buster and a couple of other locals joined them and the talk was on the recent crop returns. In general it had been a good year. They were lucky with so few transportation problems. The Air Wing had done a fine job. Costly but well worth it they all agreed.

Emmett realised he could be part of this Wing once he received his licence. Roll on that day. He had, however, to await his turn within the red tape of governmental bureaucracy. Boris told him that "it could be any time. Just be patient and get in as many hours as possible in the meantime."

Bhogal had taken his initiative onboard and would allow him use of his Cessna when fully licensed. They had two in the organisation. Each time he came to Ratilli he allowed Emmett to survey the district, and especially Melelo, on his own. His landing technique was becoming more confident with each flight. Jaswant was a very conservative and careful pilot, treble checking each step along the way. Something that Emmett took cognisance of.

Ian, who had been a champion motor rally driver, was also an extremely cautious person inside his cockpit. Only Howard showed his supreme confidence which, at times, was perhaps somewhat lackadaisical – or so it seemed. But of course he knew his engine's capabilities better than anyone.

Roy, whom Emmett had flown with in the Mandaras, was the complete daredevil. He would make his kite sit up and beg if needs be. But one felt completely secure when with him. That was what Emmett wished to achieve in the years to come. It was an ongoing project which would keep his interest focused on his days in Africa. He couldn't see how he would ever have had this opportunity in Ireland.

27

Now You See them, Now You Don't

$\mathcal{A}$ five day stint at Pope's farm with fellow wheatlanders, John Pearce and Chris Piper, both farm managers, brought untold success in the struggle against Uma.

Two patrols left Pope's to travel four parallel gorges about five miles from HQ. Gang activity had been reported with sightings of food-carrying lines of terrorists moving within this region. But the strange thing was "as soon as they were spotted, usually from the air, they as easily became invisible. Total disappearance? Lay up, ambush, look, engage and find out what the hell's going on. Okay – and don't return without a positive result." That little request came from Johnny Nimmer who was acting CO of the local FR. He was a superb pilot himself and was baffled by the enigma.

The two patrols numbered twelve each: two Zungus, four trackers and six Wazuri. Supplies for seven days were carried. Arms and ammunition were heavier in quantity and quality than Emmett's last patrol. All of the patrol meant business. He got the impression that the Wazuri had said "enough was enough now." They wanted this campaign to be terminated. And everyone else agreed.

Not a single thing moved for two full days and nights. Not even a bird. It seemed strange and eerie.

Whilst brewing tea for breakfast on the third morning one of the guards on duty spotted movement on the opposite side of the gorge. Emmett got his binoculars and lined the movement up. There were four women in his sights and he followed their movements for a full hour. They were collecting wood and disappeared within the forest with enormous bundles stacked on their backs.

Emmett took certain trees as markers so that once they crossed over to that side his patrol could then take up tracking them down. He contacted John who was in the other patrol, reported their progress and warned them to be on the lookout for these four Wabeebees.

Once in position Emmett sent his trackers on a recce of the area. Like hounds on the scent of a fox they quickly took up the chase. Within half an hour one of them returned with a strange message. They had followed the trail which was quite plain to them, when all of a sudden it went cold. Not a sign of further movement could be found. The trackers were mystified and a little afraid at this. Superstition weaves a broad vein of terror throughout the African continent.

Emmett had learnt about this from Christopher in one of their intimate discussions back on Ratilli.

They immediately set out to confront this phenomenon. Once his patrol reached the other trackers they showed Emmett where the trail ended. His four men were indeed apprehensive. Firstly Emmett asked everyone to spread out and conduct a sweeping search. The line must be the radius of a circle following three hundred and sixty degrees. Every tree must be searched, the foliage canopy above must also come under their microscope. He would remain in the centre with Piper situated half way along the line. Every square foot must be searched. There had to be an explanation.

Within a few minutes a shriek went up from one of the Wazuri a couple of yards further out from Piper. She had fallen into a pit and was crumpled up some six feet down. The opening had been expertly concealed with a thatched woven covering that completely resembled the adjacent forest floor.

When the lady in question had recovered from this frightening fall she got to her feet and pleaded for assistance to "get me out of here".

Emmett and Piper surveyed the scene and told the leader of the Wazuri to calm her down.

"I think we should take a closer look at this trap. I have a strange feeling about it," said Emmett.

A couple of them then pulled back the rest of the covering revealing a square of approximately ten foot by ten foot. Down one side lay a makeshift ladder.

"Tell her, if she is not too badly hurt that is, to feel the four walls around her."

Her name was Agnes and she carried out the search straight away. She wasn't hurting she said, only a little shaken. They watched as she pounded the wall beside the ladder. Then the one to its right and then the one opposite.

As Agnes started on the third she put her finger to her mouth and looked up.

"I can hear voices, sssh." She then put her left ear to the wall and nodded affirmation to those above.

"I'm going down Chris. Be prepared for anything. I'll shoot first and ask questions later. Okay?"

"Right. I'll be ready to follow but will keep a watch up here for any late arrivals."

This was said in almost jocular fashion but Emmett understood the seriousness of the situation, no matter how ridiculous it seemed.

Emmett jumped down and landed beside Agnes who still had her machete at the ready. On his instructions she started to pull at the lining of the wall. Away it came in one door-like panel. Darkness pervaded within. No voices could now be heard.

A tunnel lead away from the pit about four foot high by three foot wide. Emmett had a small powerful torch which he shone down the length of its beam. Nothing moved, all was silent. An overpowering aroma of moist earth mixed with leaf mould clung about the opening.

This was an awkward situation to be in as he would have to proceed along in a crouched position with stengun in one hand and torch in the other. God knows what was up front of him? But he had made up his mind to damn well find out!

With his finger on the trigger and safety catch off he set out in search of what was ahead. Agnes followed close behind with two of the trackers who had jumped down to offer backup support.

Emmett had no idea whether he was moving up, down, left or right as he lost all sense of direction. He used the torch in snatches, illuminating an area up ahead of them and at each step waiting the dreaded shot or shooting from unknown assailants.

Inching forward for however long a period, seemed interminable. His finger was itching, his brow sweating, his back breaking in this half crouch, half kneeling gait.

Every few moments he would halt and listen. Only silence rebounded back. How far had they gone? Was the tunnel safe? What if it collapsed on them? All these thoughts bounded about within his bemused brain. Was he being really stupid in going it, virtually alone?

Chris would have radioed John on the adjoining ridge with an update and he knew both patrols were present if and when required.

How long now had they been down? Although damp to touch, the earthen floor and sides, the atmosphere was close and claustrophobic. Emmett didn't know if he could continue for much longer.

Then something moved, as if a pile of logs had shifted. He flashed the torch and saw a turning to the left. It was around that corner he would swear he heard the noise.

There it was again, more hurried this time and he thought he could sense human movement. The torch flashed and caught three pairs of eyes – screams shrieked and echoed through the confined tunnel space. He held his fire and this time kept the beam on three huddled Wabeebees atop a pile of wood. The very women he had watched collecting wood from the other side of the gorge. The ones who had so mysteriously vanished without trace.

"Simama, atari, keep still, there is no danger," he called to them. His mind was all the time trying to think ahead of his next move. There were more than three women he said to himself. Where now were the others?

They cowered in submission as Emmett and Agnes got to them. This was a sort of room, slightly higher and wider than the tunnel. A store room perhaps? The air felt lighter and fresher.

Agnes grabbed the three as the trackers arrived. She wielded her machete in threatening manner. They fell to the floor prostrate.

Emmett noticed the tunnel continued and was almost high enough for him to stand. He felt it lead onto a central chamber which could be near the surface. What might they find there? As he was centred on this thought he instructed Agnes to interrogate the three women.

He got what he wanted in an instant. They, along with three others who were further into the hideout, were out collecting firewood. The gang (men) were all at a maraza (meeting), they would return in the evening.

"Right, lets lead on now. Agnes tell them to walk ahead as if nothing's wrong – otherwise they will be killed right here. Understood?"

"Fendi," and she laid into them. They were all Tuks so they certainly understood each other. Rising as one they lead on into the tunnel with Agnes right behind, followed by Emmett with his trigger finger once again primed for action.

The air was freshening. Tension was tightrope. It was only about twenty paces to the next room, a little larger than the last. And there, all covered in tightly held blankets, were three bodies in a deep sleep. Torchlight fanned the scene as Emmett crept past Agnes and the three captives. His automatic was ready for any sudden movement. He motioned Agnes to kick them awake. This she did with a deal of delight – not overly antagonistic but bold in intent. One head appeared, followed by the other two. They froze in the ray of torchlight not knowing what was in store.

Agnes spoke first, obviously telling them to turn over and lie still. They cooperated. Emmett had now got the hang of the torch and by facing it up towards the ceiling it lit the whole area.

"Ask them Agnes if this is the total number remaining in the hideout?"

After a brief moment she replied: "Yes fendi."

"Okay. Now where is the exit and which way will the gang return?"

The women all pointed one way. Emmett noticed some boxes stacked in one corner. He pointed to them and nodded to his nearest tracker. He then asked Agnes to take one of the women and find the way out.

Potatoes and maize meal filled two of the boxes with ammunition in the other three.

"Nice find," he said out loud and the tracker smiled in agreement.

Agnes returned within five minutes with the captive and reported that there was yet another chamber and then the exit/entrance, well concealed, into the forest.

Whilst making his way out of the hideout Emmett was drawing up plans for the next few hours which might well be a crucial time. One in which the two patrols should be able to ambush the male gang members.

Before returning to Pope's he would demolish this cavernous hideout. An ingenious obstacle and one of most probably many within the terrorists domain. Up until now only caves had been unearthed. This latest discovery called for a pack of Jack Russells to ferret out Charlie Fox! All this he mused was west of Ireland hunting parlance. Few would understand it here. It ma\de him smile.

After further interrogation the Wabeebees could only agree that the gang, which were seven strong, would return after dark. They had no idea where the jungle meeting was and didn't know of any other tunnelled hideouts. Their pleas of 'being there under duress' went on sceptical shoulders but their willingness to cooperate was not unnoticed by Emmett. The teams back at Pope's would be able to disseminate all their blurb.

Once John and his patrol arrived they then moved out of the immediate area and took time to formulate a master plan. They agreed that all of the gang must be taken, no matter what. They had the trump card of surprise and they must take advantage of that.

First thing to do was replace all destructed foliage at both entrances to the hideout. The gang must suspect nothing and as it would be after dark it made it much easier. Emmett found it interesting to note the method with which his trackers used leafy branches to brush the area, entrances and exit paths covering any signs of traffic. They were doing it as if it were their own secret hideout.

It was agreed that the ambush should be set around both areas. A shoot out was envisaged so Emmett and John instructed their respective patrols to dig in once they surveyed both areas.

"Lets get it done now. There will be plenty of rest-up time before dark. All agreed?" questioned Emmett who, without thought, had seemingly taken overall control. He then reported back to Pope's giving them the complete picture. Any strategic changes could come from HQ he said.

Sometime later a reply came with only one suggestion. It made sense. The trackers should be posted well above and below the area of the hideout. They were to shadow the arrival of the gang and act as backup in the event of an attempted escape.

Emmett wanted this to be the natural scenario of spider, web and intruder. No one must escape.

The captive women had offered information that suggested "all was not right in the forest". Undertones and grumblings of 'getting nowhere' and 'more difficult to get food and the like' were in everyday conversation.

They waited and waited and waited. A three-quarter moon kept popping out from behind a well fragmented cloud base. During one of these silent dark moments voices were heard, then movement could be detected around the entrance area nearest to Emmett's patrol. He whispered, into his radio, "John and Chris be ready".

Both patrols had rehearsed well that afternoon. Emmett's torch would pick them out, followed immediately by Chris doing the same.

In English he ordered them to "freeze, arms above your heads". Half of them, he thought, three in number, obeyed his command. The others turned to run and put their rifles at the hip opening up as they retreated backwards.

Two bursts of rapid fire from Emmett and Chris caught the gang, spinning them around, some falling to the ground, another one or two dropping their guns and stood aghast at their obvious entrapment. The others were kneeling with hands held aloft. No one was dead. The Wazuri had them on the ground with feet stamping them into further submission. The trackers picked up all the arms, ammunition and satchels that were scattered around. Wounds were looked at, and hands were tied behind backs. The haul was six men and six women. Had they missed one male Emmett wondered? Hadn't the women said there were seven? He asked for interrogation by the Wazuri to be immediate.

Yes, there had been seven but one was left at the baraza for some reason. Could Emmett believe that? He had his doubts but for now he had to demolish the hideout and have the captives carry the loot back down the mountain. Both patrols were called home on HQ hearing of their success.

Chris made light of how it had all fallen into place, pardoning the pun!

"That will cost you dearly in the pub, boyho," laughed Emmett in reply. He thought they all needed to lighten up after the tension of the last twenty-four hours. Another job well done on the Farmers Reserve ladder of success.

After clearing out all usable booty from the tunnelled hideout it was left to Emmett to drop two grenades into the entrances. Captives humped the boxes of ammunition and sacks of food down the mountainside, legs shackled by lengths of rope. The six male terrorists were a motley crew. Most were unshaven, two with long beards, and all had long unkempt and very dirty hair. Their body odour was gagging. Eyes were bleary bloodshot. They looked a defeated bunch as if they had had enough of this war.

"Well done you guys," was the general attitude employed by staff and followers at Pope's. Agnes was promoted as the star of the show and this did a lot for the self-confidence of the Wazuri.

28

"We would like to thank Anna, Master"

Ten days later Emmett got a call to proceed to police HQ in Urukan. The Commandant in Charge took Emmett into his office and shut the door behind him. His desk was large and orderly. Two phones were to the right of his swivel chair.

"Sit down please," he invited his guest. "What I have to tell you is good news on one hand but not so good on the other. First may I offer you our congratulations on such a fine operation. Your captives have proved most interesting."

"Oh. Why is that?" asked a somewhat puzzled Emmett.

"Well, you see one of them is the blood brother of Naded, the leader – Field Marshall they say of Uma. Now that is a tremendous prize and in time we hopefully will be able to make him 'sing', I think the phrase is? Anyhow, you will know what I mean."

"Wow! They looked such a raggle taggle lot I wouldn't have put them as better than food carriers. You never know do you Colonel?" Emmett had been told to always promote the official in whose company one found oneself. They loved it!

"It is true, one must always expect the unexpected," he replied with a smile, "however, this capture could also have a downside."

"How do you mean?"

"Well, you see we know that Naded is well connected with elements within *Makinto* and that might make you a marked man. Understand now my friend?" the Commandant said in a sterner tone of voice leaning across the desk from Emmett. His left hand playing with a pencil constantly turning it upside down.

There were a few moments of silence as this sank in. Emmett was first to reply "you mean they may seek revenge in some way?"

"Precisely my good friend. You personally have been most successful on your exchanges with the terrorists and this will not have gone unnoticed, if you get my meaning?" tap, tap, pencil tap.

"Yes, I'm beginning to follow an uneasy train of thought Colonel."

"I have spoken with Jeri Ntsemo about this and he wishes you to see him after leaving me. Is that all right by you?"

"Oh yes certainly. Are you telling me that I must now travel with an armed guard and that sort of thing?"

"Well not literally, but you must watch your back, perhaps a little more carefully." Tap pencil, tap, tap.

There was that phrase again thought Emmett: "Watch your back," but this time it came from the head of police. That was a different matter, a much more serious connotation he felt.

"I think," the Commandant went on "you should discuss the situation with both the CC and your local FR personnel. I am sure something can be worked out. I just wanted to warn you. You can be certain, my, our department's total commitment to security. We have to win this battle." Tap, tap, tap and tap.

With that he smiled, stood up and offered his handshake in friendship. The pencil remained on the desk.

On leaving the building Emmett noticed he was attracting quite a lot of attention with uniformed staff coming to attention and part saluting as he passed by. They were all grinning, their fresh round well fed faces lighting up the dreary PWD painted walls and offices of cream and off cream!

On the drive over to Jeri's office Emmett remembered him being told that the Commandant was very pro Zungu and not at all keen on corruption. He therefore would not respect any part of *Makinto* or the President's elite guard. Some day, he thought to himself there would be civil war. Somehow, he did not wish to be caught up in it.

Jeri was a lot lighter in his interpretation of the situation but did, once again, tell him to put the danger signs up and not to be complacent. He said it was a "damn lucky breakthrough" and prayed for it to reap rapid results.

"There is a feeling that the whole Uma business is winding down. They are completely outsmarted, outgunned and overawed by the popular response to their bestial outpourings. It worked in the beginning. The Kenzie were frightened into cooperating but Uma had not factored in the might and fury of the general farming community. The FR spiked their pretty balloon in no uncertain manner. They are losing face rapidly."

"Well those fellows we bagged seemed at their wits end. How they survived in that hideout Lord only knows and what good it was doing 'the cause' is hard to understand? But then again how can we pretend to know what is in their heads. Notice I didn't say brains." They both laughed.

"Am I becoming a racist Jeri by any chance?"

"Not a chance Irishman. I comprenez vous, as they would have said in the old days here."

"Shall we go to the Club for a drink or two?"

"That's fine by me. I'm not in a hurry to go home. Oh by the way could I put a call through to Anna from here? We might find her at home. I am sure she is being mothered by the family to her heart's content."

"Sure thing." He called his secretary and asked her to get the number.

"It will take a bit of time probably so read *The Standard* whilst I tidy up. Over there, pick and choose," as he pointed to a table with half a dozen newspapers neatly laid on it.

The call came through about ten minutes later on a very crackly line. Anna was bubbling and wanted to return to Urukan as soon as possible. They hadn't talked for all of two weeks and although there was some hundreds of miles between them they felt very close. It was quite evident in their rhetoric. Jeri, very graciously, left his office to the lovers.

"I'll come up for you next weekend if you really have the doctor's go ahead," Emmett said jokingly in to the mouthpiece he caressed lovingly as if it was her very ear.

"Apart from a little stiffness here and there I think I will be well able for you, lover boy. Come get me," she gurgled the last few words. He knew that tone well. He yearned for her. It had been so long without the aroma of musk around him.

"See you soon. Love you." They hung up. Emmett sat for a moment pondering his next move. A few drinks in the company of Jeri would be relaxing and would take his mind off the imponderable.

Next day Emmett had a long chat with Christopher. He had to know whom his servant thought were the most trusted staff members on the farm.

"Please don't ask questions until I tell you. Okay?"

"Yes master."

"I need four good men who you would trust with your life. Your life, your wife's, your children's. Do you understand, Christopher? It is very serious."

"Yes, fendi." A more friendly and personal note rang in that answer. His eyes showed he understood.

Emmett rose from his chair on the veranda and asked Christopher to sit down, think about what he had said and if possible, come up with some names.

He watched from within the lounge as Christopher leant forward, putting a hand either side of his head and covering his ears as if he wished to shut out any sound. Indeed, to shut out the world. He sat like that for a good few minutes until Rajah sidled up and placed his muzzle up under his arms and tried to lick his face. The dog seemed mystified by his friend's manner. He took the dog's head in his hands and rubbed his ears lovingly.

Emmett returned with two glasses of lemonade placing one on the table in front of Christopher.

"Thank you, master. I think I know who I would trust."

"That's good. In your own time let me hear their names."

It took almost an hour, such was the depth of thought and reasoning for Christopher to name his four most trusted fellow farm employees.

"This secret must remain with us Christopher, and us alone."

"Fendi," he appreciated the faith his master placed in him. He would not let him down.

In the week following their meeting Emmett managed to segregate this quartet, one at a time, without drawing any attention to their one-on-one discussions.

Emmett needed them to be his personal bodyguards and wished them to keep their ears to the ground reporting back to him daily, hourly if need be.

They would be trained at Buster's HQ, away from Ratilli and prying eyes, in close combat attack and defence, the use of arms and then accredited into the security section (SS) – the elite squad within the FR which had recently been formed. These people would lose their identities and take up code names, for fear of reprisals within their families and home reserves. Emmett was asked to propose six or eight names for perusal.

"Anytime within the following week old bean," said a jubilant Buster who was still on a high from a record crop and a splendid holiday. Emmett agreed that both he and Shirra looked totally relaxed and radiant in their seashore tans. She especially, looked stunning. Her cleavage shone bronzed and inviting. Her eyes questioned his. He moved away from the obvious intent. He had to be strong in his Lenten obligation to Anna. That was love. This was lust.

Strange things happen in the wee small hours of the morning Emmett recalled on waking with a start. He was alone. The dream had been about his fellow Irishmen who had accepted the challenge in distant climes. He had recently heard from Collins and Vard who both seemed to be enjoying themselves and held down good positions.

"That's it," he said out loud drawing immediate reaction from the pack on the veranda. Even Tippy woke up and peered down from the top of the wardrobe. Her eyes, two crimson pearls, lit up the little disneyesque façade. She was so sweet and gentle. But a pain at times.

Emmett was now wide awake and was on his way to the kitchen for a brew up of tea.

"Collins, Matthews, Mac and Vard. That's what I'll name them. My bodyguards/confidants will bear the names of my four closest friends." He spoke to no one in particular but the dogs. They looked at him with wonderment not quite getting the meaning of this outburst. They whimpered with confusion but

251

kept their tails awagging. For their obvious dismay Emmett fed them treats which were much enjoyed.

He drank his mug of sweetened tannin on the veranda. The compound was still, slightly mystic in shapes and shadows of various bits of machinery lying dormant for now, but shrouded in African dew.

Dressed in his blue lungi – sarong – he led the dogs in a camp walkabout.

He was pleased with this radical idea and would now be reminded of the 'fractious four' on a daily basis. He felt good, warm with the idea that his friends, in name at least, would be around him, close by when needed.

They in turn, when informed by Emmett, would probably think he was touched by the sun! Things – way out thoughts and ideas – did happen when one got lost in a desert under a blistering blinding sun. Or so they saw in the cinemas back home.

Let them think what they wanted He was happy with it.

Wisps of cotton wool clouds wafted around the impressive gates of Anna's home. It was certainly well named. On his previous visit Emmett had experienced the sensation of walking through the neighbouring forest enshrouded in an over blanket of atmospheric moisture.

A security guard was now stationed at the gate. His pillar box accommodation protected him from the damp. He had been briefed on Emmett's arrival so no long questioning took place.

Dogs rushed from the house to trot back on either side of the vehicle as it approached. Theirs was an enjoyable greeting – they seemed to be smiling.

An ethnic vision gracefully appeared at the head of the steps. Swathed in a green and red robe that reached the ground Anna's arms became outstretched as Emmett jumped out and slammed his door. He raced up the twelve steps taking three at a time. They held each other closely – so close that the other's heartbeat pounded closely through craving bodies.

It was probably a full minute before Emmett stood slightly back from his beautiful Anna. He put his hands either side of her face and then drew her to him – lips tenderly touching lips prior to a violent crushing, moment of passion. Her dogs crowded around with whimpering tones and most probably questioning "me, me, me?"

After this ritualistic welcome Emmett moved back down to the vehicle and lifted out his grip and a heavily laden kikoo.

Mumbi had now joined the lovers and after welcoming Emmett she took the kikoo from him and instructed his driver to follow her.

No one else materialised from the house so he asked if they could have a short stroll around the garden. He wished to breathe in the mountain air and stretch his legs. He also wished to be alone with his woman. It had been a long time. His patience had run thin. Anna said she felt fine, physically. Her mental wellbeing perhaps needed a tad more time. She was still grieving and would carry that burden for years to come.

"But I now have you again, my divine Irish. I feel so much better, so happy. Everything will be alright."

They sat on a garden bench enmeshed in mist until Anna remarked "we are getting wet, we'd better move inside." Emmett had not noticed it. He was in his own Shangri-La – an emotion he hadn't experienced prior to this. Anna very obviously meant far more to him than he first realised or appreciated. Long may it last he thought.

George and Mims returned from Kenzi about 6.00pm. They all sat in their drawing room around a lovely log fire with George dispensing pre-dinner drinks. He was most interested in the ongoing fight with Uma as most of it was west of Urukan up in the Mandaras.

"In Kenzi we don't hear much about what's happening in the rest of the country. Victor has the press towing the line towards his blinkered ways of thinking. I hear from Anna you made an important capture?"

Emmett proceeded to recount the tunnel episode and how security, even on the Punjabi Plains, had been stepped up since then for fear of repercussions.

"Evidently," he continued "there is a connection between Uma and segments of *Makinto*. Have you heard anything along those lines?"

"Yes, there have been rumblings. A murmur here, another there but nothing concrete."

"Perhaps," said Emmett "if they breakdown Naded's brother we may learn something important?"

"I'm certain both movements are interlinked by the 'boss man' but the boss man doesn't want to show any knowledge of it. Let me top you up," George said as he rose to refill his own glass. The ladies now returned and sat on the couch facing the fire between the men.

It was a homely scene and one that Emmett longed for. Perhaps his continued bachelorhood out in the wheatlands was getting to him? It had not mattered early on but since Anna's hospitalisation, recuperation and absence from Ratilli Emmett felt a pining for company.

"How are Margaret and Jeri," enquired Mimi "and the children?"

"In great form really. They haven't been out to the farm since Anna's accident. I feel Jeri is working just a little too hard and becoming stressed with the Uma problems. He gets called out at all hours, like a good GP back home, and that's telling on his health."

"He hasn't got an easy job," chipped in George "and he walks a tightrope with the President. One hell of a balancing act I would call it."

"I can imagine that all right," agreed Emmett.

Mumbi announced dinner was 'tari'.

After coffee the ladies retired. Anna to finish her packing with her mother as company. George and Emmett stayed a long time either side of the fire savouring a fine balloon each of Courvoisier VSOP. They covered many subjects and finished on what Emmett was planning to do after his initial contract was up.

"Hopefully return for a further three years and really earn some good bonuses. But I will return to Ireland for a month or so to see the family."

"I'd love to come with you," said George with a far off look in his eyes. "How about some fishing on those lakes you talk so much about?"

"What a great idea," Emmett replied with genuine surprise and pleasure all mixed into one.

"Let's call it our pipe dream young man," and taking Emmett by his shoulders he led him out into the passage to the bedroom wing "and let's keep it our secret."

Mumbi served a very early breakfast after which they all departed. The mist was still down and it reminded Emmett of an early morning in county Clare after a heavy night's rain. No sun had arisen and all was dank and grey.

Mims hugged Emmett in a fond motherly embrace.

"Look after my chicken, Emmett dear. I hold you responsible for her. She's not to go back to work for another week or so. I've spoken with Jeri." She broke away and got into George's Mercedes. She had obviously said her goodbyes to Anna.

"Take care you two. Keep in touch." George and Emmett shook hands and clasped arms. All was understood.

Anna had presents for Margaret and the children and she wanted to collect clothes for the farm. They arrived at Jeri's house to find only servants on duty. They then went on to his office and fortunately found him in. He could only spare five minutes and said he would send the children out for the weekend if that was all right? It was agreed.

Anna was overwhelmed by the reception she received at Ratilli. It started at the weighbridge where Emmett had to drop off his driver. Looks, whispers and then handshakes followed as each one standing around the buildings spotted who it was master had in his vehicle.

Anna and her Wazuri were quite a talking point since their ambush and her miraculous escape. News spreads like a bush or forest fire in these parts. And, as is the norm, it snowballs in content and extravagance. She had become a cult hero. She had escaped from the *Makinto*.

Later that evening Christopher told Emmett that Limani wanted to see him out front.

When Emmett moved onto his veranda he saw the entire workforce assembled outside his garden gate.

"We would like to thank Anna, master," said Limani and the women in the group started to sway and clap their hands.

"Anna, come on out, you are wanted," called Emmett above a mounting harmony of voices.

On her appearance the women erupted into a defining ulation of tongues on roofs of mouths. The men in the group stamped their feet and waved their hands above their heads. Then the entire staff broke into an African lullaby which lasted for a tear jerking ten minutes.

Anna broke down and buried her head in Emmet's shoulder. The dogs barked their heads off and were totally confused. Christopher standing beside Emmett had tears streaming down his face as he too kept in time and rhythm with the choral recital. Emmett embraced Anna until the song died away.

Limani once again moved forward and in Tukulu addressed Anna. It was short and obviously sweet as Anna gracefully left Emmett's side and went to Limani. She took his hand in their thumb to thumb ethnic way of greeting, firstly in her native language and then in English thanked them for their blessing and good wishes.

In these few moments Emmett saw her leadership qualities. Suddenly she became a queen in front of her loyal subjects. She respected them as much as they did her.

Anna went amongst them taking their hands and bowing to her elders. It was a regal scene, one that would remain with Emmett for years to come. He once more was proud of his Anna. He noticed that both Rajah and Rastus accompanied her on her walkabout. That was good. Rani stayed by his side. After that moving event they retired to his sofa, held hands and wafted a few drinks prior to turning in.

Next morning she rode out with Emmett before breakfast and said she felt really good. They took Corrib and Mask accompanied by the dogs and went through the walk, trot and canter routine before 'giving it a blast' as Anna ordered, on their way home after about an hour's outing. She had certainly got her fitness back with miles of walking and jogging. Her arms and shoulders seemed to be able to take the strains associated with holding and pulling the reins. She hadn't been run away with. Emmett breathed many sighs of relief as they dismounted some way off the homestead and walked home. She said her legs were a little wobbly rather like the after effect she remembered on first harnessing her Irish stallion.

29

Thank the Lord for a pile of maize stalks

Jeri and Margaret arrived with the children well before dark as they themselves were travelling on to spend two nights with the Freedos. They would pick up Anna and the children at teatime on Sunday afternoon.

It had been a few months since the children were last on Ratilli and both rushed to see and be with the ponies accompanied by Anna.

"Well, we don't have to worry about them," smiled Margaret as they sat down to a quick cup of tea on the veranda.

"How has Anna been?" enquired Jeri who seemed unusually quiet and withdrawn.

"I'd say she is as good as new. She does, however, have nightmares and doesn't sleep too soundly." Emmett then recounted her homecoming and the celebration she received from his staff.

"That must have been quite stressful for her?"

"It was, but she carried it off with regal charm. It was moving and totally unexpected."

"That shows how the general Kenzies feel about *Makinto* – even out in these arid regions."

"We're all tightening our security," said Margaret and our children are now driven to and from school each day. A hell of a bore but necessary."

Jeri said they must depart and apologised for such an abrupt stay but they wished to arrive in daylight.

"Point taken. Enjoy yourselves and give them our best wishes. We like them a lot."

The children rushed back from the stables to say their goodbyes with Anna waving them away from the middle of the compound.

It was a bubbly evening with cries of laughter and dismay over the scrabble board after supper.

A home is certainly a home with children in it, thought Emmett as he languished in a hot bath after they had gone to bed. When would he settle down and where? He loved his old style iron bath filled high and full of Badedas and bubbles. All plans seemed easier to fathom out in such luxuriant surroundings. It was easier, however when he was alone with his thoughts. Anna, bless her, didn't make it that easy when titillating his fancy on these visits. Not that he was complaining!

For the first few days when they were alone Emmett and Anna discussed her ambush and lucky escape as they sat on his veranda.

He learnt how their truck, on its return trip from the exercise up in the gorges of the Mandaras, rounded a corner on the sandy road to find a large tree trunk halfway across their path. Jaci applied brakes and swerved to miss it. At that moment a hail of bullets cut across their windscreen from an oblique angle.

Jaci took the brunt of the fusillade – the truck hurtled out of control into the culvert at the side. Tumbling over and over it came to rest on its side. Another burst of bullets hit into the vehicle as shrieks of anguish filled the ensuing silence.

Anna, sitting up front beside Jaci, had been hit in the shoulder and neck and after the crash must have become unconscious as she didn't remember anything until later.

All she heard were cries and moans as she came to. She lay between two dead bodies. There was much blood on and under her. She couldn't move and didn't wish to as she heard the gang, whoever they were, ravaging those who had been thrown out onto the roadside.

Machetes and single shots were being used at random. One person climbed on top of the cab, leant inside and struck blindly with his machete, not knowing who was already dead.

Anna was struck twice with glancing blows. She bit her lip refusing to cry out and got away with it. The attacker felt he had finished his task and climbed down.

She then heard in the distance a vehicle approaching. That evidently alerted the gang into retreat action. She heard engines start up and speed away.

For what reason she will never understand but the approaching vehicle did not stop. It changed gears a couple of times and kept on down the road. The scene was probably too horrific and frightening for the driver to halt. He had to think of his own life and those of whoever were with him.

Anna, in the hours that followed, managed to crawl out of the broken windscreen and crossed the adjoining field on hands and knees. She remembers seeing the pile of maize stalks and sought refuge within its bosom. She remembered nothing more.

It was in hospital she learnt about the magnitude of the massacre and that *Makinto* were to blame. Never mind her feelings of disgust towards them before that, now she promised revenge. She was as one with Emmett's feelings. They would bide their time. Revenge was sweet they believed

Emmett was on a bit of a roll at this time as he had been invited to join the Gymkhana Racing Committee. They felt his enthusiasm over the past two seasons, especially his input into the trial hurdles campaign, which had increased public awareness with attendances well up on previous years, deserved due recognition.

He learnt that the Shah family group had increased their sponsorship for the hurdles and were prepared to sign a three year undertaking. Emmett felt that national hunt racing, all be it a tiny segment in this embryonic industry, was now to be recognised. Another first for the Irish!

Emmett would have to find another horse or two for the upcoming season. Geronimo was a marked hero and they all knew his capabilities. He was the one to be dethroned. However, Emmett felt no one had seen him at his best. In other words there was still 'a lot left in the tank' as his chums back home would have put it. Another decent thoroughbred to work with would be Emmett's mission. But where to find it was the question? None of the polo players would let a good one out of their yards. Emmett would have to search out a 'has been' who perhaps wasn't, or an untried but problem child from a breeder's farm. It would be an interesting search and one that had to be very low profile. Otherwise he could be pipped at the post before the race even began?

How chilling a radio call can be? Just as Emmett finished the last spoonful of his creamy rice pudding, a Christopher speciality, the night guard hailed him from inside the office. He rushed out with napkin being used to clean around his mouth and took the call. "Emmett here, over."

"Buster here Emmett. Hope you are sitting down, over."

"I will, sounds ominous?"

"*Makinto* have struck again and this time in our area. I need you to get a small group of your trackers with two good shots to back you up. And get over to Three Mile Cross as soon as possible. Keep in touch. You will meet up with the others there. Okay?"

"Many casualties?"

"Another truck ambush. Luckily its not yours or mine. Get cracking."

"Am on my way. Over and out."

The four bodyguards were alerted. Three trackers were in camp as were two of his best shots. They departed within twenty minutes. Three Mile Cross was on the Urukan side of Koram so all units from and around the town had been alerted and were already en route. It seemed that it was a copycat ambush – as that of the Wazuri two months previously.

This time, however, it was within the wheatlands district and the truck with farm labour was indeed 'one of ours' as Buster had put it so distinctly.

A feeling of déjà vu greeted Emmett. The truck – a Toyota three-tonner – lay on its side off the road in the culvert. It was on a corner leaning down into a dry river bed.

Two ambulances were already in situ with injured bodies being attended to. Six dead were laid out beside each other just to the rear of the truck. It was owned by an Asian group who farmed land down beyond Jonathan's – almost at the furthest end of the Punjabi Plains. The truck had been into Urukan to collect spares, supplies and two ladies with new babies from the hospital.

One of these women had been hit in the face by a bullet – a glancing blow – but both babies were, seemingly, all right as their lungs bore witness to. They were swathed in yards of blankets and strapped tightly to their respective mothers' back. This most probably saved their lives as both women clung to each other when the truck turned over. Luckily they weren't hacked or shot after the crash.

There were three survivors including the driver who managed to give accurate accounts of the attack.

Two landrovers with militia clad insurgents wearing orange berets – probably ten to twelve in total – plundered the edible supplies, tins of oil and grease and anything else that was readily handled. They were in a hurry and just shot at anyone that moved. They then took off in the direction of Urukan.

Roadblocks had been put into position within forty-five minutes of it being reported. This made the landrovers 'take to the bush'. Once again it was night time – not a particularly dark one with a quarter moon present – but no air reconnaissance could be in operation for at least six hours. It therefore had to be a follow-up operation with as many roadblocks as could be manned hopefully encircling the area.

Half a dozen neighbouring farmers arrived within the hour. All were allotted areas to patrol, by vehicle and on foot.

Emmett had a funny feeling about this operation. He couldn't quite put his finger on it but something, dramatic and fatal was to happen. The terrain was spooky. All arid and heavily gullied. Ideal for ambushes.

Tracks, good enough for vehicles, were fewer than chicken's teeth. A giant sweep from the vehicle, eight to ten men on foot, was coordinated and put into operation. They lined up on a given sign and progressed at walking pace. The same formation was setting out about five miles to their east. Police, GSU's and Wazuri manned the main road between Koram and Urukan. It would be difficult to avoid this dragnet if *Makinto* made a break. They would be taken. Of that there was no doubt.

As Emmett inched his landrover forward, with Vard beside him and Collins taking a view of proceedings from the rear, he found himself once again questioning the rationale behind this attack. How could it be of any benefit to anyone? No answers were forthcoming – for now at least.

It was a long fruitless crawl but one that had to be done. The patrol kept in contact with TAC HQ set up on the main road. At 12.30am the message came through that the two *Makinto* vehicles were making a run for it and heading towards the road from Urukan to Kitos. Emmett and his crew could return to TAC HQ with the others.

An hour later the *Makinto* ran into a GSU ambush. All hell broke loose.

Within twenty minutes the loudest cheer rose from TAC HQ. It was like Ireland scoring the winning try at Lansdowne Road against England.

"All terrorists have been exterminated," came across the airwaves, or words similar to that!!

Everyone was stood down at 2.00am. Emmett's FR unit went to the tiny cottage hospital at Koram on their way home. One additional death had been recorded. The injured were being treated.

Emmett met the Bamjees, the Asian family from whose farm the truck and workers were returning to. They were devastated and very afraid. Not even the news of the successful follow up made a difference to their pallid grey faces. Eyes were tearful, hands and feet fidgety. They were a very singular family and not well known by many in the district.

Collins mentioned something on the way home that made the hairs on Emmett's arms stand rigid for a few seconds. This was followed by goose pimples and shivers down his back.

The truck that had been ambushed was the same model as Ratilli's – a dead ringer in fact. Could there have been a mistake made? Was his meant to have been the target? Was this a wakeup call?

Early next morning Emmett drove to Buster's and breakfasted with them both. He discussed the possibility of Collins' suspicions. Buster said there were a dozen such models in the district but he would not rule out the thought.

"In fact it was a great pity that all the bastards were dead. If we had one body to grill we might have learnt a lot – instead of nothing. Fuck all in fact."

Emmett felt the fight was becoming regional.

"Our GSU boys certainly wish to get noticed. They obviously didn't want prisoners. I detect a one-up-manship ring to their success. Great pity, as you said, but one can't blame them."

"It does show the animosity that exists in the ranks of the militia. I only hope we don't have an internal war on our hands Emmett. That would not be easy to contain."

"More coffee Emmett," asked Shirra who had been keeping a close eye on each of 'her men' as they traded remarks.

"Yes please. That's a particularly good brew I might say."

"Well it's a new blend I am experimenting with. Half Kenyan, half Costa Rican. I am glad you approve – we like it. Don't we darling?"

"What? Oh yes, very full bodied. Great after a night out."

Buster said he would put some feelers out into the Urukan/Kenzi networks to try and ascertain the reason for the *Makinto* incursion.

"Just cannot understand those bastards. Were they all high on dagga or what? Or was it a sort of bravado thing? We are the greatest and don't you forget it. Bang, bang."

"It's crazy all right, Buster, but also a little frightening, don't you think? One never knows where or when they will pop up next time."

"I only hope," interrupted Shirra, "that they don't make the road, our life blood, a regular target. What would we poor women do? Remain on the farm all the time?" As an afterthought and when neither of the men responded "it certainly would not suit my lifestyle. Would it now?" she said with pleading tones to both of them.

"Better get on with some work," was Buster's response as he rose from the table.

Emmett took the hint and in thanking Shirra for the meal he felt her warmth in their handshake. Her eyes bore into his. Moonlike they radiated sensuality and sexability. She wanted it and wanted it badly.

Emmett remembered their time spent in Urukan and how she insisted on early morning sex – every morning. How he ever played a reasonable game of tennis after that truly amazed him. Shirra exuded sex with a capital 'S'. As she was the only nympho he had ever come across he remained completely entranced by her. All his manly emotion erupted when near to her. They sparked off each other like pieces of flintstone.

Emmett had many sleepless nights thinking about her and how he repeatedly fell under her spell. She was explosive. Anna was comfortable.

At times he said to himself: "to hell with it. Live for today. God knows what tomorrow brings?" Then he would feel bad about betraying Anna. She, after all, was his first love. But did he really know what love meant? Could he have a second? She had, after all, intimated her willingness for him to 'relax himself' as long as she wasn't around. They both knew what that meant.

Emmett felt he had the best of both worlds. He just had to manage it correctly. It was rather like fly fishing – cast the fly, hook the trout, play it. If done skilfully you landed the prize. Emmett now had two trophies.

"I'm a greedy bugger," he said to himself with satisfaction. "It's worth it." He knew, however, his parish priest in Ballyvaughan wouldn't condone it!

30

"Luck of the Irish, my Ebony Angel"

One more crop and then home. That's what was on the menu. His offshore account looked impressive - £7,500 from two bonuses. His savings account with Ulster Bank held a balance of £4,800. What a party he would throw.

Emmett felt well pleased with his foray into African agriculture. From knowing absolutely nothing about wheat farming he was now in a position to hold out for a more lucrative contract. Much gratitude had to be showered on both Ian and Howard who, not only had shown him the profitable way ahead, but whose respective families had cushioned him to their bosoms. His employers had come up trumps and a respectable trust had been developed between them. Emmett would probably never understand the working of the Asian mind. Just be there with them and be prepared for any eventuality. Devious is as devious does. He had indeed learnt something.

He had made his mind up to return. He had plenty of unfinished business with agriculture and subversion. His quest to find and destroy those who had been party to Anna's ambush lay heavy on his mind.

Stories of *Makinto's* bestiality and general cruelty to their own people were increasing on a daily basis. Torture chambers had been discovered in and around Kenzi. Mutilated bodies lay in shallow graves nearby. No one could answer the obvious question, why? What were they trying to achieve? It certainly had no logical answer.

In one disused warehouse the police discovered a most horrible sight. In the middle of the floor a ten foot high letter 'M', made of timber, stood tall. Strapped to it was a male body whose skin was part pealed away from its various limbs. Cuts had been made from throat to penis, pelvic bone down each thigh, over the kneecap and then straight down to the toes. Then the pealing of the skin took place. This body had only a few inches of its left side peeled away. Perhaps the torturers had been interrupted and disbanded in a hurry? It, unfortunately, did not help the body in question. He was dead. One wondered whether he had died prior to the bestial act or as a result of it? Information, sooner or later, would come to hand and the world would hear of this incredibly cruel act.

Jeri was the one relating the incident to Emmett:

"It looked, evidently, like some ritual took place around the structure. There were twelve wooden boxes placed in a circle around it. Perhaps the hierarchy of *Makinto* were present. It may well mean something, in their language. A gruesome thought whatever."

"Not an event I would like to be caught up in," with a shiver snaking down his spine.

"Let's go to the Club for a noggin."

"I'll drink to that," said Emmett as Jeri rose from his desk and departed his office.

It was lunchtime and a Friday which meant the bar was packed with farmers. Their wives were out shopping and having hair do's. They would all meet up later on.

Talk was all about the torture chambers now splashed over the media outlets.

"Shoot the bastards," was the main comment.

"If I see any of their jeeps in my area I'll shoot first and ask questions later," piped up Charlie, the vet. His normal ruddy complexion went a cherry red during the discussion.

"A likely heart patient if he's not careful," whispered Jeri behind a hand shrouding his mouth. Emmett nodded in agreement.

"Let's get onto a more pleasant topic fellows. Have you found a new horse Irish?" questioned Mike 'Jambo' Hogg a Kitos tea planter.

"Not exactly. Have seen a couple of prospects but nothing definite. Why you ask?"

"Oh, we're interested to know what our opposition will be. Up in my district we are going to give the hurdles a hell of a go this season. You certainly won't have it all your own way this time I promise you."

"That's sounds serious Mike. I look forward to the challenge. It was too easy last time," and he turned to them "cheers." Emmett raised his glass of 'pinkers', winked and added "here's to the sponsors. Good luck all."

They all drank to that and much laughter and shoulder hugging followed. Large wooden platters of crusty bread, cheese, pickles and scallions were served to virtually all present. Some, the more senior, went to join their memsahibs in the dining room. World cricket and rugger tours were the luncheon topics with all local troubles forgotten.

Emmett collected his household provisions assisted by Matthews and Vard who had visited relatives in the township. They then collected Anna who was spending the weekend at Ratilli. She had taken on a new driver, Sarah, who would follow them in Anna's newly souped up landrover. This service had been a present from Jaswant. He understood how much she meant to Emmett and he was prepared to look after his Irish investment, no matter what it cost. Already Emmett's own landrover had been upgraded, reinforced and had bullet proof glass fitted.

Emmett, under Anna's instructions, had invited Ian, Jan, Rachel and Howard for Saturday evening. She was preparing her mother's speciality – a rack of lamb. He had managed to persuade old Findlay, the Urukan butcher to hold his finest joint for the occasion.

Emmett was allowed to prepare their first course. He decided on skewers of prawns and pineapple with a pecan sauce. Crepe suzette finished off the meal with Irish coffees as the goodnight teaser.

"An evening out of the Ritz," proffered a radiant Rachel who looked stunning in a clinging sky-blue shift.

"Incredible, you two. When did you get the time to put it all together?" questioned Jan. She had chosen emerald green, also a long elegant shift, which emphasised her green eyeballs of fire piercing radiant beneath her mane of chestnut hair.

The two lads looked spick and span in longs and open neck shirts. They made two elegant couples, thought Emmett, definitely fitting the bill of any Holywood production! His own beautiful Anna had chosen ivory for her cocktail length dress and shoes, the ethnic beadwork worn as a necklace sparkled as a cascade of water in bright sunlight, each colour caught in the candlelit surround.

It was good to dress up on occasions such as this. To forget the parochialness of the wheatlands and fantasise a little gave a luxuriant feel to the occasion.

"Sure wasn't the great outside world only a flight away?" and any one of them could facilitate of that luxury. Dreams are made of this, surmised Emmett as his eyes took in the rapture of the moment.

He wished they could all be together in the west of Ireland. He would take them to Clifden, Roundstone, stay at Ballinahinch Castle with perhaps the chance of a salmon caught on one of the many pools below the hotel. Then around the Seven Bens to Oughterard and across behind the Corrib to Cong and Ashford Castle.

Race week in Galway, oysters at Morans on the Weir and a visit to Craughwell to see the hounds and kennels of the famous Galway Blazers.

A trip on the family's hooker around Galway Bay with, weather permitting, a landing on one of the Aran Islands. Emmett could see the four of them clad in Aran sweaters, with their hair blowing in the westerly winds, their naturally sun tanned faces taking on a burnt gold complexion with the softness of the Irish climate.

"Penny for them, Emmett?" interrupted Jan as she cradled her Irish coffee in cupped hands.

"Oh, gosh you caught me. I was visualising all of us in the west of Ireland – it made a pretty picture."

"Perhaps one day – maybe sooner than later," added Ian and "by golly these are good," alluding to the coffees.

"Any more for anyone?" asked Anna who rose and went into the kitchen. "And why not, one for the road," came an unanimous reply.

The ladies wandered off to the bathroom with the men stretching their legs in the front garden. Howard joined Emmett in a King Edward cigar. Nobody else smoked.

The dogs needed a run so Emmett took them to the airstrip. It was a serene evening, a sky full of stars dotted around a half moon. On returning he found the ladies inspecting his garden.

"Everything seems so lush. Who is the gardener Emmett?" enquired Jan.

"Christopher mostly but I love tinkering around in it too."

"It has all come together beautifully and looks like a mature setting. Well done."

"I have to thank you, Jan, for getting such a response. I didn't want one plant to wither away."

"Lots of t.l.c," Rachel purred as she breathed in the aromatic Jasmine creeper and then they returned to the veranda and the men. Anna arrived with new glasses of Irish coffee and distributed them as everyone settled down in the drawing room. They departed thirty minutes later and suggested that this be repeated monthly in rotation. Emmett and Anna concurred as they waved them goodnight.

Relaxing together in their luxuriant bubble bath some minutes later Anna concluded that Emmett had been really fortunate in having such great neighbours.

"Luck of the Irish, my ebony angel." He took her into submission very easily. What a pleasure he concluded.

Emmett was called to attend a committee meeting of the Gymkhana Racing Association held at the Urukan Club. It was an afternoon meeting after which he booked a table at the Peking Restaurant for Anna and himself.

It was agreed to hold two extra race meetings in the upcoming season with the Champion Hurdle as the centrepiece of the final day. An extra qualifier was also agreed to as, seemingly, all the polo crowd wished to take part this time.

Emmett was allocated an increased budget for the construction and maintenance of the hurdles. He was also given a mileage allowance for the many trips he would have to make. This was stipulated by the sponsors. He was happy to accept their generosity.

Prize money, which up 'till then, had been minimal, was increased by tenfold which gave everyone an added incentive. Two meetings would have children's races. There would be one race for novices and one open to all under sixteen.

A racing 'ball' would be held in the Kitos Club on the night of the final meeting. All in all things were looking brighter than before. Emmett was immensely pleased and vowed to himself to find a couple of good horses to hopefully take on all-comers.

That evening over their prawn fuyong, duck in black pepper and a mountain of lichies Anna mentioned two items of great interest. One was the sudden influx of prostitutes to a certain area of Urukan. This, the Wazuri concluded, was a definite result of the ongoing war against Uma.

Young women were being driven off their homelands and not wishing to live in the fortified camps had fled to the nearest town seeking work. Little was available so they took up the oldest game in the business.

They chose a street two blocks away from the market which Anna said was now known as 'Susieland'. With more militia strutting their stuff these were their prime targets. Anna suggested they should take a drive down there on her way home.

Her other piece of news interested Emmett greatly. Having explained all the points that were discussed at his committee meeting and feeling Emmett's obvious yearning to find a new horse or two, she remembered something that was said on their stay at Jay and Jasmine's farm.

"Remember Jasmine said her family were friends of a Belgium family who bred horses in the Congo. She said something about them being too good for farm work. Perhaps they have thoroughbreds. What about finding out?"

"Great idea my love. It is about time we visited them again anyhow. I'll try and arrange it for next weekend or the one after. Okay by you?"

"I got on well with her. She seemed quite a lonely poor woman."

"Well remembered my sweet we will follow it up. Cheers. Well remembered."

They drove down Susieland after an excellent dinner. Collins and Mack were on duty and as Emmett watched them through his rear mirror he couldn't but smile at their eyes. He now knew where 'out on stalks' came from. Theirs were literally that.

Emmett curb crawled like he had seen in some movies. Anna half lay on the front seat her head out of view.

Mini skirts, white knee-high boots, tighter than tight blouses scantily covering enormous boobs, lipsticks of the brightest hues, hair styles maxi and mini in creation topped off a parade of pariahs.

Some lingered curb side, others waited in the shadows of duka doors. Emmett didn't stop but cruised openly sizing up the talent show.

He had walked along this street – Fifth – many times, in daylight, in his forays to and from the market.

266

Not a word was spoken until he pulled into Third Avenue and headed for Jeri's house.

"Well, what do you think?" purred a revived and upright Anna. "Quite something, eh?"

"You bet your bottom dollar on that all right," replied Emmett almost laughing. "What about that then you guys?" he joking questioned his bodyguards in the back.

They looked at each other mystified and couldn't answer. Then Mac said:

"I saw someones a bit like them with Jonathan one day in Koram, master."

"Yes, you are quite right. I remember also seeing them."

"Look, but don't touch," came from Anna, "they are dangerous,"

She then talked about the truck drivers who were increasing a hundred fold and that these, together with the gangs of thugs, were their main customers.

"Tell the staff at Ratilli that these ladies are Atari (danger) and to stay well away," she concluded. Both bodyguards agreed.

When they arrived at Jeri's they recounted their little excursion to Margaret who listened with much revolt in her eyes. She had not been told about "this new scourge and outrage," as she called it.

Jeri came into the room with a jug of hot coffee and was immediately set upon by Margaret. "Why hadn't she been informed.?"

"My sweetest, it has got nothing to do with you, so calm yourself. We have people programmed to keep an eye on them from within the Department. Kenzi is rife with them. Coffee you two?" and he changed the subject.

"Peking as good as ever?"

"Yes indeed, it was packed."

Back on the farm Emmett contacted Jay on the radio. Either weekend would be fine and he would have Jasmine contact the Maingards who were the family in question. They were about an hours drive from Mandalay.

"Oh, and by the way, I'll be popping in on you one of these day soon. Bye now."

If Emmett was to get another horse or two then extra stables had to be constructed. The shed in which they were now housed was full up with grain drying machinery so an alternative had to be planned. These were the sort of projects that Emmett revelled in. Challenges were his main course, there to be devoured.

He walked the compound, every inch of which was known intimately to him now. He had to be careful, however, not to annoy the Bhogals. But then again he remembered something Ian had said earlier on. "Don't worry about them, you're in the driving seat now."

267

31

"They watched five hippos peacefully grazing the lawns"

$\mathcal{I}t$ was about two weeks later when out of an uncommonly grey sky came a bird of a strange hue. All farm workers rushed out onto the compound grounds to gaze at this queer creature circling overhead. Emmett's first impression on seeing it was "my God, it's a flying bedstead."

A faint sounding engine was obviously powering this mechano like structure. A person was sitting in a tubular frame with a little propeller out front. The tiny engine was mounted between the pilot and propeller. A single wing straddled the microscopic guts of a 'stranger than fiction flying machine'.

Emmett, followed by two dozen or so staff, walked and then jogged to the airstrip and watched the 'creature' land, pull up within fifty to one hundred yards, turn around and taxi back to where the amazed faces were gathered.

A grinning Jay Freedo took off his goggles, unstrapped his safety belts and dismounted from the tiny 'no sides' cockpit.

"My God, Jay, you frightened the life out of us. What on earth is that yoke?" erupted from Emmett as he welcomed him with outstretched arms.

"Gee, its my latest toy, Emmett," and turning to the contraption with his right hand on the tiny wing "and one that is such fun to drive. I'll take you up but first I need a drink. I'm desperately dry."

Emmett asked Limani to put a couple of guards on the plane while he lead Jay to his house.

"It's called a microlite, Emmett, and used extensively in the States. I saw them last year and ordered one. I was bowled over by it. Now where's that lemonade of Christopher's I tasted last time?"

"Coming right up. Want to freshen up first? You know the way. See you back here in a mo."

They both left the veranda as Emmett had to complete what he was doing when so rudely disturbed by this amazing visitation.

Later over tankards of cool lemonade Jay explained his toy.

"I thought it would be ideal for my photographic work. And so it's proved. I've had it a month and I've been able to get some amazing shots. The animals don't seem to bother about it, not even the sound of the engine when I'm literally feet above them. Brilliant, quite amazing, I'm knocked out about it."

He was now becoming really animated and "do you know I can land it almost anywhere. Brilliant is my summation. Bloody marvellous you would say."

They both remained silent for a few moments savouring the drink. Dribs and drabs of staff were now returning to their workplace. Undoubtedly they would also return for Jay's departure.

"I'll take you up for a spin now if you like," Jay remarked as he stood up and stretched his angular body.

"By the way, Jay," prompted a slightly apprehensive Emmett, "do we have parachutes?"

"Oh my God no, Irishman. It can land on a postage stamp. Feel better now?" he questioned as he put his arm around Emmett's shoulders.

"Sort of. Anyhow let's go."

When the waiting crowd saw that Emmett was being strapped into his seat they once more rushed to the airstrip. The womenfolk ululating as they ran. Christopher had to restrain the dogs as Emmett had requested him in case they chased it down the runway.

The tiny engine was like a Briggs and Stratton unit on some large lawnmowers he had seen on the some of the coffee baron's lawns. He noted it started on a first press of a button in a scantily adorned twelve inch dial between them.

After a number of revs Jay unleashed the brake and away they went. Within eighty yards they were airborne.

Emmett reasoned it was not much different to the Cessna's he flew, just a lot more open to the elements and a lot more flimsy in form. He really did liken it to a mechano built vehicle – that flew?

They circled the nearest sections to the homestead and then returned to the airstrip. It looked as if Emmett's entire staff were present to greet their safe return. Loud applause broke out as Jay taxied to a halt.

"I must head on home now Emmett. Just thought you would like to see it. Jasmine has named her 'Screwball' – she's really talking about me you see so I have let it stand. The kids love the 'monica'."

As Emmett alighted he turned and said: "next time I want to fly this bicycle. Okay with you?"

"You bet – make it sooner than later. Bye for now," and he took off heading over the Ratilli, road and Ian's homestead. That will raise a few eyebrows Emmett thought to himself!

He wasn't more than five minutes inside the door when he heard Ian's voice calling him up on the radio. After their intros came "and what the fuck was that? Over."

"Jay's new toy – a microlite – and he took me up for a spin. Quite terrifying but alls well that lands well. Hey? Over."

"I thought it was a flying bedstead. Something out of Phineas Fogg's world. I'll think I'll stick to my type. Over."

"I agree but it could be fun to have one. He said I can fly it when next I visit. How are things generally? Over"

"All is fine here. Thanks. See you soon. Over and out."

That night in bed Emmett thought hard and deep about Screwball and how he must fly it soon. Evidently no special licence was needed. His would cover this strange creature.

Emmett took a short break, five days, and flew by air from Kenzi to Nairobi. He had made contact with his East African friend, Colin Dymmot and asked him to search out a big strong five or six year old thoroughbred gelding for a certain amount of money. He had heard from Jasmine that the Maingards had nothing available. So he decided on Kenya.

Colin met him at the airport and they spent a night at the Norfolk Hotel partying in the Equator Club. Next day they drove to Naivasha in the Great Rift Valley and met with Julius Erskine who had a stud farm on the lakeshore.

Emmett was shown a number of likely candidates all of which he rode. In all he tried five and was impressed with the strength, size and movement of one bay gelding called Grandee. He had won a few races at two and three years of age but hadn't shown anything over the past two seasons. A number of places but no wins. Julius said he was 'a bit angular' to be a good polo pony so he was for sale as a riding horse. The price was right, after some negotiation needless to say, and Colin said he would organise the transportation to Kampala. It would be then up to Emmett to collect and take him to Ratilli. Quite an undertaking in anyone's language they thought.

He spat on the palm of his right hand and slapped it into Julius's hand – the deal was sealed Irish style. The three of them then retired to the Lake Hotel for a good few gin and tonics and a superb luncheon. Sitting on the raised veranda they watched five hippos peacefully grazing the lawns that ran down to the lake.

On the drive up the escarpment to Nairobi Colin outlined how he would get Grandee to Kampala. He would lend Emmett his two-horse trailer. One of his syces would accompany the horse and he thought the trip from Naivasha would take about fourteen hours. He would do his best to contact an old school friend who had a smallholding outside Kampala and near Lake Victoria. It would take quite a bit of putting together, Colin thought, but it was possible. Emmett liked his optimistic outlook, to life in general.

The great thing about Grandee in Emmett's mind was he had never broken down or in fact had never been lame. As a pure thoroughbred he was a little lighter of frame than the half-breeds which most horsey people in Ukenza rode and played polo on. He was sorry Grandee wasn't still an entire as he could have used him as a stud stallion.

"But you can't win them all now can you?" he had heard his father so often say. He, however, was as pleased as punch with his purchase and the few days away in a different environment bucked him up no end. He was really beginning to have a hankering after Kenya.

Without much trouble and an overnight stop outside Kenzi on the farm that had provided Emmett with his two polo ponies, Grandee arrived on Ratilli three weeks after the purchase date. His overland trip had taken five days in total. A few strings were pulled and quite a lot of money passed hands at the two customs posts.

Corrib and Mask whinnied madly on his arrival but after a couple of days all three played and grazed happily together. Geronimo had returned to Rachel for his holiday between racing seasons.

Emmett would have six months to prepare Grandee for his Ukenza debut. He, hopefully, would then have a steely two-pronged attach and retain his champion hurdle trophy. He felt its place was rightfully on his mantelpiece. It looked majestic there.

Prior to then and during the upcoming months Emmett's third crop had to be tended and reaped. He had been told by Jeri that Bhogal wished him to renew his contract so he could therefore plan ahead. He himself had decided to take up his second term and had accordingly been planning ahead. His vacation would be split between Ireland and Kenya. He, however, would not take up the luxury until the time was right for the 'fractious five' to be together once more in Larry Murphy's.

A roster system for 'away duties' in the Mandaras was in operation with six to eight wheatlands personnel away on anti terrorist duties every ten days.

Emmett had brokered an aerial partnership with Ray Marsh and their airborne grenade assaults were becoming legendary. They had honed their attack and delivery down to a fine art. Some hairy moments did occur with hits recorded on their wings and fuselage necessitating them to be alert at all times. And safe.

Incessant patrolling of the Mandaras was tightening the tourniquet around Uma. Also, on a daily basis, deserters were filing into forward homeguard posts. Their up to the moment information on terrorist numbers, hideouts and movement made it increasingly easy for the FRO to make contact after contact and literally hammer the guts out of the enemy.

Naded, their leader, had managed to escape through the net on a number of occasions that they knew of. Most of the FR top brass thought it would only be a matter of time, however, before they would entrap the 'big fish'.

Makinto, on the other hand, were stepping up its particular nasty brand of violence but it also was being met with a hardening of opposition from the populous.

Patrice Lelonge was engendering a 'we will rule' cult into his DMC disciples and they were coming forward in multitudes to his rally's.

The Wazuri throughout the country were as active as an ants nest. Their weekly sorties, in the company of the FR and Home Guard, were proving heroic in determination and victorious in magnitude. This magnetism was drawing the tenor of the Kenzi people nearer their destiny.

Buster's ops room had become 'the local' with everyone contributing some little or big pub artefact to its creation and ambience. The area allocated was the end wall of their veranda next to his actual ops room.

Shirra created a masterful logo for the 'wheatsheaf' which hung suspended from the ceiling about ten feet out from the wall. A bamboo fronted bar counter defined the serving area. Books of tickets were purchased and used to pay for drinks. Everyone took a turn to be barman. It was all so simple and easy to run. As much discussion on farming matched that of the troubled areas gossip emanating from the returning patrols and recent sitreps. A mini club was in its embryonic stage and much appreciated by the farming community.

Shirra loved being Queen Bee. She flirted with everyone. Emmett wondered how many of them had tasted the fruits of her endeavours? No one showed any particular over zealousness in response to her taunts, however. Perhaps they were all dab hands at the game of poker?

Her visits to Ratilli remained quite frequent and never seemed to clash with Anna's. Some were short sharp bouts of lustful moments of release. Others were much more meaningful and adult, like trips in his landrover around the farm with her showing a keen interest in the actual farming methods used and types of seed sown. She acted as a wife would or should thought Emmett. He especially enjoyed these interludes and genuinely hoped that Buster got the same kick out of her company as he did. The dogs always accompanied them and she loved to stop at one of the tiny dams and play 'stick' with them – throwing it into the water and calling for its return to her.

These were moments when Emmett became broody like one of his mother's Rhode Island Reds in their farmyard back in Ballyvaughan He knew he wanted to settle down sometime and make a home. But where and with whom? Shirra, at his own age or thereabouts, would have been a prime target. He had met no white person who took his fancy in three years. And that meant he was three years older, perhaps wiser, but still quite lonely.

Sex-wise he had no problems. His manly needs were well catered for but when he was in the company of Ian, Howard, Buster, Jay and the like he felt a pang, a yearning, for something lasting of his very own. Someone who was there by his side at all times through thick and thin.

He was maturing like a good Bordeaux red and longed for the day when someone would uncork his passion and savour the content he had to offer.

Emmett, however, did enjoy his own company. He loved his independence. But he too was warm and wished to share this with a like spirit. Perhaps Africa would not be 'a pot of gold at the end of the rainbow' in his marital stakes. Perhaps Lizzie Munally from Kinvara who worshiped the ground his limbs languished along might be the one?

Lizzie - Elizabeth Mary Jane - and Emmett had grown up together and were raised on adjoining town lands. She of the ginger mop, freckles as big as smarties, had been in the 'Wall gang' since primary school. They were from the hill side of the road between the two villages and the 'Beach gang' was from the sea side of the road.

They First Communioned, Confirmed and Graduated the same years. Lizzie did pharmacy in University College Galway and now ran the family chemist in Kinvara. They had last seen each other at Emmett's father's funeral and wake.

She had shown interest in his African safari and had intimated a wish to travel now that she was qualified.

Emmett turned the pages back to their late teens when the summers would offer all sorts of splendid possibilities for cavorting in the hayrick, snuggling into the thrashed pile of straw stacked beside the threshing machine or just roaming the seashore looking for cowrie shells and starfish in the lukewarm rock pools at low tide. All good clean fun. Then the circus, Duffy's or Fossett's, would come to town and as kids they would peep under the big tent and crawl within the tiers of seats attempting to evade the ticket takers. Their paltry pence were much better spent on cones of ice cream and the like they reckoned.

They were a team, Lizzie and Emmett, and they empathised with each other from an early age. He would stand up for Lizzie when she was bullied and harangued for being turnip topped, pepper pot, ginger nut and the like. He bloodied many a nose on Lizzie's behalf and became known as her protector.

Their respective families were friends but not close friends as some of the other and nearer neighbours were. But it was the tradition to assist each other with the crops and the boats and this sort of life friendship had existed for generations.

Most of the young of Emmett's and Lizzie's year had attended third level education away from home and had therefore become more worldly. They never, however, forgot to return for the annual chores.

Then of course there were the annual festivals, village by village, with all the surrounding parishes attending and participating. The nightly 'hops' – dances

273

– were the highlight with all the elderly couples tripping the light fantastic to the beat of the Show Bands. The younger couples would do the Galway jive which sadly Emmett could never master. He craved the chance to get on the floor with his left hand outstretched and whirl Lizzie into step after step of a routine syncopation. But alas it never worked. He was, however, adept at the quickstep, foxtrot and old fashioned waltz.

"Not bad either," he would say to Lizzie, "at the Latin stuff. Lets go."

Those were heady days and nights. They would walk or cycle home, kiss and cuddle as the mannerly "goodnight. See you tomorrow," was mouthed. Nothing more.

Then the post mortems in respective kitchens as their Mams would still be up finishing the ironing or baking the next day's soda bread.

A style of life far from that in Ukenza and yet the rural African probably attached as much devotion to his or her cattle, sheep or goats and the much mended and patched up football that was kicked between thicket and thorn.

Emmett had once heard some sage emote "a peasant is a peasant is a peasant," somewhere sometime. And do you know he agreed with him. They, no matter where, were the salt of the earth. Genuine people with no airs or graces. Emmett somehow liked it that way. Was he being a trifle naïve he often wondered?

32

"Everybody out, guns blazing, -------"

Emmett's four bodyguards or 'heavies', as Ian termed them, had become master marksmen with Lee Enfield 303's and Greener 12 bore shotguns. Their constant practice at Melelo had honed their expertise into a much requested attribute.

Whenever herds of game entered the farms on the 'plains' their presence was urgently requested. These, mostly, came from the Hindi farmers who were not into carrying or using guns.

Emmett would always accompany two of his bodyguards and join in the hunt himself. He very quickly put a price on the trophies with seventy percent of the catch going to him. Hence his labour lines were kept awash with game meat.

Ian showed him how to make Biltong in the Rhodesian fashion. This was strips of venison cut and hung out to dry on long lines of wire. Depending on how one liked it the strips could be seasoned with salt and pepper or just plainly put out to dry.

After a few days these strips would then be stored away in a cool place for savouring in so many different ways. Emmett felt it reminded him of those old men in the West of Ireland who had a plug of tobacco, an inch or so in length, and who would cut and pare it with a little penknife for either chewing or filling their clay pipes.

Biltong had a very special meaty taste which when chewed took ages to finish and digest. It was a wonderful food on long trips or patrols.

One of the nicest ways of eating it was shown to him by Jan one evening when he arrived up unannounced. They were having soup and scrambled eggs on toast for supper. Sprinkled, quite heavily, atop the scramble was a covering of Biltong. Quite extraordinary thought Emmett but quite a gourmet's taste to the normally bland dish.

No farmer was without his strip or two of Biltong stored on the ledge above the dashboard of his vehicle. Just in case!

It must have been the bit of gipsy blood in Emmett that prompted him to bring ten pounds of his best Biltong to Urukan the next time he was on a visit. He sold it to the Club and had a regular weekly order booked there and then. The proceeds of this would cover all his grocery supplies. He was learning fast!

Emmett's third Christmas was spent as a guest of the Nimmers, on their farm in the foothills of the Mandaras. Anna accompanied him and they spent five glorious days in a totally different environment.

Salomi Nimmer was a sister Tukulu so had an immediate rapport with Anna. They hardly ever left the house, except for their obligatory sundown walk of thirty minutes.

Emmett, on the other hand, was kept occupied with co-piloting Johnnies Cessna, fishing and riding his string of polo ponies. He was shown all the trout bearing streams of the Mandaras and on two occasions drove and hiked up to a superb stretch of ice cold clear water which provided them with a couple of hours of gamey pleasure. Something Isaac Walton would have adored.

They travelled heavily armed and whilst fishing had sentries posted as lookouts. Fortunately no incident occurred and Johnnie remarked how "it was almost like old times". His son, James, the agriculturist, was a keen bird watcher and spent his time, a little away from them, chronicling his sightings.

The repartee over the evening meal with each side trying to out do the other had stories of "the one that got away" or "it could have been a barn owl but most probably was only a scops" made for a truly happy family gathering. The two younger children made Anna relate her experiences on the gymkhana circuit and in the Wazuri. Terrorist movement in the mountains had fallen off appreciably over the past four months and   Johnnie had been able to hand over his regional Farmers Reserve responsibilities and take some time off which facilitated his generous offer of hosting Emmett and Anna.

His runway, cut into and along the side of a hill, ran up to his farmyard with the end building acting as a hangar. All his farm buildings were made of timber off-cuts with corrugated roofs. The homestead was cedar shingled roof atop hand hewn stone. Hardwood window frames and doors had all come from the local sawmill about three miles away on the forest boundary.

Warm raging fires crackled and spat in large inglenook fireplaces every evening when they partook of a variety of Sundowners, rather reminiscent of Anna's home the year before.

Parts of his farm ran over eight thousand feet above sea level so nights and early mornings were extremely cold.

Somehow Emmett felt a lot better, health wise, in himself and wondered whether he shouldn't move to the highlands after his third harvest which was eight months away. Nothing was signed with Bhogal although both sides understood that the status quo would continue.

This was the heart of the polo and cricket region and their social scene was more enticing than that on the Punjabi Plains.

In a quiet moment with Johnnie on his own, he broached the subject of his interest in, possibly, looking for a position in tea or coffee after completing his contract.

"I don't think there would be any problem in finding you a suitable job when the time came," was Johnnie's reply.

"Lots of farmers are constantly on the lookout, especially those without sons to carry on the holdings they have built up. I'll keep my ear to the ground for you."

A germ of an idea was moving in Emmett's mind. He would investigate it further.

His next 'tour of duty' as these forays into enemy territory were called was almost a disaster before it truly began.

The truck, in which he and two other Zungus and twenty HG were travelling, was ambushed on a tight turn about thirty minutes drive away from Popes. They were heading for the upper reaches of the Mandaras and would be dropped somewhere into the forest.

The windscreen was shattered by a hail of bullets and the driver lost control. They left the road, hit a ditch, then a bank and rolled over before coming to a halt on their side. It all happened in slow motion – or that is what it felt like to Emmett, who immediately covered his head, as did all the others in the back of the truck, which was enclosed with a canvas tarpaulin.

They had practised this evasive and safeguard action dozens of times. Grab your gun, then bend your head down to your knees with your arms covering your face. Wait for the movement to stop. Count to ten then follow your leader.

This time a loud shout came from Tinus who was up front and team leader.

"Number four. Good luck. On three. One, two, three. Go."

That drill – number four - meant "everybody out, guns blazing, onto the ground in a semi-circle, await further orders."

It took only a few minutes for the shooting to stop – on both sides. Then Tinus took command, the troop dividing into two, with follow and mopping up operations their immediate concern.

The driver was the only bloodied one of the patrol and it was, luckily, only superficial. Primarily, wounds were from the shattered windscreen. His left hand had quite a bad cut which was the reason he had lost control of the vehicle.

On inspecting the area of the ambush they found three terrorists dead, one wounded and a few had escaped into the heavy bush.

After radioing into headquarters for the maintenance truck Tinus then drew up his plan to "go get'em, those fucking shits. Are we agreed eh?" His

277

Afrikaans accent becoming more pronounced. Within ten minutes they set off in two groups with four trackers operating like greyhounds out of traps.

The original idea was for the patrol to be dropped much higher up the track and then to undertake a wide sweep of the three gorges which evidently housed a cache of arms and food supplies. With a twenty strong patrol they could handle any gang they came upon. So far they had been extremely fortunate. Lots of superficial cuts, abrasions and no doubt heavy bruising would be felt in twenty-four hours time. Pride was dented but resolve was even greater. Perhaps revenge had reared its ugly head?

They drew a blank, however, with two former hideouts discovered but no arms or supplies. Lots of movement had recently taken place as reported by the trackers so after forty-eight hours Tinus radioed base for a truck and escort to be dispatched for their collection.

Their patrol had covered six ridges and gorges without a contact. Even the remainder of the ambush party had disappeared.

It was thought they had trekked up and over the mountain and infiltrated their kind on the other and quieter side. The one wounded prisoner would probably cough up some useful information and a follow up could then take place.

Tony Pope had just returned from a trip covering the USA and UK. His rapid fire accounting of it kept the 'mess' in hoots of laughter for hours on end that night.

"I'd never swap the life we have here for any of it," he kept reiterating. Some felt that Patricia would love to be back overseas, especially during these troubled and disruptive times. She was such a warm and kind gentle person who could have done without all of this intrusion into her lifestyle. She would be seen walking her pair of Alsatians around the perimeter fence of the farm's inner sanctum. These, Emmett felt, were her moments of solace when she was at peace with her world.

Tony was a true Cockney, born to be with people all the time. She was totally the opposite.

She invited Emmett, on a number of occasions, to ride out with her, accompanied by a syce and her dogs. She confided in him and poured her heart out on one occasion describing the trauma Tony was going through with a prostate problem. She couldn't bring herself to say the big 'C' word but it was foremost in her thoughts.

"Patrick would step in if anything happened" she said almost tearfully "but I couldn't stay here without Tony. I'd go back home."

Emmett then realised that this, the here and now, was indeed a man's world and would it ever return to the joyous times of yesteryear? He somehow doubted it.

Three letters arrived from overseas with news from Australia, Asia and the USA – only Europe was missing in this communique.

They were making arrangements for a reunion in October next. And how did that sound to "the African adventurer?" This would be some 'thrash' thought Emmett as he sailed from paragraph to paragraph.

He had to make his mind up about his future, chop, chop. If this coming harvest was a success then his luck average would be due to run out in his next tour. At the end of his first three years he would have enough funds overseas to buy a good sized farm back home or indeed anywhere in Africa.

This latter thought was foremost in his mind. His hankering after Kenya was upper most in his thoughts. But perhaps he should sign on for another three years? Surely all of these could not be drought stricken?

Emmett felt he was very much part of this African canvas but whether he should settle in or not was his enigma?

His closest mentors Ian and Jan painted a rosy picture for the immediate future – the next decade, they mused, would be good for agriculture and in their opinion would be financially beneficial for Emmett.

He mentioned his recent stay with the Nimmers and how he was drawn to the tea and coffee growers' lifestyle. His body felt much better at that altitude and there was definitely more on the social side to be savoured.

Jan agreed but she didn't like the cold nights and heavy rain periods. She was happy where she was. Ian stated "I'd never move. They will have to drag me away in a coffin."

Grandee had settled into his new lifestyle with aplomb. After the first two weeks of rest and getting to know Corrib and Mask, Emmett started hacking him around the farm. He was loath to enter the small dams until the ponies led him into a muddy abyss. They raised their forelegs and thumped the water with gusto, splashing all in close proximity.

Gradually Grandee got the message and followed suit. To some horses this is the prelude to knuckling their knees and rolling in the muddy pool. Emmett was well aware of the signs and dug his heels into his sides driving him forward and out of the dam - - in time.

The syces followed and they continued their trotting, cantering and negotiating the contours which made the horses use all their muscles. Grandee had only ever been trained on flat even surfaces so undulations like these made him really use whatever grey matter he had between his ears and each and every muscle. Plenty of stumbles were awkwardly countered.

Emmett had noticed his rather large ears, for a thoroughbred, and likened them to a lot of national hunt bred horses back home. He liked his strong bay coloured body with deep brown, almost black, stockings. Once built up with miles of trotting and cantering he felt he would have a fine, almost Irish, horse beneath him.

There were six weeks to the first hurdle race which most probably would see Geronimo back in business. He and Grandee were working out together each day. Geronimo's aggressiveness had Grandee digging deep into his reserves. This year the champion hurdler had real competition and it was right here on his own doorstep! Emmett was looking forward to their fast work together. This would be a real trial. He would most probably be able to get them 'race ready' on the farm this season without having to give them runs down the field as was the case before.

Anna would ride Grandee and Emmett wanted to land a touch first time out! If all went to plan he would get his entire expenses back in one fell swoop.

He noticed that Grandee liked to run from behind leaving plenty for his final burst. Julius Erskine had forwarded all the little idiosyncrancies found in training him for four seasons, which proved a great bonus in getting him ready for his first outing.

Kitos hosted the opening meeting of the season. Six flat races ranging from sprints to two over twelve furlongs (one and a half miles). Grandee, as a two-year-old, had won two races over six furlongs and then one over ten furlongs with one over twelve furlongs as a three-year-old.

Emmett had got both really fit and decided to enter them for the Chumbi Plate over twelve furlongs. He would ride Geronimo with Anna aboard the other. Money flooded onto Geronimo with little interest in Grandee.

On the way to the start he gave Anna instructions as to how to ride the race.

"Stay behind the leaders until the final turn and then make your run on the outside."

Geronimo would hopefully be up with the leaders but would be unable to resist her challenge. Emmett would cover the others in case she got into trouble.

As usual, for so early in the season, the field took off as greased lightening, like on the polo field. At about halfway Emmett, then lying six of thirteen, felt Geronimo gaining considerably with each stride, or else the others were wilting? That proved the case as suddenly with about two furlongs to go he found himself in front. Rounding the bend he felt someone on his outside coming very quickly up to, alongside and then passing him.

He glanced under his right arm and picked out Grandee's white fluffy noseband at Geronimo's hindquarters. He shouted at Anna to "go for it girl" as they came alongside. She was still on the bridle and passed the leader just before the winning post. She had never moved on Grandee and won 'with a lot in hand' as they say in Ireland.

Emmett was pipped on the post for third but was extremely happy with both runs. Johnnie Nimmer had placed Emmett's bets and later that evening, at the prize giving in the Club, handed him a wad of notes. Anna had to stuff most of it into her shoulder bag as Emmett's bush jacket pockets could not accommodate the loot.

Together with the winner's cheque (sponsored) the total covered the purchase price and all transportation costs for Grandee. Not a bad return on his first run smiled a very happy Irishman.

Jeri Ntsemo was highly impressed as were a number of the leading polo lights, all wanting to know Grandee's history.

"Found him in the Congo, on a farm doing nothing. Luck of the Irish you might call it," as Emmett bought another round of drinks. He could spin them any yarns so early in the season he felt, so why not run with it?

Luckily he had warned Anna prior to the meeting about his leg pulling idea and she collaborated entirely with the subterfuge. It wasn't long before various farmers decided they too should look at the Congo possibilities. Emmett wished them all the best of luck!

A new name was being whispered from mouth to mouth. Even The Standard - the daily newspaper - ran a half page editorial on Fredi Gachiru – the evident brain behind *Makinto*.

From all the snippets of information that pieced together the terrorist jigsaw, this one name kept bouncing out at the powers that be. He had not been identified physically nor his actual whereabouts or the HQ from which he operated. Both remained unknown. But the FRO and security forces were getting there gradually.

Evidently like Naded, he had been trained overseas, with many years spent in Russia prior to returning to Ukenza. He, however, was more of an intellectual and a far right radical one. He didn't have military training but someone had let slip that he had been involved with the KGB and therefore knew how to set up a revolutionary process with all the trimmings. Perhaps it wasn't his real name and was he operating under a false identity, another informant had proferred?

Whatever the exact story Fredi Gachiru was becoming increasingly the thorn in the side of the countries populous. Uma and Naded were almost a spent force and it was reported that Naded was more often than not operating out of Uganda. Perhaps, the security forces thought, he had found a radical group within that country who needed a well-tried leader and jungle fighter? They too were experiencing ethnic troubles in their far north and western regions. Perhaps easier pickings were on offer for the virtually vanquished Uma general?

281

Jeri Ntsemo had a contact, a very close one, inside *Makinto* after all this time and the dribbles that came forth were now forming a lake of Ndugas proportion.

Just as Uma had required food and arms as their life blood to bankroll terror campaigns *Makinto* now needed finance to maintain their grip on personnel within the President's Elite Guard.

A new wave of hostage taking with exorbitant ransoms being asked, coupled with a Mafia-style extortion racket on commerce and industry, instilled the worst era yet experienced, of fear among the Kenzian people.

"All I can say to you good people is that the police force within my jurisdiction will stand firm on defending your rights. If it should be a case of us or them – them being the army – I know I can back our police combined, I must add, with the Farmers Reserve Organisation. We make a fine force. Long may it last."

Jeri was addressing a meeting at Pope's which had brought together the hierarchy of all farming areas and groups. He continued, "Do not become lax in your defences for we perhaps may have to think Urban rather than Rural terrorism. For this I will need your support.

"I must tell you that we are receiving great support from the 'ladies of Susieland'" This brought loud guffaws and much light-hearted banter from the crowd.

"We have a few informants and their weekly handouts are most intriguing" – more lecherous laughter exploded from less mature and the more well travelled audience. Jeri took a long mouthful of beer and continued; "I am prepared to use any and all methods to defeat these bastards as you see. I am sure you will agree. If and when Urukan becomes a target, and it will, I want to be prepared on all counts.

"The Asian community are very scared as they have been and are being hit, some on a weekly basis, in Kenzi. They fear it will shortly come our way.

"Be extra vigilant is all I ask and lets be there for each other. Thank you one and all."

He got a rousing round of applause and then everyone broke away to replenish glasses and relieve themselves.

Pope, Barker, Nimmer and Buster got together with Jeri and shut themselves inside Tony's office.

"They are drawing up a new strategy – best leave them be," said the tall Dick Wright-Hill as he grabbed a couple of his mates and bundled them off onto the veranda.

Patricia appeared with two house servants and the biggest saucepan full of sizzling sausages Emmett had ever seen. This was the entrée to the braai that would be sampled in a little while she prompted. It was 2.00pm. The sausages were devoured in minutes, only for another pan full to magically appear.

Over the excellent braai of venison a lot of the talk centred around the gymkhana race season. Emmett kept his ears wide open and learnt that quite a few new animals would be on the circuit.

"We're not letting that wheatlands Irish beat us again," came from Tinus Cloete who had given Emmett a few nice winners last season. Various other polo players took up an aggressive but friendly exchange of thoughts and opinions. It was all good clean fun but Emmett knew he would have stiff opposition this time around. His two pronged attack would have to be the sharpest.

On their return flight and piloted this trip by Ian, he did a survey of all the roads leading out of Urukan's African townships, familiarising one and all of the complexity of the terrain and the escape routes that might be used.

"It's good to know these," commented Buster, "in case we have to do any follow ups in the future."

They all agreed.

"By the way, you three pilots," referring to Ian, Howard and Emmett, "have you a mental picture of everything – and I stress everything – in and around our district?"

Howard and Ian replied in the affirmative with Emmett saying "I'll put some time into doing just that when Bhogal allows me an hour or so on my own. I'd like to know what lies beyond Melelo for instance and how far is it to Freedo's place and over the border?"

"Might come in handy in an emergency," prompted Buster "I gather it's heavy bush out to our west with little or no habitation."

"That's about the score," answered Howard "and there aren't too many roads or tracks in that area either."

"Absolutely no water," said Ian as he swung the kite along a line parallel to the Koram road.

Emmett had noticed that whenever he had been a passenger with either them or Bhogal, they all kept a close eye on the road below, despite it not being the shortest route home.

It became more and more evident that this 'lifeline' had to be inspected on a daily basis and protected at all times.

"We will take you up as co-pilot won't we Ian?" said Howard.

"Of course and it will be a good security exercise for us too. I know a lot of the forest roads as I used to rally over them."

"Thanks guys."

33

Being alive in a coffin with wings

Emmett experienced the uncomfortable thrill of lying in the nose cone of Mustafa's 'Wasp' as it sped down the runway. Every little pebble and roughness on the strip seemed magnified one thousand fold as he lay on his back with arms braced against the fragile metal cone. He wanted to do this, it was his choice. He had been warned of the unpleasantness he would experience.

Once in the air it was only the noise of the engine and the propeller that made it known he was flying. This wasn't a spray run, "too dangerous my friend" said Mustafa before takeoff. "Your extra weight up front could cause problems." It wasn't a point to argue against.

Emmett felt the manoeuvres the Wasp was being put through but nothing more than if he had been sitting beside or behind the pilot. His tummy was now hardened to such movement.

Landing – touching down – was an incredible sensation. He felt the entire cone was being crushed around him and yet nothing moved. It rattled horribly. The roar of the engine as the flaps were let down with reverse pressure applied felt as if the casing was crumbling around him.

It was quite some experience and one he felt not to be repeated too often. Perhaps it was an escape hatch Emmett thought, with fears of a terrorist attack flashing across an addled mind, as they taxied back to his house.

As he extricated himself, with the help of Mustafa, all he could say once in a sitting position in the pilot seat was "wow". His most favourite expletive,

"Well, what you think?" questioned Mustafa looking a bit sheepish.

"I wouldn't want it as an everyday occurrence but I now know what it feels like to be alive in a coffin, with wings." They both laughed as Emmett jumped down onto terra firma.

"I've never done that before," said Mustafa "and I don't think I'd likely try it again."

"Only in an emergency," replied Emmett and lead them off to the veranda for a stiff drink. Christopher was waiting and he looked agitated and then bemused by their upbeat spirits.

That evening Emmett's mind was full of terrorists, attacks and escapes. It was a minefield of sabotage and subterfuge. One that seemed to surround his life in Ukenza and one that he had not factored into the original equation. But that was then and this was now. Too very different chapters in his African safari.

He felt he must try to work out the possible methods an enemy would use in the event of an attack on Ratilli – for whatever reason.

As hostage taking was a recent arm of terrorism being used, with some success, in the city and towns, that method might well become rural. And then what?

His mind didn't close down until the early hours with a myriad of quite amazing possibilities flashing across his puzzled brain.

At breakfast he was called to the radio. It was Ian.

"Are you at home this morning. Over?"

"All morning. I have bookwork with Gilbert. But why. Over?"

"I want to run an idea across you. Over."

"No problem. Come on down."

"Cheers. See you soon. Out."

A couple of hours later Ian arrived by landrover and Emmett settled him down on the veranda with a cool beer.

"So, what's on your mind?"

"Could you take ten days off and accompany me to Rhodesia? You would be co-pilot?"

"Wow. What an offer."

They both remained silent and gulped down a few swigs before Ian took it up again.

"My Mums not too well and my sisters think I should visit, so Jan is willing to stay at home. I want to fly down and I need a co-pilot. That's it in a nutshell."

"Well, its not a bad time – a month before planting and its between hurdle races. I can't miss them."

"No problem. Tell me the dates and I'll fit the trip in between – if that's all that's on your mind?"

"Yea. That's about it. I'm sure I can square Bhogal, especially as I'll be with you. He is in awe of you even though he won't tell you."

After a few more gulps of beer and heavy thought "yea, I'm up for it. What about visas, etc.?" questioned Emmett.

"Just give me your passport. I'll sort it out for you. We have plenty of time anyhow. Cheers," and they raised their glasses in a toast.

"A good trip and safe returns."

"Cheers."

After Ian departed Emmett asked Christopher to tell the syces to saddle up Grandee. He would clear his mind with a good gallop.

With the canines in tow he set off for a mind clearing blow -out aboard a mighty fresh gelding. It was fun with not a worry in the world on his shoulders.

He came across a break in the boundary fence and further into the farm he spotted a small herd of zebra. On radioing back to Gilbert he ordered two drivers to bring the vehicles with six to ten labourers. Emmett would circle the herd and hope to stop them breaking further into the farm.

Once the staff and vehicles had arrived it was quite easy to drive the zebra back to the fence, along it and to their break-in point. After their return to the reserve, the other side of the boundary, his fencing gang mended the massive hole they had broached. All was back to normality within an hour.

Emmett continued on for a further hour before returning to the compound. Grandee loved these impromptu outings and was somehow maturing in both stature and mind with each week that passed. Emmett thought it was time to school him over caveletties and start out on making another champion hurdler. Next season would be his he thought as he lead him to the awaiting Songuru who had taken over as his very own syce. A lovely ripe rivalry existed now that each syce had a racehorse of their own.

This season should be great craic with two really taut strings to his bow he pondered as he sat on his veranda awaiting his meal. The dogs devoured at least six basins of water and then flopped down all over the cool cement floor, exhausted.

That afternoon Emmett caught up on his diary and wrote a few letters to Ireland. He intimated his intention of returning for a month in September/October. That was when the 'fractious five' were planning on the reunion. He was greatly looking forward to those few days, for that would be the mother and father of parties. He knew he had changed appreciably and wondered about the other four?

Ian flew down almost every second day and let Emmett fly him all over the Punjabi Plains. They explored the native reserves west of Melelo and on two occasions landed at Kanzi next to Lake Nduga. Ian checked out his house, fortunately finding all in good order. They flew over the lake and circled Ncema, the town on the west shore, and near the border.

Ian complimented Emmett on his flying and said they should have a super time away in Rhodesia. They were quietly confident in each other's ability and although both were short of air hours their combined expertise should see them through any crisis.

Both of them took in the arid landscape, noting roads, tracks, bridges, villages and dams that glistened mirror-like in a sparse African canvas. Neither man mentioned or referred to their specific interest in what made up this almost uncharted region. Both knew it could hold attacking groups. It would also hold valuable escape routes.

They followed the river south of the lake which took them to Jay Freedo's Mandalay sanctuary. Ian took the kite down low enough for them to count every animal within his preserve. He dipped his wings in response to Jay and Jasmine's waves and flew off to the south of the Punjabi Plains, an area unknown to Emmett.

Ian pointed out and named the homesteads of almost all the farms they crossed over. He remarked on how dry he thought their lands were and why there were few zungus in this portion of the region. Emmett noticed and remarked on how few dams there were.

"A case of Hindi and Kenzie not knowing or practising good basic husbandry – that's all," replied Ian who was thoroughly scrutinizing every acre beneath them.

Emmett had learnt that Ian had been a superb rally driver and it was obvious his handling skills had transferred gracefully to aeroplanes. It was a pleasure being his passenger and he looked forward to their trip together.

On returning to Ratilli he told Emmett that as soon as their passports had been returned they would plan their departure and return dates.

"That's fine by me. I have squared it with Bhogal and Mustafa will keep an eye on things here. I'm really looking forward to seeing the Rhodesias. Thanks a lot for today. See you soon. Love to Jan," and he closed the side door of the plane.

Over a sweet mug of tea he told Christopher all about their flight, where they had been and what they had seen. He wouldn't inform him, however, until the last minute, of his impending trip. The fewer people who knew, he felt, the better.

A charming man, Mickey Fernandes from Kenya, toured the Punjabi Plains and stayed a few days at Ratilli.

He was the man from Monsanto whose products were used in the regions crop spraying programme. Mickey was here to tell of the new 'cocktails' they had produced – herbicide, pesticide and fungicide – and how they should benefit the crops' volume.

Two of these products could be mixed together which meant that only two flights were now needed instead of three. That in itself was a great saving in time and fuel.

Emmett and he talked for hours into the night about East Africa and Kenya in particular. Mickey's territory covered East and Central Africa and after telling him about his upcoming trip with Ian, names and contacts down there flowed as a river in spate.

He was a polo player and kept his ponies on the family farm at Limuru just thirty miles north of Nairobi. He knew Colin Dymmott and the Erskines and promised to keep Grandee's provenance a secret. They laughed long and loud over that piece of subterfuge. Mickey felt that Jomo Kenyata, Kenya's President, was

287

doing a wonderful job of governing the colony, which they all still called it, and with agriculture and tourism their only two industries, he had placed top Europeans as their Ministers. Very bright young Kenyans were placed high on the rungs of their respective ministry ladders so that a balanced and amicable handover to black rule would eventually take place. All agreed this was the correct way forward.

"No chance of that ever happening here, I'm afraid. Ubugu is too entrenched and power crazy."

"A great pity Emmett as this is a super country." After a few moments Mickey added "it, however, has one terrible misfortune and that is, it's landlocked like Rhodesia."

Mickey would have been in his mid thirties, Emmett thought. He had his own plane, left at Urukan on this trip, and had half shares in the family farm. He had been educated in South Africa and had a BsC from Wits University, Johannesburg. He was a bachelor.

Emmett and he hit it off from the moment they met. As this was Mickey's first trip into the Punjabi Plains he took him to Ian and Howard's and then they kindly passed him, with introductions over the radio, to all the other farmers in the district.

After Mickey had completed his sales tour he returned to Ratilli and spent his last night with Emmett. They promised to keep in touch. Mickey would keep his eyes open for another horse like Grandee and his ears to the ground for a suitable managerial position for Emmett. He had friends in the game department and was confident something would become available.

"I'm not in too much of a hurry as my contract here is quite lucrative but never look a gift horse in the mouth, eh?" Emmett explained as he waved him au revoir.

"Kwaherini," was Mickey's reply – a Kiswahili 'farewell'.

34

Matopos, Granite Boulders and Cecil John Rhodes

Ian collected Emmett early on a Monday morning. He said the weather reports were favourable as he circled both farms and set out for Kitwe, Northern Rhodesia.

They refuelled at this copper belt metropolis and flew east to Salisbury. Ian did the takeoff, landings and radio contacts while Emmett gazed in rapture at the changing landscapes below.

Lake Kariba was taking shape and would soon be the second biggest dam, to Egypt's Aswan, in Africa. Its waters would eventually cross the border between Southern and Northern Rhodesia. As they neared Salisbury in the late afternoon Ian explained the strange buildings and crops that crisscrossed an area of perhaps one hundred miles radius outside Salisbury.

"Those there are drying barns and that greenish yellow crop is their liquid gold – tobacco. Salisbury has one of the world's largest auction marts for that crop. It is their prime export product."

Emmett didn't answer. He just gazed down in awe.

They checked into Meikles Hotel in the city centre and ate the finest meal both had tasted in a long time at The Causerie, the hotel's top class restaurant. It was all so grand! White linen tablecloths, starched napkins and weighty Sheffield cutlery mingled with Waterford crystal. Emmett felt he was back in the Shelbourne or downstairs in the Gresham grill in Dublin.

Next morning Ian's sister, Margie, collected them and drove straight to their farm in Umvukwes, some sixty miles west of the city.

The siblings hardly came up for air, as Emmett took in the changing and very different countryside to the Punjabi Plains.

Mooi Estate was a tobacco and cattle enterprise and had been in the family since the 1920's. Ian's father had been a pioneer and had discovered this piece of land after trekking up from South Africa with a group of Boer[6] farmers. They had bred up one of the countries finest herds of beef shorthorns and had planted one hundred acres of tobacco after the Second World War. His father had died six years previously, leaving the running of the estate to his mother and sister

---

[6] Africanise speaking South African farmers.

Margie. His other sister was married to a solicitor and lived in Bulawayo, at the other end of the country.

Margie, very similar in build and facial expression to Ian, was a widow and had no children so managed the farm just as her father before her. She loved the work and was blessed with a great eye for stock, maintaining the registered herd and indeed increased its number quite dramatically.

They had brought in the son of one of their neighbours to manage the tobacco end of things which was also thriving.

Now their mother was ill with angina troubles and was a shadow of her formidable self. Margie was finding it difficult. She hoped Ian, her older brother, would offer some comfort and ideas on the future of the estate.

Emmett had gleaned all this from their conversation along the way.

Mrs. Poultney – Susan – was very poorly and he was allowed only a brief chat with her. She was confined to her room.

He was told "make yourself at home. Take yourself off and if you meet another zungu it will be Fanie, the manager. He will look after you. Okay?"

"Sure thing," Emmett replied and sallied forth.

When he wandered through the cattle Emmett felt a pang, a yearning to be with stock again. He inwardly felt he was a born stockman as was his father before him. Somehow he empathised with these massive joints of beef and suddenly felt he was missing something in his life.

Fanie found him gazing at pens of bullocks that were obviously being fattened up for the market, and Emmett was remembering the times he had accompanied his father to the marts at Gort and Athenry. Each farmer, armed with an ash plant and shod in mucky wellies, would lean over the rails assessing the weight of the batch and estimating the price they would make.

A day's outing to the mart whether selling, buying or just watching was a social event on every cattle or sheep man's weekly calendar. The 'craic would be mighty' was the most commonly used phrase – and indeed it was no matter what age one was.

Emmett was shown the tobacco plant, the leaf, drying sheds, grading sheds and the end product, a bale weighing one hundred and fifty pounds which would be despatched to the auctions where hopefully it would command top prices.

It somehow didn't hold his interest, a tad too finicky for his thinking, but pure GOLD when everything went right for the crop.

They spent the first three days on the farm and then Ian decided it was time to take a flying trip to the eastern districts to visit one of his old friends in Inyanga.

Emmett couldn't believe his eyes as they flew into a highland region, not unlike parts of the west of Ireland. Little lakes sparkled and nestled between pine forests and mountain grazing, dotted with heather and gorse. Large flocks of sheep and deer occupied these lands which seemed sparse in comparison to those of Umvukwes, Marandellas and Rusape over which they had flown.

"A much more changing landscape than Ukenza," remarked Emmett.

"Ya, it's a wonderful country alright and it's governed by the Brits. Hate to think what would happen if it ever gets independence?"

They landed on a private strip which ran along a lakeside and taxied up to a very large and expansive building.

"That's Troutbeck Inn owned by my friends, the McIlwaines. Wonderful fishing and a tough golf course. Shit but it gets cold up here in winter. Brass monkey weather. They have large log fires in every bedroom. But isn't the setting magic?"

"I'm almost overseas here, very Scottish actually, but also could be parts of Ireland. Amazing."

Two days later they flew to Bulawayo to stay a night with Ian's second sister, Vonnie and her husband Roderick. They lived in a slightly elevated suburb Hillside which was well treed with properties of no less than an acre in extent.

Roderick was in real estate and an auctioneer. He was about to visit a farm to the south of Bulawayo so asked Emmett if he would like to accompany him after he had settled in?.

"Yes please."

"It will also allow the two of you," nodding to Ian and Vonnie "to get stuck into family affairs. See you later then."

In his Datsun estate Roderick explained the terrain they were passing through. "Its mostly bush – scrub land – with grazing in between thorn bushes and ethnic trees. Farmers sink boreholes and build dams so that their stock can get water. The land here takes one beast to every ten acres so you have to have large spreads if ranching is to pay.

"You will see Afrikander cattle – big humps and big horns – they are the most adaptable. Some ranchers cross them with exotic breeds like Hereford and Shorthorn.

"Today I'm visiting an intensive farm owned by a charming widow, Peggy Patullo, who has a prize Jersey herd. She wants to sell up. Her children have grown up and left the roost. She feels a little insecure. Things are not so rosy here."

Ian had explained that Bulawayo was the capital of Matabeleland, the countries largest province which borders Botswana and South Africa. Salisbury was the capital of Mashonaland which was a richer province. The two ethnic tribes that inhabited these regions were arch enemies. Didn't seem good for the future?

Once again Emmett was allowed to roam around the surrounds of the homestead where he found the Jersey herd grazing next to a large field of Lucerne.

291

All buildings were thatched with walls of wooden poles tied together. Lovely and airy, Emmett thought but furnaces if set alight. Not a happy thought.

After lunch Rod drove to the Matopos Hills right next door to her farm and showed Emmett the grave of Cecil John Rhodes, the founder of the country.

All around the grave were giant granite boulders, some twenty to thirty feet high and in the strangest shapes. Sitting on, under and running between was the sweetest looking furry animal, quite like a rabbit.

"They are Dassies – rock rabbits," said Rod anticipating Emmett's questioning frowns.

"Their skins are highly prized and are made up into coats and bed covers."

"By the way, did you notice the hedges of Plumbago, that little blue flower, at Peggy's? That was Rhodes' favourite flower. Grows everywhere"

Ian decided to stay an extra day and night as there was more to plan and discuss about their farm and Margie's burden of responsibility once their mother passed away.

Rod brought Emmett into his office and told him to window shop, visit the museum and be back by 1.00pm when they would lunch at a superb Spanish restaurant, his favourite watering hole in the city.

Rhodes, in his wisdom, had decreed that the main streets of Bulawayo should be wide enough to turn a span of sixteen oxen and their wagons without trouble. Today this meant that there was enough room for two lanes of traffic each way with parking for vehicles between the traffic and sidewalks.

"That was some forward planning," Emmett remarked to his host over a massive pile of paella at lunch.

"This is a wonderful country. We have our problems in being landlocked and a growing tension between the two largest tribes, the Matabeles and the Shonas. God help us if they decide to go to war. My money would have to be on these fellows here – they are blood brother of the Zulu you know. No better fighters." He changed the subject with his next mouthful.

"I gather things aren't too kosher up with you guys?"

"You can say that again. I'm on my third year and never thought I'd be fighting a war. But somehow I think we are winning. Ian has probably given you a thorough update."

"Yes, well we have discussed it. He is quite up beat about the future which should please you but he does feel we, the whites that is, have only got so much time before all hell breaks loose. God only knows when. We live on a volcano, Emmett. Enjoy it while you can."

Emmett felt Roderick knew they were all living a life on borrowed time. His philosophy was 'enjoy it while you have it'. .

Africa, in Colonial times, was about as good as one could get – for everyone, black, brown and white.

Ian had been given permission to use an airstrip which was only five miles away from Mooi Estate. Margie came to collect them and reported their mother had taken a turn for the worse. She was extremely worried. Next day they moved her to a hospital in Sailsbury.

The end came two days later. The funeral was an enormous outpouring of grief from the farming community.

"It was a good call Margie," admitted Ian at breakfast that morning, "that I should have been present, before, during and after. I'm only sorry for you, Emmett, having had to suffer our loss."

"I was proud to have met her and indeed your entire family. I hope I was of some comfort in being able to assist when necessary. I too have been through it this last year so I empathise and sympathise with you all."

Vonnie and Roderick were to stay on for a week with Margie which allowed Ian to depart for Ukenza only two days late.

Their flight home was uneventful if a little on the sombre side. They made radio contact with Howard who was also in the air between Urukan and the farm.

"That was a lucky call, a chance in a million I'd say. Anyhow Jan will now know our estimated time of arrival."

"Are your dropping me off first?" asked Emmett.

"Yah, sure. We'll have a good look over our lands before though."

He dipped and waggled wings over Buster's and got a wave from Shirra out in her garden. Ian flew low over Ratilli's compound so Christopher would know they had returned and then he took in all the sections including Melelo.

"Looks like you have really good seed beds this year. Good luck with the planting and thanks a span for your company and friendship. See you soon." And with that Ian flew home.

It was only much later that night when Emmett lay awake that he fully appreciated the loyalty and team spirit that very obviously existed within his farm staff. Everything was in perfect order as if he had never been absent. His dogs twisted his arm and were allowed to 'sleep in'. Emmett appreciated their affection and company. He thought about the three other African countries – Uganda, Kenya and Southern Rhodesia – he had travelled in. His first love was still the jewel of East Africa, Kenya.

Race days were now something special in the districts hosting them. A tremendous camaraderie had emerged over the previous two seasons with inter-farm rivalry playing a major part for the African labour employed on these various farms.

A sponsor, in the guise of the local brewery distributors, Chibuku, jumped on the bandwagon organising a soccer tournament (seven a side) at each meeting. Ten minutes each way was played.

The early knockout matches would be played before 11.30am with two qualifiers for the final matching up between the last two races. This gave them the maximum audience with presentations being made on the course in front of the stands after the final race.

Emmett had been cajoled into entering a Punjabi Plains team. Howard lent one of his trucks and two teams of players from their three farms, with followers, now accompanied the horses. Rachel and Jan chose a yellow and black striped jersey, white shorts, yellow stocking as the Wheatlands strip. How many times had Emmett seen those almost same colours carried to success by the hurlers of Kilkenny? Perhaps one day they might also triumph here?

As it turned out the team was beaten quite resoundingly in the early rounds of the last two encounters. It was obvious there were too many individuals and not enough team co-ordination in an unscripted strategy. Neither Emmett, Ian nor Howard were into football and did not have the time to spare. But it was all good team fun and they agreed it was good to show 'our flag' in a different environment.

Geronimo won yet again, completely out jumping and out staying the opposition. However, there were two animals that showed great promise which might make the next two races less one sided Emmett noted as he discussed the race with Howard and Ian in the Club afterwards. This was the first time Ian and Jan had attended and they were thrilled with the day's outing. The three ladies were photographed with horse and jockey in the winner's enclosure.

Grandee, ridden by Anna, had finished third in a tightly fought one mile race.

"Another few strides and you had it won. Well done and he doesn't look as if he has had a race," remarked Emmett as he met them both in the unsaddling bay.

"Do you know he really enjoys it – I can feel it – and he got me out of trouble on that final bend. It was all my fault," said a breathless Anna as she dismounted.

"No harm done my darling. Get to the scales and I'll catch you at the stables."

All six of them stayed the night at the Gymkhana Club at Ian's request.

"We haven't been partying to your successes so feel it only right to celebrate together up here in enemy territory – and Jan concurs, don't you baby?"

"Sure do and its great to be away from the farm for once – altogether."

These 'after the races' parties were quite something. An awful lot of drink was taken, a lot of leg pulling and everyone danced 'till the wee small hour's. It was a wonderful way of letting off steam and forgetting the tense situation that existed only miles away. The Mandaras offered an impressive backdrop as they partook of an early breakfast on the Club's veranda.

Emmett had noticed, in his almost three years of residence, how early everyone got up and cracked on no matter how late they had hit the pillow. He wondered was it the altitude perhaps or the climate? He too was party to the routine. It certainly wouldn't happen back home!

Each day, around about five in the afternoon, a large dark depression appeared in the north-west sky. Christopher first pointed it out to Emmett.

"That is rains, fendi. They coming soon."

The sky darkened prematurely prior to sundown and it even made the night sky blacker than black. Something Emmett had not noticed in previous seasons. Perhaps this was to be a horrendous foreboding from which there was no escape.

This buildup lasted for nine days and then all hell broke loose.

Three inches of rain fell in one twenty-four hour period, exactly ten days after planting. Streams became rivers, contours directed the flow from the lands into gullies that became gorges all along the farm's roads and tracks. Soil was washed away, trees were uprooted, and some main roads became impassable.

Labour lines had roofs leaking like sieves. The main grain store on Ratilli experienced the same disaster.

In the days that followed this downpour farm graders worked sixteen hours a day to clear up, realign and fashion new more resistant contours and washaways in the stricken areas.

Every farm had stocks of corrugated sheeting, and old rusted roof areas were now hastily replaced.

The downpour seemed to have mostly affected farms south of the main road – the Punjabi Plains – as Ian, Howard and his neighbours only had slight damage.

Two concrete drifts on the road to Koram had been partly washed away, which kept all transport at a standstill.

The P.W.D. (Public Works Department) from Urukan, once alerted by Jeri Ntsemo to the problems, pulled all their machinery from the regions not affected and had them employed on the Urukan to Ratilli stretch of road. Altogether five drifts had been badly cut away and damaged.

"How fortunate this wasn't in harvest time, Emmett," was Howard's opening remark when he met him, by chance, at the Ratilli building. Both were out surveying the damage along the roads.

"If we don't get any more, then you will be able to rectify any crop damage once it starts to show. You will just have to replant the affected areas. Some deluge eh?"

"I've never seen anything like it. Back home we get incessant rain but never in that quantity. Quite frightening really. You guys didn't get the full brunt of the storm I hear?"

"Yea. We were lucky this time. If you need an extra grader or two just say so and both Ian and I will despatch post haste. Okay?"

"Thanks a million. I'd better be getting back. See you soon."

That was the spirit that pervaded in the district. A powerful weapon of self preservation.

It took another two weeks for this strength to be fully displayed. A second deluge – this time of four and a half inches – landed on the entire area, above and below the road.

If Emmett thought that radio/wireless communication lines had been used before this then he was in for a shock. Terrorism and its appendages were way down the pecking order, right now it was a case of self preservation.

It was a race for survival on the Punjabi Plains, the bread basket of Ukenza. Was the crop to be a right off?

The FRO HQ, i.e. Buster's, was the meeting place for the farmers emergency needs. Were they to replant? Would there be time for the crop to mature? Could harvesting time be extended? etc., etc.

Emmett was the 'new boy on the block' and therefore listened and hopefully learnt. They would all rally round to their respective needs and that was unanimous. Buster was designated I/C Harvest Relief, even though he was just as badly affected. Everyone was sent back to quantify their own respective damage. They were to meet in five days time, when a plan for survival would be presented and put into immediate operation. Time was of the essence.

Emmett now realised how fragile his lifestyle on the plains really was. He remembered his best friend back home, James, stating once "you can't fart against thunder" and translating that to the present crisis it just proved how incredibly destructive the elements could be. There was nothing anyone could do to halt them.

The rains had arrived at the correct time, but no crop needs monsoon proportions to be hurled down on top of it.

From the air the scene below resembled the destruction created by a tidal wave. Circles and curves of water movement throughout the area created a canvass of mathematical mystique.

"An awful lot of replanting would have to be done," said Howard as he circled yet another way to take in the southern region of the plains.

"Will we have enough growing time?" asked Emmett.

"Something similar happened, not as heavy or widespread as this I hasten to add, about eleven years ago. Some of us were still planting at the end of April. We did manage to harvest the crop but figures were well down. Its essential to put some cash flow into the scheme of things, especially for the Bank's sake."

"It will be interesting to see Bhogal's reaction. He's coming out tomorrow. I'm glad I've had this view of the scene prior to his visit."

"That's Jonathan's farm down to your right," as Howard banked in a wide curve to view it more closely.

"Surely this crisis will make government do something about it?" enquired Emmett.

"Maybe, but I doubt it. The C.C. will pull out all stops to have roads, electricity and things like that repaired, but it will be down to us to get a crop in. By the way, have you got enough seed left?"

"Probably, I'll check on return."

"I think we've seen enough devastation, don't you? Lets get back and have a kawa."

"Fine by me."

The area in front of Emmett's homestead was a lake. Luckily the sheds on either side of the compound were eighteen inches above the ground level, and were stone floored. But some water penetration had occurred and the stables were a little sodden.

Every man woman and child was armed with badzas (hoes) and were fashioning channels for the rain water to run off and away from buildings.

All dams were full to overflowing, and culverts either side of the avenue and airstrip were torrenting on downwards to lower lands now becoming more like rice paddies than corn fields. This would all be a muddy morass within a few days, and it would take at least another week for the place to dry out, provided there was no more rain.

Only then could one register the damage and prepare a plan of reconstruction.

Next day Jaswant recalled one season when harvesting only finished in September due to the young crop having been eaten by locusts.

Emmett felt his concern and reaffirmed the regions combined plan and modus operandi which should see them through this turmoil.

"We now have our own emergency here just like the terrorist one in the designated areas. Have confidence Jaswant we will win both. Trust the powers that be."

With that Emmett raised his mug of tea as if in a toast and Jaswant acknowledged it.

297

"Thanks for your Irish spirit," he replied. He was a courageous pilot Emmett thought as the Cessna took off while skidding to left and right as power was increased for takeoff. His landing had been quite hairy, but Jaswant had kept to the very centre of the strip which had been graded especially for his landing.

Howard had instructed Emmett the day before on what to do to keep the strip workable. He had followed his orders precisely.

Very hot weather followed for a two week period which produced a patchwork quilt effect on young wheat stems rising like an unshaven face – some areas more profuse than others.

It was then time to ascertain the acreage that needed replanting. Certain sections were less affected and these were allowed to grow without disturbance.

Section 4, however, needed a lot of work and it was decided to replant in-toto. Approximately 2,500 acres!

Emmett borrowed a second grader from Ian and with both working maximum hours a day, contours and culverts were cut in the worst affected lands. A general staff meeting was called on Ratilli at which Emmett outlined his plans.

"We may not have bonuses this season but I do want to harvest a substantial crop. I think it is still possible. I need your complete and undivided attention. These next three months will test all of us. Are you with me?"

The din that erupted would have been worthy of Cup Final day. Emmett had his answer – they were all behind his efforts.

In all he had to replant over 3,500 acres. What was most encouraging was the small amount of damage to the Melelo crop. Only about 600 acres needed replenishing.

His lodge, however, needed a re-thatching on one side but as there was no grass at this time of year Emmett brought up a couple of tarpaulins to cover the weakness.

The circular gallop for his horses had been completely obliterated. No fast work was possible for almost two weeks. It was extremely dangerous riding them on the sodden earth as it was akin to an ice rink. Their race preparation was now sorely distrupted

It was, however, possible to get two blasts on the new surface prior to the next meeting. Both horses seemed in good form.

This, however, was not the case at Urukan's meeting. They ran well below their best, finishing third in their respective races.

Geronimo never sparkled and was beaten at the last hurdle. There was nothing in the tank.

Grandee, ridden by Emmett this time, was also listless and although staying on at the finish never shone.

298

Their performances were much talked about with even the suggestion that the 'Irish luck' had finally run out? Emmett went along with their good humoured banter but was crying within. This was a failure – the crop could also fail, so what was the third? Bad luck always runs in threes was an old Irish superstition which he thought very much about at that moment.

35

"What's it like being Whiteman's meat?"

"*Ratilli*, Ratilli, come in please. Its Jeri, over"

This was repeated a few times before Emmett could wake himself sufficiently and clamber to the radio.

"Ratilli here, Jeri. Go ahead please."

"Its not good news I'm afraid. Have just learnt from Kenzi that George and Mims have been taken hostage. A high price has been placed on their heads. Got that? Over."

"Yes I have. Were they taken at Clouds? Over."

"Affirmative. Over."

"What's Anna's reaction? Over.

"Shattered. She is packing and will be leaving very shortly. Over."

"Do you think that is wise? Over."

"Can't stop her I'm afraid. She's determined. Over."

"When did you hear this news? Over."

"About thirty minutes ago. One of the servants contacted the local police. Over."

"And when did the abduction take place do you know? Over."

"Probably plus minus 10 o'clock. Over."

"They have had plenty of time to vanish then? Over."

"Yes indeed. It has to be big '*M*' I'm afraid. Over."

"Understood. Should I make any move? Over."

"No. Most certainly not. You stay put and relay this to your H.Q. Over."

"Wilco. Please keep me posted. I'll be listening out. Over."

"That's all you can do at the moment. Sad news I'm afraid. Let's hope for a happy ending. Over and out."

Two quick mugs of tea followed by a walk around the compound with a long stop in with the horses. Two were sleeping, laying down in their straw beds, the other two were standing up. He cuddled the two heads, Corrib and Mask, who were standing and tried to explain his predicament, his worries, his fears.

Was this just another of *Makinto's* high profile hostage taking or was there, perhaps, a far deeper intent?

Anna would be the negotiator, with whoever came forward as their go between. Was she at risk? Perhaps her parents were the bait and she was the real target? She was a much sought after prize in their books. She had been the proverbial thorn, with her Wazuri, in their side for a long time. They had tried once to get her and failed. Was this another more contrived attempt? And perhaps he too might be included?

Buster was informed at first light and Emmett was told to remain on the farm and just listen out.

"There is nothing you, or anyone up here, can do so hang on in there boetie as best you can. Over and out."

The region was about halfway through the build up to the harvest, mid June in fact. Some acres would commence on time but the majority would be late. The weather was pleasant and the general growth consistent. An average tonnage would be the best everyone hoped for.

Emmett was endeavouring to get away in mid September and take two months vacation before returning for another three year tour. Bhogal had confirmed his reappointment with a salary increase to boot. His neighbours on the Plains were thrilled.

It had been a topsy turvey two months after the floods when the mop up and replanting had made it most stressful.

The only bit of lightness and joy had been Geronimo's retention of the Champion Hurdle mantle. It had been a close affair this time. Emmett knew the preparation had not been perfect to say the least but the horse's 'guts' had won the title. He could retire now.

Grandee had won two more races, once with Anna in the saddle, and was voted the most improved runner of the season. Many people were still attempting to validate his provenance! The Belgian prank had worked well. Both horses were now turned out on Howard's bushveldt till next season.

It was five days before Emmett's worse fears were realised. Anna had not returned to Clouds from a trip to Kenzi. No one could make contact with her.

As it was out of Jeri's jurisdiction he had to rely on friends within that administration to keep him informed. Kenzi was the home of *Makinto*. No one knew a thing. No one was speaking. It was a difficult time.

"You are not to stir from the farm. I will keep you up to date on everything. Let's hope for the best. Over and out."

Emmett was getting annoyed by the impersonal resonance of these radio calls he was taking just recently. It was all so cold. He felt utterly useless being away from the hostage taking, it was as if he was purposely being kept out of the action. On reflection he could understand that Kenzi was a very different proposition. It had its own agenda and would sort the problem in its own specific way. He just had to be patient and hope.

> "Patience is a virtue
> Have it if you can
> Seldom in a woman
> But always in a man."

Where were his thoughts at that moment? They should have been with Anna and her parents but somehow they were not.

"I am soaring above the earth in skies of blue. I am king of all the earth. Why do I need you?" A strange thought to be running through his mind. Where was it leading him?

Anna had driven down to Kenzi mid-morning time. She and her driver had stopped off at various aunts and uncles to hear if by any outside chance they had any news. Both families were distraught and broken with worry and fear. Not a pinch of information had been heard.

Visiting police headquarters and receiving a 'no news' bulletin she did some window shopping and sat at a sidewalk café table and ordered a kawa. Whilst half looking at the daily paper she noticed a *Makinto* landrover curb crawling along the street. It turned off a good way down from her. She wodered about her parents' safety and whereabouts. Were they being brutally treated, separated and in isolation? She knew of their resolve and inner strength but paniced at *Makinto's* bestial minds and prayed for her parents' salvation. A cold shiver travelled all down her spined and she felt as though the hairs on her back were suddenly standing on end. Anna thought about her own vulnerability and questioned how she would react in a similar situation.

A waitress brought her kawa and as she went to get some money from her bag three uniformed men – bare headed – grabbed and bundled her into a *Makinto* jeep which simultaneously arrived a few yards from her table. The three abductors threw her into the back and jumped in beside her. The jeep sped off.

She was immediately blindfolded and cuffed with wrists fastened behind her back. Not a word was spoken.

Anna estimated a fifteen minute journey before they stopped. She was roughly bundled out onto the ground, pulled to her feet and pushed up a few steps into a dark room and heard the door being locked behind her.

The floor was hard and slippery, probably polished cement. She inched her way around the space for a couple of feet and came up against a cold wall. She slowly followed it, finding each corner and eventually the door. It seemed as if the room, more of a cell she thought, was empty but for her. She shuffled to a corner and sank down to the floor.

The interrogation started sometime later. It was rough – a slap across her face each time she wouldn't or couldn't, answer their question. There were two of them. They threw her backwards and forwards from one to the other, picking her up each time she fell to the floor. She tasted blood. Her nose and mouth were throbbing.

They were using fists now and one blow dislodged the blindfold. She looked them straight in the eye before another fist caught her straight above her nose and between her eyes. She saw stars and sparks and landed on her back, with her head cracking the cement floor.

She didn't remember when she awoke but felt she was alone. Through puffed and streaming eyes she took in the tiny empty cold cell. A single light bulb now glowed in the centre of a damp paint peeling ceiling. Everything was dirty grey. She was wrecked. Every inch of her body hurt, even her legs, thighs and bottom. Large black boots had kicked and damaged her, all over.

She was still handcuffed. Her arms were limp now and literally pummelled into her lumbar region. The steel bracelets had cut into her back and rubbed great welts of gore along her panty line. They had stripped her save for her panties. Her breasts were battered and bruised and for once sagged limply against her body.

"So this was the *Makinto* way, was it," she said in a whisper through cracked and blooded lips.

"I too will get what I want from them, just wait and see." She crawled to a wall and propped herself against it. She didn't think she could stand, so sat and plotted a way to beat them.

Much later she was dragged from her cell, along a narrow corridor, and plonked on a chair in front of a large desk.

Behind it was a high ranking officer of the *Makinto*. He motioned the two attendants to stand outside the door.

The officer was a big man – fat, round with a shining face, fat fingers on bulging wrists. A thick gold watch sank into folds of light black skin. Bright gold rings crowded glutinous fingers. He leeringly leant across the desk with his arms firmly welded to the polished top.

"Tell me now. You wish to see your parents again don't you? And you wish to return to your work, don't you?" His speech was slow and definite.

"In fact you want out of here. Is that not so?"

Anna couldn't answer – not yet. She had a plan but she had to be pushed to reveal it. She now played her game. Perhaps this was Fredi Gachiru of whom she had heard so much?

"I have all day and all night, missy. Take your time. But tell me what's it like being white man's meat, mbudzi (goat)?"

His questioning was slow and deliberate.

"Are we not good enough for you, hey?" There was no smile on his face.

"How do they smell? Different to us, hey?"

"I bet he's not as big as we are – so why you fall for him?"

"Was it money, mbudzi?"

"I could question you for hours – all sorts of questions – some you wouldn't like you know. I could get really intimate."

There was a pause for a minute or two.

"Is there something you would like?"

After a silence Anna whispered "water."

"Right. You shall have a glass of water."

He banged the desk twice, the door opened and a guard entered. He was ordered to bring a jug of water and two glasses.

Her inquisitor continued, and now sat back in his chair, "I will get what I need from you – sooner or later, however you wish to play it."

Anna was relaxing, as much as her wounds and bruises would allow, and was gaining confidence. But she needed a little more time and some water. It finally came.

He held the glass, taunting her to lean forward and sip from it. She did just that and sipped long and lustfully. She felt the 'wine of gods' trickle lasciviously down inward canals she never knew existed. Her cracked lips sucked in the liquid as if it were her last. Anna, however, was determined it wouldn't be. She would win whatever it took.

He allowed her finish the glass and then refilled it but kept it out of her reach.

"Now my little tukulesi, tell me how I get to your man with the jatti (pony tail)?"

"More water please," was her answer.

He pushed the glass towards her. He didn't hold the glass so she had to control it with her bruised and swollen lips. She sipped and let her tongue dip into the depth of the glass. It felt so good. Quite suddenly Anna felt a warmth within her. It was burning anger, and she was ready to spill the beans. She wanted her parents released, and she couldn't particularly care less about herself.

Emmett used to play a Doris Day tune quite a lot called "Que sera sera" and it had become her motto. What will be, will be.

Anna slumped back into her upright uncomfortable chair, with wrists aching from the tightness of the handcuffs, her face and body searing pain from the beatings she had taken. She slowly unfolded her plan.

"We have a secret saying," the words were slow in coming, "in case either is in trouble. No one else knows this. No one," she faltered.

304

"Go on little mbudzi, you interest me."

"If I give you these and you relay them to him he will come running. I promise."

"Now that is interesting. And what might they be little one?" He leaned right across the desk with his puffy frog-like face resting on fat arms inches from her.

"I will tell you if you promise to release my parents," she whispered.

"That could be done – but only when I hear the 'jati' has taken the bait."

Silence prevailed. The ball was in play. Who had the next move?

Anna edged her body towards the glass. He filled it right to the lip. She repeated her last performance and then sank back once again.

She knew she had little bargaining power, but felt she must make the effort. Her parents' freedom, for her lover's capture. To any African or Indian that was the going rate in this troubled country. Nothing unusual in that she thought, except she would not be betraying Emmett – she would be warning him. She pronounced the sentence in a slow but sure tone.

"It is 'Ella is playing'"

"And that's it?"

"Yes, that is what we have arranged to be said. Simple really." She was feeling quite cocky now and wished she could be free to taunt this fat pig as he had her.

"You send him a message with those words in it. Then wait. You will see he will come to rescue me." She slumped back once more into her dejected pose.

"It seems so simple."

"It is. That's why we planned it so."

He rose from his chair and strode around the room for a good few minutes, mumbling to himself, obviously summing up the pros and cons of this snippet of information.

His bangs on the desk brought the two guards back into the room.

"Take her back to her cell and give her a meal. I have work to do," and he strode away down the corridor ahead of Anna and the guards who manhandled her frail body for what seemed an eternity. She lay on the floor and fell asleep.

Sometime later she was awakened by a kick to her feet. The single light bulb glowed weakly from the ceiling as a guard placed a bowl and a mug on the floor beside her. He opened the handcuffs and re-locked them once she brought her arms to her lap. She stretched her arms as best she could before the cuffs were locked on once more.

Mealie meal and water was gratefully accepted and eaten by the battered and bruised Anna. Each movement illustrated another hidden hurt. She knew she was in a poor way physically, but up top her mental powers were sparking off each other like a pin ball machine.

It must have been next day she was taken out to a vehicle and bundled into the rear end of it. A whole patrol of *Makinto* were gathering around three other vehicles parked alongside each other outside a building. Anna could hear them talking, and she recognised the voice of her inquisitor now giving the orders.

"Don't return without him. He must be alive. Understood?"

There was a jubilant cheer of "ndio ndio" (yes, yes). Anna crawled into herself with revulsion at what she was doing. But surely her darling 'Irish' would counter their move and best them out of it? "He must," she thought "otherwise all would be lost."

In the drive that followed Anna started to have real doubts and feared the outcome.

From what she gathered in bits of loose talk between the six men surrounding her in the jeep, "they would be stopping in Urukan for eats and then assemble in Koram for the final journey. A messenger had been despatched earlier to deliver their commander's orders."

All Anna could do was wait. Every so often she would have a boot banged into any part of her anatomy.

"They are so strong and fearless these *Makinto*," she mumbled to herself each time it occurred.

She knew she was on the way to a showdown. Hopefully Emmett would be well armed by being forewarned. She believed she had not betrayed him.

36

"*MAKINTO* – Africa's foulest and most evil organisation"

One Makinto vehicle was sent ahead of the main group. It carried the secret message to Emmett. It had been written by the interrogating officer.

The envelope was handed to Japhet at the Ratilli who promised to deliver it personally. After looking the place over the messenger departed back along the Koram road. Japhet saw him leave and then cycled down to the homestead as fast as his two lithe legs could take him.

Emmett, on reading the note a couple of times, asked Japhet about the man?

"Came in blue Toyota with driver and two other men."

"Describe him please."

"Quite long, tall, clean clothes, trousers, shirt. I notice his shoes. Black, very shiny, smart."

"What did he speak?"

"Tukulu, fendi. He smart. Look every place."

"How long ago did he leave?"

"Twenty minutes, fendi. Heading Koram, fendi."

"Thank you Japhet. You did right in bringing it to me personally. Go now please and keep your eyes open."

When Japhet departed Emmett called for Christopher to bring tea. He sat in a worried state waiting, with his dogs around him. This was something most strange.

The dreaded message had finally arrived. But yet it was only third hand. What was written on the paper was "Ella is playing". This was their secret message of warning – only he and Anna knew it. But they personally had to say it. Something therefore was terribly wrong. It meant that one or both were in real danger. Which one? Where? When?

Alarm bells rang through Emmett's head, his body was tense, his tummy full of gripes.

He jumped into his vehicle picking up Collins and Vard at the compound's gates. He chose Buster to confide in. He would know what best to do.

307

"You are certain this is genuine," enquired a worried friend and his Commanding Officer.

"No one else would know or ever use that phrase. Yes, I'm certain all right. *Makinto* are after me. They have Anna and her parents. I'm the ultimate prize. What do I do?"

After contemplating for a few tense moments "you hang on here until I have a pow-wow with the powers that be. Okay? It's mid afternoon so we have plenty of time to plan. You're safe here so just relax awhile. Go and talk to Shirra about tennis or something. Okay?"

So much was flooding through Emmett's mind at that moment. Where was Anna? How was she? When would *Makinto* strike? Were they coming to Ratilli? What would happen if they did? He was awoken from this macabre screen of thought by "Buster says I'm to show you some t.l.c. and take your mind off whatever is worrying you. Fine by me." In almost whispered tones, close to his left ear, "what would you like me to do – except the obvious – I never shit on my own doorstep so that will have to await another time, another day."

She took his hand and led him out into her garden, a mother figure. For the next thirty minutes he received an education in horticultural and floral influence on the Punjabi Plains. Shirra flirted quite openly with him and never held back on an odd embrace and a passionate kiss when suitably enveloped in shrubbery and away from prying eyes.

This was quite surreal he thought. On the one hand his life was threatened and his girl friend could well be beaten and tortured - she must have to have revealed their password. Whereas on the other hand, here he was being cosseted by the queen of nymphs and openly seduced in broad daylight!

A bellow from the veranda brought Emmett back to reality.

"Yes, coming, be there in a minute." He tightened his grip on her hand, looked deep into those pools of pleading passion and kissed her one last time.

"Thanks for everything. I'll remember you."

He ran to the veranda and followed Buster into his H.Q. office.

"Right now," he started with "you are to get the hell out of here – I mean the Plains. Pack your essentials and hightail it that-a-way" pointing to the west.

"This situation is too tricky to argue with so please don't. It is for the best. We'll be sorry to lose you but better you remain alive than dead."

With a really quizzical expression he gazed at a mute Emmett.

"For once I have the better of you. Dumbstruck and lost you look, and so you should be. But I bet you have run this scenario through a hundred times, hey? Tell me what's your best means of escape? Go on, don't be all coy on me now in your most crucial hour."

Nothing but silence prevailed. Then:

"But I wish to fight, not flee these bastards. I have spent a great part of my three years doing just that and I'm not about to stop the trend. What makes you so anxious to get rid of me anyhow?"

Buster was filling his pipe and completed the operation before replying. He left it unlit but used it as a descriptive tool in his address to Emmett, which had the air of the Commanding Officer all about it.

"Without your knowledge I have been, with the cooperative assistance of Jeri Ntsemo, planning your escape for sometime.

"Oh don't look so shocked, just let me explain. You have been, for some months now, a marked man – not the only one I hasten to add - by the *Makinto*. Some documents fell into the C.C's. hands and we have been monitoring events aligned to information contained within them. Hostage taking and ransoms, as you are aware, have been a major threat these past six months.

"Anna's parents, then her, are part of a web to attract their prime target, their piece of 'white meat' as they refer to you. Their cult has a ritual day coming up soon and you were to be the main course. Are you with me so far?"

Silence, only wide eyed disbelief gawked back at him.

"Good. I'll continue. We didn't know about your secret passwords, but now that a signal has arrived we will put our own strategy into operation. In brief, that means you are to be written out of the scenario and we are to proceed with Operation 'Wipe Out' – the total destruction of *Makinto* with or without the President's blessing or help.

"As I speak, two heavily armed Farmers' Reserve Units are being deployed. We feel *Makinto* has already set in motion their attempt at capturing you and two other Zungus in the Kitos region. Fortunately we have had an insider within *Makinto* for sometime and he has come up trumps. Are you still with me?"

"Yes sir I am." Emmett felt like a little boy who had done something wrong and was now being scolded for it, for his own good. He couldn't quite get his head around this, however.

"You are to proceed to Fuda, go over the border and head for Elizabethville. Get yourself an air ticket and bid us au revoir. Understand?"

"But what about Anna and her parents?"

"We will deal with them, don't worry. We will keep you informed I promise. But your skin is more valuable attached to your body don't you think?"

"Yes. Very well but - -"

"No buts I'm afraid. This is an order. You will thank me in time. Trust me."

After another silence Emmett came alive with "I'm one up on you then. Jay left his microlite with me whilst he is in the States. I will fly it to Mandalay. How about that? Could be safer in the air than on the road? And with my vehicle at the homestead it will seem as if all is normal. Yes?"

"Oh, very well but I was giving you an escort. But yes, that's a grand idea. Can you leave straightaway?"

"I suppose so. Gosh. What a dreadful thought – leaving here after all this time. I'm totally gob smacked. Sorry, that's an Irish saying," he almost grinned and continued,

"Well then I'll be off. Thanks for everything."

"I promise you Emmett we have everything at Ratilli planned for. And Bhogal is in on it. Good luck. My escort will see you home and up in the air."

They shook hands. Emmett jumped into his vehicle and made what might well be his last trip from Buster's HQ. It took him only thirty minutes to pack his two overnight bags. Everything was pre-planned for just such an emergency. Now it had arrived.

Saying farewell to dogs, horses and Christopher tore him apart. He did it quickly – there was no going back.

They pushed out Screwball. Tyres, petrol and oil had already been checked out earlier. This had been a daily routine since it arrived on Ratilli.

Emmett took off and circled the homestead, flew up to Ian and waved as Jan came out to see the 'bedstead'. Same thing happened at Rachel's and then he was off across country to Mandalay.

He really couldn't believe this was happening.

Against the wind, under an approaching darkness and above an arid African bushveldt, he wondered why he shouldn't just turn back and face the music – the *Makinto* – Africa's foulest and most evil organisation. He was to blame. He was the target and he wouldn't be there to see their demise. All he thought about was Anna and would he ever see her again?

Buster called his entire squad together in full battle dress. His plan was simple.

"We will set up an ambush on the first bridge past Ratilli. I'm not saying much. You all know my thoughts. Hit hard. I only want two or three prisoners. Bring them back a.s.a.p. Go for it. Good luck."

Jeri Ntsemo's hands-on approach to these damnable assaults on reputable people within his region led to the greatest surveillance operation of the campaign.

Once the alarm was sounded by Buster a combined force went into overdrive. This had been planned, to the nth detail, for many months.

Just as UMA and *Makinto* had their secret organisations up and running in a well oiled mechanism so too had the Farmers' Reserve Organisation, but in a completely unheralded way. They obviously matched them stride for stride in a campaign that was finally leaning heavily towards the 'Farmers'.

The flares over HQ alerted two well placed FR patrols who had moved onto the Bhogal farm for the sole purpose of encircling the homestead, compound and labour lines.

"We let the enemy infiltrate the farm, then catch them with their pants down and obliterate them. Understood men?" were Buster's last orders as they set off to their waiting stations.

Both Ian and Howard manned the squad encamped within Emmett's grain shed. They had moved there thirty minutes after Emmett's departure. Instructions were given to Emmett's 'heavies' now positioned as lookouts within his house to hold fire but keep them posted on the enemies progress. Now everyone waited.

Three *Makinto* vehicles halted some few hundred yards down the runway and just beyond the limits of the compound lights. They had been turned to face the way they had driven. Obviously thinking that by entering from the east of the compound they would proceed unnoticed.

"Enemy on move towards house, fendi." It was Vard's voice on the walkie talkie to Ian.

"Keep still and report. No movement from any of you."

They knew the drill. The intruders would have to attack and enter the house from the veranda, obviously hoping to catch the Zungu – Emmett Doyle, asleep. Little did they realise, however, that their every move was being monitored by some of the FR patrols.

"These contours of Emmett's have come in mighty handy," said David Purdon to his group, who were lying down behind one not fifty yards from the rear of the workshop.

"It won't be long now." He looked at his watch. It was 23.15 hours and all was quiet on Ratilli.

One hour later it was over. The *Makinto*, all sporting their orange berets, had walked straight into the trap. Ten shots had been fired and all insurgents had been taken captive save for the drivers and any backup that were left in their vehicles.

These sped away after about twenty minutes, when they obviously feared the worst and no communication had taken place, only to be confronted head-on by two FR vehicles who opened fire as they came into range.

At approximately the same time as the attack on Emmett's homestead the other *Makinto* vanguard of three vehicles had driven into Buster's ambush.

Here there was a real dogfight with the battle continuing for a good half hour. There were casualties on both sides but fatalities only on the side of *Makinto*.

Altogether they had twenty-four combatants. They also had one prisoner in the rear of their third vehicle who was only found after the battle was over. This jeep had tried to run the gauntlet but had crashed into a tree and toppled over onto its side. The occupants crawled out with hands raised above their heads, battered faces totally aghast at the surprise and situation that followed.

It was only sometime later, after the insurgents had been rounded up, that moans and groans could be heard from inside the overturned vehicle.

There Rod Beaton found a battered, bruised and bloodied Kenzian female with her hands tied behind her back. Her legs were also tied about the ankles. So badly was her face damaged that it was minutes before one of the Home Guards recognised her.

"Fendi, fendi, its Anna – Mr. Emmett's Anna, fendi. Oh my God fendi what have they done to her?" He broke down completely and was comforted by Beaton and some others who rushed to the vehicle.

Rod saw something more worrying than the battered face. Blood was pouring from wounds in or around her chest region.

He instructed she be laid flat on the ground covered with whatever clothing was available and not to be moved from there. He pressed the call button of his radio.

"Come in HQ. RB here."

"Go ahead RB."

"Mission completed, satisfactorily but have found a badly wounded Anna in the back of a vehicle. Need doctor and ambulance urgently. Over."

"Wilco. Listen out."

Buster's brilliance in organisational skills, together with Jeri Ntsemo's total cooperation, had two Urukan ambulances standing by at Koram Clinic with two Asian doctors awaiting such a call.

They arrived within twenty minutes and set about administering the necessary medication. Altogether there were eleven wounded – four Farmer's Reserve and seven *Makinto*. Three *Makinto* were dead.

Just prior to departing, one of the doctors took Rod aside.

"I don't hold out much hope for the lady. I think the bullets have penetrated her lungs and massive internal bleeding is taking place. I have radioed the hospital and surgeons are on standby. Better be off."

Jeri and Margaret met the ambulance. Anna was stretchered into the operating theatre without delay. Just prior to surgery she came to, recognised her auntie and in whispered tones "it was my family or Emmett you know. Please tell him I loved him. Please, please." She drifted off and the surgeons asked Margaret and Jeri to leave them now.

An hour later they emerged with glazed looks.

312

"We are sorry. Nothing we could do to save her."

Jeri held Margaret very closely. They were sitting on a wooden bench inconsolable. After a few minutes Jeri took control.

"Better think positively. We have to find George and Mims now. Lets return to the children my love." Jeri and Margaret then thanked the operating team, her colleagues, and departed.

Explaining to the children was probably the worst moments of both their lives.

37

"Could we visit you at Christmas, all of us?"

Emmett saw a silvery glistening ribbon in the late sunlight which he knew was the river that snaked its way from Lake Nduga down through Mandalay. All he had to do was follow it southward and locate Jay's airstrip.

He understood it was close to the homestead which presented itself in all its glory within fifteen minutes. The Castle looked quite medieval and completely incongruous from the air. Mandalay staff appeared from everywhere and waved joyously thinking Screwball's appearance meant the return of their master.

As it was early evening a lot of gazelle were grazing the airstrip and its surround, so he had to make a number of dummy passes attempting to frighten them away.

It was only after half a dozen of Jay's staff arrived to shoo them that they took any heed.

Emmett touched down and turned the craft within a hundred yards of landing. He was surrounded by Mandalay's staff and although he noticed a degree of sorrow as he wasn't their master, they offered a jovial welcome and took his bags to the house. Others took control of Screwball and pushed it away to its hangar.

Jasmine appeared with her dogs on the veranda and walked across the garden to greet him.

"What a lovely surprise. I hope its not a two minute visit as Jay would say?" She smiled warmly as she took Emmett's hands and offered each cheek for the traditional kiss.

"I'm afraid it is." He took her body in a bear hug and broke down sobbing into her left shoulder.

"Now, now, come in and let's hear all about it. That must have been some sundown safari you undertook? Let's have a couple to still the nerves." She led him up the steps into the drawing room, and sat him down on a couch then moved to the drinks cabinet.

"Whisky or brandy?"

"Whisky please."

Emmett was distraught. He had escaped to here, but now that the adrenalin rush of flying had subsided he was swamped in grief. He hadn't thought about it on the trip over. Too many other things to monitor whilst controlling the 'bedstead'.

"Drink that, and in your own time, tell me."

Jasmine sat close to him. She held a drink and wore a musk perfume that reminded him of Anna.

Over the next hour Emmett explained his predicament and just what was going on in the war against *Makinto*.

Jasmine was horrified. She replenished their glasses on two further occasions.

Emmett could see her brain was working overtime. He felt she could have become afraid for her own safety, now that she was actually harbouring a fugitive. He had thought about this and was anxious to make the next leg of his journey without delay.

Don't worry about me," she said "I'll also go with you over the border for a week or so as one of my family is in hospital. We will leave early in the morning. I won't call anyone just in case hostile ears are listening in."

Emmett was amazed how matter of fact and assured she was. How fortunate having such friends and people like this in his circle. He figured he had been correct in making friends wherever he went. "You never knew when you might need them" his father had told him.

He didn't sleep much that night despite a wonderful dinner washed down with lashings of French wine. Emmett kept wondering what was happening back on the Plains? Had they found Anna and her parents? Had the Farmers' Reserve won the battle if there had been one?

Every question would be answered in time. Buster had promised that. Emmett would be able to phone Jeri's office once safely in the Congo and that was the last hurdle in his race to escape.

They were through Fuda and over the border by 07.30am next morning. Jasmine had brought a driver and a nanny who was Congolese and from her home place.

Before driving to her family's farm they stopped off at her mining groups headoffice in the city. There, an efficient secretary booked Emmett a flight on KLM to London for the following evening. He would be back in Dublin by noon the next day.

Something, some little niggling notion, said "hold fire with phoning Urukan". He didn't know what it meant but for once Emmett listened and obeyed. Perhaps they only wanted to hear from him from home – his home, Ireland. Then they would realise he was truly out of reach of the dreaded *Makinto*. And their plan had worked.

315

Jasmine's family estate was thirty-five miles out of the city. Her brother, Jacobus, ran the farm which was an intensive mixed operation of dairying and vegetables.

Their aunt, Isolde, was in hospital with a likely cancer and was evidently going downhill quite speedily so the entire family was being summoned. Jay would be returning from America within the week. Emmett felt it a great pity that he should have missed him. It might be a long time, if ever, before they met again?

His day and the next passed in a flash, and it was only when at the airport and having kissed 'au revoir' did he fully realise the enormity of the task ahead.

At that moment, sitting next to the final check-in desk prior to boarding, Emmett realised he wasn't as mature a man as he had thought he was. He was suddenly very alone. His entire world had been turned upside down.

Emmett kept putting off the moment – le moment critique – as Jasmine had reminded him prior to departure.

Now back in Ireland, having spent a day and night with friends in Dublin, he set out on the drive home, his home in Ballyvaughan, County Clare. He had not called Urukan as he was afraid of the outcome. It was still there, that niggling sensation within his ruffled brain.

Emmett needed the comfort of his mother and sister. He desperately craved the love and warmth of family. His nerves were shattered, even though he was safely home.

His account of his sudden arrival did not dot the eyes or cross the tees and they were not overly inquisitive.

When he finally made the person to person call to Jeri he sat in the hall alone in the house.

The C.C. was thrilled to hear his voice but knew instantly of his anxiety. He gave Emmett the terrible news right away. His account of Anna's demise was chronicled in great detail. Every effort had been made to credit her with the success of the Farmers' Reserve victory at Zumba Bridge and of the mopping up of *Makinto* in the few days since Emmett's departure.

"George and Mims are traumatised but well enough in health. Margaret has taken leave and is with them at Clouds. Anna's funeral is tomorrow at noon. We shall all be there. Three planes are flying up from your area so she is having a wonderful send off. Her last words, Emmett, were 'tell him I love him' so rest easy. Your secret message won the day – no, the battle in fact."

"The President has had to side with the police and his elite squad will be disbanded immediately. A triumph for all of us in the quest for democracy."

"Call George tonight. He understands completely. Have a good rest and get your mind off Ukenza and *Makinto*. I will tell you when you should return.

Stay well my Irish friend. Our thoughts will be with you and Anna tomorrow. From all of us God bless."

The line crackled as Emmett held the phone after Jeri completed the conversation. He slowly replaced the receiver into its console and sat there all alone. Tears had welled earlier on but now they flooded as he grabbed his handkerchief and took refuge in the bathroom.

His mother found him there on her return. He was inconsolable. She sat on the side of the bath and cradled his head on her lap. He hadn't the energy to get off the floor.

When Sinead returned, after closing the schoolhouse for the day, Emmett gave them the complete story and the truth about his sudden return. They sat around the old wooden kitchen table with a bottle of Powers Irish whisky and three glasses. His mam had not indulged since his father's wake but needed one now.

Sinead was the strong one.

"You mustn't blame yourself. Guilt should not enter the equation. You were fighting a war and you both knew the possibilities. Have another Emmett," as she passed him the half empty bottle.

"It's a terrible tragedy. You have lost your love and you can't be there for her funeral. They will understand."

"But I should have stayed and fought the battle," he cried out only to be halted in any further guilt sodden thought.

"You were ordered to leave and you can't go against orders now can you? Perhaps you too would have been captured or shot and then what. Two corpses? No my daring brother, your superiors did the right thing. I know you feel the opposite but in time you will appreciate their decision. Sorry to have to be so forthright but that's me, you know well enough."

That night was his most troubled. After supper he had phoned Anna's parents. It was a tearful fifteen minutes. They absolved him of all guilt and he must carry the memories of their happy times together.

"You are our son, Emmett, the one we never had and that will remain so. Hurry back."

All through that night he turned the pages of events over and over and over again but failed to find a satisfactory result. It was dawn before he dozed off.

At about the time of Anna's funeral Emmett visited his local Parish Church, lit half a dozen candles, and prayed for her family's strength and fortitude to carry them through the day and months to come.

For the next month Emmett found solace in going to sea with a family friend, Joe Linane, who had four hundred and fifty lobster pots dotted along the cliffs out in the bay. He worked from 6.00am 'till noon five days a week. He found it hard at first, his muscles not honed on manual toil in the sunshine of Africa, but exhilarating after succumbing to the daily rhythm of the tasks at hand. The Galway Hookers were not only a joy to be party to but were a sight for sore eyes.

His mind was taken away from the Punjabi Plains and although a number of nightmares did interrupt some exhausted hours of slumber he found himself mellowing into the intimacy of family and parochial life.

Only when it was time to meet up for the reunion did Africa once again appear on the horizon.

They, 'the fractious five', spent three full days together at the Grand Hotel, Malahide, and heard in great detail the accounts of their respective three years experiences.

None of the four, however, wanted to swap their lifestyles with Emmett?

"Far too dangerous old fella," was the Australian colonial opinion of Matthews. Emmett noticed he had a marked Aussie accent and was very tanned.

"I'm completely into the Parisian way of life darling Emmett – cosmopolitan you know and my French is pretty good, aussi mai oui?" was Vard's camp proclamation to the group. He now wore a black beret, black tee shirt and black jeans. Around his neck was a bright red silk cravat.

"I wouldn't mind a stint in Africa," butted in Collins "but I've just signed up for another two years in Gaucholand. You cannot imagine the size of the ranches I'm handling. Some are a half a million acres. We too fly everywhere."

"You will be most welcome," prompted Emmett "and we will hire a plane and see Africa."

"You're on Emmett." He raised his glass and they all drank to that pledge.

"What about you Napper and where exactly are you stationed?" He was languid in his reply and was probably the most introvert of the five.

"I'm living in Bangalore, South India and I'm a partner in a small but vibrant firm of Architects. I'm completely taken by the khama of the country and have specialised in designing ashrams, places of worship. When I'm there I dress Indian fashion in long white robes and sandals. So sensible. I ride a motorbike and have a small ground floor apartment with a sweet garden not far from our office. I'm extremely happy there and I adore oriental food."

"So do I," responded Emmett "in fact we should find an Indian restaurant in town and have a meal there before we all return. What say ye?"

There was affirmation all around.

They learnt a lot about each other over those three days and although they were very different in their outlooks and professions their boyish camaraderie remained solid in its foundation.

Three years, in some ways, was a long time away but they agreed to remain in touch, even more so, they promised, through the years ahead.

Weekly phone calls to Bhogal's office and Jeri's kept Emmett in touch with the situation in Ukenza. Nothing appeared in the Irish national papers.

Ratilli's harvest had not surpassed last season's tonnage but it was enough to show a profit and bank some more bonus in Emmett's overseas account. He wasn't needed back 'till the new year said Jaswant and he was not to worry about anything on the farm.

The news from Jeri was not so rosy. After 'the battle of the Plains' as the infamous ambush had been dubbed, there was a dreadful backlash between the *Makinto* and the police.

President Mbugu remained silent and let the civil war that erupted carry on regardless of his feelings.

The army held back until the entire elite guard was denuded of its high profile status. Police interrogation lasted three months with virtually all members of *Makinto* slung into goal and forgotten about. African justice to the tee.

Pockets of insurgency throughout the country were scooped up in the cleansing process.

Once the administration was happy with the situation the army publicly sided with them.

The President was out on a limb and called for a general election in April. This was greeted with immense joy by the populous with bonfires lit at sundown on every Sunday of the month.

"George and Mims are well over the tragedy, Emmett, so I think you should call them again. We, Margaret and I, know they would love to hear your news. Keep in touch."

Emmett had worried about making that call. He still had not completely ruled out his sudden retreat from the battlefields of Ukenza being the reason behind Anna's death and his cowardly (to him) withdrawal.

At the time of her funeral it was easy to speak with them. Grief was their common denominator with blame solely ascribed to *Makinto*. Jeri had explained Emmett's sudden retreat to Ireland and they understood fully. And agreed it most sensible.

Emmett had many sleepless nights – nightmares of horrific proportion flooding the golden wheat fields of his mind. But time cures all things his God fearing mother kept reminding him.

She also had another ploy which she hoped would keep her son at home. The lovely pharmacist Lizzie Munally was available and had never so much as looked at another whilst Emmett had been away.

"Surely she could be courted and made to make the union," his mother kept reminding Sinead. She, however, would have nothing to do with it.

"Leave him alone, Mam, he will find someone in time."

Emmett phoned George. The line, for once, was clear. They talked for many minutes as of old and before the tragedy.

"Would you like to speak with Mims. She is right beside me?"

"Yes please."

"Hi Emmett. I gather you are well from George's remarks. Life goes on here just the same. We have to keep going. We are fortunate, we have the other two. Are you in touch with Jeri and Margaret?"

"Yes, I have been kept up to date with the ongoing situation. He reckons I should return in a few months time. He has evidently discussed my future with Bhogal, so I'm being cosseted by them."

"Not a bad situation to be in especially as its your safety that's in focus. I must say the populous are caught up in the forthcoming elections, and Patrice is making hay while the sun shines as I think you say."

"That's good to hear. Are you confident that terrorism, etc., is 'out the window' and your life will return to normal."

"Yes, I think so but you should discuss those sort of things with George. Anyhow, lovely to hear you again. Please keep in touch. All our love. Here's George."

He was now much more relaxed and Emmett could detect it in his voice.

"What are your plans Emmett," he opened with.

"Oh, I want to return to Ratilli for another contract. Bhogal is being extremely kind about it all, and suspect he is being guided by Jeri and the Farmer's Reserve Organisation on the Punjabi Plains. So I shall play it by ear and await instructions. I'll get some hunting here and generally muck in with farm chores and the like."

George butted in as if he had something imperative to reveal:

"Emmett slow down a piece and let me have a say. Okay?"

"Go ahead, I'm all ears." There was a silence as if the line had gone dead.

"Could we visit you at Christmas – all of us?"

There was a pregnant pause.

"Wow. How fantastic. But you will die of the cold."

"Not a problem. We will stop off in London and kit ourselves out. I want to catch a trout or a salmon – anything in fact. How about it?"

"Absolutely marvellous. I'll plan your entire time here. Gosh what a surprise. Might I enquire – is this off the cuff or do the others know about it?"

"No – completely ad lib. In fact Mims has had to sit down and is just staring at me. She is in shock," he giggled softly.

Then there was a gurgle – a satisfied one then "such fun. I'll start making arrangements at this end. See you soon."

The line went blank. Emmett sat back exhaling, shouting, "wow, wow, wow," so much so that his mother came rushing in from the kitchen, like a clucking hen protecting her brood from an overhead hawk.

"What's up? Such a commotion."

"Nothing Mam, nothing at all. Just happiness."

He jumped up and enveloped his mother in a bear hug. Not something he had done for a long time.

He jumped up and enveloped his mother in a bear hug. Not something he had done for a long time.

"Put the past out of your mind – this will be the beginning for a new Emmett Doyle".